# Battery Life

Hi there,
   Thanks for picking up this book;
If you enjoy it — or even if
you don't — please help out
2 nice but struggling young
men by either passing it on
   to the next person or
leave us a written review
   of it on its Amazon Page.
   Just type in 'battery life book/
                  kieren hughes/
             nick white at
             — Amazon.com
             — Goodreads.com
             or
             — Barnes & Noble.
                  com

Cheers.

*For Tabitha & Elodie.*
*NW*

*For the commuters.*
*KH*

# PART ONE

## Weather The Storm

Weather the storm and rise again,
City of battered edges,
Wooden beams may creak and sway,
But sail on through the ages.

A city steeped in constant flux,
Of struggles, wars and battles,
Plagues and pits and powder plots,
Rifts and royal scandals.

Your earth has churned for centuries,
From feet making their mark,
Fires have swept and cracked your bones
But never dulled your spark.

Each time knocked down, brought up again
Through hands of sons and daughters,
Carriers and barriers,
Preserve your river's waters.

The cry of decades echo in
Chaotic blasts of violence,
Bombs and blood and broken hearts,
And yet you watch in silence.

The ignorance of mortal men,
You rise above each day,
Angry fools who live and die,
Watched like a passing play.

Each generation leaves a mark,
Sometimes a scar is made,
A tattoo of what used to be,
Where skeletons are laid.

Though ghosts may sleep beneath your streets,
You shed your skin anew,
For future fables to take place,
Around and over you.

Inside your veins a million trains,
Pump through your beating heart,
The sooty mice seek food and hide,
From cat's eyes in the dark.

Crosses and circles, lines and squares
Reshape your shifting form,
A breathing city built to last;
Forever weather storms!

## Stargazer

Five hours clocked in and there's still no word from the radio, not from anyone. The usual communication and industrial setback I guess. Still, I don't mind sitting up here; the last human outpost between the city and the space programmes. At 1,040 feet I sit and just seventeen feet beneath me stands the partially completed highest platforms and empty panels that will complete The Shard of Glass; a feat of architecture that will subsequently complete the present state of Western Europe. All of it resting in time, like me, by just a single call from that radio.

1,023 feet further, down a dangerous slope of near vertical glass, 8 million Londoners now reside. Across an expanse once deemed unimaginable to its founders spreads a complex network of intersections; intersections of cultural and physical boundaries that prevent one's view from the ground from ever fathoming it all as just one reality. I, however, get to see it as one single complex landscape; a landscape that, by day, resembles a glistening-skinned serpent trying to slither its way through an infinity of greying, turned-over egg boxes applied to the loosely wired underside of some vintage motorcar; a beautiful creature that twists its way from the sea far behind me, past the peaks of Parliament and Battersea Power Station at the ridge of my nose, to the distances of the west far beyond.

Slightly behind me, down below and across the river, stands a fortified square of grey brick that stamps onto this landscape the origin of this great but questionable city; whilst tourists surround that particular landmark like besieging insects after the Crown Jewels, just nearby, they don't seem to realise that there are the fascinating shifting layers of time (and its shifting definitions of wealth) that trail off directly from its legacy. The dome of St Paul's Cathedral for example, marks out how the reaches of religion once tried to scrape the sky like I am now. The rising roads of Tower Bridge mark the era of the modern world's industrial expansion into the wider realms (when Britain was great they say), whilst less than the distance of my forefinger and thumb are the tower blocks of different economically-charged termite hills; the peaks of Canary Wharf, again all reaching for their own personal heavens for different purposes entirely. Then of course there's me; sitting upon a single chair with a control panel and instruction manual before me, a tiny compartment behind me, cables and ladders plummeting to a vertiginous fall beneath me (all attached to tons of swinging concrete I can tell you) and me, squeezed into a tiny white box of thin windows, here, at the precipice of a new future.

"Most hate this job", they told me before I took it on, but not me. I'm out the way; just gazing and thinking as I am right now. For most, the worst part I guess, would be the ladders; you could sit up here all the time until your rotation ended but, sooner or later, you'd have to make a hell of a downward climb for whenever you'd have to answer that basic call of nature to relieve yourself. The wind and the cold (and it's strong in this country) is always somewhat unavoidable, the latch on my door isn't great, leaving a gap of maybe a few millimetres between here and the outside cold and once open, you'd be at the mercy of something of an overhang as you swing yourself, into the wind, onto the grips of the ladder's first steps. The drop that takes you down the centre of The Shard's attaching scaffold work essentially goes most of the way (it joins to an external lift on the seventieth floor) to the concrete floor of London Bridge, all those 1,040 feet below you but, taking it slowly of course, you only have to climb seventeen metres before you reach the first flimsy walkway that takes you toward the portaloos of The Shard's upper levels. The Shard however, will be revealed to be a pyramid shape in its design and so, with my crane being straight in its more functional approach, this first platform marks a rather lengthy walk across the sky to these higher levels which is somewhat worse than just continuing down 'the drop' to the next one, of which (if you paid attention to your shapes in school) has the edge of one diagonal surface meeting with a straight one, hence that next perilous walk being less long. Of course, then you have to go back up again which, when resisting gravity, this lengthier climb, its treacherous wind and its climactic overhang back into the box, can be doubly worse.

Of course, as I've often considered, with relieving myself being the only obstacle from me staying up here, what it would be like to have a quick pee out my right-side window. Would anybody notice it? Would it simply disperse into the force of the fall? I doubt I could get away with it, for then they would surely send me to that place I really just don't want to go right now? Home, or the old home anyway.

The best part of the job however, is the position's sense of peaceful serenity. Coming from suburban Newcastle, London is just too noisy for a bloke like me and up here you feel like you've been gifted with the most placid part of it, the only set back of course being that instead of having the mild, 24-hour exposure to traffic sounds and arguments that everyone else gets, you're instead exposed to a 5 minute or so rush of sudden sound intensity all at once. First there are the rota blades of the helicopters, the police, the journalists, the billionaires, whirring around just beneath me like annoying wasps, occasionally making me wonder what would happen if they should collide with my structure itself. The worst ones however, are the planes; coming out of nowhere like whales in the ocean when you're least expecting it, great jet engines so loud and close that they rattle my cage, sometimes rattling that tiny latch open and threatening to throw me out through it, 1,040 feet onto the concrete below. A few times, these passing sky tormentors have caught me out whilst in the middle of the climb. All I have to do in this situation then, is hug the bars more tightly and wait for the shaking to pass, praying that if I did fall there would be a few thousand more bars along the way to try and grab hold of. They blot out the sun all of a sudden, these beasts, and shoot forwards to what I've gathered must be to London International Airport and, although a big Northern bloke like me shouldn't admit to being a pansy like this, I do feel a little bit of jealousy that there are things operating at a higher altitude than me.

Hours are ticking by now. It's nearly time to clock out for the night but, after securing a deal with my closest supervisor (I shan't say his name) I sometimes get to stay the night; this project has to be completed soon and neither of us can be arsed with the commute. Both of us would rather turn a blind eye to that small footnote in health and safety and just start work as early as possible the following morning; delays like this unspoken one on my radio then often working to my benefit.

My mates who have gathered that I sometimes do this, often ask me why? To be honest, I just can't stand cities; London especially. I've seen it in my own life and I've seen it in theirs; life is just too hard on them. I mean just look at how far it stretches? So fabricated and so fast these places have become that it's impossible to keep up with what human contact should be about; family unity now lasts about five years at best whilst friends or even lovers have now become positioned at such polar ends of this network that any attempts to renew any interest in one another does so at the expense of their working lives. Things have truly become 'out of balance' you could say. No, it's not for me down there, I'd rather be up here, away from it all, just gazing and the likes amidst no other company other than my own.

At this height, there is something to be said for sunsets over London. As much as the mainland Europeans I've met might all complain about how much dirtier British cities are when compared with those elsewhere, in some form of yin-yang logic, the pollution, piss and rain somehow react with the falling sun to create something akin to a heaven on earth. It's as if the falling sun takes its summer heat and the evaporation of all that polluted water from its ascent and somehow transforms them into a kind of red mist that then falls back in an eastwardly swoop towards the grounds of Greenwich; London somehow shrouded for a fleeting moment in some great red sail.

These are also hours of man-made beauty too for, from this perch only, I notice that the million electric office lights as used by the day workers from say 8am-6pm, are all switched off at nearly the exact same point at which the night workers arrive to switch theirs on elsewhere. If these lights were like stars I would describe this sight as being like the constellations of one galaxy suddenly dying and being absorbed through some kind of metropolitan black hole to emerge, reborn or displaced, at some other end of the same void. This is a spectacle beheld only by those who work at these great heights and quite often, I see the flashlights of torches, communicating from one crane box to another, each erected at different points of the city, to make each other aware of its momentary beauty. I communicate back of course as it's nice. I like to think, that within *the loneliness of the high-distance crane operator* there are others just like myself, all on the same wavelength over something that only we can understand.

Construction companies are mostly all international these days, and with most of the project wrap up or festive-season bashes taking place here, there and God knows where, I often wonder whether during my contracts throughout Newcastle, Birmingham and London, whether I've ever unintentionally run into any of these men. If I should in the future, maybe I could buy them a pint and discuss this personalised phenomenon of ours.

Night eventually draws in, that radio order is now forgotten and when there's a chill like tonight's I like to enjoy a cuppa and a fag whilst looking over the overhang from my open window. I have a slyly smuggled sleeping bag as well as a load of tinned fruit and sandwiches in the back compartment where I enjoy my slumber. It's cramped of course but the alternative is 'the climb'. Can you imagine that downward climb if ice were to touch that ladder in the dark? And my team are supposed to not know that I'm up here. For those who may be curious, *relief* during these colder hours is done into a bottle that I'll discard of tomorrow.

After I've changed into more comfortable clothes and rustled into my sleeping bag, I listen to some music, look up at what I can see of the stars through the upward angle of the window and think about times past. I think of my wife, my kids and when I'll see them again, whether my Mum's recent departure has taken her to heaven and where my world and I may be going next. After a couple of distractions from overhead planes, it's back to silence and I nod off.

These days I mostly dream of falling, it's usually always the same in its abstract tones, something to do with how impressed I am with my ability to recognise the speed at which I am falling and how this grants me the ability to count the passing windows of The Shard as its sloping surface finally intercepts my straight fall and allows me perhaps, to slide the rest of the way down to my survival; the bottom of which, I never actually reach of course and don't even want to, I just slide on and on and faster and faster. The worrying prospect of these dreams is that they're brought on by the discomfort of my sleeping posture and often cause me to stir, a stir of which may one night see me slam my way through the door and into the waking realisation that my dreams have become a plummeting reality.

I tend to wake up around 5am whereby with work commencing at 7, I can relax with another cuppa and fag to await my first radio orders. This morning I've awoken to the sounds of heavy rain battering down upon the large bollards of metal above me, hitting them before anything else in this immense city on its journey to the ground, as if I'm somehow privileged to receive them first. It's pretty much still dark and what a great sound and fantastic feeling this all is; awoken inside a cloud, a heavy mist rising from the city floor with a soon-rising sun. The exteriors of my paper-thin windows are a concrete grey encased in the globules of morning moisture. Not even the closest city lights can be seen and it's like there is the feeling of being in some different world entirely. It's going to be a cold and wet day which means work (and the ladder) will be harder, but I like to be here; gazing and pondering.

As if to share the same perch as me, the pigeons have settled upon the bars outside to await their own busy day, it's like I'm getting to know them now. And the best bit for this time of the morning? Turning that useless latch, I open my door to lean out beyond the overhang and look down as best I can at The Shard. Although I can't see the view as well as I could if I had more direct aerial view of it, the tip of the structure looks incredible. In case you didn't know, the finished vision is that the tip will involve three pinnacles of triangular glass that will nearly, but not quite, pull together as a complete pyramid; instead resembling the three-clawed fingers of some creature clawing the sky. The partially completed form of this then is now protruding through the mist like the emerging mouth of some great fish breaking surface for its breakfast, with me, the maggot, dangling from the structure of a great hook. With the added addition of the air warning lights, neon bulbs of blue and yellow still visible from the thickness of the mist, it also looks up like the opening petals of some great, exotically-coloured tropical plant; the humidity of its surrounding jungle licking and hydrating its smooth surfaces and as the cloud curls itself upwards off the glass, the rain falls in beautiful precision, straight down into its black-hole mouth.

I wait away those drifting morning clouds and the rain decreases. Finally, there is the morning crackle from my radio that signifies my supervisor's early morning warning call and I return to work to await the next one. Another cup of tea is due, maybe?

If I don't get a delay like yesterday's, The Shard should be completed within a month. Could I simply stay up here for that long? How long would it take for them to notice? In my life, I once had a base of sorts in the support of my parents, both now recently gone; I had another in my marriage of which too has also recently gone. Amazingly amidst the two of those I also built for the future in my children and the money that I'd left for them, all of which, for reasons I won't go into, have also disappeared away from my life now. This, instead, is how I go about such life duties these days and so for anyone who should ever come into this city, whether it be in typical English rain or beaming sunshine, they shall see my contribution high above everything else. One day they will build a building higher than this one and if not too old, I will sign up for it; not just because of the fact that not many others will, but because the further I go from the floor, the more I begin to understand of the path I've left upon my world.

# Strange Requests - Volume 1

Friday Night at The Cellar in London Bridge. I'm in the middle of a retro-funk set when I notice a guy eyeballin' me from the pool table. I look down to crossover from *Maceo* into some *Average White Band* but when I look back up he's still standing there, rocking his head up and down slowly. I guess he's enjoying it.

I signal over to the bar to pour me another drink and look over to the Nigerian security guard, Ole. He's busy chatting to some girls at the table by the door.

I scan my fingers over the laptop to find the next track; *Peaches* by *The Stranglers*. Just as I load it up I see a tattooed hand shake my wrist. I look over and its eyeball guy.

"Nice set, mate."

"Cheers."

"Do ya take requests?"

"Um...yeah."

"Cool. I want you to play something you can stab someone to."

I almost miss the crossover and stare at him.

"What?"

He repeats himself.

"You know. Play something you can *really stab* someone to."

To enforce his point over the music he starts moving his hand back and forth furiously in a mock stabbing action. I try and smile and look over to get Ole's attention, he's still distracted. I think about asking him who exactly he wants to stab but change my mind in case it's me. I simply turn back to him and say "Alright then mate".

Eyeball breaks into a big, yellow toothy smile and says "Cheers pal. I owe ya one"

He pops a cigarette in his mouth and heads over to the outside area.

I furiously scan through the tracks to find something that will put Eyeball in a killing mood but not kill the mood. *Peaches* is coming to an end. I start to sweat as it counts down - 15, 14, 13. The red light flashes and I hear *The Stranglers* begin to fade. Eyeball looks over expectedly. For some reason only one track comes to mind. With hesitant fingers I load the track and press play:

**SL2** - *On A Ragga Tip* (Original Mix)

Some of the crowd are up and at it now. I look over to Eyeball. He sticks one thumb up in the air and starts skanking. I line up the next track as Ole says goodbye to the girls and looks over to me with a nod.

## Suicide Sally and Ludivine Miss Lucifer

There were things that mothers would tell and warn their teenage daughters about that were obvious, there were things that they'd warn them about that they knew were going to happen anyway, boozing (definitely) sex (if we were lucky) and drugs (maybe), but the plan that was hatched between my best friend Ludivine Picoult and I through the girls' toilets, classrooms and bedrooms of our little suburban town of Fareham, Hampshire, would really, truly, absolutely, take the piss. If caught, there would be no excuses, no alibis through which we could explain ourselves, this really would break the bond of respect between a parent and a 16-year-old girl so profusely as to be (as we thought it) absolutely fucking hilarious. They would be so flabbergasted, perhaps even brought to tears by how honest and inexcusable it all was in its level of disrespect, that the very notion of us even thinking of doing it was a funny thing to be existing in itself. That's *why* we did it. It wasn't that we didn't respect our mothers, far from it, it's just that after we'd had our fulfilment of underage drinking amidst the familiar faces and locales of Fareham High Street, we needed something more, something epic, something akin to a great quest in its piss-take-stake of things.

Through a friend at our school, whose dad worked for the music industry, we had secured tickets to our favourite band Primal Scream (aka, "The Scream" or "Primal "Fucking" Scream") at London's Brixton Academy for the tour of their most recent album *Exterminator* and by purchasing tickets for the South Western Service direct to Waterloo we would go and see them; oh fuck yeah, we would go and rock our little princess hearts out to them and then get back in time for Saturday morning without anybody, parent or school, ever finding out. Ludivine (my sexy Belgian friend) had convinced her parents that she was staying at my house for the night, and I subsequently had told mine that I would be staying at hers, and with both our parents having never really properly communicated, it was a sure-fire bet that they'd never bother checking up on us. We snuck out, met up at the train station and jumped the crappy shit-stinking South Western all the way to Waterloo.

### *Inner Flight*

The nature of our mission was even more deliberately sinister than just the physical proximity of our distance from home. It was also miles away from the womanly decency our parents had come to expect of us. Hidden in both our handbags, were several sets of lingerie knickers and bras that we'd bought from an Anne Summers shop; sewn into the insides of them, we had placed notes describing various sex acts that we would like The Scream's front man, Bobby Gillespie, to do to us, followed by a reference number and one of our mobile phone numbers. Once inside The Academy then, we would lob these onto the stage and hope that afterwards Bobby, (or at least one of the band members) would call us back stage to perform such an act (and here's the funniest part) whichever one the reference number would then refer to, we'd have to go ahead and do. Of course, nobody ever decides on their own sex acts, do they? I had written Ludivine's and she had written mine and we spent the first half of that 90-minute journey pissing ourselves laughing over the depraved filth that our cruel friendship had conjured up. The funniest addition to all this was that we had stolen a rather conservative pair of underpants off our friend Ingrid, whose family were devout Christians, (believing in no sex before marriage and all that shite) in which Ludivine had written 'Give me some Christian bum love' followed by sketch of a crucifix that closely resembled a cartoon bum hole. Since Ingrid had not yet got her hands on a mobile phone, the number that was sketched down would go directly to her parents' landline of which was just sheer, cruel genius. If it were one of us and not Ingrid who was called up then, we would, as we had promised ourselves, have to go through with it, (if we didn't we would be a 'chav', and nobody wanted that). Now, as those tiny suburban stations shot past our windows and the sun began to set over the passing greenery of South East England, we knew there was no turning back.

Ludivine (a typical mainland European) had by this point, had had one, singular experience with intercourse whilst I (aside from a few cases of fun with Dick and Jane) was still technically a virgin and so the prospect was slightly scarier. For reasons of style as well as escapism from some of our insecurities, missions of this level required pseudonyms and so for tonight, as this was a rock gig, I, Sally Rains, would be Suicide Sally and Ludivine (after several name changes) would be Ludivine Miss Lucifer; what absolute fucking pussy cats!

After a few sips of the beers we'd bought from our local offie we began to become restless and went for a walk around the train. We hung out in the smoking carriage where we pretended to flirt, and hereby wind up the mouthy, chain-smoking chavs who were becoming briefly visible through the nicotine clouds and the shadows of their Burberry caps; ugly mongs en route to London from Gosport or Portsmouth or some dump near us. We kept this up until they sunk into their predictably crass ways upon reaction to our rock gear and our beers and so we gave them our own brand of mouthy abuse before heading back to our seats. A few more sips of our beers and the booze started to take on a mild effect, the clickety-clacking passing electricity poles began to remind me of rock music and our anticipations grew. Then came the build-up of the third-world-like high rises that marked the outskirts of London and their piss-stained concrete began to remind me of the aggressive darker edges to the *Exterminator* album of which many fans had had a problem with. Personally I preferred 1990's seminal *Screamadelica* and the two of us fell into a conversation over which of the two penultimate Scream albums was better (since we were so young, we had, incidentally, encountered all six at roughly the same time); *Screamadelica* I argued was not only a beautiful evocation of the band's innocent youth finding its musical voice but also as an historical document of the rise in hope and ecstasy culture that had arisen in the absence of Margaret Thatcher. Having both tried half a pill before, we were both familiar with the album's association to ecstasy but Ludivine, originally being from Belgium, had no idea about what Thatcher was all about and so therefore didn't particularly get this angle (neither did I if I was honest).

*Exterminator,* however, as Ludivine argued, was simply just the modern equivalent and that it was currently too present tense to be appreciated yet, she claimed that it would, in time, bookend our former decade with the notion that *that* party was now well and truly over and we were about to enter meaner, darker times to come; every reason, she concluded, for living our lives to the grittiest extreme whilst we still had it tonight. What was it with the French, (or Frenchified culture if you want) where they were always so bloody political about things? I still disagreed.

One year later, terrorists would fly two hijacked aircrafts into New York's World Trade Center, killing thousands in the worst terrorist atrocity in western history. Two years later this would instigate the U.S and the U.K into entering an illegal war on global terrorism via the invasion of Iraq, kick starting a much more fucked up world. The album's comments on political corruption and modern warfare would hereby hit the level of historical cultural significance that Ludivine was speaking of. She was right. Bitch.

Finally, the train pulled to a halt and we jumped off into the hustle and bustle of Waterloo station; we both needed a piss and so went to its public toilets where we had to dish out 20 pence just to enter; *'20p!? How much for a shit?'* I asked the porter.

We later went outside and found ourselves near the South Bank where the night's walkways were lit up by great neon lights of blues and greens that shone from the above cabins of the newly erected London Eye as well as from the glass walking panels beneath us, whoah, despite the British pessimism that had greeted the millennium celebrations, the year 2000 really was quite futuristic we thought to ourselves. Anyway, enough of this evocative bullshit, we had totally failed to realise that access to the Underground was back inside Waterloo Station and we'd just wasted 15 minutes of our young lives looking at both Europe's biggest Ferris Wheel and the back end to some theatre. Back in we went where we purchased an underground ticket and rattled our way through the claustrophobic confines of the Northern and later the Victoria Lines to emerge upon the streets of Brixton.

Brixton at night merely resembled a street of lit up chicken and kebab shops where its heaving crowds of mixed cultures, but mostly black, made their way between the collapsing structures of the street markets that were packing themselves away for the night and allowing the honking traffic to continue. By the looks of the markets they too also seemed to sell chicken and kebabs which struck us as pointless. Cigarette and ganja smoke were everywhere, as were the shady characters who were smoking them, 'Brixton was a troublesome ghetto' Ludivine told me, 'and it was true' because she'd read about it, apparently. A short walk away, behind its prison-like barrier fences, the Brixton Academy wasn't quite ready yet and so, with us being out of beers, we decided on a quick trip to the cash machine, find a nearby pub, get tanked up before maybe trying to make some friends. Of course, this then took us to that dilemma that was somewhat universal amongst all teenagers; that terrible barrier of getting served alcohol. Furthermore, in rough old Brixton, there was an extra barrier of having huge motherfucking doormen. There were three known methods to get past such things, the first was that beautiful (but short lived) method that came upon the dawn of the computer age that enabled more tech savvy teenagers to create fake I.Ds that could fool adults, the other was specific to our sex in that all we had to do was push our tits up a bit, apply some make-up manipulation and pull an innocent smile and there would be no problem getting in at all, ('girls never start fights, do they?' Hahahaha, fuck you and your face!) needless to say, voluptuous, sexy-broken-English, Ludivine Miss Lucifer was fucking excellent at this. These first two methods seemed to work upon our gum-chewing mammoth man as we approached but we also adopted the third since it was something that could be continued all the way up to the bar. This third technique had been created mostly by boys (since they couldn't pull off the second) and was named 'the conversation technique' whereby, if you appear to be in deep, enthusiastic conversation and not concentrating on the presence of these massive men, then they'd automatically assume you were past the nervous wreck stage that would normally befall such an underage drinker and would just assume you were mature enough to be going about your everyday adult, conversation-based lives.

The place was rammed with Scream fans, which was good for making friends but shit if you wanted a place to rest your drink (i.e: a table) so we smoked and waited, the booze now reacting to some pretty good tunes and running nicely through our systems like some fucked up, cross-eyed ferret. Everywhere, as we had taken notice, the crowd were, for some unexplained reason, throwing packets of crisps at each other of which seemed to be making the bar staff look somewhat suicidal. Eventually, we heard "do you girls want a seat?" and by some miracle, there was an otherwise rammed table that had two spare seats for us. We took them and found ourselves in the company of a dreadlocked woman called Helen and her friends (I only remember two of them) Jaqueline and Paul. They were around their early thirties and were doing PhDs in medicine. Lying about our true ages as to not draw attention to ourselves of course, we began to discuss at length the works of Primal (fucking) Scream, and with them being old enough to have truly understood Thatcherism I thought I could win one over Ludivine (and negotiate my way out of one of my later sexual shenanigans – this bitch was dirty) by proving her theory of *Exterminator* being the best to be absolutely wrong. To our great surprise then this older group began explaining the complexity of their previous album, *Vanishing Point,* of which I was told was designed to be the imaginary soundtrack to a film I'd never heard of. This group were so generous in buying us round after round that we at first became somewhat suspicious of them before simply deciding from their welcoming smiles that they were just simply, sound-as-fuck people. Pretty soon then, being suitably pissed, we decided that we were bonding with this generous bunch rather well (but not well enough to have revealed our diabolical plan) and so we asked them if they would like to join us for the gig. They revealed however, that they had actually sold their Scream tickets to instead attend something better at *Fabric*, a massive nightclub in Farringdon, which was somewhere in the north of the city but not too far away. Suddenly understanding that they had one Scream ticket still yet to sell, they just gave it to us free of charge, suggesting that we could sell it outside the Academy and maybe make a tenner for ourselves. The mystery as to why they were so sound with us and not especially to anyone else in that establishment was something that would always stay with me. Maybe med students had enough money to not care?

Anyway, eventually this group left and we were by ourselves again. A strange, wild-eyed black guy in a massive winter jacket was prowling the place, whispering strange words into people's ears that I immediately associated with a drugs sketch from TV's *Brasseye.* The moment he leant over our table I was able to make sense of a few of them through his thick Jamaican accent, 'weed' 'E' 'Coke' 'for The Scream' of which Ludivine somehow made sense of as 'We eat cocks and scream', why ever the fuck she thought someone would be saying that, I don't know. As he leant over our table however, the massive hand of mammoth man caught hold of this dude and in a hail of Jamaican 'fuck yous" he was dragged outside. Caught off guard, as we were at this moment, the doorman then locked eyes with us and our sixteen-year-old selves was revealed through our veneers; he could smell the morning dew that was teen pubescence and also made us leave in a manner that was far more polite than what happened to this drug dealer. On our way outside, the booze still running around our systems, we decided that we still weren't munted enough to go to the gig just yet and so we approached the mad man who'd been thrown out before us of whom was now hassling the crowds outside.

"What you after baby?" he asked.

"Just some weed" we said, and he began to lead us under some sodium-lit bridge way. He was scary, he stank and his eyes were massive and had it not been for our poison currently taking effect I would have considered this situation more suspicious than I did. In the shadows he undid his winter jacket and from inside, beyond a smell of B.O like I'd never smelt before, were a series of protruding compartments containing, god knows, all kinds of shit I suppose. He eventually pulled out from one them, a bag full of weed and said "purple haze, fucking beautiful girls".

"Okay".

At which point, he dramatically and frantically began ratcheting up the price throughout the short time that it took us to assemble our notes. We managed to cut this process short at £40 and his exchange was surprisingly honest. Noticing the flashing blues of police lights intercepting the sodium yellows of the night, he then disappeared his own way into the darkness and we went ours.

We were now in the orbit of bars, food vendors and alleyways that surrounded the Brixton Academy and we found our own private alleyway, somewhere next to some great disused warehouse, where with some Rizlas we were able to construct a joint. It was good stuff and the giggles started. It was during this moment of stoned contemplation that we decided it would be a good time to call our parents and further convince them of the accuracy to our alibi. I went first, the usual shit, and then went Ludivine; however she was managing to blag her way past her parents isn't especially relevant as it was all Belgian for bullshit anyway. Her call however was then suddenly interrupted by the emergence of some very strange high-pitched whistling rebounding off the concrete walls that surrounded us. Then, as if this very whistling had pulled him into existence, there appeared a young black man dressed entirely in yellow clothing strutting towards us with each leg stretching out to an almighty distance before him as he walked on. He was gripping a huge bottle of beer in one hand. This was all we needed to make a convincing phone con and I could tell by Ludivine Miss Lucifer's expressions that she was making some excuse to her parents as to what this background auditory presence was supposed to be. What excuses could she have possibly been making? Then he stopped and spoke in what I can only describe as the most ridiculous high-pitched voice I've ever heard;

"Hey sexy ladies, what's happenin'?"

My gestures to make him shut the fuck up came to no use.

"Do you know the best thing about being a man, baby? It's that you can get your thing out and you can piss wherever you want" His flies came down, his knob fell out and he began pissing on the bins...

"...and now I'm pissing right here, you get me?"

Ludivine was quickly saying her "au revoirs" and hanging up. How the hell would she get out of this one? And if she got busted I sure would be too. Who was this interfering prick?

The booze and drugs then decided his fate without a moment of doubt; my fingers flicked forward and the burning end of the spliff shot through the Brixton air like a perfectly homed missile and reacted with flecks of hot ash like a meteorite collision upon his knob. His eyes widened first before the pain set in and following a scream that nearly broke glass, he began bouncing around like a comedy rabbit and clutching his member, his still-streaming piss bouncing off every surface available to him and spraying back upon him until dripping wet from head to toe. Two forms of justice in one I thought.

"Ah shit girl, you just burnt my dick!" he was saying as he bounced up and down. Finally, some sense came to him and he placed his injured piece into the top of that big bottle and presumably into the cooling beer within, his eyes now expressing his relief.

"Why did you do that? You shouldn't have done that Sal" declared Ludivine at me. How dare she complain at me avenging his thoughtlessness toward us I thought, and the two of us fell into a mini scrap that tumbled back onto the floor, all to the high-pitched sounds of "Yo baby, yo baby, calm down".

At this point, headlights appeared up ahead and we stopped as a lone Rolls Royce drifted past us and from inside some elderly, affluent types (we hoped it was the royal family) looked upon two young wrestling women on the floor before a piss-dripping man with his dick in a bottle of which of course from their angle, and when silhouetted beneath the sodium yellows, must've looked like a massive, deliriously oversized member. They drove on past and all three of us found this hilariously funny. I apologised to this man, whose name he revealed was Bodrin, and for a man who'd just had his goldfish head burnt by a teenage girl, was surprisingly sweet about the whole thing. This had made me feel more guilty than I cared to feel about the matter and with time now pushing on and with us not being arsed to sell on that third ticket Helen had given us, we decided to take Bodrin with us. It turned out he used to be something of a fan and so everybody was more or less happy. Punch the sky, a freeze frame happy ending...for now.

### Accelerator

The three of us got into the auditorium to be struck by the smells of nicotine, ganja, booze and sweat. The supporting act, Asian Dub Foundation, were already halfway through their set. Although their sound and back lighting effects were quite striking to our stoned and pissed little minds, they weren't really our scene, and after all, with much work so soon afoot, we scrambled through the crowds to the bar to further prep up. It was here that we concluded that for all the years the government had spent in trying to tackle the dangers of Brixton (of which were often mentioned on the news) all of it had finally amounted to nothing but.....the creation of the plastic, anti-violent pint cup, an odd observation that once again began making us feel strangely politicised in readiness for the prospects of the aggressive, angry power of *Exterminator* being played live!

The crowd were waiting now, whistling and cheering into the darkness as the silhouettes of techies could be seen setting up various stuff on stage, the silhouettes to the fingers of Suicide Sally and Ludivine Miss Lucifer however were going into our bags and pulling at panty strings. A few more silhouettes appeared on stage and upon recognising that it was them from their figures we laughed about which one of them might have the bigger dick and which one of us (maybe both) might receive it. Electric lights flared up and they burst into the intense behemoth of unstoppable guitar energy that was the track *Accelerator,* surely one of the angriest tracks ever recorded? The crowd went fucking bat shit! A mosh pit had started at the front of the crowd and was spreading wider afield whilst Bodrin was for some reason screaming like a girl.

Ping, ping, ping, and the first sets of our gorgeous panties were flying. I got some on the stage and at least one caught over Martin Duffy's keyboard, most of Ludvine Miss Lucifer's just landed on the floor or got caught up in the ocean of dreadlocked and Mohican haircuts before us.

*Accelerator* melded into *Motorhead,* that then melded into *Rocks, Exterminator, Swastika Eyes, Kill All Hippies* and so on and so on, at one point Bobby glanced in the direction of where his sex missiles were coming from, wherein we lifted our tops and flashed him our tits (we were braless, naturally), he seemed to ignore this whilst we did seem to get a laugh out of Mani, of whom being the band's newest member, having jumped off from *The Stone Roses,* was striking us as the soundest and made me wonder about what special treatment Ludivine Miss Lucifer might grant him if he was to call her. Suddenly two pairs of massive hands grabbed us from behind with a force worthy of bruising and we jumped aside, taken aback to be greeted by some massive tattooed biker type and his mates laughing at us. We gave him Suicide Sally and Ludivine Miss Lucifer's own foul-mouthed brand of abuse before, it seemed, Bodrin had tried to intervene and start a fight with them...*all of them*. The widening, Viking eyes of this man and his group, pretty much suggested that Bodrin was about to get well and truly shat on, and although we thought it sweet of our odd new friend to stick up for two teenage girls like this without any real reason to do so, we quickly took the advice of some nearby long-haired type that "The Scream don't write for this kind of vibe", and we were quickly moved to some other part of the crowd. Oh well, we had experienced some rough stuff; had to happen at some stage. Ludivine Miss Lucifer and I would surely dream up some kind of revenge later on, maybe upon his Viking balls.

Needless to say, the rest of the gig was shitting great and amidst the screams and smoke that met the darkness of The Scream's short break, we decided we could get away with a sly spliff. The clearly-more experienced Bodrin rolled it for us and the colours of our vision began to stream for every time we turned our heads. It was strong shit and we were now pissed and stoned simultaneously. This state then followed appropriately into the encore song of *Higher than the Sun,* of which the deliberately retro lighting made us feel like we were lifting to the sky whilst trapped amidst the reds and yellows of some crashing videogame; reflecting off Bodrin's eccentrically yellow attire of course, it made him resemble some sort of fluorescent, squeaky-voiced god lifting back off the earth after having previously failed to fit in anywhere within it, probably because of his rancid smell of piss. Upon the more mental *Come Together*, we started on the bras, implying to our targets that maybe there were two nubile girls in their audience who were prepared to run around bottomless before they went topless; what absolute fucking pussycats, yes! Whatever then happened behind the sprays of the smoke machine, I don't know, but one of my precious bras, our arousing weapons of choice, must've got snagged on something and somehow caused a technical fault, bringing the gig to a temporary darkened standstill, drawing everyone's attention to both the sound and the massive arse of the woman in front of me who thought she could get away with pissing into her plastic pint cup whilst the crowd would be too psyched to notice - her face went red with embarrassment. Finally, like a sputtering car, The Scream's light show and smoke machine started back up and they continued. Most of the gig's second half had consisted of their *Screamadelica* stuff and finally it was over whereby amidst the dispersing crowds we realised just how well and truly trashed we actually were.

We had no more bras and panties left of course and neither were any of the band yet calling us so we joined everyone else in the 'funnel of I-desperately-need-a-piss hell' that constitutes the end of any half decent gig and we were led back outside onto the Brixton streets where the buzzing crowds were now drinking and smoking on the curbs and spilling into the fast food places (the French ones were all talking politics). One lone knobhead, clearly led on by the rage of *Exterminator,* was trying to kick the glass out of one of the bus stops only for his foot to go through it rather than break it and secure him in his own unmovable trap that enabled the police to arrive to arrest his hopping, gimping self.

Giggling, we waited with further anticipation for our phone calls (surely our missiles, our delirious silk boner makers had been disruptive enough for them to want to take notice) but nothing came. It was on this corner of the street that we then became re-aquainted with Bodrin who was now laying his bizarre rhetoric upon some poor street guitar player. We then noticed that a short distance away, that biker prick who had earlier grabbed unpermitted the o'royal tits of Suicide Sally and Ludivine Miss Lucifer had fallen into some kind of argument with our other encounter of the night, that mad-eyed Jamaican drug dealer from before. It was obviously concerning drugs and with both sides of the party clearly being absolute psychos it was quickly getting out of hand. With the crowd now parting to stand transfixed like the blood-thirsty apes that they were, nobody seemed to see exactly how, what happened next, had actually happened; after a couple of typical pushes and shoves then, a blow seemed to have been made to our dealer's face of which then sent some of the contents of that massive jacket of his to go hurtling through the Brixton air and land just before our feet. Whilst this fight was temporarily (albeit, even more aggressively) being separated by one of the biker's mates, Ludivine went on to pull an expression that drew my attention to what the contents of this man's pockets were. Amongst some other shit, there were two plastic bags in particular, one of which contained another of this dealer's exotic poisons in a powdered form, and the other, two slips of paper with the word *'Fabric'* printed upon them. Our outrageous behaviour had clearly led the gods of our friend Ingrid's world to abandon us and now it was the lord of sin who was granting gifts upon us.

'No', I whispered to my sexy friend, of whose red lipstick then seemed to resemble the newly-sucked blood of some vampish nymph as she pulled a terrible, wicked smile before squatting down to slyly place these contents into the pockets of her tight jeans.

It was at that point that we saw the dealer patting down the bumps in his thick jacket to realise that he'd lost what he had and then, *it* happened. Turning back to the biker he shouted;

"Where's my tickets? Where's my gear? You thievin' white cunt"

"What? You callin' me *a cunt!*?"

"You fuckin' thievin' cunt", at which point a blow was thrown back, and then back again.

The faces of the surrounding sadists lit up upon the promise of more bloodshed and we figured it was no-turning-back time once again and began our sly walk away.

The faces of the gathering crowd turned to white-eyed horror and everyone dispersed in what felt like slow motion as our most generous of mad men then reached into a further compartment of his jacket and pulled out something resembling black lead. Screams, shouts and pounding footwear was then everywhere and that street musician that Bodrin had been harassing (with a guitar strapped to his back!) seemed to pull off a perfected somersault over a 6-foot brick wall into a courtyard or somewhere and now the three of us had entered one of those nightmare, slow-motion dream runs. From behind there was a *Blam-Blam-Blam* and the streets lit up like fire. Turning onto the next street, Bodrin and the two us ran towards the direction of the flashing, streaming blue sirens that were coming our way from an unknown distance. From out of them we saw the silhouettes of the police quickly running towards and past us with their batons out before them like waving, comedy erections and we weren't sure whether to laugh or scream. The sirens lit up the streets to a maddening blue and all I could think about was that we were young, we had thrown our knicks at The Scream, we were high, we had just had some form of disturbing revenge and we were going clubbing, *for free!* Absolute fucking pussy cats indeed!

Whilst Suicide Sally and Ludivine Miss Lucifer would never receive the phone calls of their expectations that night, something curious had later happened over subsequent years; The band Primal Scream's next album *Evil Heat* (another that was also inspired by the world's ongoing political depressions) would contain a track entitled *Miss Lucifer*, whilst the one after that, 2006's *Riot City Blues,* would contain a track called *Suicide Sally and Johnny Guitar.* Whether or not these tracks were indeed, inspired by the names sewn into this duo's underwear is left unproven, although they're inclined to believe it's a 'yes'.

### Don't Fight it, Feel it

We quickly found a black cab, which span the three of us through the darkened streets en route to Fabric; we remembered briefly crossing the river but other than that didn't know where the fuck we were going. Bodrin's legs wouldn't stop bouncing as if the music hadn't stopped, which seemed to irritate our driver who was just trying to concentrate on some political debate from his radio. Eventually we screeched up before the pounding front doors of Fabric and this area struck us as even rougher at night than Brixton was but we were just too fucked to care by now. We'd survived one mad ordeal of violence (although the weight of it was beginning to take shape upon the backgrounding sober self of my tenderer Sally Rains) but Ludivine Miss Luifer and I could easily survive some more, we thought. We joined the queue and the prospects of Fabric's even bigger doormen finding our substances began to sober us up slightly but we decided that if The Scream were too pussy to go all the way with us tonight, then we would go all the way with the night itself; there was no turning back...again. The powder of which we had acquired, as Bodrin had informed us, was MDMA of which Ludivine then decided was best hid up herself, something of which I then did too with the little weed that we had left. Finally we came to the doorman, what did we do? Conversation method – you know the drill, works every time. This time it even got us and our drugs past what looked like weapon scanners; *just how dangerous was this place?*

We were inside; if Primal (Fucking) Scream had put on a spectacle of a light show from the distance of the stage, then the inside of Fabric made us feel like we were a part of that gig's electrical circuitry itself; the place seemed to suggest a history as some kind of storage place, since its layout consisted of a vast network of rabbit-warren-like brick tunnels that seemed to lead further and further underground, each of these tunnels was alive with intense light and the pounding sounds of dance music of which then connected, like great cables, to immense chambers of dance floors through which an ocean of faces could be seen through flickering lasers and smoke. If the concoction of booze, drugs and music were making me feel like some kind of uncontrollable parasite was running through my blood stream, then now I felt like the uncontrollable parasite running its way through London's bloodstream. And this music? This bass? It was so heavy as to shake the walls around us, the progression of the music throughout the night, like the states of Bodrin, Ludivine Miss Lucifer and myself, had progressed from rock music to something that seemed to have just lost the plot. Something about it all just didn't feel quite right, yet. We explored the place further, going from tunnel to tunnel, it was dark, confusing and occasionally scary before we were led out into one of the same chamber dance floors that we'd been through several times already. Overall, we had counted three of these dance floors, the smaller one seemed to be the most intense with somewhat darker, harder dance music; the second, of which appeared to be in some kind of basement, was playing music resembling electronic punk whilst the main one, the biggest one (where we were now) seemed to be playing more conventional hard house.

From the balcony that overlooked this particular dance floor, there stood a bar that shone out of the darkness like some kind of hazily streaming, neon cloud. At first we were surprised to see that there wasn't a heaving queue like there was at the Academy and at the fact that the bartender then approached us, did so in the fashion of an inquisitive insect like we were something unfamiliar to his realm. This was less surprising, of course, when we realised that one lager and two Smirnoff Ice's came to £25 and we began to fear that the exploits of our nightly duo would soon run out of cash and we'd be forced to go home; this of course, for the purpose of us truly taking the piss, just *could not* happen! We leant over the railing of this balcony and watched the dance floor where we began to feel a strange sense of detachment from both the creatures of our newly discovered universe and its strange, otherworldly music. Its inhabitants were dancing in an erratic fashion that was faster than any human should be able to move, they were hugging and kissing each other with more apparent love than any of us had seen in the outside world, it would have been somewhat amazing if the first two weren't compromised by them all seemingly talking absolute shit. This was not a place whose vibe was dictated by the influence of lager and Smirnoff ices we then decided, and so it was time to try something else and try to get on their wavelength. After giving Bodrin his own cut, Ludivine Miss Lucifer and I entered the ladies toilets together; every cubicle was closed and behind them was more sniffing than a flu pandemic. Finally three girls emerged from one of these cubicles with the grins and eyes of something that might live under a bridge, and now it was our turn.There was a shelf in this cubicle that seemed to have been placed here for exactly the purposes of what we were going to do next. We locked the door, used our national insurance card to cut the stuff into lines across the shelf. Brief paranoia turned to giggles and with a rolled-up tenner we snorted the stuff up our little pussy cat noses! Yes!

We returned to meet a newly grinning Bodrin back at the bar, and we waited. Then I noticed somebody I thought I'd recognised choosing the sensible option of a drink back over at the hazy neon cloud. Who was he? A tall man in a leather jacket. Where do I know him from? No. *No*, it couldn't have been?! *Holy shit!* Oh no! It was Mr Hawling, teacher of maths at our school! For sure, (in retrospect) he was young enough to be going to this type of establishment, but this place didn't fit with his reputation of sitting at home in his spare time and reciting mathematical formulas. Not at all! I, Suicide Sally, had formerly repressed my feelings that Fabric might had been a piss-taking stake too high and this was its backlash, he would surely see us any moment now and we'd be done for? Our parents would know, our school would know, and the terrifyingly conservative forces that ruled our world would permanently sever the glue between Suicide Sally and Ludivine Miss Lucifer forever. I told Lucifer that we had to go, only for her sexy Belgian face to turn and place two lips against mine and say something exotic and French as she pulled away. Knowing that I didn't understand French, it was clear that our substances had suddenly taken effect, she had joined them, she had joined the same state as our surrounding minions and so I turned to Bodrin, who was stood grinning motionless, the UV lights reflecting off his stupid florescent clothing like some kind of alien - he had gone too, I was alone in this world now and so I ran back to the toilets to hide.

It was at this point in my life that I learnt that when one is on strong drugs, one should not sit still, for sitting still, (like I was, on the toilet) is when the heebie-jeebies are able to catch up with you, and at that moment, all the tiny moments that had made up the night so far began to fit together as one big painting of absolute menace. Shit! The unknown goings on of my home, the money, the booze, the sexual promises I'd made, the drugs, the shooting (what *the fuck!!*) and now Mr Hawling?! All of this would surely have consequences? It was all a mistake! Where the hell were we? How would we get back?! Shit, fuck! The room was beginning to spin and the morning would be drawing closer. Somehow, I'd acquired a bottle of water from somewhere and tried to sober myself up by refilling more and more from the sinks, the pounding music was still thundering through the walls and the one hundred sniffs coming from behind the cubicle doors weren't helping. Spots. Oh shit. Spots were appearing on the walls that hadn't been there before and I drank more. Suddenly my mind switched to the headlines of the UK's continually negative newspaper stories about the teenagers who'd died in similar places from taking ecstasy, oh shit, that was from ecstasy, what the fuck had I just taken? Why had I believed that prick Bodrin? Wait, those girls had never died from ecstasy, it was from the water they'd drunk to hydrate themselves, their brains had drowned, I remembered, shit, shit, I had to stop drinking water I realised, but I was dehydrating, *dehydrating!* Oh fuck, this is how it would begin! The women emerging from the cubicles, their nostrils flaring, were beginning to notice my state now, and the spots on the walls had become beetles, lots of them, hopping in and out of each other. I had decided that I didn't want my young life to end in this toilet and so panic set in. I thought of the heartbreak I would inflict upon my parents upon my death here and so I screamed. It was at this point that Ludivine entered with a face of twisted euphoria.

"Ludivine, I think something's going wrong" I told her.

"Try to calm down. It's all in your head" she explained.

Beetles.

"No, no, I'm going to die here" I cried.

"You are not going to die my sexy –

Beetles

– Suicide Sally, you just have to come outside –

Beetles

- and join in with other people" She went on.

"Mr Hawling's outside, the maths teacher."

"No he's not" She denied. Could he have been a hallucination, like the beetles?

"He is. It was those guns in Brixton –

Beetles

"...this is our punishment. He can't see us like this".

"Where is he?"

"At the bar"

"There's nobody at the bar!"

Beetles, beetles, beetles. Sniff, sniff, sniff.

"He is Ludivine, we're fucked".

"No, *you're* fucked, come on" She took my hand and was leading me outside. I dragged myself free, nothing was going to take me outside now.

"Let me stay here for a while, please".

The beetles were fucking everywhere and I felt my brain drowning, or did I?

"Okay, we'll stay" said Ludivine, who then began stopping me from overdoing it on the water. My breathing slowed in pace, I consumed less water and the beetles began to return to their homes behind the tiles.

At this point, a woman emerged from the cubicles after a long time sniffing; we recognised her and she seemed to recognise us too. She was from the pub earlier, one of the sound-as-fuck crowd; the prettier one, Jaqueline, we remembered her name and she hugged us, frightening me slightly but making Ludivine love her even more. As we then remembered, she was a medical student and I began to feel some hope from whatever expertise she could bring to my conundrum. Ludivine explained proceedings to her and after telling me about both better, medical-textbook breathing techniques and that this bohemian bathroom was not doing my mind any good, she began to relax me back to a state of normality and we all linked hands, two sexy girls and I, and we began to leave the place back out into the madness. I was led downwards through the tunnels (no sign of Mr Hawling) and into one of the brick archway chambers that had temporarily fallen silent from the music. We descended an iron staircase through a cloud of cigarette smoke and entered the crowd where Jaqueline's sound-as-fuck crew were awaiting and we were all suddenly more than enthusiastic about seeing each other as if we were all such long-term friends or something. Suddenly I then realised that whether or not it is drugs or a lifetime that make you feel such a way towards another human being, whether it is a reality or an illusion, shouldn't really matter, it all felt good, and we all fucking knew it. We chatted about the gig of which we had completed our diabolical plan whilst they began to explain that everybody here was waiting for some kind of DJ set to begin; this was the set they'd sold the Scream tickets for; I had failed to pay attention to what the name of this DJ was and still, to this day, can't remember. Anyway, the lights went down, everyone screamed or lit up fags and then the set began; at first a slow build-up of weird ambient sounds before a sonic collapse into intense energy and laser work. I remember developing the strange notion that those pesky bathroom beetles may had appeared at that moment to take me away with them. It was gorgeous, beautiful, every wave of bass that vibrated through my body felt like the touch of love, and the lasers that flickered off our faces were like the refreshing sprays of some kind of warm shower, warm or cold, whatever temperature your body needed, they were providing it. I could feel how the muscles in my face were feeling strained by the stretch of my smile and my friends, Ludivine, Bodrin, Helen and the others, were all doing the same. We loved the music and we loved each other, finally then, it had taken me all this time, until the age of 16 to understand that the 'love' that had been mentioned throughout the stories of my childhood had finally been granted to me and the negative state that I'd felt in the bathroom was almost inconceivable now. I leant over and kissed the beautiful Ludivine Miss Lucifer and she held me tightly; I looked over her shoulder into the crowd and saw that everyone else was looking back at us with equally ecstatic smiles and the two of us tried to discuss over the sound how this was how society was supposed to be, how it was the positive alternative to the political troubles that *Exterminator* was talking about and how such techniques of music and light should be harnessed as a means of creating global peace. This, my friends, was fucking amazing, *this* was the answer!

A balding, middle-aged man winked at me from within the crowds, not in a creepy way, but in a sort of fatherly gesture of 'now you get it, girl'. I thought he looked vaguely familiar and I winked back at him as if to say 'being bald is cool' to which he smiled again. We had joined the men like him, on their new, heavenly, bald universe.

Despite the love that was going on in that chamber that night, a clearing had once again formed around Bodrin, whose long, florescent limbs were going fucking Jedi ape-shit, and then we realised that unbeknown to Bodrin, his dick was still hanging from his flies from earlier on and was doing the best moves on the entire floor. We left him to it, maybe we'd tell him in the morning. God knows how long we were dancing for but we were covered in sweat and our muscles hurt...

...Suddenly, (what the fuck?) all eight of us (and some others) were sat on the staircases of the corridors, our teeth gnawing and chatting about some shit that everyone, my new best friends, seemed to be so deeply involved with. I had smoked nearly a whole pack of cigarettes and had half a pint in my hand although fuck knows where it had all come from.

Whatever we were talking about, Ludivine Miss Lucifer seemed to be very involved (probably politics); I didn't really need to join in, I was just enjoying the feelings of this new substance I'd discovered, all I seemed to really be able to focus upon was how the lighter was somehow being worshipped by my group, passed about like some unnoticed conch that was allowing them to express their opinions. This conch then brought forward the very thing I'd forgotten about but had always been fearing. A hand, at the end of a long leather jacket, slapped Helen on the shoulder and asked for its turn with my lighter, Suicide Sally and Ludivine Miss Lucifer then tried to hide from the sudden appearance of the chain-smoking Mr Hawling but couldn't as his own fucked self then proceeded to sit down and join in with the conversation. All we could do was stare; stare at each other, our pretty, pussycat mouths open wide in disbelief at what was happening, had he recognised our pubescent 16-year-old selves behind our gorgeous babe make-up? Holy shit, this couldn't be happening, surely we're fucked?

"Don't freak out, that would only draw attention to ourselves" seemed to be the only idea that was being psychically expressed between our sexy, young selves; "he must go soon, surely?" Whatever the fuck our sound-as-fuck crew were talking about before, and how the fuck Mr Hawling had managed to interject his own opinions into the equation seemed to now suddenly be fascinating Helen and her friends, spooling off their discussion into a whole new direction. From what I can now remember of it however, I too, was also fascinated. It went somewhere along the lines of that; as based upon patterns throughout history, our society, through a combination of technological progression and industrial, corporate expansion (his example of the recent trend of the mobile phone encapsulating both), was more than mathematically likely to move on from the liberal 1990s into an age of absolute, complete conformity; this being a conformity of art, of music and of beliefs and social structures before eventually reaching a tension point whereby it would all then fall apart and be forced to redefine itself as something new; I read this, simply, as something meaning that cynicism would evolve into optimism, was I right? Even on all the drugs that they were, the medical students were able to get their heads around this and were left aghast with looks of having just discovered the meaning of life. Could this be true? Had our school's Mr Hawling, the man who stays at home to recite maths theories, have just turned up at Fabric to announce that he had ways of predicting the future? At least for the upcoming decade? To our future doctors? And why, oh why the fuck, was he *here*? And had he recognised *us*? His theory finally ended on the note that during his said era of conformity, things that had been previously dismissed from the various sub-groups of a liberal society would somehow come to be recognised by everyone, whereby Ludivine Miss Lucifer (oh Ludivine, oh Ludivine, my typically voluptuous mainland European) intervened with,

"Have you recognised us yet then?"

What had she done? By Jesus, titting Christ! Love was over! Now we were fucked and I would well and truly kick her Belgian arse back to French land and its stupid French, fucking, aarrrrgh!

On second thoughts, I was too loved up to care.

Mr Hawling scanned the two of us; the terrified face of Suicide Sally followed by the devilish face of Ludivine Miss Lucifer and he simply responded with;

"Yes, Ms Rains and Ms Picoult, I believe".

That Belgian bitch was going to die when I got out of here.

"Are you going to tell?" she responded.

"What is there to tell? That people have individual lives? I'm not here to do a fucking register." and with that, he was gone, and we were suddenly reminded that Mr Hawling might had been the soundest teacher in the history of all teachers.

Helen and the med students were somewhere between spooked and mind-blown and the conch had stopped being passed around, stopping the flow of conversation somewhat. Therefore, Helen suggested that we all move on, back to her place for a *Big Brother Finale* party; Jesus, this shit was never ending! We grabbed our things and left whereupon on the way out, I had a second encounter with that same, balding, middle-aged man from before; we hugged and an unspoken goodbye was felt between us. Such moments of drugged up love then, I began to realise, as this MDMA stuff was beginning to mellow, would, and could, only ever be temporary.

As the two of us parted, Helen and her company began cheering me and I didn't fully understand until they informed me that the man in question had been a popular and revolutionary radio DJ known as John Peel. It was then that I recognised him.

Four years later, the champion of independent music would die of a sudden cardiac arrest whilst holidaying in Cusco, Peru. Losing the influence he had over radio (coupled with the rise of the internet and the changing the ways in which we discovered and bought music) commercial radio stations began granting less and less time to more eclectic musicians, preventing any truly exciting artists from ever emerging onto mainstream channels. Eventually, of course, corporately manufactured pop music (most of it consisting of cover versions) became the mainstream, turning television's *The X Factor* into one of the most commercially successful TV shows both in the U.K and the U.S and making producers such as Simon Cowell, (not the artists) into the new musical superstars. The spirit of music (all kinds of good music that is) could be said to have died with John Peel.

### Higher than the Sun

Where was I? Back south of the river I thought, somewhere in Vauxhall, in Helen's student place; I too, would later go to university and it had to be said that out of all the student places I ever got to see during my life's adventures, this was a *very* good one, we were in a large front room with two huge sofas and it had a nice kitchen and bathroom too, the place alone made me think that perhaps medicine might had been a good career to pursue but for some reason I ended up studying music theory.

The curtains were still drawn and although I was worrying about the prospects of the journey home my sexy Belgian friend and I would soon have to take, the drugs were now mellowing me into a state of carelessness, everything seemed great simply in the moment, every distance seemed walkable, every problem seemed solvable and everybody in the world was presumably in the same state of mind as we were.

Something was attached to my head, something elastic, I reached up and felt the face of a paper mask pushed up over my forehead, I pulled it down to see the image of that sand bag-like face of the *Big Brother 1* contestant, Craig Phillips, with the eyes cut out. Looking around the room, I saw that everyone else was wearing the same thing; oh yeah, I thought, the *Big Brother Finale* party, that's where we were. The fact that everyone was wearing these was either a sign of two things, either, because the finishing episode of Channel 4's social experiment (of which had played earlier in the day and of which Helen was currently rewinding the pre-recorded footage of), was so immensely predictable that my company were already sure of the winner, or that they'd already been *told* of the actual winner and had purchased or made these stupid masks within a time frame that made no sense in relation to the chronology of this night's events. Then again, although it all seems stupid now, *Big Brother 1* had actually been taken rather seriously by the general public back then and people had placed bets on this shit. Anyway, despite the sofas, we were all sat with our backs to the walls and spliffs and bottled beers were doing the rounds; Helen finished rewinding, pressed play (these were the days of VHS tapes) and we all pulled Craig Phillips masks over our faces to make stupid animal noises as we awaited the climax.

That *Big Brother* gas chamber seemed somehow important in its lonesomeness at that moment in time and Craig was hugging the other last contestant under the spotlights, (some Irish girl, a nun from what I can remember) as they stood somewhat unaware of just how many viewers this stupid show (a first for Britain) had attracted. It kept cutting back to the studio where Davina McCall was awaiting the results of the votes on a headset, and then she announced it, "the winner is Craig Sandbag-head Phillips!", before the house's electric doors flung open and fed him to a legion of his caged-up audiences like something out of a zombie film. Jesus, they were going titting mental! Ludivine Miss Lucifer and I then concluded that all this shite must've been being televised at somewhere around the exact point Primal (Fucking) Scream must've been finishing their set and that this crowd was bigger than anything any of us had seen at any of our night's venues.

Being the virgin that I still was and, of course, being particularly curious of about televised sex, all this *Big Brother* fuss seemed to have actually been about was whether or not someone would either have sex on live television, have a fight on live television or possibly get a boner or shit themselves in the shared pool. It took us back to the still-worrying violence that had happened outside the Brixton Academy around that time of whose audience were no different to this one, so this was what celebrity culture was evolving into? Pure, basic, urges; curious indeed.

Now, if beforehand, most people who were involved in this crazy night of ours had already been talking mostly just shite, then now we had entered the arena of the night, where *everyone* was talking *complete* shite. The euphoric mellowing of the MDMA was colliding with the highs of the weed and the intake of alcohol and now, whilst squatted around the ash tray of their glass coffee table, nobody could truly express anything that made any coherent sense. Instead then, this made me turn my attention to the music that was being played, of which seemed to had fallen to Jaqueline's responsibility; wonderous, meditative chill-out electro that seemed to complement the dim lamp lights of the room and move in sequence with the luminous globules that were pulsating through the lava lamp. These drugs were dynamite!

By this point, Bodrin and some others had shut their eyes for too long and subsequently passed out onto the floor and so I moved over to the CD player where Jaqueline began introducing me to the sounds of *Underworld, Aphex Twin* and *Air;* some of the finest electronic stuff of the previous decade. It was somewhere between the question and the answer about one of these bands that Jaqueline gave me a brief look that I couldn't quite understand but made me feel something back towards her; what the hell was happening?! I thought. It happened again, it was definitely flirtation, seduction even, a look of "let's let the music dictate our emotions and let's get it on". We both moved back to the table, where the shit-chatting was beginning to founder amidst those who were left standing and we realised that, somehow, we were both the most sober characters left in that situation. Helen clocked off to bed, hugging everyone as she left, whilst Ludivine Miss Lucifer had fallen asleep on the unconscious shoulder of Paul. Jaqueline and I tried to make conversation with the last man standing who was one of those types who could just go on all night, snorting or rolling this that and the other off the table, however his questions about things were a lot more quickly intense than our slurring, one-note answers and so things began to wind down to a standstill; one of those standstills where you realise that this night had gone on well and truly, too long and fuck me, it was *still dark*! How long was this night? That train-viewed sunset over the countryside of south east England now seemed a long time ago.

There was silence and I felt the vibes, uncomfortable at first, coming off Jaqueline. Then as if everything suddenly came to a standstill with that time-freezing music, the finale of the night came over me like being hit by a suddenly-refreshing wave of cold water, all this made sense, *Underworld's* music was trailing upwards from the speaker like a smoke to settle forever into these student digs' walls, to conclude our wild night of piss taking then, what happened next, was simply meant to happen. Jaqueline told me to come to her room to check out what further ambient music she had and of course, I followed. I was led into a room where the open curtains brought moonlight onto walls of David Bowie posters and shelves of medical textbooks and a room that had mostly been taken up by a giant bed of mostly red linens. Upon closing the door, she faced me, looked into my eyes with a look of half loneliness, half sexual need, her arms came forward to wrap around my hips and then it was me who made the first move to bring her lips forwards to mine and embrace our tongues. What the hell was I doing? I didn't really care. Jaqueline then stepped back into the moonlight and began on her shoulder straps, she took off her top to reveal her rather small breasts behind an ordinary bra, she then began unzipping her jeans and pulled them to the ground. She gestured for me to do the same, of which I was embarrassed about, as I had deliberately gone out bra-less of which would put me ahead of the game in the erotic stakes, oh what the hell, I'm Suicide Sally, rock bitch, and I'm going to make love to you! I went down to my knickers where I felt the sting of my embarrassment meet the early morning cold and I trembled slightly. Jaqueline stood naked amidst the dust particles that were dancing in those shafts of moonlight and I observed her. She was slightly rounded around the waistline which left her vagina in shadow, but her light breasts met gravity rather well, and I thought that this is what I might look like when I'm a mature woman. All I wanted now (or at least as the drugs were telling me) was touch and I took down my knickers and hoped that my skinny self wouldn't make her clock my actual age; I actually *wanted this!* In my nakedness I began to feel a sudden sense of what it was to live on earth, I could feel my heart pumping life around my body, I could feel the slow rotation of the earth and I tried to imagine how each little particle of cold might be colliding with my skin. She stepped forward and with her touch these senses doubled, oh my God, we were suddenly upon the red linens, her touch was soft, and as she caressed me, I caressed her, everything was beautifully smooth and soft, very different to what I'd experienced with the dominating, harder touch of men. I shut my eyes and felt her tongue upon my nipples, her hand squeezing my breast, go Sally go! Her tongue then moved down to my vagina where I had never experienced such a sensual overload before, I guess this was the difference between same sex and opposite sex intercourse, in that a woman knows *what* to do to another woman. Then it was her fingers, going in gently, I was wet now, I couldn't help it, and then she started making me feel sexy in a way that I'd never been able to achieve by myself. Oh my god, what was happening? Would I ever have a night as mad as this ever again? Is adult life like this all the time? If so, I can't *wait* to grow up.

Suddenly through the walls, came the sound of my dear, beautiful partner in crime, Ludivine Miss Lucifer, screaming and ranting in French pleasure from what must have been a guy (I never found out which one). Belgian whore! I then tried to practice the same techniques that Jaqueline had done to me back to her and although she began to make the correct,

.

convincing sounds, I wasn't completely convinced that I'd been much good which then bothered me since in this state I felt it more important to pleasure her than her pleasure me. Jesus, these drugs were making me consider someone else's pleasure over my own; 'the end of human selfishness' I thought, why the fuck was this stuff illegal? Quickly it was then her turn again and she had me face down to work her magic from behind; and whoever instigated this strange synchrony of sounds I don't know but for everytime I felt the pains of pleasure have me scream out, it was followed almost immediately by Ludivine; one step, two step, I remembered from dance class, Suicide Sally, then Ludivine Mis Lucifer, one after the other, like there were four of us having sex in this equation which seemed to turn me on more. It wasn't long before I came and seconds afterwards, came Lucifer, with an immense Euro howl that must've woken everyone else up in the building.

We had all fallen quiet now, Jaqueline had put some more ambient music on her stereo which took her into the world of sleep. To this music, I stared up at the ceiling into some strange pagan patterns that had for some reason been painted on the ceiling. The earthly rhythm of this music seemed to make the patterns move as I comprehended the events of our night. Slowly, the music began to push my train of thought into the history of my country and where the origins of these pagan symbols had come from, it took me to sleep. As *The Four Seasons* once said "What a lady! What a night!"

Just as popular music, Britain's first great and solely positive, 20th century export, was about to lose its true soul to the weight of mass commercialisation; so too then, was that of British television. *Big Brother* had been so popular as for the series to expand itself out into a fifteen series-and-counting franchise, saying goodbye to the rebellious, risk-taking days of the likes of *Monty Python* or other great British comedy or intellectual talents, in favour of a 24-hour live feed of people sitting in gardens. In one terrible foul, digital swoop then, the entire cultural landscape had been changed; the contestants who went on *Big Brother* were no longer the normal, rather likeable everyday people like Craig Phillips, (intrigued, perhaps, by a televised social experiment) but weirdos in search of quick shot at cheap, talentless fame and so people too became more shallow. The thing that had disturbed me most about all this was that on both accounts, the prophetic words that had been expressed by our maths teacher, Mr Hawling, upon a drugged-up staircase in Fabric on one night in 2000, words regarding the mathematical probability of the noughties entering an age of extreme conformity, proved to be true. Yeah, the noughties were both bleak and tedious; two things that never needed to go together.

### *Out of the Void*

What must've been less than two hours later, I awoke to the lights of a dawn sky making its way through those open curtains and onto the crumpled folds of the disturbed red linen, reminding me, as it did, of the overload of lipstick that I had encountered at various points of the night before; the smell of feminine sweat was everywhere, dust was in the air, and although I knew I had to get home, I lay there still, letting the last of the MDMA flow through my system as I admired the slow motion quality to the stillness that was around me. I rolled to the side to see Jaqueline's naked body still lying next to me in an almost perfect posture; her form was no longer as sexual as it had seemed but had more of an aesthetic beauty of which I too, spent some time admiring. I was head-fucked of course, but nothing was detracting from the insane, sensual wonder of everything that had happened between the two of us.

Shit. We had to get home. A digital clock told me it was 5.00am and so we still had time to maybe make it back to Fareham for about 8.00. I had to find Ludivine. I got out of bed, pieced together my various items of clothing, kissed this strange encounter goodbye and left. Despite her own sexual conquests that night, I found Ludivine Miss Lucifer, for some reason asleep across one of the sofas in the main room; other members of our party were still scattered across the floor, half clothed and still wearing Craig Phillips masks over their faces. I shook her, she awoke and we both agreed it was time to leave. We scribbled our mobile numbers followed by a 'stay in contact' down on the back of a newspaper that we then left upon the coffee table. Bodrin was still asleep, sat upright against one of the walls and after applying further lipstick, we left him two smackeroonies on both sides of his face as a means to briefly cheer him up when he awoke before realising that he was in some strange flat and would inevitably be subjected to one of those difficult social situations where one doesn't know how long they're welcome. With a character like Bodrin however, that difficulty could be more on Helen's flat's side than it was ever likely to be on his. That problem was not for us however, we were fucking off to get away with it whilst we still could, Suicide Sally and Ludivine Miss Lucifer, uncaught, undiscovered and still together as one. We quickly used the toilet, silently closed the front door behind us and made our way down a thin stairwell to the ground floor of the complex that then led us outside.

The weather was grey, drizzly and we had no idea where the fuck we were until we walked around this area (it was Vauxhall) and saw that between the tower blocks, there were the top two cabins to the London Eye, peaking out over London a not too far distance away. Thank god for 21st century landmarks we thought. That was our destination, and like the pussycats that we were, made perfect navigational sense of our jungle and skipped onwards. The fact that we didn't mind that the rain was getting slightly heavier, was merely proof that last night's substances were still making their way through our systems, instead of rain, it felt like a refreshing shower, the birds were making sweet, sweet music and we felt that we were enjoying our walk. At the end of a series of small parks, we came out by Vauxhall's giant bus station of which had some kind of structure built over it resembling a ski slope. Our fucked-up state seemed to send us into autopilot however and we just continued walking on to Waterloo.

A short distance ahead came the pounding music to some nightclub that was *still open*; its punters, all gay men, had spilled out into the street with their beers and were just getting it on. Jesus, we thought, if these dawning moments were the beginning of the end for our night, it was simply just the end of the beginning for those guys. The gay community knew how to party, what were the opening hours for that place? And what drugs were they on?

This of course, then brought me onto questioning myself, had my brief moment with Jaqueline classified me as gay? Now, for the record, I am not, but I liked that I had had the experience and that the true story of how I came to lose my virginity, about how I'd set out to fuck Primal Scream and ended up sleeping with a woman, would be a strange and unclear one indeed. These topless gay men seemed to take themselves rather seriously indeed and so we gave them a little wink of suggestion that with us being so fucking hot and, at this stage, a little sexually confused, would send them into their own brief moment of confusion from which we might be able to straighten them.

Next up was the back end to a great cubist-looking building of which I had to inform my idiot foreign friend was the headquarters of MI5. Mentioning this was a mistake of course as it then sent Ludivine off into talking about politics once again and claimed that compared to the Belgian Intelligence's headquarters, the MI5 building looked especially insecure and that she could easily get passed its guards with her Belgian, ninja cat skills.

We walked on and reached the Albert Embankment of which ran along the south side of the Thames, a beautiful straight walk all the way to Waterloo. From out of the drizzling greys that blurred our horizon stepped small numbers of suited men carrying brief cases and with the majestic architectural beauty of the Houses of Parliament and Big Ben's tower just across the river, we assumed these men to be either intelligence workers or politicians; spies, politicians, hard-partying gay men and drug-taking medical students only a mile apart from each other as if pretty much neighbours?

What a strange city this was.

The great wheel of the London Eye approached and we re-trod last night's early evening footsteps to find our way into Waterloo station and board the next South Western train back to boring old Fareham. This first train was pretty much empty and we suddenly felt fucked and in desperate need for sleep; this could have had deadly consequences however, for if we fell asleep on this particular train we could wake up somewhere around midday in fucking Plymouth. As it happened then, the third-world tower blocks, the graffitied, concrete tunnels and the electricity poles that signified outer west London were this time experienced as snippets of waking life merged with dreams. Although silent in this state, both of us were wondering how much of the night we might had got away with; would Mr Hawling say anything? Would our parents have discovered something suspicious? And had we missed a phone call from The Scream? More music was the answer right now, Ludivine pulled out a set of old headphones and with the sun rising over the green fields of south east England, we rode our journey into both the noughties and our more adult lives to the darker edged chills of Primal Scream's *Long Life*.

Yes, fourteen years later, I can honestly say that we still seem to have had got away with our devilish expedition. Yes, it would seem that after turning up at our different doorsteps a couple of hours later, our parents hadn't noticed a thing. Mr Hawling (a strange character at best) never seemed to have mentioned a thing as if he hadn't even been there in the first place, and had he? And whilst I no longer particularly listen to Primal Scream outside of nostalgic reasons, we never did receive the phone calls of our expectations although our devout Christian school friend Ingrid was known to have been particularly distressed during the following weeks afterwards. As is always the case, the friends we had made that night never contacted us again, shy British repression at its best perhaps? Nobody wanting to break a second ice despite seemingly being best friends in the moment, although in saying that, I do seem to recall making brief eye contact with a dreadlocked woman, who may have been Helen, many years later in the crowds at the Glastonbury festival, nothing came of it of course, but there was that moment of recognition that will undoubtedly be undone by the long passages of life. As for Ludivine and I, we seem to have both returned to London although not together; it is during my morning commutes, when passing through Vauxhall underground station, that memories return and ideas of getting in contact begin to click. Now we appear to only be friends in that way that the digital age only permits you to be, via the likes of Facebook and so on, virtual friends, separated yet somehow linked by millions of digital zeros and ones.

Oh Ludivine, Ludivine, my sexy, stupid, Belgian princess friend, do not let the weight of passing time, of bleaker more complex decades, of subsequent duller friends or relationships stamp out your renegade soul, and maybe one day, we will glance our beautiful pussy cat selves over the crowds of the same carriage.

# MAKE IT!

"Dylan!"
The alarm on the phone kept beepin'.
"Dylan! Where you at?"
I reach out and swipe it onto the floor. I hear mum walking up the stairs. Then the knocking.
"Dylan! Don't make me come in there. You know what time it is?"
"YES! *Fucksake*."
"And don't you be swearing in my house. Your sister can hear you. Now up, out of bed. You got a big day today."
I roll over and switch the radio on. The newsreader narrates as I contemplate facing the day.

*London is set to soar to record temperatures today. Meanwhile, in Tottenham, protests continue over...*

I stumble out the room and into the bathroom. I run a cold, cold shower.
Downstairs mum is serving up porridge. My little sister, Tanya, is staring me out. She pokes around her bowl and smirks at me?
"Dylan, you look awful."
"Shut up, Tan"
Mum turns around from the stove.
"Dylan, I told you to put your father's suit on."
"It's too big, mum."
"I don't care. This family has worked hard to get you this opportunity and you are not going to mess it up you hear?"
I turn back upstairs and go into mum's room. Dad's stuff is still untouched in the wardrobe. I pull along the rails through out-of-date suits and look for the least embarrassing one. I end up picking a grey pinstripe one. I put on a loose shirt and pull on the baggy suit. I catch myself in the mirror.

This ain't me.

I grew up in Deptford. I wouldn't live anywhere else. People think it's a shithole. They're the same people who won't walk through here at night but will buy a luxury apartment on the Creek Road as soon as they hear a Waitrose opening. This is where my family are. Third generation Jamaican and proud. My grandfather opened a market stall here in 1963. He'd sell all kinds of fruit and developed a good reputation in the community. He died in 1999, when I was 6 years old, and my father inherited the business. He was into selling too, but it weren't fruit. Man pushed drugs, drank the profits and ran the business into the ground. By 2001 the stall was gone and the only time you'd spot Dad on the high street was outside the bookies in a hat and vest. When mum found him stealing from our flat to pay off his debts she threw him out on the street. The last time I saw him he was with the pissheads by the anchor statue at the other end of the market, shouting his head off at no one.
Mum tries her best but she struggles to balance shifts at the Albany with looking after the two of us. I've been trying to get my head down in LESOCO but it's hard to study business when your business is trying to just keep food on the table. Then one day mum rushes in with this great big smile on her face, waving her phone around in the air laughing.

"Dylan! You've been blessed. Lester got you an interview!"

My mum's brother, Lester, was the local boy made good. He used to be a troublemaker in his time and got collared during the Brixton riots in the 80s. In fact, he did some time for it. When he got out he was a changed man. He went back to college, passed his exams and got a place at the LSE. He now works for an investment bank in Canary Wharf and drives a Porche. Mum don't shut up about him.

"Come from nothin' and made somethin'." She says to me and sis 10 times a day.

So mum gets in touch with Lester one day and tells him I'm doing well in maths at college. He says his firm is offering internships for young talent in the south east and, without arksin, she fills in an application form and sends it off. Next thing I know I'm in this baggy suit lookin like a prick.

Mum takes a photo.

"You look so handsome. I'll be praying for you."

The interview is at 4pm in Heron Quay so I need to get the DLR from Greenwich. I look at my watch. I have 5 hours. Best get there early. I turn to go out the front door but mum shouts back from the kitchen.

"Hey!"

I look round and she hands me a £20 note.

"What's that for?" I say.

"A haircut."

Tanya starts laughing. I look at myself in the mirror and see what she means. Looking back from the mirror is a skinny boy in a big man's suit with a tall, messy afro.I started growing it back in school when I used to board. I had a girlfriend at the time who loved to play with it so I kept it for her. We broke up last summer but the afro stayed put.


I head up Amersham Vale and make my way up to the New Cross Road. I put my headphones on. The sun is blazing down so I put on some Bizzle. I head into my man Danilo's barber shop, *Top Knoch*. People always arksin' why Dan couldn't spell *Notch* when he opened the place but he always says it ain't a real word anyways. The place is always buzzing with the local chat. I walk in. One of the barbers, Bam, turns and points at me.

"Ayy! What's happening, Mr D?"

"All good, Bam. Danny about?"

"He's not here today, Bossman. Just me. Come sit down."

Bam is old school Rastafari. He used to be another baller but has slowed down in recent years and now just cuts hair for Danilo, despite having the longest dreads in SE14 (although they're greyer these days). Bam has Sky Sports News on and keeps looking back. Usain Bolt is being interviewed about the Olympics next summer. On the bench next to him are two more ex-Yardies drinking beer, watching the screen.

"Dat brudda mean business."

"True say"

I jump into the vacant leather barber's chair. Bam smiles and shows his gold teeth. He stares over his spectacles and looks at me in the mirror's reflection.

"So what you sayin, D? You looking for a trim, Earthworm Jim?"

The boys on the bench start laughing. I sink down in my seat. Bam covers up my neck. He lights up a cigarette.

"What you lookin for, brother? Rows?"

"Nah man. Clip it."

Bam opens his bloodshot eyes wide, staring at me perplexed.

"What? *Why* you wanna cut it down fa?"

"I've got a job interview innit."

Bam let's out a deep, bassy laugh and looks round at the hyenas on the bench.

"Ay, Dylan want a short cut to go wit the baggy suit!"

The whole shop erupts. This is one of the reasons a haircut takes two hours in New Cross. I look at my watch.

4 and a half hours to the interview.

Eventually Bam settles down and starts setting up some clippers.

"How deep you want clipping?"

I stare at my Afro for the last time.

"Close. 0.5 into a 1 blend."

Bam takes a pull on his cigarette and shrugs.

"Ok boss. Here we go."

I hear the buzzers clip on and vibrate with electricity. I close my eyes and wait for Bam to take the first swipe. I listen to the news in the background.

*Protests in Tottenham last night have spread to disquiet in different pockets of London. Our reporter is currently in Clapham High Street. Sarah, what can you see there?*

Bam mutes the TV and turns up some old Barrington Levy shit. I feel the metal press against my forehead and buzz deep into my scalp. Bam digs it in a couple of times. I can feel tufts of hair drift down my chest. I start to relax. Then I hear the clippers stop buzzing. I hear Bam cursing.

"Fuck. Sorry D. I need to change to another pair. These ones keep cuttin' out."

At first I say no problem. Bam walks off cursing through some beads and into another room. Then I open my eyes and look at myself. The two guys behind are crying with laughter.

Bam has fucked up my barnet. He's done a massive circle from the front of my scalp to halfway into my afro. What's left is like a massive Dracula collar where my fro used to be. I look mental.

"Ay Bam. Hurry up yeah?"

I see a guy cycle past the window outside then stop and take out his phone. He shouts into the shop.

"Fam. Smile for the camera yeah?"

I throw him an evil.

"BAM!! Where you at?"

Finally, Bam walks back in with some new clippers.

"Sorry D. All good now."

"This ain't a fuckin joke, blood. I've got an interview. Clip me down. This shit ain't funny."

The hyenas are still laughin' it up. Bam looks at my stupid hair in the mirror. Even he is chuckling.

"No worries D. Here it go."

I hear the clippers switch back on. I close my eyes and relax.

Suddenly, there's a huge boom outside. Everyone stops what they're doin. Bam drops the clips.

"The *fuck* was that?"

We look through the window. I see a woman pushing a pram hold her hands to her mouth, then turn it round and run. A kid runs past and shouts into the shop.
"Oi. Someone just torched a car down the road and it blew."
"Shit. Anyone hurt?"
"Nah man. But there's kids on the street causin' trouble. You need to close the shop."
Bam lights a smoke. The two hyenas walk out.
"Like fuck am gonna close de shop. Kids are kids. Just some shit and it will blow over."
Bam blows out some smoke and turns the TV back on. I catch the TV screen. A fucking building is on fire in South London.

*Riots are spreading throughout London. People are reporting large scale looting, vandalism and arson throughout the city. We are also receiving reports of disturbances now in other UK cities. Police are advising everyone to stay indoors or head home as quickly as possible.*

I get all these buzzes on my phone. My messenger is going nuts. It's friends from my old school.

*Get over to the stores in New Cross Gate. We storming dem!*

*We taking down some shops.*

*Fuck the Feds. Fuck the government. Take back the streets.*

*SE crew meet us in Greenwich for the next move.*

Not Greenwich. Not today.
We hear more noise outside. There's shouting and then the thunder of feet. About twenty kids go past. Some laughing. Some lookin' mean as fuck. They're running towards Deptford Bridge.
Bam locks the door and puts up the 'Sorry. We're closed sign'
This is bad. I look at my watch.

Less than four hours to the interview.

Bam is still staring out the window. Two police vans hurtle past. I look in the mirror. I've still got fucked up hair.
"Bam. Ay Bam. Come on man. Finish the job."
Bam looks round stressed.
"D. I gotta put the shutters down. This look serious."
"Bam, please, just clip me down and I'll go. Come on man, look at me."
Bam walks over and puts the clippers on for a third time. Third time lucky. He's just about to dig in when there's a knock at the window. A boy is banging to get in. Bam looks round.
"Hey. It's Danilo's boy."
He's banging, pointing up the street and mouthing something.
"Let him in." I shout.
The boy looks behind him, up the street, then back at us before running off.
"De fuck?" says Bam.

We both stare at the window as four figures enter the frame. One has a can of something in his hand, one has a Staffy on a chain, one is on the phone and the other is holding a huge fuck off baseball bat. They all have their shirts off, which they've wrapped around their faces as makeshift balaclavas. They stare into the shop like the four horsemen; skinny, shirtless, still and menacing. The one on the phone gestures to the others to move on. Just before they do one of them swings back with his bat and takes Bam's front window clean out before running off. Glass shatters into the barbers and spills all over the floor. Another one throws a red flare into the shop. It starts spurting out bright light and smoke into the room. Bam goes crazy.

"YOU FUCKIN' PUSSYOLE PRICKS! I'LL FIND OUT WHO Y'ARE, YA HEAR."

He kicks the flare out into the street and runs up the road like a madman, carrying the clippers with him. I'm still sitting on the barber chair holding my breath. I run out coughing and spluttering. As I head into the street I hear choppers soaring overhead. I walk past a homeless guy outside The Venue. He mutters something,

"Any spare change mate?"

Then he stares at me and looks puzzled.

"What happened to your head?"

I catch a glimpse of myself in the reflection of a window. What's left of my hair is now covered with broken glass. I need to sort this out.

There is another barbers I can use further down the road. I cross the street over to the Amersham Arms and spot another pocket of trouble brewing. Three police cars are blocking New Cross station. The New Cross Road and the road behind to Fordham Park are closed off and there's a mob of about thirty yutes hollarin' at the officers. Now there's no way into Greenwich at all. I look at my watch.

3 hours and 15 minutes to the interview.

Outside the Amersham are two old punks with facial tattoos and Mohawks. One of them looks me up and down.

"Fackin' ell mate. Have you looked in the mirror recently?"

I ignore them and walk over to two coppers standing by their car. I can see one of them radio for assistance, the other looks wary.

"Don't come any closer."

"Look, I'm trying to get to Greenwich."

"This is your last warning."

"You don't understand. I've got an interview."

I notice the two coppers stare at me and then look at each other, smirking;

"You look like a fucking monk mate. Now get on with ya. Move on."

I can feel a swelling of force behind me. People are shouting and throwing things. I hear a bottle smash right next to the copper's feet. The two coppers retreat back a few steps. I spot a riot van speeding up the road. It pulls up and 12 cops in vests with shields jump out, create a boundary line and start pushing the crowds back.

I can hear some chatter behind me.

"Let him through man."

I feel someone shove me forward, I trip up into the copper. I feel a hand grab me by my tie. Something is sprayed in my face. It stings so badly, I fall down coughing. I hear people shouting.

"Ay, ay! They've fuckin' gassed him. FUCK YOU!"

I curl up on the floor as more stuff is thrown. The chopper is right overhead. I hear the police retreat. The mob are standing right over me. A couple of them pull me to my feet.

"Bruv? Bruv? You alright yeah?"

I murmur at them "I can't see. I can't see."

"Pepper spray, innit. Ay Bred, get some water."

Someone throws water over my face. I feel the sting rush again.

"Don't worry though, yeah? We gonna fuck em up."

My vision starts coming back. I can make out a few blurry figures.

"Ain't you Dylan Palmer?"

"Yeah, that's Tanya's brother. She's in my year."

"Bruv. What is wrong with your hair? You look like a toilet! Ay, Riki get this shit on Instagram."

The group of lads are laughing as they huddle round me.

"No, get in closer yeah. Deano show your blade. And those new trainers."

"Everyone say *G-PAG Crew*! Yeah?"

They all shout *"Get pussy and guns!"*

I hear camera shots being taken. I try to pull away from them but one of them grabs the sleeve of my suit jacket. I feel my left sleeve pull away and rip.

"Upload it yeah. Haha. Dylan, safe yeah?"

"Say hi to your sister innit. Come on let's go."

I hear the lads run off. I stagger down the New Cross Road towards Greenwich. Every now and then I stumble as my eyes adjust. I can smell burning plastic in the air. The chopper is still hovering over my head.

*We're going to go live now to Christy who is in Deptford Bridge which is experiencing some trouble. Christy, what can you see?*

*Richard, I am just behind a police cordon which has been pushed back from New Cross due to high levels of hostility from local youths. Several cars have been set on fire here and rioters are currently throwing missiles towards us.*

*That must be very frightening for you, Christy. Can you describe what the assailants look like?*

*Well if we can zoom our camera a bit further up the street you can just about make out a line of several people in sportswear with their faces covered up. Most of them are keeping a distance at the moment but occasionally a few of them can be seen breaking ranks and rushing towards the officers.*

*Yes. I can see someone now walking towards the police, Christy. He's not wearing sportswear though. He looks like he's drunk.*

My eyes are getting better now but I'm still struggling to walk in a straight line. I can make out blue flashing lights just ahead of me. I have to make it to Greenwich. Time is running out. I hear the sound of things flying over my head and whistling past my ears.

*Richard, as you can see we are getting all sorts of things thrown towards us. Bricks, bottles and occasionally flaming objects. The police are just asking us to move back a few metres as things are intensifying.*

I keep shuffling towards the line of officers. I can hear them shouting at me so I raise my arms in the air and keep walking. I shout out to them:
"I need to get to Greenwich"
The officers are gesturing for me to get out of the way so I shout louder.
"I NEED TO GET TO G...."
Suddenly I feel something smash by my feet. I can smell petrol. Flames start to snake up from my legs. I panic.
"HELP ME! HELP!"

*Richard, I.... I don't know if you are seeing this at home but the drunk man has been hit by a flaming missile and he is on fire.*

I run around flailing my arms. Two officers bundle me to the ground and cover me to make sure that the flame is fully out. All I can smell is petrol and smoke. An officer looks down at me.
"You're alright, mate. We got you just in time. Andy, can we get an ambulance to the scene please. What's your name?"
"Um..Dylan."
"OK, Dylan stay lying there. An ambulance is on the way."
"But. But..."
As I look up at the two officers and the gathering crowd I can hear a commotion. A lady pushes through the crowd, followed by a camera man.

*Richard, I am currently with one of the youths who has just been caught up in the riots in Deptford Bridge. Just minutes ago he was hit by a flaming missile which has burnt through some of his clothes and a substantial part of his hair. Sir, why are you rioting?*

"I'm not."
The police officers try and push the woman back.

*What are you protesting against?*

"Look. I need to get to a job interview."
The reporter looks blankly at me for a moment before the police force her back and she turns around to the camera.

*And there you have it, Richard. A young, black teenager who is fighting to get more work opportunities. But one can't help but feel that such vandalism and destruction is the wrong way to achieve this goal. This is Christy Fuller reporting from Deptford Bridge.*

As the officers get distracted I spring to my feet and make a run towards the Big Red Bus Pizza restaurant by the roundabout. My burnt shoes slap the ground as I pace towards Creek Road. My legs still singed and raw. I need to make it to Greenwich DLR. The High Road is closed off so I'll have to try Cutty Sark instead. I pull the loose suit sleeve off my arm and check my watch.

2 hours to the interview.

As I turn down onto Creek Road I see more police cars race down towards Greenwich. I see pockets of gangs moving this way and that. The mid-afternoon sun is burnin' the shaved part of my head. I feel my phone ringing. It's mum. At first, I ignore it but the ringing doesn't stop. I swipe to answer it.

"What?"

"Dylan! Where are you child?"

"I'm on my way to the interview."

"And you've got your haircut?"

I watch a car pass by me slowly. Two kids in the back seat are pointing and me with their mouths open.

"Um....yeah."

"Gladys call me and say you're on the television."

"What? No... that must me someone else mum."

"Ok baby boy. Good luck. You call me when you get there. And when you get out."

She puts the phone down just as I walk past *Up The Creek* and head towards the nearest barbers.

Greenwich is like a ghost town. Most of the shop windows are boarded up. Including the barbers. I bang against the shutters but hear nothing. I throw my hands up in frustration and run them over the bald patch. The situation is fucked. I look at my watch.

90 minutes to get to the wharf, get a haircut and make it to the interview!

I head to the DLR station. Just as I reach it someone's pulling a barrier across the entrance.

"Station's closed."

"Why?"

"Trouble at Deptford Bridge. Trains start at Island Gardens."

"That's on the other side of the river!"

"Sir. Just take the foot tunnel."

I don't have time to argue. The foot tunnels are a mission. It'll take me 15 minutes from here and the clock is ticking fast now. I run past the old boat and down the spiral staircase towards the tunnel. It stretches far out in front of me. I look down at my burnt shoes and then at my watch.

1 hour!

I take a deep, deep breath and start running. Hard. About 45 seconds in I can feel my lungs burning. My head is pounding and I feel dizzy. I see people walking towards me like bodies without faces. They are all leaning away from me against the rounded walls. In the distance I can hear laughing. The middle of the tunnel is blocked by a load of people sat on the floor, drinking beer. Some of them turn their heads and look over to me. I hear one of them shout out.

"Look out! It's a zombie!"

I hear them laughing. As I get closer I recognise who it is.

"Rex?"

One of the kids stands up

"Fucking hell. Dylan! Is that you?"

Rex was one of my skating mates. I met him at the ramps beneath the Southbank Centre when I used to board. He's with a few of his mates who are smoking a joint. Rex takes a swig of beer.

"D, what the fuck man? Your hair, mate."

His mates start whisperin'.

"Look man, don't ask. What are you doing down here?"

"Taking cover mate. It's like a war zone out there eh?"

Rex scratches his thick ginger hair. I look back at my watch.

"Where you going, D? Fancy a smoke?"

"Mate, I've got to get to Canary Wharf. I've got a job interview."

The stoners burst out laughing.

"What for? A fucking horror movie?"

"I got to get there. My uncle sorted it out for me. If I don't go I'm in deep shit. I need to get to Island Gardens. I've got 40 minutes.

Rex looks up towards the end of the tunnel.

"D'ya think you'll make it?"

"I have to."

Rex looks back at his mates before taking another swig of beer. He stares at me for a moment.

"D. Do you remember that time those little chavs beat the fuck out of me and stole my board?"

"Yeah I do."

"You remember what you did?"

"I lent you mine."

"Yeah man. You did."

Rex crouches down behind him and bounces back up, pushing a skateboard into my chest.

"Well now I'm giving you it back. Now go! Get to the wharf, bruv!"

I stand stunned for a bit. I look down at the seriously splintered board. It had seen better days. Rex shakes my shoulder.

"Dylan, go! You can make it."

I nod and place one foot on the board. As I push up to speed I can hear the skaters cheering.

"SKATE FAST ZOMBIE BOY!"

"AND GET YOUR HAIR CUT!"

I haven't even been on a skateboard in the 3 years since I last saw Rex. It takes me a moment to get my balance but soon enough I'm gliding towards the other side of the Thames. I look at my watch.

30 minutes!

I can do this. I may look like shit but I will make it. After all this shit I have to make it. As I skate faster I start to relax, people in the tunnel start to blur to the sides again. I catch a couple of fitties giggling at me. They call back after me and laugh to each other,

"Lookin' good skater bwoy!"

I look behind to check them out. Just as I look back round I smash into something. Hard. Everything goes bright white for a second and I land on my back. A rush of pain surges towards my face and I feel my nose running. I look up and see the end of the tunnel is partially gated off.

An old woman kneels down next to me.

"You alright, son? You just went straight into those shutters. Oh Christ, lad your nose is bleeding something terrible."

I try and mouth something to him but my mouth is full of blood.

"Arghhgottttooo"

"Don't speak son. I think you've damaged some teeth. And it looks like the impact has knocked some of your hair off. We need to get you to A&E."

I panic and stand up. Blood runs down my shirt and tie. I try to speak again.

"Nooo. I've dot a dob inderview..."

I start to walk off dizzily. I see the old woman reach into her shopping bag. She brings out some kitchen roll and some frozen peas. She rips off some off the paper and hands it to me with the peas.

"Ere you go lad. Put these over your mouth. It'll calm the swelling. Keep 'em. They was on offer at Iceland."

I look back at the old girl. She's looking all concerned. I mouth to her through the bag of peas.

"Dankoo."

I pull myself up the stairs towards the light of Island Gardens. The blood on my hands is sticky and this seems to fuse the peas to my face along with the ice. I see the DLR in the distance and pad towards it. I look at my watch.

20 minutes!

I get to the DLR platform just as the train is pulling in. I can get to Canary Wharf and find a toilet to clean myself up. As soon as I step on the train the carriage goes quiet. A large group of French schoolchildren gasp and move away from me.

I hear someone whisper "It's a beggar. Ignore him and he'll go away."

I stand staring at the carriage of people as the train pulls away. I try to pull the bag of peas away from my face but it stays stuck to my lips and splits. The peas shoot everywhere and crash to the floor like marbles. The French school kids are screaming now and their teacher is moving them to another carriage. For the last two stops I stand alone. I head to the unmanned front carriage and watch as the glass buildings reach higher and higher over the clear blue docks.

I stay on the train one stop past Heron Quay and head into the Canary Wharf shopping precinct. I look around dizzily for a sign for the toilets. Then something catches my eye. In the window of an electrical store a Plasma TV is screening the news. The newsreader is talking over footage that is replaying the same clips over and over again. The first clip is of the building on fire. The second is of a load of kids kicking in a shop window. The third clip is of the New Cross Road - a line of police facing a mob of kids throwing missiles and in the centre of the shot, clear as day, is me, Dylan Palmer, arms up above my head walking towards the camera with that stupid fucking haircut. To the right of the TV is another screen, split into four. Above it is a camcorder pointing at me. It is filming all the shoppers walking past. I move into the camera's view. For a moment I just stare. My Dad's suit is ruined; one arm is missing. My tie is loose and my white shirt is stained blood-red. My face is puffy and swollen and my eyes are bloodshot. And on top of my head is my beautiful afro - half shaved and glittering with glass and dirt. I crack a manic smile and notice my front left tooth is badly chipped.

"HEY YOU!"

I turn around to see two security guard walking through the shopping centre towards me. I've left a trail of red blood spots all the way from the station.
"WAIT THERE."
I look at my watch.

10 minutes.

There's no time left to clean up. I turn and run through the shopping centre. The security start chasin' me. I take a wrong turn and find myself in a dead end of Salons and Coffee Shops. The two guards stand at the end of the corridor and speak into their radios.
My phone buzzes. It's a text from mum.

*Good luck baby. We love you and are proud of you. Tanya and Mum xxx*

The security guards walk closer cautiously, like two cats approaching a wounded mouse. For a moment I feel sad it's ended like this. I feel and look like a bum. I feel like...
My Dad.
I feel an anger surge through my chest. This ain't how this is meant to finish.

This ain't me.

As the guards get to within ten metres of me I burst towards them at full pace. I see their eyes go wide as I thunder into them. I bowl them both over to the floor and race towards the light doors at the end of the corridor. Just as I get towards the door I see a cleaner mopping the floor. He stops and looks up to see me running towards him. The guards shout for him to do something.
He puts his mop down and opens the door for me. Daylight spills into the corridor. As I run through I turn to the cleaner.
"Fucking legend!"
The cleaner shuts the door behind me and I run across the pavement past Canary Wharf underground, I just miss two moving black cabs as I fall into the rotating doors of Ordell Investments.
The foyer is huge with shiny marble floors. In the corner is a huge tree and some leather chairs. I walk towards the desk. The receptionist stands up straight away.
"Can you leave please?"
"No, you don't understand. I'm here for an interview."
"If you don't leave right now I'm calling security. Get out!"
The anger returns. I can feel my body and my voice shaking violently
"Fam, do you have *any* idea what I've been through to get here? I'm here for an interview...."
I look behind and see the security looking around for me outside.
"If you don't leave I'm calling security."
I slam my hands down on the desk.
"NO! LISTEN! I have been cut, blasted, sprayed with pepper, set on fire, humiliated on TV, broken and chased to get to this interview. It is 4 o'clock in the afternoon and I am on time. My name is Dylan Palmer and I am here to interview for an internship at Ordell. Now pick up the phone and tell them I'm here, motherfucker."

The guards spot me in reception and run towards the building. The receptionist stares at me. I feel rage beating through my body. I want to smash this building to pieces and burn it all to the ground.

Then I hear an old familiar voice.

"Dylan!"

I look up. At the top of the escalator is my Uncle Lester. I watch as he glides down and walks towards me. Just as the guards make it into the foyer Lester walks up to me and gives me a huge hug. The guards and the receptionist stand still as Lester puts his hand on my cheek.

"Dylan. What happened?"

I stare at Lester. I can feel hot tears run down my face.

"I'm....I'm here for the interview."

Lester smiles

"Well here you are. You made it!"

Lester looks up at the guards.

"Can I help you gentlemen?"

The security look at each other.

"No sir."

"Good. Now on your way."

The guards shuffle off back into the street as Lester puts his arm around me. He swipes me through the security barrier and towards the lifts.

"Don't worry, Dylan. The interviews are running behind by about an hour or so. Now let's get you cleaned up. I'll take you up to my office; I have a shower there and you can shave your hair too. Samuel?"

The receptionist looks over to us.

"Yes, sir?"

"Go to Boss and buy a new suit for Dylan. And a shirt and tie. What size are you Dylan?"

"Um...I don't know."

"It doesn't matter. Samuel, just bring us a selection. Put it on my account."

We step into the glass elevator. I feel my ears pop as the lift rises fast. As it pulls up into the sky I watch the city unfold in front of me. The afternoon sun glistens over the winding river. In the distance I see pockets of smoke rising from different boroughs. Lester leans towards my ear.

"Can you see our block?"

"No."

"It's right over there."

Lester taps on the window of the lift.

"You know how I know, Dylan?"

"No. How?"

"Because I look out from my office at it every single day. Never forget where you're from, Dylan. You get me?"

"Yeah. No. I won't."

I feel a text buzz in my pocket and smile. As the lift flies up to the sky I look out over the skyline. I've never seen so far before. And I want to see more.

One hour later I step back into the elevator, press the button and go two floors up to the interview. I catch my reflection in the mirror and hardly recognise myself. A skinny youth in a £500 suit and a smooth, smooth trim. As the doors open I see a girl at a bright white desk. She looks up and smiles at me.

"Can I have your name please?"

"Dylan Palmer. Can I have yours?"

She gives an awkward frown and looks towards some glass doors.

"The board will see you now."

As I walk over I see four figures behind the glass. I step closer and the doors swish open. The panel look up.

"Mr Palmer. Take a seat."

I sit down. I feel pain from my bruises but try not to flinch. I try to focus in on them but my vision is still a bit blurry.

"Did you have any trouble getting here Mr Palmer?"

I go to speak but stop myself.

"No....no trouble. I'm kind of local."

The head of the panel raises his head.

"Oh really. Where are you from?"

I give a wide grin and show off a new gold tooth cap.

"Deptford. South East London."

# Many Rivers To Cross

That dream again. No different from the last time. It starts so simply. As always. So simply that it took Drew a while to notice that although the setting was familiar, it was nonsensical for there to be a path in the centre of the River Thames.

The rest seemed the same. The motionless, carbon-grey sky above watched over him as he paced steadily towards the jetties of the Dome, past the still towers of a lightless wharf and onwards upstream. No miracle feat was this though, despite being neither North or South of foot. Beneath his feet were a series of secure, rectangular paving stones leading him on towards the capital. These impossible slabs were set strong in grassy turf and short, red-brick walls rose up to his hips, allowing him to run his hands along the cold concrete and moss. The river lapped tranquilly on each side and Drew remembered thinking, "who would create such a thing?"

Then he noticed the silence. Like the city was on mute. The river passed by without intrusion and although he could feel a soft breeze on his skin he could not hear it. His suit felt baggy, his tie loose and his feet were bare. Above his head, the cable cars dangled. He stopped to look up, leaning against one of the walls. He shouted upwards without sound. He was sure he could make out a figure in one of those cabins but he guessed they couldn't see him; perhaps they didn't care.

The river splashed up against the sides of the wall, startling him, before returning to its placidity. The water was higher now so he felt it best to move on, onwards along this great wall of London.

As he passed along between the banks of Greenwich and the Isle of Dogs he felt the breeze pick up. A seagull swept over his head and landed in front of his path. It gave Drew a cursory glance before hopping up onto the wall. It watched as Drew walked on. The Thames water was now almost level with the top of Drew's walls. He felt no panic from this but picked up his pace towards Shad Thames. No lights could be seen from the thousand windows of riverside apartments. Maybe they were all asleep? Like him.

Finally, as he approached Tower Bridge he saw an opening in the wall. He stumbled into a jog and could make out a shape. A bench? The breeze had now become a strong wind and drizzle began to prick his cheeks. The river lapped onto the top of the brick work as he ran towards the bench. Beneath the blue arches of the bridge the walls gave way to what seemed like a small garden. The pavement ran into a circle and waves rolled up against the turf. The rain was falling heavily now but Drew could see he was no longer alone. On the bench sat three old men in raincoats and flat-caps. Two were engrossed in conversation. The third sat reading the Racing Post.

Drew mouthed silently to them to draw their attention, but as he did a great wave rolled over their heads, missing them all and crashing into the other side of the Thames. He froze in shock, but the men maintained their intense, wordless conversation. Another wave shot overhead and crashed the opposite way. The river churned and rose around them. Drew stood petrified. The high walls that led up to the bridges' engine rooms were too far to reach but surely they couldn't stay here?

A third wave rose up and over their heads. Drew screamed, red-faced into the silence as freezing sleet lashed against his face. The two men stopped talking and looked over to the third man. He brought down his paper and the sound came flooding back into Drew's world. In a friendly Bermondsey drawl, he exclaimed,

"Storm ahead, son."
Drew looked over to the north side of the bridge by St Katherine's Docks. He could see a figure waving. Jessica.

"You'll be late for work."

Drew lay in bed, half-dressed. He still felt uneven and it took a moment to adjust. Jess was standing in the doorway swapping her nurse's uniform for pyjamas. It was morning.
"Are you ok, babe?" he offered gruffly.
"Yeah, just fucking knackered." She said rolling into bed and giving him a warm but tired kiss. "I've made you a coffee. It's in the kitchen."
"I slept in my suit again." he said half to himself. Jess was already asleep.
After showering and changing Drew took another look into the bedroom and leant over to kiss Jessica's cheek.
"Will I see you later, baby?" He whispered.  She smiled and stirred.
"What time will you finish?"
"Around 6."
"Maybe, babe. Just. If not I'll leave you some food in the oven, yeah?"
"Ok…thanks. Love you, yeah?"
She gave a grumble and drifted away. Drew closed the bedroom door and headed downstairs and out towards the daylight.

By 7pm Drew knew he wouldn't see her. The train at London Bridge had sat stationary just beyond reach of platform 4 for 38 painful minutes. He looked out of the window from the train as an adjacent one rolled past. He watched the gallery of abject faces pass his. Faces of people he would no doubt never see again. You could see a thousand different people in London just once in your life every day. He was only thinking of one.
When he got in there was a note on the dining table: 'Pie in oven. MISS YOU! xxx'. He opened a beer and put on the news. London was to host the 2012 Olympics. Scenes of unbridled joy from Trafalgar Square.

The walk began again. Still waters. By his feet he now occasionally stumbled past lost objects. A dolly, an umbrella, a tooth retainer, coins and crates. He ran his hands along that red London brickwork hoping to meet some more strangers. But the path seemed even longer and lonelier than before. He passed under London Bridge and kept an eye out for the seagull. In no time he found himself in between St Pauls and the Tate. He looked up at the bridge, climbed onto the wall and tried to grasp the metal beams. Again, it was too far.
As he jumped down he was startled by a man in a black uniform running past. The man shouted something back and hurried off. It was getting dark. Cold. Unlike before, he could hear the gentle breeze and in the distance Ben chimed one, two, three, four, five. The waters began to rise. Six. He started to jog once more, past Charing Cross. The waters began to churn and wrap like rope-knots either side. On the South Bank a string quartet played while at the other side of the water, near Embankment Gardens, was Jess. But she wasn't alone. Behind her stood two men. Drew called out to her. The water churned and sloshed aggressively against the wall. Jessica blew him a kiss. One man put his arm on her shoulder. She turned and walked away. Tears ran down Drew's cheeks and as they did the Thames buckled, stretched and shot violently up into the heavens, leaving nothing beneath but

shingle, sand and bone. Drew watched it swirl away into the heaven and the stars, the universe and the unknown.

"You fell asleep on the sofa, Drew."
"I know. I'm sorry."
"Don't be sorry, silly!" She kissed him. Slower this time. She'd brushed her teeth too.
"I've overslept. I'm going to be late." Drew shot up to leave.
"I thought later we could…" Jess started but Drew was gone.
She sat down on the sofa for a while and tried to drift off. Her eyes drew heavy and she slept for a while. The next thing she became aware of were noises outside. Helicopters. Sirens. She turned on the television and went numb. Panic set in and she reached for a phone to call him. And call him. And call him.
Three days later she left the hospital, pale and tired. Her brothers put their arms around her shoulders as they had done when they were children, whenever she tripped and fell. Whenever she felt lost or scared. She missed him. How she missed him. Her brothers made her sugary tea and watched her finally get to sleep. It was time for her to sleep.
She found herself walking alongside the pagoda in the park. She'd never walked this path before and certainly never in her pyjamas. The sun shone down through the trees and the Thames shimmered in the light. Maybe she'd walk a bit further today. She draped her arms over each side of the wall, running her fingers through the cool waters. Overhead a seagull swung down close to her ear, the breeze hitting her face. She watched it swoop skywards before descending gracefully down to a post by the south side of Chelsea Bridge.
By the roadside someone was waving. She smiled and ran and ran.

## Thoughts and Memories from Beyond the Flashbulbs

### *2006: "Casino Royale" Royal Premiere*

This was not the only time this had happened to me but I remember this time distinctly because after some fucked up dream about my Dad boasting some weird metal teeth I had again awoken on the back seat of Screening Room 5 to find that the lights had gone up, the credits had rolled and the old dears who typically made up the audience for *The Queen* had already arisen to see me crashed out behind them as they hobbled past me to be unaided back down the stairs.

In the main screen next door, nobody would've noticed you sleeping around 24 rows back, but in the Screening Room screens there was no hiding since these shitty, cramped screens only consisted of just 50 seats each.

At least on that day, the complaints weren't able to manifest themselves for the majority of the managers and team leaders were fretting next door, not only about the wide range of celebrity attendees due to turn up, but the arrival of the actual Royals themselves; this being for the World Premiere of the new James Bond film, 'Casino Royale'.

I was late now, I was supposed to be helping Anwar, Paddy and Brian O'Bastard in 'The Airlock' as soon as my film had finished and I'd cleaned up.

Why the fuck had they put me in *The Queen* again? This probably would've made it around the 21st and a half time I'd sat through it and it was always on those sweeping establishing shots of the Scottish Highlands about halfway through that I'd nod off. It had played here for *six fucking months!* How many times could a man watch such a thing? And, another thing, even when I'd been appointed duties to a different screen, *The Queen* would suspiciously move with me. The old dears' complaints would always be the same of course; '*why?*' they would ask '*had the film been at the top of five flights of stairs to which they were too old to climb?*' and yet, Stephen Frears' award-winning Royal drama would forever be moved upwards whilst on the ground floor's Screening Room 1, fifty or so teenagers or twenty-somethings would squeeze in to see *Children of Men.*

Still, at least this crowd hadn't been the type to leave a mess of which I'd normally be pressured to clean up, and this meant I could still make it to the Airlock in time without anyone noticing.

The strangest thing that really struck me about that day was that after having sat through that film over and over again, the real Queen was about to make her arrival in a little under an hour and this had never been a situation I'd ever imagined myself to be in.

Let me tell you about this place I was working for in those days; our cinema, (along with two other competitors) dominated the glitz of Leicester Square to make itself known as the company's flagship auditorium and was, I'm sure, definitely the first of its kind. It had previously been one of the West End's leading theatres before making the 20th Century conversion in 1937 to host the film *The Prisoner of Zenda.* Much of its theatre decor had remained intact; between its lower Stalls Floor and Upper Royal and Rear Circles (those two forming a grand balcony), the auditorium boasted something like 1,700 seats. The same great crimson curtain concealed the biggest screen in the square. On the walls, 1930's Art Deco sculptures of gold naked angels still remained as did an old, silent-era organ that could ascend and descend into the stage; incidentally, there was only one man in London who still had the means to play it. Whilst the notion of attributing different price ranges to the different sections of Stalls, Rear and Royal circle always struck me as stupid in the case of a cinema, it was nevertheless, an impressively atmospheric place to see a film. Its history was legendary too, it had somehow survived The Blitz, had hosted the European or World premieres to practically *every* major film ever released, it had, until just a few months ago, hosted the BAFTA award ceremonies and somewhere in the 1950s, a young actor named Maurice Micklewhite Jnr had been sitting in his agent's office nearby with his entire career on the precipice of failure should he not successfully choose a catchy stage name for himself; as the story then goes, he apparently looked out the window to contemplate these fateful passing minutes and saw upon the side of this historical building, the poster for the film *The Caine Mutiny,* and there and then named himself Michael Caine; *that* is how legendary this place was.

Of course, we all had to memorise the place's more impressive shit as a means to get through the interview and so far it had earned me two happy months as an usher on a 35-hour contract. Back home on the estate, my Mum had just got together with Steve, yet *another* boyfriend, and with my younger step sister and brother both understandably wanting separate rooms as they entered puberty, it was insisted that I could only stick about at home so long as I paid her rent. This had all been fair enough. The job would get me by as I worked out some way of getting into the film industry and I couldn't stand Steve, so the irregular shifts, most of them at night, enabled me to stay out of his way.

Like most historical buildings in England, modern times hadn't been kind to it. I don't know what you know about the exhibition industry but cinemas don't actually make much money from the films they screen. Instead, most of their revenue is made from the confectionary stands. In the Thatcher years then, the rental price of any business in Central London (plus utilities) shot through the roof and so the cinemas in this place ratcheted up their retail prices, kept their maintenance costs to an absolute minimum and paid their staff the lowest wages possible. This cinema in particular later realised it could make some revenue off the films themselves if they screened some of the big, selected titles independently for a short time after their normally-agreed exhibition runs. As a result they built The Screening Rooms, which took over the cinema's adjoining alleyway space (which itself had apparently once been the scene of a violent poll tax riot). It was basically five, box-like fifty-seater screens that were stacked up on top of one another in a space no bigger than your average fire escape; tickets cost a fortune, yet it succeeded, sweat would congeal on its walls, yet it succeeded, mice ran about its floors and yet it succeeded.

To pass the time, my colleagues here would share a YouTube video of a premiere once hosted here back in the 70s of yet another Bond film, *Moonraker.* I think it had something to do with some kid who'd had his dreams fixed by Jimmy Savile to be a cinema manager and so this was it; in it, the staff were all tuxedoed up, white gloves, the lot, they lined up and met the stars, they sipped champagne and were apparently paid pretty well, the building even had a cloak room for the aristocracy and the building's old dressing rooms (once the abode of theatre stars awaiting their stage calls) were then our luxury staff rooms. Now, however, we wore dirty, stained uniforms, we were predominantly kept from socialising with anybody from high society and our social area was now in a tiny room in the basement with a broken table and three uncomfortable chairs between thirty or so of us, with much of this place's historical back rooms just left unused. Like a crap Hogwarts, it was a place with chambers of ever so slightly less magical secrets. Yes, everything about it that had once been a staple of London class had had its costs cut to such a degree it had descended into plain and simple tat. I would wonder to myself, as these Royal Premieres took place, whether the same could be revealed behind the scenes of Buckingham Palace?

Still, despite my grumbles, I'd been happy there; of all the menial jobs to be had in London, getting paid to embrace my one true love, films, all day was by far the best of all of them and the staff, like London itself, were made up of different nationalities, different faiths and different races; most were Europeans roughing it for a few years while they picked up the language (and some of the girls were gorgeous). Others, like me, were made up of wannabe filmmakers, artists and actors, whilst others were just general, charismatic drifters or petty criminals and yet we all got on so well that still, to this day, I've loosely kept in touch with some of them.

Anyway, I reached 'The Airlock' where two of my mates, Anwar and Paddy, plus Brian O'Bastard had already assembled. Anwar, the world's laziest Muslim, who'd already been here for years, and Paddy, an insanely ambitious Dutchman who could beat most high-flying city boys in his desires to milk this city for everything it had were simply fucking about whilst O'Bastard turned and whistled breaths of disapproval through his nostrils.
"You're late" he said monotonously.
"Sorry. One of the old ladies needed help down the stairs". He couldn't argue with that, I thought.
Brian O'Bastard was clearly not his real name; we called him that because he was just, unapologetically, a complete bastard. Every menial job has its own version of Brian O'Bastard; those kids who'd grown up the hard way, had been bullied, and without the credentials for anything more aspirational, had settled into retail jobs to slither themselves into management positions so they could bully others now beneath them. He was bitter now however because we always had good alibis that stopped him in his tracks.
'The Airlock' was also not this place's real name, instead it was merely a staff corridor that was conveniently located halfway between the Screening Rooms, the main cinema's grand foyer and the security doors, making it an ideal place to hold back anyone who could leave one part of the cinema but not yet enter another; that idea of having to strictly close one door before opening another merely reminded all us film fans of the spacecraft airlocks used in all those science fiction films, hence where it got its name. The four of us awaited by the door to the main foyer where through a small window we could see what was happening inside.
Now, Royal Premieres, unlike normal premieres, followed an incredibly strict procedure; only the staff not subject to having criminal records would be invited to work, throughout the day we would merely set up & place pamphlets for the film upon the chairs. Police with sniffer dogs would scour the building and every bottle of water, every item and every person who'd enter the building would be systematically checked and rechecked.
By about 16.30, the general guests would be let in from outside and into the auditorium wherein most of our workforce would be positioned as ushers, these would then be followed by the lower key members of the film's crew. Then, at about 17.30, would come the film's top players; the actors, the director, the writer. First they'd come in from the madness of the outside red carpet where every journalist and fan could interact with them before entering the main foyer where they'd await to meet the Royals before specialist journalists and photographers would capture such historical events. Now, after they'd all entered the auditorium, Royals and all, and the foyer had been cleared, there'd then be a second wave of lesser known celebrities who'd be escorted by the PR gang through the back routes of the building and into the foyer, where for reasons of basic publicity, they'd have photos of their own during, perhaps, the first 10 minutes of the film, before we'd then escort them, through the darkness of the screen, to their allocated seats. These 'celebrities' in question

would normally be trends of the current moment, *Big Brother* or *X Factor* contestants or lesser known performers with only minor roles in the film.

Through the window we watched with anticipation, none of us except Anwar had been here that long, none of us had been especially privileged and yet, we were about to see, first, Bond and then the fucking Queen! Two British institutions in one; one of which had a long and healthy, international fan base.

The cameras kept flashing, and in the electrical miasma of everything, as I can recall, I could make out a line up consisting of Mads Mikkelson, Judi Dench, the beautiful Eva Green, the director, Martin Campbell, the franchise's long-term producer, Barbara Broccoli and of course, the man of whom everyone had been questioning, the most unusually cast Bond yet, Daniel Craig.

In a weird way, I remember feeling strangely sorry for Daniel Craig; so far I'd followed his career through TV and independent films and he never struck me as one for the spotlight of attention, yet the screams he had already received as he stepped out of a Rolls Royce a short time earlier had seemed to shake the city to its core. He was now *big;* big enough anyway for the photos of this night to be kept in a cultural archive longer than any of us would be alive.

Another Rolls then pulled up and out stepped The Queen and Prince Philip. Now I'm no Royalist but there's star struck and then there's the type of star struck that, as I could sense, could even make stars star struck; the line-up might have just become movie royalty but in the face of actual royalty, their status had just shrunk to that of just everyday people. All I could really think about was how little old Liz looked like Helen Mirren.

So wrapped up in all of this was I that I hadn't noticed that O'Bastard had opened the door into The Airlock and let the second wave of minor, publicity-hungry celebrities inside with us.

One thing that I always thought was cool about The Airlock was that everyone in there was subject to the same strict rules and so, ironically, before the presence of the Royals, all other preconceptions of a social hierarchy seemed to disappear. Here we all were then, three minimum-wage ushers, some security guards, a few celebrities, their PR people and O'Bastard, all shut into this cramped corridor as just mere people pushed together in an awkward silence like strangers in a train carriage. It reminded me of some strange fantasy I'd once had regarding the notion over how in times of war, celebrity came to mean next to nothing, and that I could end up in some World War trench alongside people from the 90s that I'd looked up to as a teenager; the Gallagher Brothers, Quentin Tarantino or Fatboy Slim, just having to survive together under the same bad conditions; this was a bit like that. I think it had been Paddy who started it off; of course in any kind of pressure cooker environment, it is human nature to do or say something stupid.

Upon seeing the Queen, Paddy just openly posed the question; "How much do you reckon I could charge her if I pimped myself?" The reaction in The Airlock was mixed, there were some sniggers and some sniffs of disapproval but nobody stopped us.

Anwar was next; "What if you just walked up to her and directly asked for a couple of quid?" I knew then that I had to get one over the two of them and so began impersonating my finest Fred West impression.

"Alright Queenie, don't mean to bovver you but I got six years experience in Tesco, I've pulled pints down the workin' men's club and am usin' my savin's to open a family chippy. Mind if you gimme an 'ead start?"

In the crowd, this fit red head then just burst out laughing as if being unable to contain it.

"Alright, that's enough now" one of the security guards hissed at me.

She laughed on, sniggering into the sleeves of whatever designer jacket she'd been asked to promote and was reddening in the face, cracking up.

I recognised her vaguely, she was certainly familiar, one of those young faces you sort of know from background telly but could deduce she was definitely an actress. On and on she laughed and I could tell it'd pissed off her PR person. She was one of us, one of us who could treat social hierarchy like the joke that it was and I liked it. I liked *her.*

Outside, the Royals and stars were being led into the auditorium and the press began reforming their previous positions in readiness for this next lot.

"Ok, let's go" declared O'Bastard and the four of us led them through into the foyer.

As she passed me, she gave me *that* look, that slight side look girls give you when they give away that they might be interested. They say that women find humour a turn on and I don't know if it had been an illusion of the camera flashes reflecting off those beautiful green eyes, or whether she'd been twirling that red hair of hers in the implied way that I remember her doing, but this seemed to be one of those looks that proved it. Her eyes flicked down as if to get my name off my name badge before flicking back up again to catch mine and she smiled pleasantly. I smiled back at her and then she walked out to do her bit with the press.

Moments later, I was stood in the great auditorium, waiting just inside the entrance to the Royal Circle for her and this second wave to then be seated. The place was rammed with all kinds of famous faces, and I was fixated on those traditionally styled, psychedelic Bond credits, wondering if she played any part in this film and if her name might appear as something mildly recognisable.

From its opening sequence, I gathered that this Bond film was a reboot, a return to the character's origins, only updated to the 21st century. It was interesting how in the 21st century the movie world's biggest, most iconic franchises were now pursuing the theme of 'origins'; such unforgettable, recent troubles, 9/11, 7/7, had, it could be said, instigated the mainstream consciousness into looking backwards into the past, to ponder where the culprits of this new age of terror and villainy may had come from. For anybody who knew anything about anything of course, we'd all root this back to the shady goings on of the Cold War, but it made me think about what other forms of villainy might had been being underestimated and brewing up somewhere in the distant corners of the world at that moment and then manifest themselves in some way through future blockbusters.

One of the PR girls opened the door slightly and I was there straight away. Instead of getting *her* however, I got one of those now obsolete reality TV contestants and with his ticket. I guided him via torchlight to somewhere in Row D, four rows behind the Queen, Phillip and the Bond ensemble. I wondered how they would get on if they should meet?

Through the darkness, I could see Anwar leading *her* to her seat, and again, as she sat, she saw me and I saw her; I couldn't wait to get home and get on the net to work out who the fuck she actually was. What was going on here? I kept thinking to myself.

As soon as the film had gone into full swing, Paddy, Anwar and I retreated to the Bollinger Bar (a promotional product that had been traditional to shift during Bond films) which was located just before the upper foyers and under the seated slope that made up Rear Circle's balcony seating layout. Inside, the shutter had been closed down and the girls who'd been serving were already cleaning up and so we had to help to chuck away the heavier shit, desperately trying not to make our noise pass under the seats and disrupt the film. Inside, we were listening for the booming action scenes of the Bond film, but this one seemed more dialogue heavy.

Paddy and I lifted two boxes of unused champagne bottles whilst Anwar, using the laziest excuse of his faith not permitting him to handle alcohol, just grabbed a lighter bin bag full of sweet bags and we made our way out of the bar onto the Circle Foyer and towards the corridors & staircases that led down to the storage rooms. The very second we stepped out onto the Circle Foyer however, some highly intimidating security guys in black suits appeared, ninja-like, from out of nowhere; they'd inspected the contents of Anwar's bag and were patting down his overweight form before he'd even had time to comprehend what was happening; not me or Paddy you understand, just Anwar.

"Back inside, please" one of the men said forcefully to Anwar.

"Oh my *god"* Anwar replied before returning inside the bar.

The question, 'where *the fuck* did they come from?' Was written all over the expression Paddy gave me, and, "Yes, being a Muslim is certainly hard when working alongside Royal security" was all over the one I tried to telepathically give him in return.


Whenever anyone down on their luck is confronted by the intimidating ways of a higher class, it is natural to formulate your own way of rebellion, no matter how juvenile or stupid. As we were restocking the bottles in the storage room down below then, Paddy stopped and asked me;

"Have you ever wondered what else is in this building?"

"Not really, I mean, there can't be that else much to it, can there?"

"Aaron" he said, "think about it? There's the auditorium, right? The projection booth is just slightly above that, and the staff room, the office and the storage places are all down here in the Basement, yeah? Now think about how much bigger this seems when you look at it from the outside".

He had a point.

Paddy then began telling me the same history of this place as I told you earlier, concluding with; "there's loads of old hidden bits higher up. Shall we go up there?"

We'd never been explicitly told that those areas were out of bounds for the staff; there were no locked doors for example, just the implication that with this being a Royal Premiere equating to no fucking about, that for that day at least, such an adventure was probably strictly forbidden, which of course, made it all the more exciting.

"Come on" he laughed, "all the managers are distracted, security will be watching the Queen and if the cameras see us we'll just say we'd been told there was more stock up there, or something. We'll be back in the bar before anyone notices".

It was a good alibi, and so we did it. Up the lost stairwells we ran, past the entranceways to the Circle floors, past the doors to the enormous projection room above and further. Every now and then we'd find a freely opened door where inside we'd see rather large, old theatre-style dressing rooms; bulb-surrounded mirrors were still on the walls collecting dust and there were vast wardrobes designed for costume changes, some of them even had old, never-used en-suite bathrooms. On all the upper levels to this historical building, we found more and more of these dressing rooms, most of them now used to store either mysterious boxes or cleaning equipment.

These dimly lit, upper stairwells then began to change as we presumably got to the roof, the stairs became more ladder-like as if only maintenance people were allowed to go up there. Paddy, who had been leading the way, stopped before me with another of his sinister grins; before us was the door to the roof, and of course we *had to* do it.

Pushing the bar, we creaked it open, shitting bricks over whether it might activate an alarm system; it didn't and with a sudden hit of November cold, we stepped out onto the roof.

The place basically consisted of rain-sodden vents, electrical huts and pigeons that grouped together to coo gently. We took a few steps outwards and could see the tacky neon glory of the West End emanating from the balconies of the expensive bars, restaurants and casinos trailing all the way back into the steams of Chinatown and Soho beyond. For that night however, the entirety of Leicester Square had been turned into a red-carpet event, *Casino Royale* was now screening in three cinemas simultaneously and the flood lights, erected news screens and the further decorations were being taken down, and from the ground below we could still hear the screams of the fans still waiting out the duration of the film in the cold as a means to potentially have chance encounters with their cinematic idols.

"And what *the fuck* do you two think you're doing here?"

Jumping in fear, we turned to see that behind us, perched upon some higher level were two specialist police marksmen, both wearing black and with balaclavas. Next to them I saw an empty rectangular box, and next to it, ready for use, this fucking massive, laser-guided *sniper rival!*
As their hardened eyes stared into our very being, I began to sense that there were more of these guys upon several other of the rooftops. Of course there were, this was fucking *Queen Elizabeth II''s security* we were talking about.
With one aggressive finger, the marksman in question pointed back towards the open door we'd come through. We nodded, walked back to the door, and gently closed it behind us.
We both let out a massive exhale, knowing that once this got back to O'Bastard, we were almost certainly going to be fired and considering the type of authorities involved in this event in particular, probably even worse.
We hid for the rest of the show with the girls who're still cleaning up the Bollinger Bar where we had supposed to have been; the shutter had been closed and the camera in there had always been crap. We didn't tell anyone what had happened and yet the girls still observed that we were nervous.
An intimidating knock then rattled on the other side of the shutter, bewildering the girls. If it had been the staff surely they would've just come through the door? This was it, Paddy and I thought, we were about to be escorted out and have electrodes applied to our balls.
Elisa, who was Italian, turned the key and slowly lifted the shutter. I don't know if she knew who this guy was but I did, it wasn't any of the managers, it wasn't any of the security or the police. It was 90's rapper *Vanilla Ice.*
"Can I help you?" said Elisa with her broken English.
He stared at us all somewhat unpleasantly, as if about to say something that he might somehow be sick of saying, like it might have been the brunt of some tiresome, bad joke.
He held out a plastic cup of Pepsi towards Elisa.
"Gimme some *ice*". Which Elisa than kindly did, not quite knowing why we all found his emphatic usage of the word so funny.
The humour of it all had made us both somewhat more relaxed about this strange experience of ours but we were still certain we were about to be immediately fired and although I should have, perhaps, been more concerned, my intrigue around the actress who I'd met in The Airlock just grew and grew.

# Cobham Services

As one heads towards the weaving lanes that summon the weary, hungry driver towards the impressive, modern veneer of Cobham Services one immediately gains a gratifying sense of anticipation as to what treasures may be in store behind the glass frontage. The car park has been built on a slight curvature, creating a wave effect that leads one down towards the front entrance. Whether this is intentional or not I cannot say but it does have a calming effect; one of respite following a long journey.

The main terminal itself consists of a *Days Inn* on the left and a food court on the right. Both buildings are housed by impeccable curved rooftops that, again, complement the sense that one is bobbing gently on a calm sea.

Just towards the entrance stands a totem style advertising hoarding that clearly highlights to the visitor what lies ahead. But nothing can quite prepare you for the first time you pass through the automatic doors. As one enters the main arena the initial response is an overwhelming assault on the senses. The circular design of the shops and cafes houses a spectacular food hall abuzz with various global delicacies. One standout stall has to be *El Mexicana* for the more adventurous diner, which provides its own take on Latin American cuisine. You will also be delighted to know that Cobham even has its own Carvery counter that provides the traditional British roast dinner in giant Yorkshire Puddings! Little touches such as this exemplify this station's ingenuity, ground-breaking ambition and sense of fun. I must admit I was chuckling about this unique concept for quite some time after I left.

Of course, for the more financially cautious traveller there is also a *Greggs* Bakery onsite; an addition that has revolutionised the service station industry and provided a low-cost alternative to families who at one time would have been unable to enjoy the full culinary experience these transport hubs provide. It is worth noting that in the 7 hours I spent in the food hall I only spotted two or three people eating their own packed lunches; praise indeed! The toilets let the premises down slightly; they are functionary without luxury. Added to this the hand driers were out of service when I visited which soured my trip somewhat and remains the reason I cannot award this station the full 5 Stars. They do however provide shower facilities. Other features worth noting are the *Regus* Meeting space and a facility with Massage Chairs to help you relax before that big presentation!

Before checking into the hotel that evening I visited the *Starbucks* coffee shop, which boasts a stylish mezzanine level where one can relax and watch the crowds slowly rotate around the floor below like milk in stirred coffee. So many people. One wonders where they are all heading.

The *Days Inn* hotel was the final stop on my visit and provided a comfortable and affordable respite from the excitement of the station itself. Rooms are clean and my one had a terrific view of both the M25 and the Heathrow flight path.

At around 11pm I rounded off my trip with the lights in my room switched off. From the window, I watched the traffic circling the periphery of the great city beyond. Planes would occasionally fly in and out and for a moment and I felt like I was watching some great toy town in motion; like the train set my father kept in his workshop all those years ago. He is long gone now but the memories return sometimes.

The room also has free tea and coffee.

**4 Stars * * * ***

# The King Commute

To his knowledge, Spain, or anywhere for that matter, had never encountered a problem like this before, thought Danny Fonseca. Nothing like the problem he and many others had encountered three days earlier on the 25th March. For the 25th March had been the day that London inadvertently created the 'King Commute'.

Danny had left his Somer's Town hostel and entered King's Cross underground station under the intention of riding the Piccadilly Line westbound across London to Heathrow airport where he would catch the 17.00 RyanAir service back to his home city of Madrid.

It was around 13.30 that he began to notice that it was becoming abnormally crowded amidst those tunnels, a number of failing Oyster cards and a strange high demand for croissants at the sandwich bars were building queues of increasing lengths that were then merging with the paths of the passers-by.

It was after twenty minutes of queuing to get through the Oyster barriers that he became aware of both his luggage bag and the guitar he wore on his back becoming an irritation to those who stood next to him. Although he was aware of their frustrations, he was also a tall man of which meant two things, firstly, that it was unlikely anybody would bother trying to push past him and secondly, that he could see over the heads of the smaller commuters to work out what the origin of this problem was. The problem with this advantage was that even beyond the barriers and on the escalators etc, the origin to this problem never seemed to reveal itself.

Eventually a blockade of police and security appeared along the barriers to stop the crowds, claiming that many people were apparently falling onto the tracks below due to overcrowding, and that people would have to turn back to find alternative methods of travel. Danny had an ability to notice this before everyone else had and so began to use his size to make his way back, with great difficulty, to the streets above where he was met with an even more shocking revelation - that from the entrance to the station, to as far as he could see to the edges of this area's wide streets beyond, were a further ocean of faces, clogging up both pavement and road, all looking in various directions in equal befuddlement to those emerging back out from the station behind him.

"What had caused this madness?" he thought to himself; there were a number of elements to consider here – first, a football match was coinciding with the concert to a highly popular rock band, people had been granted half a working day and both transport and shops all had offers on. All of these things, it would seem had come together at the wrong time and place and had led tourists, workers, consumers and sports and music enthusiasts to descend upon the busy city at the same time.

Now, a rumour was spreading from one commuter to another across the King Commute, towards him and beyond, that all the tubes had been temporarily shut down due to processions of falling passengers leaving the underground trains immobilised in their tunnels, meaning everyone would surely have to walk. He too then, had no choice and so stepped into the streets (that new path of the King Commute) to try and make his way forwards, somehow, to Heathrow.

Surely, the police, the town planners, somebody, he thought, would have this problem resolved in the next couple of hours and things would surely disperse? It was then that the buckles on his bags and clothes seemed to connect to those of the people next to him and he unwillingly became a symbiotic component of the King Commute.

28th March: It was only after he had passed his hostel three times, after his flight had left over nearly seven times and after he'd used his physical dominance to pickpocket those nearby of their croissants that his degree in sociology began to take on usage in his life. Indeed, the theory was true, that without clear directions from an appointed leader, people would instinctively form a natural pattern of order – and now the King Commute (some were calling it The Lord) seemed to be endlessly flowing in a clockwork motion around the city towards... who knew?

Those who had starved to death or who'd fallen ill were now entangled up in its mass and were being dragged along for the ride, food or information had become the new currency, people's luggage was being used as makeshift toilets or sources of shelter, the vehicles that once had such important parts to play in this city's motions, were now being trampled on beneath the millions of feet of one great, gormless creature and the amount of people trying to contact their loved ones had resulted in an overloading of telephone networks, rendering this great organism without communication to the rest of the world and where was it heading to?

He had assumed that most were trying to make their way to the suburbs where the crowd would presumably disperse but he was as guilty as no doubt everyone else was in simply agreeing to follow the first immediate person before him. What had caused this was that the police officers who had initially been assigned to take control of the King Commute by operating the newly erected direction panels, had, due to an alarming decrease in personal space, no choice but to also step into the King Commute and have their position replaced by the next person directly behind them, of whom no doubt with London being London, was of a different nationality entirely; henceforth, the direction panels read a new language every five seconds and gradually a new language of mixed phonetics began to take hold as the city's leading one.

Indeed, Danny now concluded, the problem he had encountered three days prior had, well and truly, never been experienced before. Yet, he began to wonder, was it actually *a problem?* For it was here that his sociological interests began to take note that The King Commute, interestingly enough, was slowly eroding any former notions of racial or religious prejudices...

### The Third Age of Knee Movement

After what may have been something around a period of three weeks (society's very definition of time was now henceforth being based upon the obvious choice of the movement of the human leg) mixed Chinese whispers had begun to pass through the flow of people that an eventual destination for the King Commute had been chosen and so it had been generally accepted as gospel truth that the mysterious direction of the King Commute was set to resolve itself.

Danny wanted to believe such rumours but basically didn't. After all, the functioning of the King Commute seemed to be quite effective and was in some ways better than what they had had before; the windows that had been removed from the shop faces had enabled the King Commute to flow through them with further fluidity, supplying itself with all the material possessions that it might need to survive with when concerning warmth, shelter and food etc. Even when Danny wanted to relieve himself from the boredom of the commute and would take to playing his guitar, he realised that he now had a far bigger crowd than he'd ever had when playing in the backs of some of the bars in Somer's Town.

The question of human reproduction (that old chestnut) was largely based upon where one would be positioned within the King Commute; the men fortunate to have been positioned in close proximity to a woman would simply get it on when the time seemed necessary and after a while, sex no longer seemed like an embarrassing subject for the English and, more so, social status was no longer focused on an individual's sexual prowess as it once was in the old world, for that in itself, was something that largely stemmed from capital demographics, things that no longer made sense in the King Commute for an advert would no longer know which component of it it would be communicating to and when.

When proceedings came to childbirth, the components surrounding the pregnant women, would be getting increasingly skilled in their midwifery abilities and would simply all help to deliver the child and then place it upon the shoulders of the nearest adult male whereupon its view of the ongoing commute ahead would grant it natural leadership skills. This child would then (as they had all settled on) presumably grow to adulthood to trample the previous generations beneath its feet, the remains of which would then be discreetly discarded with down manholes; this was the sewage system's original purpose after all. The sex of this particular newborn would also then dictate in what formation the King Commute would then reshape itself when it came to further, future reproductive activities.

### The Seventh Age of the Knee

When the rumour of the King Commute's overall purpose was eventually discarded and it began a natural quest for wider spaces, Danny, and the son he now carried upon his shoulders (his height and the view ahead had been the things that had led the others to elect him for potential continuation) found their section flowing down the wider streets of Regent Street toward the direction of the opened out arenas of Piccadilly Circus, Leicester Square, Trafalgar Square and, God he hoped, St. James' Park etc.

Some of Danny's son's first wondrous visions of the human world henceforth were of people throwing themselves from the rooftops of some of Regent Street's loftier buildings; for once, after all these years of refusal, the repressed upper classes had come to realise that, thanks to gravity, the benefits of the King Commute and its resources, were now something that weren't reaching the higher floors of the buildings and with great tumbles of liberation, such suited men were throwing themselves in awe at the King Commute, their lives now better as if they'd just survived the end of World War II.

When eventually passing through Piccadilly Circus, Danny looked up at the Circus' great electronic advertising panels where he saw that knowledge of the King Commute had finally leaked out to the rest of the world and its first news reports – now in a mixed language of its own – were being transmitted for all to behold. It would seem, just as Danny had suspected, that instead of the announcement of some great final destination, The King Commute was actually an ongoing phenomena, and that due to even further overcrowding, further cities of the world had developed King Commutes of their own and furthermore, many of the world's shipping and airline routes had also become so cluttered as to find new purposes out at sea...amidst that great King Commute of the world. It was during this sudden global acceptance of things that Danny began to think of the future for him and his new family and like most people who once came to London out of will (and not the commute), he began to look back retrospectively as to why he had wanted to come to London in the first place; some kind of half-arsed dream of becoming a musician he thought he remembered. But now with a family, it was time to think of the simpler life. The King Commute, he had learned, had actually made its way to the entrance of the Channel Tunnel, and so, if possible, if he angled his reproductive positionings in the right way (perhaps with some negotiations made with the 'upper generations'), maybe not he, but perhaps his son or future seedlings, could get through that tunnel and back into mainland Europe. Upon the other side, perhaps, they could then slingshot themselves into that other orbit that what was now being dubbed 'The Great European Tract' that would then, with a bit of luck, take his gene pool back into Spain, back into Madrid, where the heritage of his old world had once begun...

May the hopes within The King Commute of the World continue to flow...

## Pisshead

The office cleared out early at 3pm so we could get a prompt start on Dicko's drinks. I had tried my best to wriggle out of this one because a.) Dicko is a passive aggressive prick b.) I'm supposed to be home for baby bath time and c.) This is the third leaving do this month; all of which have resulted in nothing more than a damaged bank balance and a world of regret.

By the time we arrived at The Metropolitan, Gina had sorted out the cake and the 'Good Luck Richard' card and banners. She was already celebrating with her third glass of Prosecco by the time we reached the reserved area.

The bar itself was an anomaly; giant opulent red walls were decorated by huge oil portraits of mysterious, powerful-looking men. The symmetrical support pillars to this place were painted gold and on the ceiling were further mysterious coats of arms that too, may have referred to the same, elusive potraits. It seemed like it might've once been a grand old hotel from England's empirical times but now it was merely a Wetherspoon's pub, a peddler of cheaper priced booze and food to the city's less privileged pub goers. This was typical of London of course, all of *this* hidden within the surrounding enclaves of Baker Street's dirty underground station and even that was hidden behind the label of a popular tourist hub; a veneer behind a veneer and the Russian doll effect could also be said of the characters who frequented it.

When Dicko turned up it got lively pretty quick. Needless to say we all got a few evils from the assorted drones and late afternoon interns on their fucking macs.

As soon as the GM turned up the shots got lined up pretty quick. Ties were loosened, buttons undone. Harry got a bit larey with one of the barmaids. I saw her pointing at us all from the bar and shouting something at him. She still served him though. I overheard his parting shot; 'something something minimum wage cunt'. Gina was laughing for no reason; she was well on the way.

Dicko was holding court as expected. Each well-trod story got a bit more risqué and I could see a few more heads turning. It was embarrassing to be honest but by three and a half pints in I was starting to relax more. Harry said I was 'double-parked' so I sank the half empty glass, started on the next one and turned to head to the gents. He said there'd be another cold one waiting for me on my return and called me a 'lightweight pussy'. I smiled and tried to let it slide, even though I can't stand the prick.

I climbed the staircase with the laughter not too far behind me. I was texting Sophie to say I'd be back before 9. Train delays at Baker Street, what could I do.

*Home asap xxx*
*Ok. Luv u x*

As I reached the top of the stairs I felt someone's shoulder brush me.
"Watch where you're going. Pisshead."
The bloke was halfway downstairs before I could respond so I decided to leave it. 5pm is too early for a punch up, even by our fucking standards. I pushed open the door to the gents and headed over to the urinals, unzipping my flies as I went.

I made it to the porcelain just in time and let out a satisfied sigh as my bladder emptied. I started reading the advert in front of me about premature ejaculation and waited for the stream to finish. No one else was around so I tried to fill the empty wine glass by my feet too.

The next urinal along was taped up with bin liner. Dark orange piss brimmed near the edge of its white cracked well, totally clogged up. It stank. Badly. A badly written message was scrawled in biro on top

*OUT OF SERVIS*

Above it was a message carved into the wall paint but it had been scratched out.
I turned towards the sink behind and washed my hands. As I went to brush my hair I spotted something in the mirror.
The bin liner rustled.
I thought it was a fucking rat. I stood staring into the mirror at the reflection of the urinal.
*If the little shit goes for me I'm stamping the cunt out.*
I heard a screeching sound. Like a rusty tap being unscrewed slowly. I watched as the broken urinal suddenly drained like an amber sand timer, through the pipes I heard it go.
*This is fucking weird. Is anyone watching this?*
And then I heard it.
A gentle exhale. Behind the wall.
Not too loud. Gentle but clear. I looked at the toilet cubicles. All empty.
There it was again. A slight sigh, like panting. And then, a splashing sound. Like a washing basin. Behind the wall.
I could feel my heart beating as I walked towards the now empty urinal. I crouched down close to the scrawled note and black plastic. The shuffling suddenly stopped. I grabbed the bottom of the bin liner and lifted it slowly.
The bowl of the urinal was chipped, revealing a hole, no bigger than a two pound coin. The noise had stopped. And then I saw it. Something bolted past the chink of light and I saw wet fur.
I rocked back violently and crashed on my back, pushing my legs away from the wall breathing fast. I must have been shouting because one of the bar staff ran in and was holding my shoulders.
"Sir, are you ok? Sir"
I mouthed for words like a fish and pointed at the wall. Harry burst in and started holding his nose.
"Fuckin hell. What's this all about?"
I looked up wide eyed. "There's an animal. Behind the wall".
The bartender looked behind him bemused. Harry started laughing.
"You're on fucking Ket mate!"
The bartender reached for a radio.
"I'm calling the manager. You can't do drugs here."
"I'm not on fucking drugs. There's an animal. It's a fox, or maybe a dog. I saw it."
The bartender made a radio call. Harry started fucking about, knocking on the wall and laughing.
Then it started again. The splashing. But this time more aggressive. Harry looked round at me. It sounded like something was trapped or struggling.
Harry shouted out of the toilet door "Get a fucking manager here now!"
The bartender returned with a short, podgy manager and what looked like a caretaker. Behind him were some punters and a seriously worried looking Gina peering in from the doorway. Harry had got his ear to the wall and was dragging it along the tiles. The banging and splashing stopped again. Harry ran his fingers around the corner of the hollow wall until

he reached a waste paper bin spilling over with old paper tissues. He moved it to reveal a bigger hole stuffed with tissue.

"What's that?" he pointed to it, looking over at the manager.

The manager and the caretaker put on gloves, knelt down by the hole and started dragging the paper out of the wall. Reams and reams spilled out onto the floor and the struggling, splashing, panting sound started again. The people behind me and Harry were getting proper chatty and nervous.

"Get ready" said the manager "If it's a fox it'll be startled and aggressive."

The hole opened up like a bowling ball had gone through it. I watched as the caretaker went to grab another handful of paper but instead grabbed something stronger. I turned to hear Gina scream as the caretaker seized a long, slimy sock attached to a human foot.

"HELP!" Screamed the caretaker. I could hear Gina start to wretch. As I stood up I watched the leg start to kick like it was in spasm.

"Give me a hand!" Shouted the caretaker. The manager ran over, reached into the hole and grabbed another foot. The panting inside turned to whimpering.

Harry and I grabbed the shoulders of the two staff members as they heaved at the kicking, slippery legs. I started to make out some pinstriped trousers, followed by a belt buckle. The clothes were drenched in an oily liquid, like those birds you see on beaches after an environmental disaster. The manager saw the belt buckle and grabbed it. The smell was truly overwhelming.

"On the count of three, everyone PULL!"

The whimpering turned to an echoed shout from within the wall's chamber.

"Noooooooooo!"

"One"

"Noooooooooo!"

"Two"

We heard a squealing from inside the chamber. It sounded like an abattoir.

"THREE!"

As we all pulled backwards I watched as the men fell in slow motion. There was a squelch and through the greasy cavity slipped a limp but well-dressed male, lying unconscious on the plastic floor like a newborn calf.

The voices behind me groaned and screamed as I stared at the stricken individual, ammonia in my nose as the piss smell intensified.

I heard a commotion from the staircase. A policewoman walked into the room and stared down at the man, lying in the foetal position, his office tie draped over his soaking shirted belly. As he regained consciousness he began to writhe like a snake; his back arched as he opened his eyes and began to whimper. The policewoman turned to us and screamed "Get out. Now!"

As we hurried downstairs we heard her request back up. Gina was in floods of tears as more officers ran upstairs. Dicko and the lads walked over to meet us.

"I'll call her a taxi." Said the GM.


Two days later and I was on the train back to Stratford. I noticed a leftover Standard on the seat ahead of me and read the headline:

*POLICE UNCOVER FESTISH DEN IN LONDON PUB*

*A thorough search uncovered a small but inhabitable wormhole behind the urinals with access to the plumbing and room for a small change of clothes in plastic bags. The pervert they found was a local data analyst called Tom Pembridge. Journalists say he was a regular in clubs for those with 'special interests'.*

I heard someone click the toilet door of the cabin next to me as the train rattled out of Liverpool Street. I looked round before reading the last paragraph of the article.

*This is the fifth incident of its kind in London this year.*

As the train slowed to a standstill I heard the toilet flush and the door click open.

# Five Flats, Seven Years

## Flat 1 (Clapton):

We had two front doors, one ordinary, one metal. The second, we later learnt was to keep out the maniacs. There was the screaming crack head somewhere below, the man who played his music at full volume somewhere above and that strange noise that appeared at around 11pm every night from somewhere near the fried chicken shop.

"We are free to decorate" says our Rasta landlord, except for removing his weird wicker work that he insisted stay hung on the walls. *Why?* We thought to ourselves.

The mechanics in the garage next door didn't like our skin colour, the petrol station didn't fulfil our nutritional needs and cockroaches climbed our walls.

To secure a job, Christmas was spent alone here where with my lights off, the bugs and I watched next door's brothel getting ram raided; shapes scattered into the night from the windows and the two-mile police tape rerouted all the buses, once again threatening my job security as the trains and the cabs no longer wanted to come to Clapton.

Eventually, our housing benefit exposed our Rasta landlord's illegal renting to the system; "shit" we thought, "he's got keys and we have no locks on our rooms", our tensions rose as we were forced to sleep together. He never came yet we ran away, past the maniacs, past the corridor's soiled mattress that had sealed the fate of next door's senile elderly, our stuff crammed into bags with our own disappointments; our deposits not returned.

## Flat 2 (Bromley-by-Bow):

Our flat is nice. The lights of Canary Wharf are viewed from our windows, and finally we sense the future sensations the 21st century.

Our landlady is now an invisible, well-spoken voice on the other end of our phone and our country and the locals are less threatening than where we'd moved from- even their racial feuds between two parts of India have nothing to with us and so they frequently let us through their war zones unscathed – chatting away casually, as Raj takes another Mumbai-based deck chair to his head.

The building is divided into two however, ours is the top half of a maisonette, and below, the irritating fashion designers who have full possession of our fuse box. The power goes out unexpectedly and we have to bitch at them just to get a shower.

Our frustrations over these problems loosen the glue in our magnetism, we hate having to appoint who should confront the downstairs' bitches next and so our tensions rise, I eat and wash when they are sleeping and I am back to the creeping status of a child amidst a divorce, aware that from now on my journey through this capital shall be taken alone.

Their conversations about the concerts they'd failed to attend, the films they'd failed to catch become the forerunners for a boredom about to polarise these two and so they break up. I decide to leave, and as I pass my way through the rainbow-painted security gate for the last time, I finally meet the repair man of whose previous absence had contributed to the angers of this couple and I. I confront him about where he was when jobs needed doing and he responds in a language that makes no sense. I know now why our landlady always seemed so secretive of him. One mystery solved, another begun.

**Flat 3 (Oval):**

I am now renting in the south, on the 4th floor of a tower block, let out by a suspicious Italian colleague and accompanied by a company of international friends. Our nights are kept lively by the exciting tales of Milan, Johannesburg and the French Alps. Outside, on occasion, we hear gunshots and screams, and flowers of remorse coat the floor; inside however, our team of four remain good, plus an empty room where a procession of strange characters come and go, nipping into the front room to tell us of their own peculiar tales of origin and their intentions.

In just one day I am mugged and later called into the courts of justice regarding a housing tax discrepancy that isn't mine, I owe them 3 grand, the nervous sweats begin;

"This is the bastard landlord's fault, what shall I do?" My friends return to their luxury countries, I am left alone. Suspicious Russians move in. They play poker all night.

The landlord is forced to pay the money I was supposed to owe, what the hell was going on here? I get mugged again. I run. I never see this company again.

**Flat 4 (Golders Green):**

My girlfriend and I move in together to a flat share where two Irish sisters deny sticking tampons to the walls, there is a holed ceiling that fills buckets every time it rains, and there's the psychopathic, closet-gay Italian musician who thinks he's John Lennon.

The area is prone to burglaries, the lock on our front door breaks and the landlady complains from behind her clouds of chain-smoked Silk Cuts at the prospect of its repair;

"No other landlady would do this fo ya" she creaks;

"Urm, *why?*" I think to myself.

Our relationship becomes strained by the inconsiderate filth of others; a loud, semi-incestuous threesome takes place in our shared living room in the middle of the night and the landlady's dog shits outside my bedroom door become the last straw. We move out again.

The landlady says to stay in contact, I say "okay" with the half-obscured intention of calling her up in ten years time and inviting her to Alton Towers where I shall return the shits to her handbag as her irritating tobacco-ridden old body dangles bewildered from the Nemesis ride.

**Flat 5 (Cricklewood):**

My girlfriend and I get our own place; she insists we take the ground-floor flat since it's already furnished, unaware that we'd already sealed our dooms. The colds of hell rise through its broken tiled floor; there is no carpeting, every utility is broken, mice scatter the floor at night and we hear the neighbour's toilet and bedroom antics through its paper-thin walls.

The landlord is an Indian with limited English. We ask him for the repairs, he contacts his cousin on the cheap, who in turn, contacts more cousins on the cheap. 7 cousins later one comes around to fix the shower and can't. I want to go for a pint to drink off the misery but discover that my local Irish pub has no windows, they don't seem to like the English much and their strange, secretive negotiations suggest something illegal.

Later the sneaky Indian puts the rent up just after we learn that our electricity meter is connected up to some dodgy bloke next door and we find ourselves broke. The heater goes off for the last time and we're back to the freezer box again, just as the *long*-frozen winter comes in; too cold take off our clothes, our sex lives soon dwindle and the relationship falls apart. I come home one day to find her gone, the furniture is no more and she's taken the deposit money that I now have to pay again. I am broke and alone, in my ground-floor freezer-box of a home as the flood warnings come in.

I eat dried cornflakes for 5 months before eventually managing to leave.

I later express my woes to a Chinese herbal medicine man with a history in numerology, he tells me to use the numbers associated with such negativity to pave something good for my future; I later use the numbers of these addresses to play the lottery. I win an extra lottery ticket, it fails.

# The Arab Connection

Even before his Uncle Talal had advertised the prospect of abandoning the scope, heat and progressing wealth offered to him by his home country of Yemen to instead help him run his business in the great British capital, Amar had, if he's honest, expected something better than the cramped and frequently freezing cold kiosk that he and his family now operated at Embankment Station.

Although the family shoe-making business had indeed been dissipating over the last twenty years over in old Yemen, he'd nevertheless been enjoying the sinking prospects that had still been part of his life there. He and his wife Neima had had a home, petrol was still relatively cheap and the nation's faith system was keeping things simple. Uncle Talal however, (now pushing 70), still believed in the outdated notion that London was still an industrially lucrative city of the future and when the making of hot-weather shoes had failed to pick up on the island of mud and drizzle, kiosk management seemed to be the next best thing.

So this was his life now, sentenced to lengthy hours of light snacks, badly made sandwiches, celebrity magazines and fizzy drinks; the most entertaining part of his day now being when he got to use his physical girth to scare away the alcoholics who frequently tried to steal cans of beer from his fridge, the funnest part of this particular exploit being when he could see them coming from a distance and had the time to place tins of Shandy Bass in front of the real alcoholic drinks just in time to watch them legging it away to the nearby park in an attempt to get drunk on the 0.2% ABV soft drink. That's the placebo effect for you.

It was a shit life really but compared to *what*? Their business was probably making more money for them than the more suited people he saw jumping on and off the trains every day, sweating with strain as they struggled to even afford a mere transport ticket. He and his family on the contrary shared a pretty neat house in Marylebone and so could often walk to and from work, life was stress-free since the management of the place was shared between three of his brothers and two of his cousins (others ran other kiosks elsewhere) and having most of his immediate family around him felt good, there was a true unity amongst them and with them also being so many, meant it was easy to take the odd trip back to the homeland whenever they wanted. Also, since most people's money in London got swept up into the extortionate costs of transport and living, he had never needed to drive and with the family property wrapped up in some kind of cheap-rate legal contract that neither he or anybody else had ever really cared to understand, his savings were getting pretty good and so perhaps soon he and Neima would probably be able to afford a place of their own and eventually send their daughter, baby Soraya, to a decent university. Even if Europe actually had lost most of the stature that Uncle Talal had claimed still existed, it still offered some of the greatest universities in the world.

The U.K had of course been Amar's first real sense of life abroad and the idea of unity as the tool to financial growth had often been an unappreciated philosophy in his homeland, purely because he'd never had to consider its existence until he came here. It was a principle that seemed to exist within all the ethnic communities that had come here; the Jewish had embraced it in the north, the Chinese were a world unto their own, then of course his people had emerged around the 1970s and now the city was seeing the same thing amongst the dawn of the Russian influx.

What had struck him most about this country's natives however, and indeed perhaps the wider field of Europe itself (perhaps the Spanish being an exception) was the alarming lack of this particular principle, and hence it seemed to be the reason why all the ones he met seemed to be poor; strange, considering 'United' was part of the country's title after all. The main point to this observation being that whenever a Brit or a European would purchase something from him, it was always a formal, quick and silent affair, the recognition of one's nationality or faith never really being an issue. The Arab on the other hand would always recognise, and potentially get to know, the other; perhaps this was that inner human need to connect once again with that homely sense of the familiar? And so subsequently, in the time that he'd been here, the characters of whom he had become most acquainted with were of his own origin.

One such gentleman, as far as he could understand, referred to himself as AJ and was rich to high heaven; first you would smell that approaching waft of lavender aftershave and then he'd appear, always smiling weirdly from behind his expensive Italian suits and golden aviator sunglasses (Amar and his family all swore they'd never actually seen the man's eyes, even at night) and he'd appear with a long enthusiastically drawn out 'Heeeeeyyyy Big H' in the style of some kind of New York-set mafia film (Amar was the biggest of his brother's and his family name was Hassan...hence, Big H), although Amar never had a clue as to how this guy came across such information. Anyway, AJ seemed so alarmingly rich that all his money seemed to be kept within his eclectic collection of laminated credit cards and with the idea of small change being the equivalent of picking up dog shit, AJ's strange enthusiasm for drinking Diet Coke had frequently ran up a small tab on the till. At first this unpaid tab had worried Amar and his family only for AJ to show up out of the blue one month later and settle his debts with a brick-like wad of notes that he would then allow them to keep the change of.

Opinion of AJ was divided between his family. The brief, often bizarre exchanges that any of them had ever had with him had never fully amounted to any true explanation of the man; he never seemed particularly threatening – especially not in the "now-you-owe-me-money-back"-type way – the reasons for his income never made sense, he never seemed to drive, he insisted on talking in English (with an American twang) his frequent offers of going for a drink suggested he wasn't a strict Muslim and the girls he sometimes showed up with may even have been high-class escorts, it was hard to say. For Amar anyhow, AJ's funniest quality was the one that divided his family the most, in that after his brief small talks on your usual, everyday bullshit (of which even some of his brothers were cautious of revealing) he would always offer to help you out with the question;

"Do you neeeeed anything Big H? You need any caaaaaaash?" followed by that weird giggle of his.

Amar would always turn down such offers of course but he had, after years of amusement from this character concluded that he quite liked the man and that he was just, put simply, very, very eccentric. Every city had an AJ somewhere and Amar respected the existence of this particular strain of rich man for their ability to just swagger throughout the cities of the world just being 'nonsensically rich' and not adhering to the rules of normality whatsoever.

Anyway, AJ's most bizarre offer of hospitality was yet to come; the cancer that had stricken Uncle Talal had thrown inheritance of the family home and business into a complex legal loophole that was then taking its strain on his relationship with his family. Ibrahim, his youngest brother, simply hadn't bothered to show up for work over the last couple of days and this was all coinciding with the pressure to get baby Soraya, who was now four, into a school. This had instigated a heated argument between himself and Neima and instead of being left to settle matters, Ibrahim's absence had left him instead to do a twelve-hour shift in the kiosk. Honestly, twelve hours of fuse bars and vegetable Samosas? Can a man even take such a thing? It was also pouring with rain and was cold. Amar was, to bluntly put it, pissed off that day.

Then it came, that Lavender smell followed by;

"*Heeeey big H, how's it haaaanging Arab?*"; He had a large suitcase with him of which Amar had never seen before.

"Oh okay AJ, how are you boss?" Along came the usual weird handshake.

"*AJaaaaaaay's doin' just fiiiine, my man*"

AJ always spoke of himself in the third person.

"*Do you have any Diet Coke?*"

Of course we had Diet Coke, what kind of a question was that? We've always had it, what kiosk doesn't? Amar's cold gesture towards the fridge had accidentally given away the fact that he was secretly pissed off and didn't really want to be speaking with AJ today. Nevertheless, AJ got that strange sugary passion of his from the fridge, pulled its ring and took a massive gulp followed by one of his usual, babyish exhales of breath.

"*You're looking doooown Big H, is it the raaaaaiiiin?*" Rain never seemed to hit this guy, except for the globules that formed upon his aviator shades.

"Nah man, just an argument with the Mrs. The usual domestic bliss, you know?"

"*Aaaaah Neima?*"

How did he know his wife?

"Don't worry" he continued "she's a good girl, stuff will change."

Another gulp of his beloved Diet Coke and;

"*AJaaaaay was speaking to Ibrahim the other day, he says the family's got some problems?*"

"You've seen Ibrahim?"

"*Of course I've seeeen him*"; a cheeky eye was now leering over the gold rim of his aviator's, "*we're the same colour skin, same religion, Muslim to Muslim, Arab, that's the connection, you dig me?*"

"What?"

"*Anyway, he said that yooouuuuu had some problems?*"

Amar was perplexed; "Well, yeah, sort of".

"*It's a good job you know AJ, 'cause AJ's always here to help. Arab to Arab*"

Although visibility was virtually impossible behind those darkened aviators, Amar could somehow sense that his eyes were forming expressions that would suggest he was thinking of something he could do to help him. Finally he says; "*how about this?*"

He lifted the suitcase to the counter but didn't open it.

Amar suddenly felt a slight unease, what the hell would be in a suitcase belonging to AJ of all people? Would it be drugs? Stolen money? Was he now forcing him into keeping it for him? Maybe AJ was dodgy after all?

"*AJ knows when times are haaarrrd big H, this should tide you over with the concerns your brother told me of. Arab to Arab brother. Muslim to Muslim, see you around Big H.*";

Following another slurp of Diet Coke and his stranger-than-strange laugh, AJ had walked back out into the rain.

Amar was stunned, what the fuck was going to be in this suitcase? After his eyes rolled a few times in apprehension, he unzipped it. What it revealed was in some ways equally a great relief, an immense disappointment, yet also something so typically strange of the man, it also solidified AJ's reputation of eternal eccentricity in a way that made him somehow pleased. Wrapped in plastic, folded and crimped to perfection, were fifty or so pairs of pure white boxer shorts. They looked different to regular boxer shorts however, thicker and far from sexy, and so he looked even closer; they were medical boxer shorts, used for... *incontinence sufferers.*

A multitude of questions abounded, was there something he was yet supposed to find hidden amongst the folds? He double checked, no. Why was AJ carrying these? Had AJ stolen them? Was AJ expecting him to sell these on as the solution to some kind of financial problem? Would he be back for them? And what the *hell* was the problem that Ibrihim had told him about? Was he pulling some kind of joke? He could only simply conclude that AJ must've assumed incontinence was his problem. But then again, why so many? Had he assumed it then to be a *family problem?*

The next day, Ibrahim reappeared and in his typically hot-headed way tried to justify his absence on the family stresses driving him to take a short break up in Leeds. But after getting the bollocking he rightly deserved, he explained that he had *no idea* of the meeting A.J had spoken of.

What the hell was AJ on?

The answers could now only rely on a return visit from the great man himself but to their strange sadness, the paths of AJ and the Hassan family kiosk business never crossed paths again.

They would ask their neighbouring shops if they had heard of their strange friend but nobody had, they had asked around the local Mosques to no avail. Time went on, the brothers settled the small amount that was left on AJ's Diet Coke tab, Uncle Talal, the founder of all this, eventually succumbed to his cancer, the legal loopholes were cleared up with not much fuss at all and so they went on to keep the family business and Marylebone house after all. Business continued to expand, Amar and Neima eventually bought a family house of their own, their little Soraya went to school and Amar was forever left with more questions than the white incontinence shorts his family now owned. Arabs are indeed a united people, he often thought to himself, but what this experience had taught him about such matters he could never truly fathom.

# The Supermarket at the Edge of the World

A few years before the nearby 2012 Olympic Park would grant some sense of colour or aesthetic, cultural interest to the area, the East London district of Bromley-By-Bow, in the borough of Tower Hamlets, really came to signify the true outer boundary of what East London was all about. Only being on the border of Zones 2 and 3 of course, Bromley-by-Bow was nowhere near where the far reaches of this city officially ended, it was just that everything about the area looked, smelt and sounded like the end of all of what London was capable of commercialising for itself before the effluent of the River Lea would break its land mass apart into odd little sub divisions of just plain, simple non-entities. It was in many ways like it was forcing a barrier of concrete and water upon one's own unconscious interests in the city to say 'there is no reason for you to venture any further than here'. The occasional rough pubs, shops, takeaway outlets, train links and even the roads that constituted this area's crumbling feel of community all seemed to just simply stop or give in to the kind of bleak modern landscapes designed for something heftier than the simple human stroll. This area then, was and still is, defined by merely a very long and eternally busy road (the A12) that would either connect up to the enormous ugly flyover of the A11 that took people further east or would take you about a mile and a half downwards into the amber pit of the Blackwall Tunnel where, indeed, the odd stupid soul would occasionally be brutally reminded of own his true place in the 21st century when fatefully trying to take it on by foot.

The last edges of true London society itself had also seemingly stopped spreading across the land horizontally and had instead turned upwards to inhabit the 26 floors of the nearby Balfron Tower, a building that once designed to inspire hope via its space-age design now felt like it'd been turned on its head and slumped headfirst back into the earth to accumulate dirt and decay ever since, a building so big and starkly bleak upon the landscape it had garnered its own odd strain of respect.

Shape and even colour had come to its end by Bromley-by-Bow; all the wit, curves and morphological wonder that were now staples of the city's 21st century architecture had ended suddenly upon their journey east in sharp, brutal corners of rigid square and enormous, formidable walls; and the greenery and palace whites that had become utilised by the city's tourist boards had here worn away into pedestrian greys in which the years of downward hammering rain with rising car exhaust had resulted in messily organised stripes of black like the hind of some feral hyena.

Beyond Bromley-by-Bow there never seemed to be anything more but a seemingly eternal ocean of gas works, sewage works and warehouses; yet upon the final edge of this place, if one were to brave crossing either its dual carriageways or its network of dangerous pedestrian underpasses that tunnelled beneath them, one would also find what was presumably the region's final supermarket putting up a fight for the motorists' attention against what may also have been the last McDonald's drive through between the flyover and the rest of the world. Cars would pass north to south, cars would pass east to west, and in their ensuing, eternal vacuum, a vast number of crumpled brown McDonald's bags would meet and waltz with the plastics of the supermarket in the exhaust-filled air that situated the in-between. Judging by how many McBrown bags would settle on this supermarket's car park however, it was clear which company may had been winning the battle.

The insides of this supermarket offered no real respite from the depression, its sterile columns of refrigerated, processed ready meals were coated over by a piss-green sheen from the enormous and seemingly eternally broken suspension lamps that hung from above; they granted grotesque shades of shadow across the faces of its staff, highlighting the kind of inner expressions that would be more discreetly hidden by any other minimum wage worker that would simply infer a lifetime spent too long in this place. Somehow, these same lights also seemed to position a strange darkness over the place's furthest stretching corner; the same kind of strange fearful shadow work that an imaginative child might stare into the darker depths of a diving pool with, and beyond it, the factories and the world. Near this ever-darkening corner, was the first in the columns of cashiers; this was Cashier 1 and these are the people who were in the queue of Cashier 1 on that particularly woeful day...

**11<sup>th</sup> in line:**

Fuck me, I've been in this area for just two months and I'm already pissed off. I know that your student years are meant to put you through the grind and all that but I've already had to move out of Hackney due to fucking psychos and weirdos and can't be doing with them anymore. I mean is London *always* this way? Nothing ever fucking works, trains and buses are always delayed, my housing cheque never turns up when they say it will and the shops are always closed 'cause of some stupid religious holiday when your key meter runs out and this seems to be the only local place left to get a top up! Hurry up for fuck's sake, what if my freezer defrosts? I mean, they work very hard to advertise London as a great place to come and study yet they cram you into a flat the size of a wardrobe so you can't get your shit together and then there's the badly wired electricity that threatens to burn you alive while you sleep.

Why the fuck is this queue taking so long? I bet it's another bloody 'communication issue', some foreign bastard can't explain his shit to another foreign bastard because of the so-called 'language barrier'. I never used to think of myself as a racist person but when I consider that this is my country yet nobody can make any sense whatsoever out of any of the languages crossing between the nine or so people in front because of political correctness it's a joke, I mean when did political correctness mean an invite to social chaos? Then again, the government don't care about London's little pockets like this one, even though they should I guess since this place is probably the first and last port of call for those coming from or heading to the Tunnel.

This Muslim guy in front of me is looking edgy and knows what I'm thinking. Hurry the fuck up for Christ's sake...

**10<sup>th</sup> in line:**

Come on and get a move on bruv. Fuck me I'm getting the shakes, all I want is some Rizlas so I can get back, grab a Maccies on the way and squeeze in another smoke with some FIFA before the day off ends innit? They're only like 80p, couldn't I just nick 'em and pay them back like a quid another time, this is takin' the piss man. Stupid spoiled white bitch behind me is givin' me the evils an' all innit? Blame the Muslim, blame the Muslim for everythin'. Same with dose fucking video cameras innit? They're looking at me all over, get a move on.

**9<sup>th</sup> in line:**

Come on you fucking plebs, what's goin' on here? I've only got 20 minutes 'til the game starts. As long as I pick up what the 'ouse needs she won't mind me sneaking in these tins but the risk is all lost if I miss the fucking kick off. The cunts will probably play well for once with me not being there an' all. Come on hurry up I've still got to drive back yet.

"Lily, stop hittin' your brother, behave like I told you".

"No you can't have anymore sweets son, I told you, not until when we're in the car".

As per usual the wait is down to some shirt lifter a few people down kicking off. What's he gettin' at? Fuck knows, always makin' a scene out of amateur dramatics that lot. Still, you've got to respect the gay boys, I don't like the way they're gentrifying my old boozers but they don't get lumbered with this fucking life like I've got here, a walking talkin' middle aged Jonny advert, me. Fuckin' done for, forced to watch me matches through cracks in a door. When the fuck did bog roll, a few tins and the kids' lunchbox supplies become so heavy?

"I said stop fucking hittin' him, didn't I?"

Oh, don't start fucking crying.

"Right, I'm taking 'em off ya"

"Well you had it comin' Lily, I told you to be quiet and ya didn't, did ya?"

Come on and hurry up.... fuck this place is depressing.

## 8<sup>th</sup> in line:

Oh, now the bloody man ape behind me has to kick off, getting edgy because of the football no doubt, yes I'm looking forward to your crass remarks when, on top of whatever the hell's going on at the front of this queue, I have to hold up your miserable existence further by running this lot through the scanner because I want my bloody *discounts* and all.

I bet you've even parked next to me, haven't you? I bet after our argument in this place I'll get another bout of your utterly needless brutality as I'm pulling out of this hell hole, you can never just simply pass through London without encountering some kind of set back or witnessing the dredges of this country in full swing. Then again, I bet he's more of a local man, probably squeezed with those kids of his into one of those nearby tower blocks. God, I remember how downbeat my brief, youthful flirt with London was when I was in my twenties but imagine *growing up* here? Growing up with nothing, with this place on your doorstep? Happy to have left it thank God, happy to never go back, happy to have settled in Margate. What the hell is going on with this queue? No doubt those wretched kids of his are going to get more cantankerous the longer this bastard stretches on.

I smile at them as they catch my eye but *look* at them? What kind of a father pierces his kids' ears and crams them into football clothes before they're even of age to understand? That's what's wrong with this country; it's the parents. If my girls had done that at whatever age these kids are, they would've got a clout and gone to bed early and now they're doing well for themselves. At least I like to think they're doing well, actually they're probably on coke for all I know but what the hell are these little shits going to grow up to be? They're restless and aggressive now, imagine when they're as big as him? No wonder you hear so much about this bloody knife crime in the cities now. Every generation seems to just collect the dirt of the previous. Like this place. Jesus, how long has this place been here and how many people have had life-long jobs here? The thought of stagnated lives makes me shudder sometimes, how, perhaps if in my twenties and if I hadn't met Jess, how I could've become like that, rotting away behind the concrete, paying extortionate rent to some prick who can't speak my language. I want to get on the road, out of London and back home to my house, back to Jess, my lovely wife of whom in two and half hours will have my meal ready for me.

What the hell is going on with this queue?

## 7<sup>th</sup> in line:

What the hell is going on now? I can see it again, the cashier at the end of this queue is another lazy bloody white man. Their behaviour is bloody unbelievable sometimes, I still can't get over what that Robert on the bottle cap line said to me this morning. I've just got to get these spices for my mother and then I'm tempted to fire that bastard when I get back. Calling *me* an incompetent manager, saying that I'm nothing but a, how did he say it, a "cock slave" to my father's business, surely no worker rights can protect him from that? My father's managed that factory since it began and there's no way anybody else is in line for that management role, that's traditional Indian culture I can tell him, surely then that counts for racism?

"We could do with him out of the job anyway" I can explain to father, "save money during the crisis", I can say. Why the hell do they want Derek as manager anyway? Surely my experience is family-earned? We Indians know more about business here than any of these...*cockneys*. All they do is work for a couple of hours before demanding a smoking break.

Yes, the idea of him off the workforce is good I think. I've seen him you see, leading the others on, I try to relax on a tea break of my own and I see them all, sat there laughing at me, with Robert as their leader; I come in one day with a moustache and he shouts something about it being "useless" and that "I couldn't even get a woman under arranged circumstances"? Yes, I live with my mother and father, that's Indian heritage, you stupid bastard, and if I'm not married then yes, that's because of the parents. Why don't you go to India and see how long it takes you to find a bride? We're not like you, spending all that we earn on beer and having sex with whatever we can find, we value our principles you see, those kids a little behind me are what happens when we behave like you, you annoying little bastards. And we're not like that man two in front either. These bloody gays, having sex with men, what the hell is this bloody western shit? What's he bloody shouting at now? Come on you bastard queue.

## 6<sup>th</sup> in line:

Oh my god it must be about twelve hours since it happened now, how long does it take to become official? Why didn't I do this this morning? Why did I lounge about at home for hours in denial that everything would be okay? How could I have been so stupid?

That's it, I'm never drinking again, why is it that even after your best friends warn you about his reputation for sleeping around, after a couple of rum and cokes you still can't help yourself? Not even halfway through a house party and away you go back to his room so that everyone knows what's up. This could all be treated as something of a laugh of course if it hadn't been for the combo of being unprotected suddenly turning you into the office idiot. Oh my god, I'll probably have to get a new job too. Can Anton be fired for sleeping with a subordinate? Probably not, I'd imagine.

Krysta, where are you? You're supposed to be here with me through this, I thought you were my best friend here.

How would Anton respond if this test turns positive? Last night it was all laughs and caring gazes, yet when I left this morning, there were no goodbyes, no nothing. I left him to sleep of course, but there was just this feeling about him not caring, like he was slumped there like some overweight teenager late for school or something. Men don't get it generally until they have to confront fatherhood, British men *especially* don't get it. For them, their liberal ways are taken for granted and they would probably treat leading a girl to the abortion clinic like going to pay a bill discrepancy. We Brazilians however, are made to feel like we're committing child murder, and so now on top of motherhood and possible unemployment of which then may lead to deportation, I may have to confess everything to my highly Catholic family and potentially be disowned or even some kind of surgical mutilation. I bet you couldn't even be bothered to escort me to the clinic, could you? The future of my life now hangs in the balance and you treat it as just one of your hang ups, yeah, thanks Anton; English gentleman when he wants what's in your pants, the child everyone says he is once his responsibilities pile up.

I'm scared; all I want is for things to go back to the way they were, all I've got to do is piss on this thing and then it could all be over, back to work to deal with the embarrassment but not the uncertainty. How the fuck am I supposed to have a baby *here*? I don't even get paid enough to survive by myself in this city. God, I wish I knew somebody here who'd been through this. Where the fuck is Krysta? Just somebody who could tell me that I'm just overthinking things, somebody who could tell me that this is just an everyday thing here, that pregnancy is perhaps more unlikely than people say, or that a first abortion might not even be so much of a big deal.

Come on queue, what are we waiting for here? What's going on? All I want is to buy this test and then have some form of focus upon the rest of my life.

Come to think of it, just look at this place? I hate England - you're grey, you're cold, why the fuck would anybody want you as a nationality for their child anyway? And just look at that prick three behind me? That's what British men amount to, overweight, tracksuit-wearing football morons, I'd like to see you strip down and get by with that beer gut on one of our beaches my friend. Jesus, is that the kind of family life, or physique I might be in line for? I suddenly miss my family more than ever, I want to be home, back in the sun with people who might care... What the fuck is going on with this queue?

**5<sup>th</sup> in line:**

It's nobody's business, nobody's business what I buy. I can feel you all looking at me, thinking that I'm some sick rapist 'cause I'm buyin' a stack o' lads' mags yeah? Well I got a couple o' cans o' tinned fruit too an' all haven't I? So I'm not that sick.

Shit, got to rush this shit through quickly, thing is, the porn I want, the transgender stuff I can get from that Bulgarian Food and Wine place on the corner but they always give me transparent bags man, they're takin' the piss. So I have to nip 'round here to get one they can't see into and then get it in the 'ouse past Mum in case she comes home from work early. Those Bulgarians always laugh at me when I'm in there too, yeah? Well it ain't your business either, is it? They think I'm some kind of faggot buying this stuff. Yeah, well I wank off to lads' mags too, don't I? What do you think I'm buying these for? So fuck you.

Fuckin' hell, what's goin' on with this queue? Don't be bothered if people start lookin' at what you're buyin', you've got *every right*, every fuckin' right and it's none of their business. "Come on, man, what's goin' on here?"

Shoosh Naveed; the more you make a scene, the more they'll notice what's in your transparent bag. What's this chichi in front goin' on about? Something about better service. Poofs, they always have to draw attention to themselves. Homosexuals go to hell and I don't like being near them 'cause they give you ideas that'll make me go to hell. They have sex through their arses and spread diseases, why did I have to queue up behind him? I might have tranny porn, but that ain't gay is it? Especially if I got the lads' mags with it too.

Come on people, for fuck's sake, gettin' edgy now 'cause eyes and surveillance are on me and Mum's gonna be back home from work soon, I would use the net but she keeps tracks of my history so better to use the mags, just wanna crack one out before she gets in and need new material to get a stiff one.

Bitch behind is lookin' at me too, probably also thinks I'm some kind of freak 'cause of what I have a right to buy. Well fuck you bitch, what are you, some sort of feminist or somethin'? If I had my way, you'd be punished, slow and real dirty, girl. Yeah you'd love it too. Who'd the Bulgarians be calling a faggot then?

### 4<sup>th</sup> in line:

Oh my word, Simon is going to hit the bloody roof by the time I get to Poplar, I mean I expected some kind of wait in a queue at this hour but not like this.

"Service, hello, can we get some service over here please?"

What the hell is going on here, there was a man at the cashier here a minute ago, what's happened to him? I'll ask the man in front...

"Did you see where he went? What's going on?"

He just shrugs, I don't think he even knows what I'm talking about. Well, this is recession-era London down to a tee; companies trying to save money by employing less people and so put one person on the tills at a time and then wonder why they get service complaints. And then, if that person in question turns out to be a retard like this one is then everyone's in a world of pain. For god's sake, I've just been dealing with problems like this at work and don't need it here.

What really takes the piss is that Simon is cooking for me right now as part of a make up for that spat we had the other night, another spat about me always being late. Our unspoken deal always works out that if I provide the wine for these situations then it sort of negates itself and after a couple of glasses always results in good healthy make-up sex but this will tip him over the edge for sure. Why is he so temperamental anyhow? What's his problem? He's got his promotion now, he has his nice flat in Poplar and yet he always seems to be in this eternal hurry and angry. I guess I'll have to bring that up in tonight's argument. Well, I guess six months isn't long enough for me to sever the relationship if I think he's not my type. Never have been too into the aggressive types but then again I guess I must always pick them for the reasons of some unconscious attraction I guess...

What's going on? Wait, what's that?

"What's happening down there?" The mother just two in front of me has begun screaming...

"Are you okay, love?" Oh my god...

### 3<sup>rd</sup> in line:

What's everyone screaming about? Every time I arrive in London, whether it be delivery or collection, and wherever it is, there's always delay, always drama, a man can't even buy a packet of cigarettes without this bullshit. Would love to know what it's all about but every time I try to learn English I just find it all sounds like the same sound; that '...shion' sound that's in every bloody word, God knows how it became the global language. Still, should probably try and pick it up at some stage of my life.

Come on for Christ's sake, got to be in Munich by noon tomorrow and I need to get at least some sleep at some stage along the way. What are they always delayed for? It amazes me why England remains such a respected place and Romania has trouble when everything seems to run much better there. Our roads have no pot holes, our food doesn't come in these stupid microwave bags and even that Charles man in their Royal Family has been buying up our properties for cheap. Next time I come across some illegals offering to pay me a lift into the developed parts of Europe, I should just take them five minutes down the road and drop them off at my Dad's house.

Jesus, now they're really shouting, what's going on? Have to see closer...

**2nd in line:**

*£102.90?* How did all that come to that? And where did the cashier go? Said he was going to find some more till roll and suddenly he's disappeared, I really hate the UK sometimes, you pay so much for so little. How long must our business run out of cash before I can convince Pavel that we're better off raising the kids back home? That the crisis is more or less over there now? That the only view he has of Ludz is from the point of view of his stupid unemployed, alcoholic friends? How can I convince him that we were tricked into buying that business in the first place?

"Tenants in London are too poor to own their own cleaning machines" was *his* thinking;

"It's the landlords that own them, not the tenants" I'd told him but did he listen to me? Nothing in this city ever lasts, everything just stands to survive in the moment and once it shows any sign of its purpose decreasing, or its expenses increasing, people just sell it on to the next gullible buyer. It's kind of the same way that we've been treated since we arrived here too but Pavel never saw it, the Polish arrive, Poles hard work for nothing, Poles start demanding more and so Poles have to go too. At least in Poland there's a degree of care for our people and businesses.

For god's sake I need to get back and reopen, where is this bloody man?

"Where is the service here?" I call out.

"Mummy, I can see blood" little Ana calls out.

"That's not blood, it's just sauce...."

Wait; that *is* blood. What? Oh my god... It's coming from behind the cashier, oh my god...

I cover their eyes and I look behind the register to see the young man lying on the floor, what's he doing? He's sitting. No, wait, he's shaking and he's pale, and he's bleeding... oh my God.

Cover both their eyes. Stop screaming, *please* stop screaming.

"Help, we need help over here". Somewhere over the other empty cashiers I see another man in uniform coming our way.

"Please, someone needs help over here" I am saying the same thing as the man two behind...

"I think something's happened to him" I say to the approaching man.

Oh please don't let them see this, I pray for my children not to see this. Just got to get my card out of the machine and get out of here. This is too much, I have to get them out of here...

**1st:**

Fucking hell you've done it, you've *actually* done it, after a life of pussying out and not standing up for yourself, Adam, you've finally made a decision worthy of reaction, something you'll finally be noticed for, just don't let them save you or you'll just be back here and you'll just be your pathetic little self again. How long did it take me to go through with this? Six months? Maybe longer? A lifetime of just imagining just how much those box cutters would actually hurt as they entered your wrists, I'd never known any survivors to tell me, you see. It's agony, *fucking agony*, but physical pain's nowhere near as bad, it'll all be over soon. I'm looking up now at those dirty shelves of till roll papers, disused scanners and discarded chewing gum, finally now in these last moments I'm seeing a part of this wretched building I've never been to before and its sort of an escape down here compared to being up there with *them*. Seven years I've been in this fucking place, *seven years!* At this same fucking seat and I can't remember anything else, I can't remember the good times with my friends, I can't remember school or college, my life has just been this place, this fucking place; that walk, that same old fucking walk I make from Grandad's, along the junkie canals, under the underpasses to here, back and forth, over and over again, six days a week, all over now. And these people will all be gone soon too, the co-workers there was never the time to get to know properly; just the occasional crap conversation while setting up in the morning, and these customers, I fucking hate these customers. Every day, day in day out, always in a rush, always desperate, never having a thing to say to you beyond discounts, school vouchers, membership reductions or the same old stupid jokes. They look at you like you're nothing, like you're nothing beyond the cashier boy, never even considering that I had thoughts greater and deeper than this. Well I *am* nothing; I never pursued anything, I never achieved anything, I couldn't even get any further than this position, I applied for the warehouse position so that I could just get away from people, to get away from customer service but I couldn't even prove myself to be worthy enough at scanning barcodes to justifiably be given anything more responsible, nothing was ever going to go further than this place, the supermarket at the edge of the world. I couldn't just go out simply though, a statement had to be made, something had to be done to make them know just how low I had become. The trade unions were all gone, the C.A.B advice never amounted to anything and so these middle-aged psychopaths had been given free-reign to run places like this, to pay and employ you in whatever conditions they felt suited them best, it doesn't matter about your fate or your feelings, just keep the customers happy. Well they're never happy anyway.

The idea had begun as a fantasy of course but that was before things had become unbearable and then it hit me that this could truly hurt them, it could attract the media (let's hope one of these customers is a journalist) and staff treatment would have to be called into question, maybe not just here but everywhere. London would have to care about its workforce again.

I hear them all screaming now, especially the kids, and here comes Faizel, my idiot supervisor, with the folder of emergency situations under his arm... for the first time I actually like him because I know that his hesitation with that folder is just going to delay things. That way I'll be certain to fulfil my plan and then, in being Faziel's fault that I'd died, company policy might finally have to do away with relying on that fucking folder too.

The light of the lamps is making things go cloudy, it fucking hurts like hell and it's getting cold but I no longer give a fuck. Here it is - my grand, sweeping statement to the world!

I smile and prepare to let go and stare at Faizel with wild eyes but he has been pushed out of the way by people in the queue. The giant cockney is wrapping his football shirt around my wrists whilst some student girl shouts out advice behind. An Eastern European guy is calling an ambulance and my head is resting on the knees of some beautiful Brazilian girl. She's stroking my head and whispering something in my ear about everything being ok.

"Please just let me go. Please. There's no hope for me here. I just want to go".

The cockney guy is tying his bloodied claret football shirt into a tight knot around one wrist and the gay guy is doing the same on the other wrist with a bag-for-life.

I start to fade in and out as the paramedics turn up. Some gangster looking guy is now telling them what happened with wild gestures as they gently lift me onto a stretcher.

An Indian guy offers to jump in the ambulance with me. He holds my hand as the ambulance women shuts the door. I keep looking up at him and staring into the depth of his eyes.

My grandfather once told me that your guardian angels are always just over your shoulder. I didn't expect ten of them to be waiting in a fucking queue for me though.

I hear the sirens wail and feel my body moving further and further from the edge. I close my eyes and feel myself crossing a distance greater than I'd ever dared to travel.

# Yumi Tanaka's Greatest Gig Ever!

Hi! I'm Yumi. I'm 22 years old and I'm from Mure, Mataka-Shi in Japan. It's just outside of Tokyo, yeah? Anyway, I tell you bit about me. I study computer engineering. I live with my brother, Kyto, as well as my parents and grandparents. We have a happy life.

I like baseball, romantic movies and the keyboard. These are all favourite things for me but I should tell you there is something even more special to me. I love *The Rolling Stones*! Greatest band of all time! Haha!

Mick is my favourite. My dream in life has always been to meet him. I like Keith, Charlie and Ronnie too though. My favourite tracks are *Street Fighting Man* and *Gimme Shelter*.

People say to me "Yumi, why you like them? They old men!" and sometimes they laugh at my T-shirts but I don't mind this. The truth is my Dad is a big fan. He has seen them play in Tokyo and has all their albums. When I was a little kid I would put on his big headphones and play the CDs. I have known their songs since I could talk. I knew how to sing all the words even before I knew what the words meant.

I never dreamed I would actually get to see them but on my 21st birthday my family bought me a very special gift. Tickets to see them in Hyde Park in London! I was so shocked I cry when I open the card!

Any true *Rolling Stones* fan knows that Hyde Park is very special place. It is where they did famous concert in 1969 after Brian died. Everyone got together in a movement of peace and solidarity. It would be a great honour to see them play there again and experience feeling of the sixties!

My parents booked me hotel near to the park because they were worried I'd get lost in the city. I told them I would stay safe and not talk to any strange people. I was to fly out on a Thursday and fly back on the Sunday. Crazy trip, right?!

I left Narita airport very early on Thursday morning. I had never flown so far before. When I landed in Heathrow airport it was only Thursday afternoon but I felt so tired! I waited for the tube train to take me to Hyde Park Corner. The London Underground is similar to one in Japan but I think at Heathrow the monitor was broken because it said that next train was coming in 2 minutes and it still said 2 minutes ten minutes later. In Japan you would get in so much trouble for lying to a traveller!

When I got on the train I tried really hard to stay awake. Heathrow is far from city centre, similar to Narita. I looked out of the window. It was very sunny and I could see British-style houses outside of the window. I took picture because it made me think of style house Mick grew up in back in Dartford.

I arrived at my hotel at 6pm London time on Thursday night and went straight to bed. I woke up at 4am on Friday feeling wide awake. I opened the curtains of my hotel room and could see the big main stage inside Hyde Park. Instead of sightseeing, I decided to stay close to the park and make plans ready for the next day.

The ticket said that there were two main entrances to the concert. One entrance was for people who had paid lot more money than my father could afford. They got one half of the front enclosure of the concert and could arrive whenever they liked, knowing they would get good view. However, the other side of the front enclosure was open to whoever got in first. My mission was to get to the very front! The gates were to open at 1pm. I would get there for 5.30am.

With plan in place I had 24 hours to explore local surroundings. I left my hotel and walked past a showroom full of very expensive cars. I thought that this must be an area where very rich people live but then I walked under foot tunnel and saw 15 people all sleeping in bags and boxes. I wanted to stop to see if they were ok but all the London people were walking past so I felt embarrassed.

I decided to walk onto Oxford Street. Oxford Street is bit similar to Shibuya. It's very busy and everyone is rushing to get somewhere. I am quite small so I got bumped into a lot by people talking on the phone. At Oxford Circus I took tube to Victoria to see Buckingham Palace. Haha! Guys, Victoria tube smells like burnt hamburgers! Why is this?! I decided to get some food by the palace. I saw a place that served ramen and really wanted Japanese food.

I should tell you something important. The ramen by Buckingham Palace is not real ramen, ok! Please don't think Japanese eat ramen like this because it has much more flavour in Tokyo! I could not eat this bad food so instead I was directed back to Green Park, walked to Hard Rock Cafe by my hotel and had club sandwich. I saw Kurt Cobain's sunglasses too - super cool!

After dinner I checked my tickets were ready for the morning and put them in the safe in my room. I looked out of the bedroom window again at the park.

I tried to sleep but was too excited. When the alarm on my phone went off at 4:30am I was already in shower. I opened my suitcase and took out my Rolling Stones T-Shirt. I also wore bandana with Japan rising sun on it and had a Japanese flag with Rolling Stones tongue logo in the centre. I wrapped this around my shoulders. Finally, I opened the safe and took out my ticket, keeping it very close to me.

I walked towards the entrance, by the Marble Arch. I went into McDonalds and ordered some breakfast. There were lots of very drunk people in there. One person was asleep and I even saw a lady being sick on table! I decided to leave and sit by lake with giant horse's head. It was 5:15am.

At 5:30am I walked over to the gates. The sun was just rising and I felt confident that I would be one of the first people there. But as I approached there were hundreds of people already at gates! As I got closer I could see flags from all over the world - Brazil, Canada, Russia, even New Zealand! I walked towards the crowd and could hear friendly voices talking to each other. A young guy looked up and called over to me.

"Good morning!" he said in a French accent "Come and sit with us."

I am quite shy so I pretended not to hear him but he did a big whistle with his fingers and everyone started looking at me.

"Are you from Japan?" he shouted.

"Yes." I said.

"Great! I'm from France. Come and sit with us."

I decided maybe he wasn't so strange so I went to sit down. He held out his hand.

"What is your name?"

"Yumi." I said quietly.

"Hi Yumi. My name is Pascal. Are you looking forward to the concert?"

"Yes. I travelled all the way from Tokyo, Japan to be here."

"Awesome. I came over from Paris. Not as far as you, no?"

This made me laugh. Pascal started to introduce me to the other people waiting by the gate.

"This is Patrija, she's from Poland. This guy is from Argentina. And these guys are from...where did you say?"

An old couple in Rolling Stones T-Shirts smiled and said "Bristol."

I waved hello and started to relax in their company. I looked around and could see people of all ages and from many countries all sat by the entrance gates to the concert at 6 o'clock in the morning. We still had 7 hours until the gates opened!

That morning I talked to *Rolling Stones* fans from every continent. I am ashamed to say that before then I had only really ever spoken to other Japanese people! Everyone was so friendly and we all shared excitement for the gig. *Rolling Stones* are the best! Every few minutes more people would join and sit down with us. By 10.00am hundreds had turned into thousands and it started to feel like true concert crowd. I stayed with Pascal and our new friends. If we needed toilet they kept our place safe by front of gates.

By 12 o'clock the sun felt very hot. I wrapped my flag over my head and Pascal gave me some water. Everyone kept people feeling positive, saying "Not long now." We anticipated the gates opening at 1pm.

By 1 o'clock the gates had not been opened. The crowd outside was now huge and the friendly atmosphere was starting to turn to frustration. I started to wonder when the gates would open. Beyond the fence I saw a large group of security officials arrive in bright orange shirts. They looked very serious. The *Rolling Stones* fans looked through the fence at them pleading to be let in. They watched us through the partition but said nothing. I felt like prisoner!

By 2 o'clock they still had not let anyone in. Some people behind me started to shout very loudly at orange security men. People also started to push us against the fence and I became very scared. Pascal shouted back "Hey, stop pushing! Please!" The security men just stared. People were getting so angry! But then something very strange happened. Behind me the old couple from Bristol started to go "Whoo, Whoo!" like Mick does at start of *Sympathy for the Devil*. Suddenly I heard other people copy it further away until before long the whole crowd was going "Whoo, Whoo!" Then people started to clap too! It sounds funny to say but it felt powerful.

The security men looked hesitant and turned to look at a giant man in a blue shirt wearing a headset. He was shouting orders at them all but we could not hear what he was saying. Then suddenly he signalled towards us and lines of orange security men started walking towards us like storm troopers in the Star Wars!

Each security guard opened a different fence up and then we were put into separate lines and made to walk between new vertical lines of fences. It was scary and didn't make me feel like I was in the sixties anymore. Me and Pascal were separated but I could see him in the next row along. He smiled at me through the metal lines and said "Don't worry. We're nearly there! We can do it!"

Each row's security guard checked our tickets, our bags and walked us through a scanner like the one in Heathrow Airport. Once we had completed these checks we were allowed into one final gated enclosure where the big security man stood with more men in orange shirts. Some had big dogs! So cute!

The sun was really hot and we didn't understand why we couldn't be let in to concert. The big man in blue shirt watched us all fit into final enclosure. He raised a big speaker to his mouth and said;

"We're going to open the gates now. When we do you must not run. I repeat, when we open the gates you must not run."

I was worried because everyone behind was starting to push again. Everyone had one thing on their mind - to run to the front! The main stage was far away; about a quarter of a mile from the front gates on the other side of the park. I looked over to Pascal who gave me a wild stare. I knew if I didn't run all the hours of waiting would be for nothing.

The man in blue turned to the men in orange, raised his arm in the air and shouted, "Open the gates!"

As soon as the orange men did this it was like start of marathon! It was crazy. People started running very fast to get to front row of *Rolling Stones*! The sun was still very hot and, as people ran, dust burst from their feet. I looked over to Pascal who was just ahead of me. People kept tripping and falling over like a war movie. One person wasn't looking and ran into burger tent! My lungs started to hurt but I kept running. Suddenly I saw Pascal trip over. I slowed down to a jog. He was holding his ankle.

I shouted "Pascal!" and went to stop but he looked up and said "Yumi, keep going! You need to get to the front!"

I hesitated but Pascal kept shouting for me to go so I did. I made it through the final gates of the front enclosure and could see my destination up ahead. Less than 100 people were ahead of me and I could see a perfect spot. It was a V-shaped corner between the main stage and a long cat walk that separated the VIP section and us. I made one final sprint and reached out for the metal bars of the front barrier. As soon as I did I felt others press against my back, just missing out on the front row. I had done it! It was 2:30pm. I had waited for eight hours to get to this point. The Stones would not be on until 8:30pm, in another 6 hours. "What now?" said a voice behind me.

An American guy stood next to me said "We stand and wait. Front row baby!"

The first warm-up band came on at 3:15pm. I didn't really know who they were. I felt very hot and missed my friend, Pascal. I was also very thirsty but didn't want to drink much in case I needed toilet. However, there were more orange men on front row who were handing out little white cups of water and people kept handing them over to me so I took a little drink. Occasionally I could smell cigarettes and beer. An Australian guy passed me a very smelly cigarette but I don't smoke! He smiled and passed very smelly cigarette to some other people.

By 6:30pm we had watched three warm-up acts and my legs were feeling very shaky and tired. I also really needed toilet. The Australian guy noticed I looked worried.

"You ok, love?"

"Yes. I just need toilet but don't want to lose my place."

He laughed and turned to some girls he was with, "No worries! Hey girls, can you help this lady out?"

Three girls with blonde dreadlocks said "Sure" and came and huddled around me. At first, I didn't know what was happening but then one of them whispered "If you squat down no one will see you." and smiled at me. I had never gone to toilet in this way before but really needed to go so I did what lady said, squatted and pulled my jeans down. As soon as I started to go I felt so relieved! I looked around. All I could see were people's knees, feet and lots of empty beer cans. As soon as I finished I quickly climbed back up to the dreadlock girls. They all patted me on back.

"Feel better?" one of them said. I just gave a relaxed smile back. I was ready for gig now!

As the sun started to go down the sense of excitement started to build. It was 8:00pm and I heard whistles from all over the crowd. I put my phone on a selfie stick and took a picture of the crowd behind me. When I looked at the shot I couldn't believe my eyes. It was like an ocean of people. And I was at the front!

We watched as the roadies tested the guitars, drums, piano and microphones. Everyone around me started clapping their hands. The roadies all left the stage and the lights suddenly snapped off. A huge roar went up around Hyde Park. Then huge cinema screens started showing old footage of the Stones being mobbed by fans and clips of their first Hyde Park gig. A voice boomed over the loudspeakers.

*Ladies and gentlemen. Back in Hyde Park for the first time in 44 years -*
*THE...ROLLING...STONES!*

Everyone started screaming. I watched the stage lights go up. From the side of the stage a little guy with a light blue jacket, scruffy grey hair and a bandana picked up a guitar and lit a cigarette. It was Keith Richards! He went to strum the first chords to *Start Me Up* but got it bit wrong. No one cared because everyone was jumping up and down. He managed to get the chords back on track and everyone started clapping. Then from the back of the stage Mick Jagger ran straight up the catwalk and started doing his crazy dancing!

*If you start me up, If you start me up I'll never stop...*

A huge wave of joy ran over everyone. 100,000 voices knew all the words. Mick stood over the corner where I was standing. I reached up to touch him but he didn't see.
I looked around at millions of happy faces. Different faces. People who looked from the sixties with long grey hair and handlebar moustaches. Scary biker men in leather jackets with really long beards. Very beautiful women, like models. Cool children sitting on their parents' shoulders. And, of course, teenagers like me. Maybe I wasn't so weird after all.
Mick was a master of crowd control! Every time he pointed his fingers towards the crowd a huge whoop would go up. People were ecstatic. In fact, during *Honky Tonk Woman* a lady behind me took her bikini off! I was so shocked to see her naked but she just laughed and cheered. This would not happen in Japan!
Song after song the Australian girls and boy put their arms around me. We sang along to *Ruby Tuesday* together! Then I heard someone shouting my name.
"YUMI! YUMI!"
I looked across the thousands of faces to see one I recognised. It was Pascal! I reached across the rocking crowd and managed to grab his hand. I pulled him towards me and we hugged as Mick ran back past us. I felt a huge sense of relief to have found my friend. He spent the rest of the gig with me.
As the sun went down I could see smoke drifting over the crowds in Hyde Park and into the trees. I looked up at the sky and noticed the tall London apartment blocks. I wondered who lived in those little windows and whether they could see the concert. Maybe someone was looking down at us!
Mick was so funny. He did lots of costume changes and after each song he'd do a little wiggle and shout "Are you feeling goooooooood?" And we were all like "YEAH!"
The night had fallen and all I could see were little lights everywhere. When *Gimme Shelter* started to play I started to cry. Mick was joined onstage by the most amazing singer, who sang Merry Clayton's famous chorus

*War children, it's just a shot away...*

During *Jumping Jack Flash* the catwalk lit up in rainbow colours. I looked up and watched Mick, Charlie, Keith and Ronnie play together and thought they looked so cool. In tales of ancient England there are legends of old knights of the Empire who maintained mysterious enigma as they grew older. They would become immortalised in mythology. I think *The Rolling Stones* will be remembered like these ancient heroic knights of England.

The lights on stage went out. Everyone wanted more. Being so close to the front I could make out a silhouette of Keith lighting another cigarette. Then I heard the opening drum beat of *Sympathy for the Devil*. We could hear Mick's voice going "*Whoo, Whoo!*" but couldn't see him. The energy built up in the crowd and everyone started to "*Whoo, Whoo!*" again. I heard a wave of cheering from behind me and saw Mick coming up from the end of the catwalk in a black fur coat. He looked like a giant crow!

*Please allow me to introduce myself, I'm a man of wealth and taste...*

I missed some of *Brown Sugar* because a man was filming with a big iPad. I was annoyed and I think when he plays it back he will only hear himself singing and I can tell you he COULDN'T SING!!!

The night finished with a big finale of *You Can't Always Get What You Want* with a live choir. I watched couples singing to each other as the words resonated across the fields of people.

*You can't always get what you want but if you try sometimes you just might find you get what you need!*

The band finished with *I Can't Get No (Satisfaction)*. There was a huge bang and red ticker tape started to rain down from the sky. Everyone started jumping up and down to that classic, hypnotic guitar hook! Then the group took their bow and waved farewell. I stared at them for as long as I could and watched them go backstage. I didn't want them to leave. I didn't want the concert to finish. Why couldn't it go on forever?! Pascal looked at me.

"What a fucking gig!"

"Yeah! Best ever huh!"

As the crowds dissolved the two of us were left in a field of trash. We stared at each other. It felt funny how music had brought two complete strangers from different countries together.

"Come on" said Pascal "I'll walk you back to your hotel."

He offered me his arm and we walked slowly back across the same park we had ran across earlier. Fireworks exploded over our heads. It took a while to get back onto the road my hotel was on and there were police on horses everywhere we looked. We didn't want to rush too much anyway. We just tried to remember all the amazing moments. When we finally reached my hotel it was 11:30pm. I turned to Pascal,

"Where are you staying?"

"St Pancras" he said "My train leaves for Paris in a few hours. I gotta go."

I suddenly felt very sad. Pascal zipped up his jacket.

"Wanna hook up online?"

"Yes." I said. I ran to give him another hug.

"Thank you for your kindness today, Pascal."

He kissed my hair, "It was my pleasure. Now, get some sleep ok?"

And with that he turned, walked back along the pavement and into the distance. I didn't want to go to sleep so I took a walk down the street. I walked past windows full of rich people eating food, past busy bars and then past an expensive-looking hotel. It was noisy with lots of people outside so I turned the corner to walk around the back way. I then saw a big black car pull up to the back door of the hotel by the bins. Two big security men jumped out and opened a kitchen door, letting light out onto the street. As I walked closer I then saw a skinny man in a baggy white shirt and shades climb out of the car. At first I couldn't believe who it was but at the same time I recognised him instantly. It was Mick Jagger. I ran towards him but his security walked over to stop me. I didn't know what to do so I shouted,

"Mick Jagger! Mick Jagger! My name is Yumi Tanaka and I came all the way from Tokyo, Japan to see you tonight!"

Mick stopped, turned around, took off his shades and smiled,

"That's great! I love Japan!"

And one second later he was gone. I didn't even have time to take a picture and I know no one at home will believe me if I told them but I must tell you it was the happiest moment of my life. I went back to hotel feeling so strange. For a while I listened to the silence. I went to close the curtains but then noticed how peaceful London looked outside. The stars sparkled over the trees of Hyde Park. I took a snapshot of it in my mind and thought of the birds sleeping in the trees. The next day as my plane took off back to Japan I looked back over London one last time. I could see the big wheel and red buses going around like toys in a big little city. I tried to look for Hyde Park but clouds got in the way.

## Thoughts and Memories from Beyond the Flashbulbs

### 2007: The 51st London Film Festival: "Eastern Promises" Premiere

Whether or not that Royal marksman's word ever got back to the management about our forbidden adventure on the rooftop to that establishment I don't know but for some reason, nothing ever came of it and so I worked at the cinema for another year.

Paddy however, had frequently been getting himself in trouble and whilst rumours abounded that my fearless Dutch friend was due to be fired, the management forgot to ever give him the formal disciplinary. Paddy had waited and waited, he'd just keep turning up to work before eventually coming to the conclusion that they had simply *forgotten.*

Times had still been pretty relaxed; good films came and went, as did the premieres and at this stage I had never really understood why so many of us were complaining so much about the place; for sure it was badly managed and the pay never improved but being the easiest job in the world, why should it have done? What were these complainers leaving to do exactly? Pull pints? Scan barcodes? Harder, much more tedious jobs for pretty much exactly the same shitty pay?

Also, now that Steve had moved in with Mum, the job enabled me to move out from home and into a flat share in Peckham, - good in some ways but not without bringing the fear that now I was paying rent properly, I couldn't just get up and leave like I'd done with most of my previous jobs.

The best thing about that first year I'd have to say though, were the characters I'd got to know – for sure, all those young city boys would be making a packet down in the financial district – but they wouldn't have found the same interesting mates you'd find down here on the breadline; everyone from everywhere was batched in here together and had been watching everyone's back like it was some sort of global stagnation point for the world's disenfranchised youth.

So then, after one year I'd found myself with one such character, Big Momo, squeezed up awkwardly close in a tiny Box Office, staring out at a cold, October West End, serving tickets to the Screening Rooms whilst the main screen next door set up for the opening of the Film Premiere.

Momo didn't really hang out with the rest of us socially – one of those guys who had his own thing going on – but rumours about him flew about the place – he was, for certain, mixed up somehow with one of North London's Somali gangs – this was obvious because his wide-boy, gold-toothed mates would turn up, 'bitches' in tow, for free tickets, practically *every fucking day* – nobody just seemed to know to what extent. His coolest attribute however, was that despite our different walks of life, we could talk for hours, completely objectively, about any subject we wanted, whether or not we agreed or disagreed on them and his insight was always fascinating.

"The thing is bro, when you come from my area, you gotta have connections to a gang, innit?"

"But why, though? Can't you just not get involved? You know, do something else?"

My own personal take on all this was that the cause for all the gang stabbings that had then been hitting the headlines, had nothing more to do with than the fact that the criminal life had largely been made fashionable via gangster films and hip hop culture and that by *not joining* that way of life could be considered unfashionable and so of course, those types of guys would then get the bullying that came with it; I was genuinely interested on being proven wrong though.

"Yeah but that's just the point of view of the white-boy, Daily-Mail crew bruv, the ting is, if you're black or Muslim and you grow up in an area like mine, eventually someone comes 'round to pressure you into joinin' their crew. Now you need to have connections to somefin' in the first place, just to get out of *that*, you get me? Listen man, I ain't in any *serious* gang, yeah, not in any of the serious ones, but if any crew comes 'round lookin' for me, I can just get on ma phone bruv, and in about *five minutes* about ten a ma mates can turn up with knives and bats, you know what I'm sayin'?"

He always had an interesting slant on things.

"If I want a gun, if *you* ever need a gun bruv," he went on "I can get you 'ooked up through just a couple of phone calls. Girls fuckin' love 'em too, man".

Aha, here came the engine behind *every* male-centric conversation.

"You into Eliza, innit?" he asked.

The thing is, yeah, I'd had a bit of a thing for Eliza – our fit Italian colleague - recently but if I told Momo, that shit would be known by more people than whoever was watching the shitty Hollywood blockbusters we'd been playing.

"Come on bruv, it's obvious. You ain't doin' nuffin' about it though, are ya? That's pathetic bruv, honestly."

Maybe it was but I'd never been that confident with girls; it wasn't that they didn't not like me per se, my issue had always been around once you got past Stage 1, which is your cheesy first approach, and before Stage 3, which is full on conversation, I never really knew what Stage 2 was meant to entail.

"You know what I do?" Momo went on, "You gotta play 'em. One day, this girl came round ma place with all my brothers and suddenly, they all just leave, leaving me alone wiv her in the house an' shit and she just looks like she ain't into me, you know what I'm sayin'? She's lookin' all mean an' shit, so I just says to her "listen love, ma mate's just got this new Playstation and we were thinking of goin' 'round and playing some GTA and shit so you're gonna have to make your way out", and so I start preparin' to leave and she's sucking me off within the next two minutes, bro, swear on ma mother's life".

Impressive, if only it had been true.

Our conversation stopped briefly as Big Momo had to refund someone's ticket over, yes, the state of the Screening Room screens.

"What's the deal with shaggin' before marriage in your religion then?"

I would often find myself driving things towards the hypocrisy of religion, a frequent point of conversation in this unholy place.

"There's exceptions, man".

The door opened and Anwar shuffled his overweight self into our small space to avoid doing work elsewhere – the worst person you want in any debate about religion, the worst person you want in a small space with two other, relatively large men.

"What do you mean *exceptions?*" I asked.

"It all comes down to whether you really believe in Allah or not. D'you believe in God, Aaron?"

"God's a possibility but I *can't do* religion mate." I said.

Anwar buts in here of course; "Brother, *what the hell?* You say you believe in God but you're not *religious?* How the fuck does that make sense?"

Anwar just couldn't accept science or spirituality, no matter how hard you pushed either to him.

"Well God's about the possibility of a force bigger than us, religion's about following orders written from a few thousand years ago, the first part I can sort of accept as a possibility".

Then Momo took over with the most ridiculous thing I'd ever heard.

"Do you know what 'appens when you die though, bruv? Do you know what 'appens? This big fucking skeleton with red eyes turns up and asks "are you Muslim?" and if you say "yes" he lets you into heaven, innit? If you say "no", he smacks you with a hammer down into hell."

I burst out laughing.

"Where the fuck did you read that shite? I'm pretty sure that's not in the Qu'ran?" I declared.

"You can laugh brother, you can laugh all you want, but you can't *disprove* it either, can ya?" Momo said.

"Yeah" I went on "but why is it, whenever I ask god for answers, he never presents himself, yet if I want to explain, say gravity through science, I can just read any physics text book and it explains it to me in less than a paragraph? Nothing in any religious book has ever been proven true."

"And where did you read *that?*" Anwar ranted on.

"In any good science book, my friend" I said.

"Oh, he read it... *in a book.*" They both said while high fiving. Their genuinely interesting argument was then suddenly interrupted by O'Bastard knocking on the door;

"Alright, you two, shut down while we're quiet, we're having a pre-premiere meeting downstairs". My god his voice was dull I always thought to myself, as if like slowly drowning in a vat of cold, cold tar.

Then he turned to confront Anwar.

"What are you doing in here? You're supposed to be setting up the screen."

"I just came to tell them *exactly* the same thing you were, don't shoot the messenger" he lied in a brilliant, lazy fashion.

I never told you about the manager of this place; Geoff Wilton had run this place since the '70s and it was a quietly known fact that had once been something high up in MI6 and this was supposedly his chosen chill-out-job-of-choice post those days; the theory we'd all shaped however was that he was still a member of them and had, no doubt since the days of the Irish troubles, volunteered to be placed here to keep an eye on the surrounding square. He spoke with the etiquette of a since-lost London aristocracy and with his red-cabbaged nose and occasional slurs, he clearly drank like them too; his years here had made him something of a West End legend, he was personal friends with the local police force and could swagger into any local casino, bar or restaurant and basically just get shit for free. Unlike the pathetic bully-boy tactics of O'Bastard, Wilton's stature had made people feel genuinely intimidated by him. This is all funny to think back on *now*, but my memory as to how this man conducted that meeting was the first of many painful stings that'd stay with me to this day.

 "Okay, settle down everyone and start speaking in bloody English, please!!" he snapped as he stepped before the noisy circular table of the Meeting Room, his tongue like a whip that shut the Frenchies, the Spanish and the Italians up in an instant. Then, in the ensuing silence, he said...

 "I'm sure I don't have to tell you all about the troubles we've faced here in London since 7/7. Now I've just come from a meeting with the Charing Cross police and I've been told to inform you *all* that *this* cinema has gone into red alert; we *are* a potential target now and I want you all to be extra vigilant."

I heard one of the Spanish merely whisper upon hearing this man's ridiculous poshness; "Que?"

Wilton went on; "Obviously we have security helping us out today but, but they won't be here tomorrow, will they? So, this means be extra vigilant on your ticket checks and make sure you continue to check the bags of *all* customers, no matter how seemingly innocent they may look; any questions?"

Niroshen's hand went up.

Niro was another character – he'd apparently come from a rich family of British-Bengali barristers and was doing a medical degree – he claimed his reason for being here were for the reasons of the flexible hours fitting in with his son's childcare – only that seemed to had been a long time ago now and unlike everyone else, his rich background could had enabled him to leave any time he wanted – we all theorised instead then, that he might've instead been a muse to Wilton, a younger agent drafted in to shadow him and take over the said position beyond Wilton's retirement. Niro had also been a handy person to have around since his family legacy meant he knew a fuck load about employment law, and so we'd turn to him whenever we thought this place was trying to fuck us over. His 'apparent' medical degree also came into great use when none of us were able to get the time off to see our GPs, especially when I needed some clarification over the testicular hernia I'd suffered the previous February. Anyway, his privileged social status allowed him to be somewhat cockier than anyone else and do so without losing any work.

"Yes, what is it Niroshen? Make it quick." Wilton said.

"Well, sorry if this sounds a bit frank Geoff but" ...Wilton was *actually* listening..."even though we're all trained on what suspicious signs to look *for* when doing bag searches, none of us really know what to do if we should *actually* find something, you know, *dodgy.*"

The staff went into wild sounds of applause upon hearing this; it had clearly been something we'd all been thinking about. O'Bastard, who'd been stood obediently by Wilton's side all this time, clearly hated the success Niro's question was getting and started to frown.

"Well, I'm sorry to say it" Wilton explained "but should something be revealed to be explosive, it would, in most situations..." here it came... "already be too late".

*What!?* Should we declare a pay rise now or after the premiere then?

Wilton went on; "The best thing to do would be to pretend you haven't seen anything and keep the person talking as a means to stall them long enough so that you can consult the police or for somebody *else* to call the police".

With respect, all of that had simply been lost on most of the foreign ears in this room.

Wilton then inflicted his own need to be getting out and on with matters but there was of course a burning question I simply had to have answered and if Niro had the bottle to question the building's security measures then, surely, so should I?

I put my hand up. My noticeably working-class Irish roots clearly wouldn't consult such a polite, constructive reaction however. Still, like a towering monument of authoritarian English grey, he beckoned for me to challenge him.

"Also, are there any plans to change the security codes on the doors? I don't think they've been changed since I came here." I asked.

"Why?" he said, like an angry police station.

"Well, I mean, we've had some strange characters come and go in this place, and presumably they can still remember the codes. I mean, is that really enough of a security measure for the same place that *The Queen* comes to?"

For some reason everyone just went quiet as if already knowing of Wilton's upcoming wrath.

"Look, my friend, there are already measures put in place for such possible events, *do not* worry about them. Now, if we don't have any other stupid questions left to bring up, I'd say it's now time to be getting on with our responsibilities, don't you?"

In that moment, he just stared and stared at me while everyone else just waited nervously. O'Bastard was loving it. Then, with O'Bastard at his side, he turned back towards the door and whispered something under his breath before striding off like The Emperor pursued by Darth Vader.

*A stupid question? Really?* I didn't believe for a second that nobody else hadn't thought of the same concern. There had been some real freaks who'd started and left this place over that first year; there had been that bloke who kept telling us and telling us the *really* graphic, in depth descriptions as to what it had been like, during service in Iraq, to hide amidst the bloody entrails of a dying friend as a means to avoid capture and that his odd bouts of aggression were down to PTSD, only for us all to later learn that, yes, he'd *never been* anywhere near the army!! Then there was the other guy, that Parisian, who used to go mental and start on everyone whenever he'd be asked to remove his baseball cap.

And they wanted to leave security codes the hands of *those lot?*

As we then vacated the room to attend to our posts, I couldn't help but think that my perfectly sound debate had only really been ignored because of my class background implying to them that I wouldn't have the education to back up my claims. After all, it was equally as grounded as Niro's had been. No wonder those of my surrounding colleagues with minimal English skills hardly ever spoke up. There had always been the assumption that the only people who got offered positions in roles of politics or intelligence work had been highly connected, elitist toffs; even if that had been true I never would've believed that they'd be so ignorant to walk away from such a sound point because of a person's financial level, but I was now beginning to think that that could've been true.

Oh London; my home town. Whilst any race or culture could come here and more or less be accepted, it was, at the same time, always disconcerting for me that 'classism' had to even be questioned as to whether it was even a real word or not.


Growing up in Russell Nurseries, films had always been a source of escapism for me (and yes, Belsize Park *did* have its rough parts) and occasionally I'd think to myself which films, future or otherwise, when I die, would I never get to see? The realities of their experiences to be left as wonders behind what I knew of their iconic stills? Then again, I wonder whether, if fate turns out to be real that is, *why* I had seen certain films? Had those that I'd never actively sought out somehow *found me* like I was *supposed to* see them?

David Cronenberg had been one such director; his films had been an unintentional companion of mine through those long, wintery, rainy nights of the soul and to now be in the same auditorium as the man meant more to me than being in the same one as the Queen. That was the power of art I guess.

As the lights were still up for Cronenberg's on-stage intro, I scanned the ocean of heads before me for that particular shade of red of that girl from last year. I had researched her after that flirtatious encounter of course, 'She' had alternated between TV and film and I was, genuinely, familiar with some of her work. Like the seats in this place however, there were simply too many shades of red to really be sure.

Cronenberg, followed by Vincent Cassel, followed by Naomi Watts, and then followed by Viggo Mortensen went up on stage to an ocean of camera flashes and the Canadian legend himself introduced his, unusually, very British film; a film about the Russian mafia operating people trafficking services behind the scenes of this here city. After his famed legacy of allegorical body horrors, the guy was now looking behind the veneer of the London that the world so famously knew & into the real, tactile horrors then secretly emerging. What a legend.

Towards the end of the film, I'd been appointed duties at Front of House – basically a very boring, usually lonesome and, at this time of year, cold job in which we just opened and closed the front doors for people.

The great foyer itself, unlike the 1930's auditorium, had instead been stuck in the 1980s, perhaps the last decade when anyone had truly given a shit about maintaining the place's flagship status, now however any notions of caring about its class had been frozen in the blue neon light strips and reflective glass floor panels of which once being the height of cool in the decade of Duran Duran and Queen, now gave it the lonely ambience of a sterile warehouse.

Nobody had been about here then except for a few of the premiere crew lingering about the foyer behind me; now, if you lingered about *near them* you just looked like you were trying to get their attention as some shit way of getting in with their circle, so instead, I paid them no attention whatsoever and stared out through the foyer's enormous glass front to the remains of the red-carpet decorations on the square that were now being removed. The most annoying part of that, at any premiere, was that fans of the celebrities in question would linger about for hours in the outside cold in the hope of an interaction with their favourite movie star and I would, with no immediate colleagues to talk to at that point, be forced to stand directly opposite them and stare back. This, they would then see as an invite to come to the door asking questions about them and I'd have to open it again, standing in that bitching cold in my flimsy uniform trying to make them go away. On that evening, the occasional group of hormonal teenage girls who'd knock on the glass wouldn't be fans of Cronenberg films of course. No, these were *Lord of the Rings* fans who cared nothing about what the film was about except for the fact that Viggo Mortensen was in it.

As another group walked past with their Aragorn posters then, I pretended to let my mind drift and focus on something else in the hope that they hadn't noticed me notice them. Instead I became fixated by a guy outside who had been taking down the lighting rigs; some tall guy with tied-back blonde hair and I knew I'd known him from somewhere; with the occasional glance that he gave me in return, I could tell that he was thinking where he'd known me from too. A whole bunch of blurred images were failing to pull together but then I remembered something from when I was a teenager, something about a time when I'd been well into weed and had acquainted myself with a bunch of other youngsters with whom I then went on these sort-of odd quests throughout the city to try and score some and then, in turn, find a safe place to light it up. I think he was one of *those* guys. *The '90s man.* Legendary times. Those memories of mine couldn't have been longer than ten years old and *already* the country felt like a totally different, more cynical place; a place in which old acquaintances perhaps now actually *chose* to forget each other?

The premiere bunch behind me began to dissipate to fuck-knows-where but I was still aware of at least one other person still hanging around.

"Excuse me" a young female voice said, and I turned to see *her!* Whatever was going through my head I can bet my face expressions made me look like a right twat.

She held out a flyer, an invite to the standard post-premiere party and on it was a small map of the local area; "The people I was with have decided not to go to this and it seems a bit stupid for me to get a taxi to somewhere so close, you wouldn't know how to get there on foot, would you?"

I scanned it quickly; Pineapple, Covent Garden.

"Yeah, that's Pineapple, it's a famous place, you know the way to the Market?"

"No" she said in a way that implied a shyness that I hadn't expected.

"Oh right, you basically just take a right round here" I felt like a dick giving her tour-guide hand gestures.

"Cool, thanks" she replied. Her eyes *wouldn't leave mine.* Could this be true? Could this be *real*? Was there *actually* some sort of chemistry happening here? They were the only two things I could think to myself at that point.

"You're not from London, then?" I asked.

"No, Surrey" she said "I know London, you know, but I normally get about by cab".

Then we went into an awkward silence, that issue I'd always had with talking to girls now coming back to me; I thought back to the words of the ever-confident Big Momo from earlier, *play 'em,* he had said, play 'em. So I did, or at least tried to. I mentioned one of her more arty films.

"You've *seen* that?" she said with a suddenly-more-charming smile than before. That flirtatious hair-twirling started up again.

"Yeah, I've seen it a few times. Are you in *this*?" I asked, pointing back towards the screen, "I didn't get a chance to see all of it".

Her smile was widening at this point, her pretty eyes reflecting ever more of the West End glitz. It seemed it might had been *me* that was delivering her first euphoric realisation of stardom; not any agent, not some other star, *me.*

"No, I just got invited for the publicity again, my agent works with a lot of the people in the film so I just got put on the list, you know".

"Ah, that's a shame" I said, keeping my eyes fixed on hers. "What are these celebrity bashes like anyway?"

She laughed; "If I can be completely honest, they're kind of bullshit; they're always filled with these ridiculous formal rules and have just a bunch of people offering coke instead of film roles; it's all front. I only want to go so I can meet David Cronenberg", she laughed again before the awkward silence started again. Stay confident, I thought, I couldn't run away from this position after all.

"But..." she went on "I'm amazed you've seen that film. That's pretty obscure man, I don't even know many agents or producers who've seen *that*."

*Play my cards right*, I kept thinking to myself, *play my cards right* and then came the bullshitty part.

"Well, I know it didn't do much business an' all that but me and my mates used to get high to it, I was studying film and media and it kind of did the rounds around our uni; a bit of a cult film then I guess."

I could see that she was loving *this,* I had been making her feel famous before she really was, and famous for being a *cult star* at that, probably the coolest type of fame there is and I could tell she could remember me, *me,* that funny guy from the Airlock one year ago.

"Perhaps you're one of those cult stars you know?" I continued "like Rose McGowan or something? Maybe that's a better thing to be if you're trying to get in with David Cronenberg?".

Her eyes were glaring now.

"I remember you from last year now. You were funny".

Fonzy and Elvis have just officially declared me 'cool'.

"Thanks" I said.

"What's it like working here? With all these premieres and stuff?"

"Kind of shit. Just a bunch of toffs ordering you about; there's no coke getting offered down here".

She laughed; "What's your name?"

"Aaron" I replied.

"Listen Aaron" she said, nodding towards the teenage girls who were screaming at something from over the red carpet's perimeter railings opposite , "I think those girls might be fans of mine and I can't be bothered with all the hassle. You said Covent Garden is behind us, didn't you?"

"Yeah"

"Is there any other way out of here? Like a back entrance, a fire exit or something that could take me out directly to the street behind?"

"Sure"; at this point Anwar wandered his fat arse through the foyer like he should be followed by someone playing a trumpet, and of course, he had no issues covering me, - any excuse for him to just stand there and do nothing was good enough for him.

"Follow me" I said and so she did, back through the double doors, into the auditorium and downward along the far reach of the seats I took her, where next to us an ocean of heads were still fixated on the film. A giant Viggo Mortensen and Vincent Cassel were arguing about something or other at the water's edge of the Thames, their giant images stretched as we walked to the side of the screen, through a fire exit door and through another onto the stone stairwell that led downwards to further-alternating corridors.

All this time I could sense her eyes had been on me from behind, then, she suddenly stopped.

"Wow, there's a lot of secret places to this place, aren't there? It's *quiet*"

"Yeah"

"And what do they use all these extra spaces for?"

"Nothin'. Storage I guess".

"Storage for what?"

The first place I could think of in all my nervousness was the door right before us, the door to the under-the-stage organ chamber. All I could do was keep the bullshit coming.

"Well, in here's where they keep the organ, it's been in here since the thirties."

"Really?" there was an air of fakeness about such enthusiasm, "I love vintage instruments, can I take a look at it?

"Well, we'd get..."

"Aaron?" she interrupted "do you mind if I try something really stupid?" – suddenly she's smacked lips into mine and she's got me up against the door with her left hand on my chest. Then, her hand ran its way down past my stomach and onto my groin. As we briefly parted lips she then signalled to the chamber door. I went into autopilot and pressed in the door code (it never changed) and she basically pushed me inside.

The place was dark and the organ was covered in dusty sheets but the film played ever louder above us and its light was beaming down through the few narrow cracks of the stage above, tiny streaks of *Eastern Promises* dancing off the rippled dust cover.

She pushed me against it and before I'd even realised it, she went down on me. The fingers of my first hand were running through that beautiful red hair at my waist level whilst my other slipped downwards, through the front fabrics of that designer dress she'd been wearing and onto caressing the erect nipples of what must have been beautiful tits.

Another one of her hands then began to caress my balls, it was all happening too fast, those final scenes of *Eastern Promises* must've been pretty silent and I feared screaming out, *fuck, fuck, fuck*...

Then the light beams from above disappeared upon what must've been the closing credits, the audience began clapping as it happened...

She pulled away in the darkness and her wolf eyes were looking up at me with the glare of a dominatrix; she pulled up one strap of her dress stood to her feet, kissed me and said; "See you next year, Aaron."

Had that been a question or just a finishing statement? She winked and then just turned and left to, presumably, mix amidst the parting crowds to blend in as normal again.

The whole situation felt utterly surreal. Had anything like this ever happened to anyone before? Well, it must have right? As these thoughts swirled around my head one stood out clearer than the rest. Beat *that* Big Momo.

## N21: The Fall of Man

I specialise in the peculiar.

When I say this it's not to say that I myself am a peculiar person. Quite the opposite. You wouldn't look at me twice in the street but I'm always there. Looking over. And I'm looking for a story. Something beyond the normal set of circumstances.

I run a web blog; it's called *Underground*. I look for the stories between the cracks of the day-to-day rumblings of London and try to seek out the story that makes you think - *how could that be?*

I'm fortunate in that this city can still throw up its fair share of abnormality thanks to its wonderful mix of abnormal people. And wherever they are, I am too.

You may recall the story a few years ago about the recurring appearance of VHS copies of the cult 80's horror film '*Hellraiser*' on top of a bus station outside Lidl on the Old Kent Road. Quite a peculiarity. I broke the phenomenon on *Underground*.

An observant member of the public would spot a sun-faded copy of the film on top of the bus stop en-route to work one day. The next day it would be gone. Tidied away by a keen-eyed member of the council, perhaps. Only the next day another copy would appear. A newer copy, a few inches from the light rectangular space that the previous copy had inhabited.

Some days there would be two or three copies on that bus stop roof. Other days just one. But they were always VHS and they were always, always '*Hellraiser*'.

How do I know?

Because I'm always nearby.

Looking over.

The story became so well known that it made it into national newspapers. Just think about that for a second. People all over the UK picking up their morning paper to read about an infestation of cracked VHS tapes more usually found at a bad car boot sale. Who cares?

It seems many people care. People love a weird yarn. It's click-bait. And that is where I come in. My task is to seek out these odd occurrences and report them.

So when police helicopters were summoned to a disturbance involving a stricken N21 bus from that very same bus route, I simply had to be there.

But I get ahead of myself. All tales must start at the start....

Halloween in London has become a very American affair. Gone are the days where you could make it through late-October with a ghost story and a pumpkin from Tesco. Now it has become big business, more of a national holiday than a novelty. Each weekend leading up to the night itself is an ever-increasing parade of bad fancy dress. Of course, most of the year if you get on board a tube train carrying a coffin most commuters naturally won't bat an eyelid anyway. Particularly in Camden.

Ah, Camden. The place that so yearns to be the weird capital of London but, alas, finds most of its weekends pushing Essex boys in and out of its 'alternative' bars. And lo, it was here that Adam Harris boarded the 88 bus to Vauxhall with four of his friends.

The bus was packed with drunk revellers and they certainly blended in. On the top deck alone a keen eye could pick out the Wolfman, an Alien, several zombies, Margaret Thatcher, Elvis Presley (both alive and dead), Michael Jackson (likewise) and the Blue Man Group. Adam and chums had elected to dress as animals. His friend Niall was a Shark, his work colleague Gaurav was a Zebra and his flatmate Dai was a Lion. Adam chose to be a Gorilla.

They had picked the costumes drunkenly from a bizarre boutique in a Camden Basement after a day-long drinking session. Adam liked the thought of the Gorilla suit because it was a freezing cold day. The suit was a onesie with a zip at the back that you could pull up with a long black drawstring like a swimsuit. The gorilla's face was an all-encompassing mask that pulled all the way over the head, meeting the zip at the back. It looked quite incredibly lifelike once the suit was on and far outshone the other costumes in the shop. Adam had to have it.

They paid for their costumes and threw them on immediately over their shirts and jeans.

They went from bar to bar along the Camden Road getting a great response from the drinkers in each bar. After several pit-stops they settled on shots in the Black Cap before hightailing it to Vauxhall. After a few persuasive arguments with the doorman at *Fire*, who Gaurav fortunately knew, the menagerie made it into the club.

The atmosphere was building at this point. Niall lived up to his spirit animal and managed to cop off quite quickly. He disappeared into a darker part of the club and that was that. He must have shed his skin because a shark's fin was later found by the side of the DJ booth. The three remaining zoo animals decided it was time to find a new enclosure.

They jumped onto the N87 to Trafalgar Square and fell into the *Player's Lounge* for last orders in the piano bar. The booze flowed on. The euphoria built. Adam pulled his mask back on and soon they were laughing at the back of the queue to *Heaven*. There was a big act on that night and most people had already picked up wristbands on Old Compton Street but the zoo animals thought they'd try to blag it, which they managed to some success.

The zebra and the lion linked arms and after a quick pat down were heading downstairs into the reverberations. Adam, who had taken his excesses perhaps a little further than the others, stumbled forward and caught his gorilla suit on the stern looking female bouncer. "No chance. You're ruined. Go home."

Adam, left with little choice, headed back to Trafalgar Square with the hope of making it back to his apartment in New Cross. And it was at this point he took the ill-fated N21.

Being only 12.30am it was comparatively quiet for a night bus. Adam went for a front seat on the top deck and passed out. The gorilla mask stayed on. Adam's body rocked gently as the bus pulled along Whitehall, across Westminster Bridge and down towards Elephant. The chatter faded in and out. At one point he could sense people sitting either side of him posing for a photo. He opened his eyes as the bus lurched to a stop next to the Lidl on the Old Kent Road. A distorted voice crackled:

"*This bus terminates here.*"

He heard people walking downstairs but felt too tired to move. Just five more minutes and he would be fine. He fell back into a deep, deep sleep. So deep in fact that he didn't notice the lights switch off. The top deck plunged into darkness. The *out-of-service* bus turned off the beaten track and weaved through fairy-lit suburbs. Just another bus heading back to the depot. With a sleeping gorilla on the top deck.

But this bus wasn't heading back to the depot.

It is unclear what finally shook Adam out of his stupor. It may have been the wind from an open window. Perhaps the bump as the roof caught a low tree branch. I like to think it was fact the bus was hitting 97mph on a country road with no sign of civilisation.

Adam looked around in the dark. He pressed his big thick gorilla fingers against the glass of the front window just as the bus veered into a nearby field. He gave a muffled cry through the mask.

All he could see on the horizon were the beams of the bus lighting field after field as the vehicle ploughed through endless hedges. The visibility from the mask was limited and he was sweating profusely. He decided to stand up and try to head down to the driver. He got as far as the centre aisle before the bus hit a bank and lifted up from the front hurtling him to the back of the deck. As he landed badly on his back he screamed in agony. The bus drove on into the night.

Adam grasped for a pole on the edge of one of the chairs and hoisted his bruised body back up. He pressed his mask against the back of the vehicle and stared into the thick black night. *Who was the maniac driving? Where was he taking him?* In the far-distance he could see flashing blue lights. Overhead he heard the rumble of a helicopter. A thin spotlight pierced through the night sky and lined up alongside the bus's path helping Adam to see more outside. He spotted little pits of sand. The bus was driving over a golf course.

A sudden smash took out a front window. Adam threw up his long gorilla arms to shield himself. Millions of little pieces of marbled glass rushed down the aisle towards his hairy feet, along with a broken wooden pub sign with a painting of a horse on.

Adam could feel a strong winter wind rush in through the front of the stricken bus. He made another attempt for the stairs; hanging onto seats, walking through the glass and climbing over the pub sign. He looked behind to see the blue lights flashing further away. The helicopter noise also sounded quieter. The bus drove on. *Why had they stopped chasing him?*

He looked through the broken window. In the distance he could see the moon reflecting over what looked like the sea. Adam looked further still and could see the beam of a lighthouse. Still the bus drove on. He looked down at the beams of the headlights and could see that the land was about to run out. It looked like it was approaching a sheer drop.

Adam roared with fear. He reached behind his head and scrambled for the zip to undo his costume. He fumbled around the back of his neck to discover that the zip-cord had been crudely cut off. It was gone.

Still the bus thundered towards its conclusion. The edge neared. Adam lost hope. He sat on the front seat and watched as the bus reached 20 yards from the edge. He curled up into the brace position and waited to go into free fall.

He heard the bus slam on its brakes and spin around violently. Adam hugged his body tight. The bus spun again and again and again before then grinding to a halt.

The next thing Adam noticed was the gentle sound of waves lapping against the shore. He checked to see if he was still alive. He looked out of the left-hand side of the window and saw the edge of the cliff. The bus was teetering by mere inches on one side. He gently stepped back to the middle of the aisle and tried to counterbalance by carefully walking towards the centre aisle. Suddenly he heard movement downstairs. Something was running around and making lots of noise. Adam called out through the mask:

"Hello?"

The noise stopped. Then Adam heard the sound of something moving upstairs.

"Who's there?"

Adam stepped back with shock as a sheep clambered up onto the top deck and stared at him with its rectangular pupils. For a moment there was a sheep/gorilla stand-off as the two creatures observed each other. The sheep broke the deadlock with a loud baa before clambering onto a seat near the cliffside window. It nuzzled its mouth through an open window shutter. The bus rocked again.

"NO!" screamed Adam.

He had to take action or they would both be dead. He ran towards the sheep, startling it. The sheep ran between Adam's furry legs. A scuffle broke out. Adam managed to rugby tackle the animal. They wrestled for a moment. The bus rocked from side to side. Adam rolled far enough with the sheep that they both fell down the narrow staircase to the bottom deck. They hit the ground with a thud. Adam released his grip on the sheep and watched it trot off bleating through the open bus front door and off into the night.

Adam pushed himself onto his knees and clambered up to his feet. The bus was still rocking so he ran as fast as he could and jumped off into soft, mossy grass. He looked around to get his bearings. It was still very dark. The bus's lights were still on full beam. To his far left he could make out a footpath sign:

*BEACHY HEAD - 1 MILE*

He walked towards the sign, carefully tracking the edge of the cliff. Steam rose from his mask into the freezing air. He could start to trace white chalk beneath the wild flowers and grass. He had developed a limp but tried his best to walk it off. He had no time to wait. He just needed to find out what had happened whilst he had slept.

The beams lighting his way suddenly wobbled making Adam look back. The N21 bus gave one last uneasy sway before leaning over the precipice and swan-diving into the void. Adam shuddered at the sight. He heard a huge boom from the depths. In blind panic Adam upped his pace and limped almost manically toward the footpath. He felt an amber light blaze into the side of his vision. He turned towards the sea to witness dawn over Eastbourne. A giant red orb rose ahead of him. No sooner had he seen this the skyline was met with a police helicopter rising above the white cliffs. Adam watched it rise higher into the sky before spinning round to witness 2 police vehicles careering towards him across the grassy planes. He raised his arms to the sky and let out a huge wail. In a state of delirium he continued limping onwards.

The police footage from the sky, as you may recall from TV footage at the time, indeed looks like a wild ape was wandering the cliffs along Beachy Head, looking up to the sky from time to time and shaking his fist. I watched it all from the viewing gallery at the Old Bailey, whilst making furious notes. The next thing you see at approximately 3 minutes and 52 seconds in is the police jump out and surround Adam with tasers. At first he seems to comply by keeping his hands up in the air but it is clear the poor boy was not in a good place mentally by this point. At 4 minutes and 13 seconds the jury gasped collectively at the quite extraordinary sight of a gorilla (now known to be a man dressed as a gorilla) making a run from the officers before being struck in the back by several taser guns at once.

Several people left the courtroom as the footage goes on to show smoke rising from the gorilla costume before Adam flops helplessly onto the ground. It was only when the paramedics turned up that the startling discovery was made that this was no gorilla. By the time the local press arrived the story was already live on *Underground*. By the time the national press picked it up it was already trending on social media. You probably remember reading it yourself.

At the local A&E they had cut through the fur to reveal a fragile and trembling Adam beneath, like a moth from a larvae. What followed was two days of rehabilitation, several hours of police questioning and psychiatric tests. Five days later the Metropolitan Police decided to charge him with vehicle theft. Adam had evaded more severe charges due to the bus being empty. The bus driver on duty that night had not been logged on TfL's roster system and evidence of a body was never found, suggesting to the authorities that the bus had been left momentarily unattended and was consequently stolen by Adam for a long-distance joyride. Curiously, the onboard CCTV had been disabled. This sheer lack of evidence coupled with the fact that at no point had anyone reported to police the sighting of a gorilla driving a night bus meant that the case was thrown out of court as a strange but inconclusive incident; at great cost to the taxpayer I may add.

Adam Harris left court that day a free but changed man. He gave no victory speech on the court steps. I watched from afar as his lawyer bundled him into a waiting taxi, which sped up the road in a hurry. I'm always there. Looking on.

I closed my notebook and went back to work. Taking my place back in the driver's seat and closing the cabin door to start the engine of my bus. The air hissed out. I changed the *Out of Service* sign on the front and pulled away down towards Trafalgar Square. As I drove along The Strand I caught my reflection in the wing mirror. '*Another story tonight*', I thought, '*is waiting out there for me to discover*'. There are so many stories to be discovered on these streets.

But I specialise in the peculiar.

# PART TWO

## Everyone Gets Off At Goodmayes

There beneath the blinking boards,
Grey pigeons and the suited hordes
He scrambles through the cattle,
Of the Liverpool Street battle,
To fight for a seat,
Or stay on his feet,
Until everyone gets off at Goodmayes.


The trundle past the West Ham ground –
The old Olympic merry go round.
Now shadowed by the Westfield lights;
Flashing ads of girls in tights.
The crowds crush,
The station staff push.
This is Stratford bound for Goodmayes,


Maryland, Forest Gate,
By Manor Park it's getting late.
He calls his wife on the phone
"8 more stops and I'll be home".
The train driver hits the brakes
"We're not sure how long this will take"
There's trouble down at Goodmayes.


He looks around at tired eyes
Opened windows, loosened ties.
Cranky couples stare at screens,
Adverts promise all your dreams.
The carriage rattles,
The speaker crackles,
"No update yet from Goodmayes."

From Ilford down to Seven Kings,
The ghetto girls with hoop earrings
Argue about "What Danny said" -
The next time they see him he's "fuckin' dead".
Old men in thobes pat their knee,
Drunkards shovel katsu curry.
We trundle towards Goodmayes.


The train once more has overrun,
No time to see his little one
"We're sorry for today's delay,
A passenger was in the way"
Another lost soul on the tracks,
Swept aside like bric-a-brac,
To clear the route for Goodmayes.


Beyond the carriage the city lights
Glow in the distance burning bright.
Along the tracks he sees a fox
Padding past until it stops;
Its green eyes watch
People packed in a box
Waiting to pull into Goodmayes.


The doors swing open and all fall out
Some with a whimper, some with a shout.
At last he grabs the corner seat;
He'll get five stops to rest his feet.
From gasping for air,
To nobody there.
They all got off at Goodmayes.


For the last few stops he sits alone,
10% battery left on the phone.
Romford onto Gidea Park,
He stares out the window into the dark,
Then peace from 10
Until 7am,
When everyone gets on at Goodmayes.

## Manchester to London

*Good morning ladies and gentlemen, this is your driver speaking. This is the 9:06 service to London Euston calling at Stockport, Macclesfield, Stoke on Trent...*

As each stop was monotonously listed I began to feel lightheaded. I placed the side of my hungover head against the cold glass and watched the Northern city streets blend into quiet countryside. I could feel my eyes getting heavy.

The BBC Christmas party in Deansgate had led to me checking back into my Premier Inn at 4am. I had woken up at 8:25am still in last night's suit with the driest of mouths and burning eyes. There had been no time to shower. There had been no time for anything except to try and make the 9:06 to Euston. Fortunately, a cabbie wearing a *Bah Humbug* black Santa hat was flagged down with sheer minutes to spare and I made it just as the train doors were beeping to close.

The tinny announcements continued as I drifted in and out of consciousness. I suddenly felt a pang of blind panic. Had I left something important in my hotel room? I wracked my sleep-deprived brain before remembering the cabbie shouting at me from his car window,

"Ay buddeh, aren't you forgetting somethin'?"

I then remembered him pointing to the back seat of his cab. In a panic I had run back, opened the passenger door and grabbed a giant Teddy Bear from the back seat. Looking up to the luggage store above I saw the large toy staring back at me and feeling reassured began to settle down. For a short time I drifted in the midway of consciousness; aware of the train's rattle, my jaw hanging open, I felt detached from my surroundings. People spoke in the carriage but it came across as incoherent mutter. Time started to slow down. Then I heard a clear voice which pierced the haze -

"You're dribblin'"

The voice shocked me back to reality. It was delivered in a strong Mersey accent. When I opened my eyes someone had taken a seat on the opposite side of the table. A skinny, almost skeletal boy sat opposite me - like a vision of death, but with a Nike sweater and earrings. Two dark, sunken eyes locked into my view. He must have been no more than 19 but his face looked closer to 50. It looked worn and used. His short black hair was shaved into a short, cropped Mohawk and scar lines were so visible across his scalp it looked like tiger print. I scanned along past his left ear to see a name written down his neck. *Kayleigh.* I stirred in my chair, trying to comprehend if the boy was talking to me.

"Mate. You're dribblin'."

Feeling self-conscious I sat up straight and wiped my chin.

"Sorry."

"S'alright. I weren't sure if you were spastic or summin."

Unsure of where this conversation was going, I looked around for support from other passengers but none were in sight. I picked up a stray newspaper from another table and opened it to avoid eye contact.

"Where you from mate?" the boy persisted.

I looked over my paper at the tough but inquisitive face ahead of me.

"Um....London?"

"Oh yeah? Whereabouts?"

"Shepherds Bush."

The boy stared at me intently, like a boxer at a weigh-in.

"That's not where you're from though is it? You're accent ain't from Shepherds Bush."

I squirmed in my seat.

"No."

"So" the boy opened his palms expectantly "*Where* you from mate?"

"Cardiff. Originally."

The boy's face lit up excitedly. He laughed out loud and started pointing at me.

"Yes! I fookin knew it! I knew you was Welsh from yer accent."

I started looking around for help again. I thought about staring at my iPhone instead but changed my mind due to the nature of my fellow traveller. I continued to leaf through the leftover newspaper.

"What football team d'you support mate?"

Being more of a rugby fan I panicked. I knew from the boy's accent I had a 50/50 chance of red or blue. So I took a shot:

"Liverpool."

The boy laughed again.

"Mate, if you're a Liverpool fan why the *fuck* are you reading *that*?"

He pointed at my choice of newspaper. Feeling humiliated I placed it in the bin next to him.

"I'm only winding you up mate. My name's Callum. You heading to London?"

"Yes." I sighed. How long would I have to talk to this guy?

"Me too!"

*For fucks sake*!

Realising that I had another hour and a half of captive conversation to engage in I scrambled for some generic filler,

"Do you have family in London then?"

"Sorta mate yeah. I'm going to find my daughter."

I hesitated.

"Find her?"

"Yeah. Never met her."

"How come?"

He smiled.

"I've been in Young Offenders for 5 years mate. I was released today! Woop woop!"

I almost said *'Congratulations'* but cut myself short. For a short moment, there was silence. A man in a train uniform pushed a trolley up to them.

"Any teas or coffees?"

I reached into my suit pocket and found some change.

"Do you want a coffee...Callum?"

The boy looked suddenly shy.

"Erm. Can I have a tea please?" he mumbled.

"One tea, one black coffee please."

The man poured hot water into two plastic cups.

"There you are. £4 please! Happy Christmas."

The man moved on through the carriage. When I looked back towards Callum he had placed some rolling paper and tobacco onto the table. He then took out a small plastic pouch and sprinkled little green buds into the tobacco. They gave off a strong pungent smell that enflamed both my self-consciousness and my devastating hangover. I decided not to make a scene and sipped my coffee instead. Callum carried on his story as he mixed the buds into the tobacco with his fingers.

"Me and my girlfriend got into some trouble when we were younger. She got pregnant and her Dad flipped out. Couldn't handle it you know?"

Callum started to sprinkle the mix into the paper and began to roll it. I looked around again in case anyone was watching. Callum licked the paper.

"We were fourteen mate, d'ya know what I mean?"

"No." I said, perhaps a little too bluntly.

"Yeah well, her old man didn't take to the news too kindly. He was a somebody where I was from. I was.."

"*Tickets please!*" Came a voice from the top of the carriage. I panicked;

"Um. Maybe you should…"

"So anyways, he threw my girlfriend out on the streets and then came over to see me. A fight broke out. I got me head kicked in."

"*Tickets please!*"

I tried hard not to sweat.

"So, I did what any guy would do in that situation and stabbed the cunt…"

"*Tickets please!*"

"…fookin' blood all over the place…"

"*Tickets please!*"

A little shell-shocked, I reached into my suit for the train ticket inside my wallet. My hand entered an empty pocket, then another. And another.

"FUCK!" My eyes widened towards Callum "My fucking wallet."

Callum stopped talking. I *knew* I'd left something! The penny dropped.

"I think I've left my tickets in my wallet in a hotel in Manchester."

Callum burst out laughing.

"Hahaha! You're fooked mate! The ticket checkers over there!"

Callum pointed at the inspector heading down the carriage. I began to breathe heavily.

"My oyster card. My bank cards. My train tickets. What the fuck am I going to do?"

Callum stood up.

"Relax mate. I've got I've got it covered. Follow me!"

Callum popped a stupidly long spliff in his mouth and headed down to the toilets at the end of the carriage.

"*Tickets please!*"

The inspector was about ten feet away now. I panicked and followed Callum.

The toilets were occupied. Callum started banging on the door.

"Come on! Fookin' ell!"

The curved automatic doors slowly glided open like in a science fiction film. A frightened man walked out in a hurry. Callum smirked.

"Worked like a charm. Come on."

Once inside Callum sat on top of the toilet with the seat down. Legs perched like a griffin.

"What was yer name by the way?"

"It's Rhys."

"Cool. Rhys could yer do me a favour mate?"

He took off his jacket and threw it at me.

"Could you hold that up against the smoke detector up there?"

I looked up at the ceiling.

"I don't think this is a good…"

Callum fixed those sunken eyes at me again.

"Mate, I thought I was doing *you* a favour."

There was silence again between us. Begrudgingly I held the boy's zip jacket up against the detector. Callum shook a lighter and lit his spliff. The small cubicle immediately began to fill with smoke like a tiny hippy sauna. The smell was overwhelming. Callum continued his story.

"So following my…erm…altercation I got put away for a while. My girlfriend left Liverpool and headed to London to get away from her Dad. She called me mum when she got there. She was on the streets for a bit."

"What did she do?"

"Me mum contacted a charity. A shelter for women, like. They took her in for a bit. Looked after her until she had my daughter."

"Kayleigh?" I said

Callum stared at me through the smoke and nodded.

The toilet door began to bang.

*"Tickets please sir."*

I looked over to Callum who stayed silent. The door banged again.

*"I need to see your tickets, sir."*

Callum took another drag from his spliff. The door banged for a third time. Callum sighed.

"FOOK OFF WILL YA, I'M HAVING A CRAP!"

The voice behind the door paused.

*"There's no smoking on this train."*

"I'M NOT FOOKIN' SMOKIN' AM I? Rhys, do you want some mate?"

I nervously shook my head and kept my arm desperately aloft against the smoke detector. I could feel the blood draining from it. The voice on the other side of the door continued.

*"Please extinguish whatever it is you're smoking. I will need to see your ticket as soon as you come out."*

"YEAH MATE. CHEERS THEN. HAPPY CHRISTMAS TO YOU TOO. SEE YOU IN A BIT."

Callum stubbed the spliff out against the cubicle wall. "Jesus Christ, they're worse than the fookin' screws this lot."

I finally relaxed my arm. Callum looked at himself in the small mirror opposite from where he was sitting and started messing with his hair.

"When Kayleigh was born they put my girlfriend into a small flat so she could look after her. She kept in touch with me through me mum. And now, finally, I can see her."

I stared at Callum.

"Does she know you're coming to see her?"

"No way! She doesn't even know I've been let out."

"Won't she be a bit shocked to see you?"

Callum lit his spliff again, prompting me to lift up my other arm to the detector.

"Look. I wanna meet me daughter. I'll do anything to see her. Do you have kids?"

I nodded "Yes. I have a two-year-old."

"So, you'll know what I mean then." Callum puffed. "I even tried to get her something from *Toys R Us* before I got the train but it was fookin' shut! All locked up. On fookin' Christmas Eve 'n' all!"

The door started banging again.

*"Sir, open this door now!"*

My phone started ringing. Callum grinned.

"Aren't you goin' to answer it?"

I pressed answer on my phone.

*"Good morning Mr Smyth this is Angela calling from Premier Inn, Manchester. Just to let you know we have found your wallet and are holding it in reception for you…"*

The door banged again.
*"Sir! Open this door now!"*
Callum smoked peacefully, staring directly at me with a glint in his eye.
*"Mr Smyth? Mr Smyth are you there?"*
I hesitated. "I'll um. I'll call you back."
*"Mr Smyth?"*
I put the phone down. The door kept banging. I looked at Callum.
"What should we do?"
Callum took one final long drag. The amber glowed. He let out a waterfall of pungent vapour and smiled.

As the train pulled into Euston Station a crowd had gathered in front of the toilet cubicle. The ticket inspector, the frightened old man and several others watched intently for 'The Smoker' to emerge. The inspector radioed for platform assistance. Over the intercom a pre-recorded message heralded the arrival to London.

*Ladies and Gentlemen, we have now arrived at London Euston. Please remember to keep your belongings with you as you leave the train. Thank you for choosing to travel with us today and have a very Merry Christmas.*

*Shakin' Stevens* began to play. As the track reverberated around the carriage the toilet door began to glide open.
*Snow is falling, all around me...*
Smoke began to cascade out of the cubicle, into the cabin.
*Children playing, having fun...*
The passengers rubbed their eyes, some holding their nose.
*It's the season, love and understanding...*
From the shadows stood our two silhouettes.
*Merry Christmas Everyone!*
Without warning we burst out in opposite directions. The inspector went to grab Callum but missed. The fellow travellers muttered and yelled.
I didn't look back. Pacing down the platform towards the gates. Fortunately, they were open so I darted through and into Euston's busy departure hall. Panting heavily, I looked around. I'd made it out. I picked up my phone and called my wife.
"Hi love. It's Rhys. Yes. Yes, I've made it to London. Just a bit of a nightmare journey. Look, it's a long story but...if I get a cab could you please pay the driver when I get home? I'll tell you when I get there. Love you."
As I put the phone down I heard a voice behind me.
"Ay! Rhys!"
I turned around to see Callum holding my travel bag and a large brown Teddy Bear.
"Thought I'd lost ya. Don't you want these?"
I stared at Callum for a moment before taking my things.
"Thanks, Callum."
Callum turned to leave. I shouted after him.
"Callum."
Callum turned around. I held the bear out to him.
"I want you to have this. Give it to Kayleigh when you meet her."

For the first time that day I swear I saw a flicker of warmth in those tired, sunken eyes. Callum hesitated, like a wild animal approaching a handful of seeds before seizing the gift. He held my gaze for a moment.

"Nice one, Rhys. Up the Reds yeah!"

"Yeah mate. Happy Christmas. And good luck!"

Callum grinned and disappeared into the shoal of people heading towards the underground station. I headed outside to the taxi rank. A black cab pulled up and wound down the window.

"Shepherds Bush please."

The cabby, wearing a Bah Humbug Santa hat unlocked his doors and let me in. As I settled into the back seat the driver looked at me from the rear-view mirror.

"Who'd work on fackin' Christmas Eve, eh mate? Supposed to be family time innit"

"Yes." I said looking out of the window "Yes, it is."

# The AntiTrain

So far, any knowledge of it had only amounted to the brief announcements the local newspapers would make about the engineering, severe weather or signaling problems that were holding up the city's Underground trains. Then, of course, there were the other, bigger stories regarding the Underground staff going on strike over wages or benefits that would bring the city to a standstill to the great frustration of its millions of commuters. The latter had become such a story of local significance, it had made the headlines of national newspapers, it had caused some of the population to pack up and seek careers elsewhere, it had even become a debate in both local and national parliaments. Needless to say, *it* was, finally, making an impact, and that only fed its hunger for further trouble.

The people of London had always had trouble swallowing the excuses as to why the trains wouldn't be working; the pay disputes never truly made sense since the tube drivers were amongst some of the highest paid mid-level workers in the city, the weather excuse never seemed to work since if the bloody system had been successfully *built* in the 1860s, pre-dating the car and in apparently *even worse* weather conditions, then why the hell couldn't it function in the 21st century? The fact that MI5 would use the Underground for secret surveillance operations was perhaps their worst kept secret and so people's reasoning was that the shutdowns may have been a way of keeping things secret while they foiled some kind of terrorist atrocity down there.

The reality was that they were *all* wrong, the reality was that nobody knew and the London mayor, as well as the company chiefs, were under increasing pressure from the press to explain the set backs, especially when the upcoming twenty-four-hour service was vital to securing their popularities and so the usual excuses were entering the red.

What then, was really causing the endless problems to the railway? The engineering staff who inspected and cleaned the lines every night could never find the source; after cleaning out the accumulated newspaper pages and, weirdly, the collected masses of human hair that wind and static would stick to the rails, they would still find sections of the track knocked completely out of place; not worn down by years of use, not stolen, just knocked slightly out of place, more than what the train energy or any stray animal could really achieve, and too pointlessly small for any troublemaking teen.

The problem had been getting worse and so the police had been down there, specialists had been down there, MPs had been down there and even after asking for any 'tip-offs-of-the-unusual' from the Intelligence Service, still, *it* hadn't been found.

Every morning and evening when rush hour came, dozens upon dozens of newspaper pages blew into the tunnels around Kennington loop, a few of course would become snagged on the tracks as explained but most would be gathered up by *it*. There were the free London papers such as *The Metro* or *The Evening Standard,* the free magazines such as *Time Out* or *Shortlist,* and then sometimes, it would be lucky enough to acquire one of the bigger national or international ones. The world of newspapers and magazines would become more and more as the city evolved and so after many years *it* had educated itself on the ways of the outside world, of politics, of people, of the arts and sport.

It would disappear under the forgotten brick archways, through the cramped spaces of the old, forgotten, pre-industrial realms of the underground, through the rat and mouse-infested sewage puddles and towards the rancid smell of its home. The outer walls of this home were formed from stories of the late 1980s, so rotten and blue in colour now that if it were to touch it lightly, it would crumble apart like drying mud, if these stories were still to be read you might be able to read of the end of the Cold War, the Lockerbie bombing or even the end of Margaret Thatcher. This was old, *old* news to it.

Behind the blue mould, distant echoes of the 1990s such as the first Gulf War, Britpop or the death of Princess Diana could be made out behind colours of shit brown and piss yellow and then of course, to slightly more visible whites, it would enter the 21st Century.

If its home were one day to be found, it would to a human eye, resemble something of an enormous womb-like structure, and so it was through a similar, portal-like entrance at the base of such a structure, it took its fishing with it.

For as long as it had known, it had been able to see in the pitch blackness and so with a scoop of its own excrement and some saliva, it began applying its new layers of wallpaper to the insides of its abode and after it had finished, it first sat there and studied whatever the walls could teach it about its outside world, from above, below and around.

The news of train problems were there as always of course but today they hadn't been the main issue, today every paper seemed to be on about the same story and so with what first struck it as being frustratingly boring soon turned to the potential for excitement.

Everywhere there was a picture of that same man again, his name was David Cameron but it had only managed to muster the name DaCa, and beneath DaCa's image were three words, 'Leave or Remain', followed by an upcoming date of 23rd June, 2016.

Its years of studying had taught it something of the concept of both Democracy and of the European Union and so concluded that the date DaCa was referring to would mean a vote of great significance. The columns in the London papers had been more repetitive than those of elsewhere and so it had also become familiarized with some of the complaints the upper world had to deal with; rapid career changes, rising prices and problems with landlords had caused the city's inhabitants to constantly migrate around their realm, leading it to conclude that people's polling stations could, indeed, remain at different parts of the city to where they lived; this would mean that the trains could be used in great abundance on that day, and they'd be used for something important indeed. Imagine, it dreamt, if one, or many journeys could be delayed on *that* day?

The date printed across this wall's new additions read 19th June, 2016; it still had time.

It turned to look at the tools it had accumulated during its existence, a few hacksaws, some hammers and rope all hanging from its walls from strings of knotted human hair and began to masturbate ecstatically upon its potential.

The night and day, from the 22nd to the 23rd of June, would be the finest moment of its life; for years it had only affected the city and sometimes the minor other tracks that led slightly further; that day it could affect the whole of Europe. Possibly the world.

Upon that fine, wonderful realisation, it gave a name to itself; The AntiTrain.

## Thoughts and Memories from Beyond the Flashbulbs

### 2008: The 52nd London Film Festival: "W" Film Premiere

It was only in retrospect to what had climaxed the previous year's *Eastern Promises* premiere, that it began to become apparent to me just how much cinemas (as in the places themselves, not the institution) had always harboured a strange sense of repressed sexuality; was it their darkened auditoriums or their parting red curtains or that sense of a secret retreat from the real world that had led so many a teenager to their back rows for their first up-the-shirt feel around or hand job? Whether or not it had been because of our particular establishment's flagship status or because it had bordered on neighbouring Soho, I don't know but sexual activity had seemed to be particularly rife at this place.

There was that seedy Japanese businessman who'd turn up with expensive escorts every Saturday night, there'd been that time when Paddy had caught an Arabic teenage girl sucking off a guy through the hole in her niqab and then they'd both pleaded with him not to call the police for fear of it reaching their families who'd shame them in the face of their religions.

Upon cleaning the screens, we'd also find bags of pornographic DVDs left behind for the lost property cupboard of which, of course, nobody would return to claim back.

Yes, it would seem that for some customers, once those lights had gone down and everyone else's eyes would look elsewhere, the cinema auditorium could become like a type of lawless nirvana, enabling them to act upon their desires, free from whatever constraints their version of society might had pulled over them.

Indeed, the inner-city cinema auditoriums of that time, might had been dowsed in more drugs and spunk than the club dance floors nearby. What *I* had experienced, what little old me had experienced in that place then at last year's LFF, might well have been the most interesting sexual encounter in the history of cinema going.

Needless to say, nothing as interesting as that had happened throughout 2008 by that point and for some reason I'd chosen to never tell anyone about it because no one would've believed me anyway.

For other reasons however, for reasons of historical relevance really, 2008 had actually proved itself to be a rather significant year on the whole and things were about to turn *seriously* political. Rumours had begun to fly from across the pond regarding a new economic crisis that would soon arrive here and to the rest of the world.

In my younger life, my knowledge of such things had been inferred by pop-cultural images of the Great American Depression or of the stories my old man, who'd once worked for the council, had told me about the '70s in which the streets were blocked with uncollected rubbish bags; I had to expect then, as all generations do, that I would live through one of this new century's sadder first chapters.

The dawn of this event had already begun to rise over the city and with those perched at the top of its kingdom already having a greater view of the economic tides to come, it didn't surprise me that precautions had already begun to be put in place. The strange changes hereby being implemented into the working man's world, for all those who resided at the base of this great pyramid had not struck me as particularly coincidental.

The first event of which to make this explicit to me had been to do with the apparent thefts the management had kept mentioning, of both stock and money apparently; yet, even amongst the secrecy of mates, nobody had ever boasted about having anything to do with them, not even accidentally. Such denial was somewhat unusual for the motley crew of this establishment and so we had reason to suspect that this may had been the perfect fabricated excuse of the management to begin driving people out; after all, forty or so people on 35-hour contracts (and in an industry that had already been losing its battle against online piracy) would inevitably prove to be an immense fiscal dilemma.

As a result, throughout the early summer, some of us had (and most of them involving the men) become subjected to a series of bizarre interrogations. I myself, no doubt due to my reputation for enjoying a drink, had, on one shift, had O'Bastard threaten me with dismissal for apparently being drunk on duty when I hadn't even touched a drop. Luckily however, Niro had once again stepped in to inform us all that it was our right as employees to declare witnesses to such scenes and so I chose old lawyer boy himself. Niroshen claimed then that without any true evidence of intoxication, only a breathalyser or urine test could truly threaten my employment. Such a thing, of course, could only then be legally conducted by a police officer and to do that, of course, would only expose to them the cinema's own illegitimate ways. Upon hearing this, O'Bastard of course then shat his NHS-provided fat pants and simply went quiet.

Their next technique then came under the guise of them enhancing surveillance for reasons of, quote: 'the increased threat from terrorism'. This of course was a far cleverer tactic than their first, for with all of us being prone to the odd bit of misbehaviour here and there, such a thing could potentially catch us out at any point. Then, throughout the remainder of the summer, workmen could be seen installing newer cameras into practically every nook and cranny of this bizarre business and the manager's office now bared a wall of intimidating, flickering monitors of which would become something of an addiction for whomever might had been in charge on the shift in question. One time, I even caught two of the leaders giggling as they zoomed in and out of my female colleagues' arses. Hey, who were we little people to put out and stick up for human rights? Especially other people's?

*Little people;* how those four pitiful syllables still fuck me off today, for that's what we had been becoming in the managers' eyes – cattle of which to be pushed, herded and moulded into whatever they'd wanted us to be and under such feelings of vulnerable defencelessness, our first sweats of paranoia also began to rise with it.

Anyway, concern had followed concern, event had followed event and here we still all were, rolling on through life and time and ending up here in the winter daylight warm up to yet another evening of the London Film Festival.

I was on my break, sat with my back to the iron railings that surrounded the inner greenery of the square, looking up at that strangely familiar guy from the 90s. That afternoon he was plastering up an enormous poster of George W. Bush, or rather Josh Brolin's rendition of the famous idiot president in Oliver Stone's forthcoming *W* – the biopic of Bush's still-ongoing presidency. Bush, or Dubya, that very man whose actions may had led in some way to the very economic woes of which I told you. The weird thing about this was that one week before, the Festival had opened with the premiere of *Frost/Nixon* – a retelling of the 1977 David Frost interview in which he managed to get old Tricky Dickie to crack and shame himself on live TV over the Watergate scandal. We were something like one week before the new American election (Obama would win of course) and American cinema was clearly mirroring the present troubles of Bush and Iraq etc, with what had happened regarding Nixon, Vietnam and Watergate. Would that fucking country *ever* learn?

If truth be told, I was more fearful of politics back then rather than genuinely interested in it, instead something else entirely had gripped my mind regarding that night's screening;

"See you next year" had been her final words last year. Had she meant it? Or was it just something said out of awkwardness. Why had she done it? I wondered what I should say (if I should say anything at all) if I was to bump into her again? I still hadn't even been too sure about how I felt about last year's incident but if I could get more of it, then I wanted it.

The problem was, I wasn't even working that day's Premiere per se, I was working the Box Office, and although I was more than welcome to finish banking the day's takings and then go up and watch the film for free it meant that if *she* was there, I'd have no idea as to where she would be or how to reach her. And, if her words of last year had actually suggested more, than I had to make her know that I wanted it. No, no, no, this is such bullshit, there's no way she could be thinking *that,* especially *one year later.*

The queue at the box office window was piling up in my absence but today's co-worker, Abdul, had as always, taken the piss regarding the length of his *prayer time* and so thought I'd leave him there a little longer; I'd leave him to those queues of families who wanted to see the Christmas films in the Screening Rooms and would, no doubt, be complaining sooner or later about its tiny, uncomfortable screens.

Jesus, that Box Office had been making me home in on the worst of people; all I could see were just a bunch of arseholes wandering aimlessly through a world of too many trivial options, unappreciative of what they really had and how I hated how the job had been altering my outlooks on what had been, after all, perfectly innocent people.

With a young son, a father approached the gold-plated celebrity hand prints that had been mounted on the ground of the square.

"Dad? Dad? Who's Jeremy Irons?" he asked as if ready to further question whatever answers his father might give.

I could tell the father had been thinking of a child-familiar title to refer to. I couldn't resist it and so leant in good and close to this kiddy wink, all nice and as friendly as I could be like, to answer; "He played the paeodophile in Lolita".

Before the boy could open his mouth to question the *P* word, the father had picked him up and carried him away. Man, I'd learnt my skills in getting rid of them and I couldn't stop laughing.

Then another approached me with a distinct accent. An *American.*

"Hey buddy".

I turned to see this bloke dressed in an odd sort-of suit.

"I, uh, see by your uniform that you work here, am I right?" He asked.

"Yes."

"So you're working the Premiere tonight? With Oliver Stone?"

"Yeah."

He grabbed my hand and shook it enthusiastically;

"Hi, my name's Tim, I run my own private jet company in Albuquerque."

From inside his jacket pocket he pulled out a wad of business cards and handed me one.

"How close do you think you can get to Mr. Stone for me?"

"Mate, if I even speak one word to those people without being spoken to first, I'll be out of a job. You want me to get one of *these* to *him?*"

"Yeah."

"There's no way mate."

Then this dude returns to his inside jacket and takes out a wad of cash.

"What if I offer you sixty dollars, you think that'd be worth the risk?"

"You mean *quid*?"

"Quid? Oh, pounds, right? Sorry, yeah, sure".

"The thing is, there'd only be two ways of doing it. If I stood next to him I could slip it in his pocket, but that's providing that I *get to* stand next to him and of course, *if* he has pockets. The other would be to plant it on his seat, both would be a put me in the firing line of security though mate, to be honest".

At that he began shuffling more of that money through his fingers.

"Okay, I get ya" he went on "I'm an American with a goddamn private jet company and sixty dollars ain't much, right? Look how much d'ya want?" He went on.

Could I actually do it. Could I *feasibly* get it to Oliver Stone himself? Nah, it would be totally out of the question.

"One hundred and fifty. I'll chance it for one hundred and fifty".

"Alright kid, you got me. And thanks by the way".

"I'll try mate, I promise you" I said as he handed me the cash "and if I get fired, get me an ushering a job on one of your aircrafts."

"Yeah sure" he muttered to the side of his mouth as he wandered off to mingle amongst the other goings on of the Square. I think he knew I was unlikely to do what I'd promised.

The thing was, if I could have spotted the opportunity to do what he'd asked, I would've done it, but whilst I could, potentially, get the thing to him, Stone could just kick off about people privately hawking him and then I'd be done for, and after all, I wouldn't even be there to know that he'd received it. Fuck it, no, it wasn't worth the risk.

I was back onto my financial fears again, I began thinking to myself about how all those people at the top of the pyramid might had been plotting to survive whatever economic turmoil was to come, and so I invented a theory for myself, one that I believed was grounded in a very concrete reality indeed; this being that everyone was about to fuck over *everyone* anyway, so why the hell does it matter anyhow?

Abdul signalled for me to return from my break and so I thought it was time; we all called Abdul a 'lifer'; he'd been in that place since like forever, yet, despite the number of hard-working people who'd been unfairly dismissed over the years, Abdul was probably still the worst member of staff there – he was an old and ugly Bengali man, his age was a mystery although he claimed to be younger than what he clearly looked, his English was as bad as his people skills, his perverted nature caused the girls to refuse to work with him and so unsurprisingly, as I returned to my position at the box office, his ways had triggered yet another wave of chaos. Unsurprisingly again, this had stemmed from a complaint about the Screening Rooms... again.

As I entered the box office booth with him a short old gentleman, dressed in a sharp grey suit, with crutches in both hands and his hair greased back had fallen into an argument regarding something being wrong with his seat.

"Why do I 'ave to stay there? There's a bloody shit stain on my seat." The old man said aggressively; a fair enough point. I don't think Abdul understood.

"My friend" as Abdul referred to everybody as; "these are small screens, you have to stay with seat you choose. If you didn't want that seat, why you choose it?" Abdul then turns to me; "Oh god help me, these stupid bastards, day in, day out" trying to keep it between the two of us but with no thought as to turn off the two-way microphone.

"Listen to me you cunt, I been in this city a long time before you lot came 'ere, this is my fackin' turf and 'ere we have this thing called English service here, *proper* English service".

I looked at him and did a double take, I knew I'd recognised him, I'd recognised his fearsome blue eyes and that cockney twang, it was Mad Frankie Fraser! Anybody who knew anything about the previous generations of London had heard *something* about him. Everyone's heard about the Kray Twins, haven't they? The Richardson's? Yeah? Well *this bloke* had been rumoured to be the torturer for one of those parties and not only that, was apparently also the man who informed on them to the police. This bloke had balls and if he was no longer the real deal he most certainly was *back then*, and now he was *starting a fight with Abdul!*

"My friend, if you're going to be rude, then I don't have to serve you."

Abdul, like a small meditating troll, then simply swivelled his chair to one side to avoid him. Mad Frankie Fraser was left in the cold, staring at him menacingly through the glass as thick breaths of winter air exhaled through an angry old smoker's mouth.

"You *what?*" he asked through gritted teeth?

I butted in over Abdul's computer, "It's alright sir, I'll sort you out. What film you watching?"

"The Bank Job" Frankie claimed. A true story about the robbery of a Baker Street bank back in the '60s. I wonder who'd been behind that one?

Abdul's screen was displaying plenty of spare seats; Abdul you prick.

"He's not much of a gentleman, your colleague, is he?" said Frankie to me.

"Sir, my friend, please" Abdul kicked off again "I can tell *you* what a gentleman is, you cannot tell *me* what a gentleman is."

"Oh is that so? I think I should teach you some good 'ol fashioned London manners."

"Abdul, shut *the fuck* up" I whispered to him. Change the subject, change the subject *now*.

"It's fine sir, I've put you on an aisle, I thought it might be more comfortable for you considering the crutches and stuff" I explained.

"Aaron my friend, do not give in to him, I explain rules when he arrive".

"It's fine Abdul". With my heart pounding through stress, I pressed return and dispensed his ticket.

"Ah cheers son. You could learn somefin' from 'im", Frankie kept up the evils on Abdul as he crutched away back to the Screening Rooms.

"Abdul you fucking prick, do you know who that was?"

"My friend, I don't care who people are. If they .."

"He's a gangster Abdul, he's a fucking gangster, and I'm not getting into that shit because of you"

Abdul continued his non-sensical rants as the Box Office door swung open. It was another type of gangster, it was Big Momo.

"Aaron? What you up to?" Momo asked.

"Nothing"

"I need a witness, innit?"

"Eh?"

"Wilton's givin' me a disciplinary down in the office bro. Remember what Niro said? We can legally demand witnesses, can't we? Cover me, bruv".

"Why don't you ask Niroshen?"

"Nah man, geezer's bein' a dick head, innit, he don't wanna do it." Big Momo stopped to watch Abdul rant to himself a long string of *Bastards* and *fucking* in some incohesive blur of an Anglo Bengali dialect.

"The fuck's wrong wiv 'im?"

Upon thinking of having yet another break from Abdul's chaos, I accepted to accompany Big Momo, leaving Abdul to his further string on non-sensical obscenities as a family of four approached him.

All I had to do was sit in the office and witness Big Momo's disciplinary from Wilton. O'Bastard was there too just to take notes. It went something like this; Momo had lost some of his money when he was cashing up on one of the previous evenings, it was something around twenty-five quid; the crux being as to whether this had been a case of 'theft gone wrong' or if it had been a genuine mistake. Momo claimed that it had been because he'd forgotten his glasses that day and could easily have made a mistake, Wilton then claimed that they'd put the issue on hold for a few days and then reveal to him the outcome after it'd been discussed at a further managerial level.

He was later fired of course, but on what grounds? What *exactly* did the managers need to discuss further to come to such a conclusion?

Firstly, all of us, *every single one of us*, had made mistakes with our money from time to time, such things would only be an issue if they proved to be consistent, which this hadn't been and of course there wouldn't have been any clear evidence to either side of the story so what was there for them to *discuss* exactly?

Things in this place didn't play by fair rules of course, and such a truth would of course eventually be decided by those with financial interests. 'Downsizing' then, had become word of the year in this city, everybody had been shrinking their work forces and everything was against Momo. The managers hated his rude-boy persona and he was still on one of the old-school, full-time contracts. I was also on one of those contracts. What I didn't get though, was that the guy was badass, if they *really* wanted rid of him, all they had to do was track him on the CCTV for a few days and he'd eventually do something to incriminate himself anyway.

To avoid going back in the Box with Abdul, I dossed about in the screen for a bit and found Niroshen helping the others to place the festival guides upon the chairs.

Upon the screen, the projectionists were testing parts of the film, the lights in the auditorium would go on and off and random disconnected scenes of *W.* would play out before us.

The thing that upset me about this whole Big Momo thing, was that he'd once openly confessed to me that he'd accepted this job as a means of escaping whatever the fuck might had been going on in his neighbourhood. He was one of the few who'd *willingly* taken the escape route from that way of life, it wasn't much of an escape route to be sure, but it had *something*, and now these pricks were going to send him back to where he came from for something that might not even had been his fault, for something that was grounded in nothing more than someone else's financial interests. And what kind of defence was a dude like that going to have against it? Nothing.

And then they wondered why these guys turn to crime?

I felt sorry for the man, I *really* did and so I asked Niroshen what legal advice he might be able to give.

"Nah, Big Momo's fucked mate" was his response.

"Surely *you* could do something, you've threatened these pricks with legal action before, you know *how* to do it, even if you bullshit them, you know *how* to bullshit them."

The festival guides were getting slapped down upon seat after seat.

"I do know *how* yeah, but that's only if I wanted to do it, isn't it?".

"Why, have you fallen out with him or something?"

"Nah" Niro went on, and this is where he *really* shocked me "it's just that we've all got to look after our own interests at the moment, if you know what I'm saying?"

I said I hadn't understood what he meant and he explained in the fashion of a cunning strategist.

"Look, if they're getting rid of the old contracts, that means they have 'a list' of people, doesn't it? Well, you won't find me on there. If I leave them alone, they leave me alone, and that means not interfering with their interests, doesn't it?"

Still to this day, the arrogance of his statement has stayed with me.

"Why do you think I get to put my 35 hours where I want?" he boasted.

It was here that the young, naive man that I was, learnt that just because someone could be trusted to *know* the powers that can protect, doesn't mean they could be trusted as people to *use* them correctly.

At that moment, I saw the last scene of the film; Dubya had stepped out onto a dream-like baseball field, a baseball had been smacked high into the air and it was failing to come down. Then it went to the credits.

Through a strange twist of fate, Niro then tripped on the stairs and sprained his ankle. He was sent home and I was accepted to stand in as his replacement; my heart was thumping, I would get to work this motherfucker, and I would at least have a chance of finding *her*, if she was due that was.

Shortly before the show, I flitted up to one of the PR people and got a quick look at the guest list; she was coming, she was *coming* and she'd be sitting in Seat 18, Row D, Royal Circle. She was *coming*.

It had been, of course, a slim slice of fate that had enabled me to even talk to the girl the first two times and you could place any bet that such a scenario would not present itself a third time. This time then, I would simply, have to find a way of contacting her.

Her positioning in Royal Circle was a bitch, for I'd be appointed duties downstairs in the Stalls. How the fuck would I do it? I kept thinking, merely trying to separate her from the crowds later would be an act of desperation too far. Then I thought of it, the business card that American guy had given me, I knew her seat number, what a perfect messaging device. In the privacy of a toilet cubicle, I quickly scribbled down my message, the first thing I could think of;

*"See you next year?"* Meet me by the downstairs ladies' toilets, right side, you already know the way, final scene as Dubya Bush steps onto a baseball field.  Aaron.

I worked out I had about five minutes to run up to Royal, plant my message and get back down before any of the management suspected me of doing anything weird. I got up there and things couldn't have been better laid out for me, it was perfect, I merely slipped the card behind the first page of the Festival guide, she was bound to at least open it.

The crowds poured in and my role in the Premiere had begun, I was suddenly hit by the strangest form of tension, like the way some pervert might feel as if he were about to be caught, about to face the branding of a criminal label without having formerly considered himself as one. What if it all went wrong? She could complain about it to her PR people, the security, my managers or O'Bastard and I'd gone and stupidly written my name on it. They'd all know it was me and worse still, what if there'd been a last-minute re-planning of the seating and it got to the wrong person?

As a result, I really wasn't concentrating much on the ins and outs of that particular Premiere, all I could think about was how stupid I'd been.

Finally the crowds had settled comfortably into the Stalls and up above, I could see the same for the balcony and so I leant against the side wall and waited for the usual cast and crew intro. Who was there exactly? I can't really remember but there was Josh Brolin, Elizabeth Banks, Toby Jones, Thandie Newton and I think maybe James Cromwell but Oliver

Stone was the star here for me, amid the flashlights he came to the front of the stage and said something about how "this man had lived a life not worth living".

It was upon the exact full stop of that sentence, that moment the applause went up, that I felt something of a static surge hit the back of my head and trickle down my spine. It was like those religious experiences people tell you about when they'd been touched by the hand of The Lord, it was just like that, and with it, I knew she'd found my message and was watching me from the balcony. My view of the balcony seating from where I'd been standing was awash in shadow, more and more so as the digital photography flashes steadily faltered in respect for the film.

Seat 18, Row D, Royal Circle, she had seen me and I'd felt it. Two beautiful green eyes in a head of perfect red hair had homed in on me from the direction of the projection light. Whatever she might have been thinking, I had to respect my own balls for reciprocating last year's events, no matter how insane it all felt in that moment.

The red curtains parted.

I had previously identified a spare seat and hid amongst the audience so that even if my little trick had put me in trouble, none of the managers could have found me to pull me aside, I could at least then, see this situation through to its conclusion. Here I would wait and see if I could spot her from behind if she would make her way to that right-hand door that led to the toilet. No way would *I* be there first, waiting for potential trouble.

I don't remember much of the film; just counted down the scenes to that final one. Then it came, that scene with the darkened, flood-lit baseball pitch and it was as if the beats of my heart were disturbing whoever had been sat next to me.

I turned and saw a female form making its way down past the audience towards the door in the shadows. Was it her? This time it was some designer white dress of some sort, hugging those thighs, those hips whose sultry sways carried a hint of nervousness. Her hair had been died brunette but I could tell it was her. I let her slip through the door.

I stood up, shuffled my way to the end of the row and followed her, could this be *it*? Could it happen *again*? What if it's the wrong person? I went through the door, there were a few milliseconds of either denial or disbelief I don't know which but it was *her* again for definite. Whilst the previous year she'd been the dominant force, this time it would be me and by the brief look those green eyes gave me before I grabbed her, she fucking knew it.

The kisses we exchanged somehow negotiated that we both knew the toilets would be the wrong place to do our deed and so I turned, punched in the security code to the same staff corridors as last year.

I took her by the hand and led her down that same stone staircase, this time I took her past the organ door down a further staircase and into the basement corridors. She laughed as I led her onwards through corridors so narrow we had to practically squeeze sideways through them and I took her towards the door to the popcorn storage room. Another security code (they never changed) and we were inside. Before that same heavy door had shut behind us again she was already sat up upon the metal shelving unit with her legs apart. The sides to her panties were practically coiling themselves around my fingers as if they'd been *led to me* and so I just ripped them off. Embarrassingly, she seemed a lot fitter than I was and so with her arms around my shoulders and legs around my waist she tightly pulled me in, practically shaking that flimsy metal shelving thing apart as we went at it.

The sounds of the passing trains shook the walls and pipes of this place, one thousand and one lonely tunnels of overlapping non-directions existed just behind those walls, the cluster fuck labyrinth of reality to which all this city's, and every cities' glitz had been built upon.

Fuck films, fuck pornography, nobody ordinary had ever hit the heights of cathartic sexual fantasy like I was achieving then, *nobody.*

My hands were on her arse, and I'd practically forced her dress so high up she was practically nude. Then we came and fell backwards onto the cushioning of the great plastic popcorn sacks, both of us catching our breaths.

No way had this just happened. Many people had no doubt fucked a celebrity before but I bet nobody had done it in a place like this, the last place you'd ever find one, hidden in the bowels of the West End, amongst the spiders and mice, hearing the rattling commuters pass them by.

"I guess you had some bigger roles here this time, didn't ya?" not knowing why I'd decided to say that.

"Your little trick with the business card was very smooth, I must say. Whose business was it anyway?"

"Want to use a private jet?" I so cleverly responded.

"I'm not *that big* yet Aaron."

She had remembered my name, she had remembered my name, and suddenly all kinds of thoughts about being a celebrity boyfriend came into my head. What if she gets more famous? Would she take me with her? Could I actually *be* her *boyfriend?* And so I had to ask.

"Why me?"

She leant over, placing a hand upon my chest.

"I liked you, didn't I?"

"Really?"

"Yeah, why are you so surprised?"

"I mean, you could get *anyone*".

"Do you *really* think so?" She asked.

"Well, you're in with *them,* you know, them up *there,* those who have jewellery".

She laughed, "And you think that *that* gets me laid?"

And I guess in my thought of thoughts such embraces hadn't perhaps been so strange after all.

"Listen, in my line of work, I have to get up earlier than you can even imagine, I work *all day,* sometimes with no real breaks at all. Every friend I've ever made in this business is always working to the same degree as I am but on some other, random point of the planet and so there's no opportunity for me to have any kind of normal relationship even if, say, I'd ever wanted to settle down. Everything I eat or wear has to be controlled by marketing people, my behaviour has to be monitored and every party I ever attend is controlled all the way down to whatever bloody Hors d'Oeuvres they're serving. Privacy is a paradise Aaron, in my line of work it's a fading privilege but you, you're in a strawberry field".

I thought about all those newly installed cameras, what problems they'd caused; thank fuck this was one of the places that didn't have them.

"Don't take what you see at face value"

She began assembling her things;

"Besides" she went on "if anybody ever recognises me in a public place, none of them would have the balls to chat me up anyway."

I guess by that then, she meant that *I* had. I wanted to tell my Dad.

"I have to go, Aaron".

"No, stay a while" I insisted "nobody'll come down here on a Premiere, not even the cleaners."

"No. I have to get to the last of the crowds, my PR people could be looking for me. You see what I mean by privacy?"

I agreed and led her out undetected.

In those eternal five minutes afterwards, lying there with her in a fog of disbelief I began to wonder why this experience had been given to me and so rewound to the strange twists of fate that had led me to it; the strange Private Airline owner who had just happened to be outside as I'd been smoking there, the way that Niro had sprained his ankle just after confessing how prepared he was to use employment law to his own means, and so I rewound again to the earlier discussions I'd been having with Abdul just before the Premiere began – the crux of it had been to do with Karma.

Despite what we all thought we had known about Abdul, other than the typical things we'd find hilariously funny about him, nobody really knew *that much* and so, with the Screening Room queues having since left, I took that moment to try and get to know the man. It began with an apology about the Mad Frankie Fraser debacle.

"Sorry that I shouted at you earlier Abdul".

"My friend, you no need to express forgiveness to Abdul, I see in your eyes that you are good man, Abdul sees these things in people."

"Yeah, I'm sorry, it's the way they treat us here just stresses me out that's all".

"My friend, no man is a bad man, he is only turned that way because of environment. Abdul can tell you from experience what problem with this place is".

"What is it, you reckon?"

"One philosophy my friend, one philosophy, the money-and-greed philosophy, it is all around us in this place. I'm from Bangladesh, I've seen many things, you have to see through all pairs of eyes before you can see the true picture. I've been here long enough to see how this place has changed, used to be good men managing here, now they give up, only care about money."

I didn't know where he was going with this so I thought of something more playful.

"Go on then, what was the first film that was playing in the main screen when you started here, Abdul?"

"Living Daylights."

"What?"

"Living Daylights, James Bond, my friend, nice movie"

I nearly spat out my Evian as I realised he'd been here since *1987!*

"You've been here *that* long?" I continued.

"Yes my friend". The idea of it gave me a sting of fear for I too had started on a Bond film.

"Didn't you ever think about leaving?"

"Oh my friend, I am very qualified, I can tell you".

"What subject?"

"Social Politics, I have PhD".

"You have a *PhD in Politics?* That's amazing man, why don't you use it?"

"No jobs here, my friend, I need English to get job and can't understand it. Abdul need English teacher"

This had been mentioned before - Abdul had, at one stage, somehow got the idea that I could go to his house and teach him English for the bizarre payment of authentic, home-made Bengali curry alone.

"I used to be big in Bangladesh my friend".

"So why did you come here?"

"Bengali government put me here, paid for it, they said, 'Abdul, take this and *go!*'. London, my friend, took me and gave me and my wife house in Marylebone, used to be good place, London".

He'd been living in *Marylebone?!* You needed city boy money to be living *there.* He must had been given a stash.

"What happened in Bangladesh?"

"Bangladesh then, was not called Bangladesh my friend, it was East Pakistan and there was terrible war with Pakistan. I was in resistance but we failed".

"You fought *in a war?*"

"Yes, my friend. Abdul was shot five times".

Abdul then opened his shirt and showed me some scar tissue next to his heart, then he showed me another on his arm, and then on his back and another on his foot; and this Box Office was *cramped.*

"And this one my friend, this one was nearly very bad" Abdul explained as he began undoing his belt and sliding down one half of his trousers until I could see his underwear, he was ignoring my hand gestures to make him stop, to stop him exposing himself to the outside world beyond the window, or even to the newly installed cameras. He pointed and pointed enthusiastically at an entry wound just next to his groin.

"This one, straight through Aaron" which I guess meant it must had come out of his arse.

He stared and stared at me for a while before I heard his zip and belt buckle refasten themselves; "Abdul survive because Abdul was gentleman to them, Abdul kind, so instead of death, they send me away to London, they send me to" a perverse look of disappointment came over him as he looked at the cramped environs encasing us in that place, "the cinema". He sat back down.

I remember being stunned, those bullet wounds had seemed pretty authentic to me.

"My friend, beliefs in my country shape our look at reality. In my country, all people see ghosts, they are as physical as this glass" he touched the glass, "they are as physical as you and me. Ghosts are not story but everyday things, I see this in Africa, I hear this in China, but over here I no longer see ghost."

"Why not?"

"People only see what they *want* to see here, here now has the same problem as Pakistan and Bangladesh, one philosophy my friend, just one philosophy, this culture only want money so they see it everywhere, they no longer look for ghost. What man see is reality, what reality he see creates his destiny. Eastern philosophy likes Karma so Karma work, people see it, people feel it but there's no Karma in the Money philosophy, the Money Philosophy only make bad people".

Then, as if his lips were moving in unison with the naked woman I had had with me, he said "Don't take everything at face value".

If you were to open the door to the Box Office, pass your way through the corridors, head downstairs, turn a corner, pass the minute staff room and turn right into the men's locker room, you'd find on the inside of Abdul's locker door, a small black-and-white, passport-like photo of a young, handsome afro and moustached stud-of-a-man smiling respectably back at you in a military uniform.

"Don't take what you see at face value" were what both she and Abdul had said to me merely hours apart.

Fate is real. I can tell you that now. Karma is real also, but like all things, fate clearly has its negative side and Abdul had been hit with it.

To my knowledge, he still resides in one of London's cinemas even now.

# Clacket Lane Services

The approach to this particular station, found to the south of the London Orbital, creates a sense of mysterious anticipation as soon as one clears the junction. Clacket Lane services is tucked away behind leafy trees and once the traveller arrives at this humble but tranquil stop one could almost be forgiven for thinking they have chanced upon a woodland lodge in a remote forest reserve. The homely feel continues as you enter the station itself. Magnificent wooden beams prop up the windows and skylights like an ornate cathedral and, much like a cathedral, there is a slight timelessness to this station. The shopfronts; a trio of classic British shops - *WHSmiths, Cotton Traders* and *Spar*, give a sense of nostalgia from simpler times. Indeed, it must be said that standing within its confines the year could be 1979, 1987 or 1995 and there would be very little to suggest that it wasn't. The only new kid on the block is the slightly more modern *Fresh Food Cafe*; where healthy alternatives are on offer to the hungry traveller at (reasonably) affordable prices. I ate a roasted vegetable wrap and I would be lying if I said I didn't enjoy it.

To the untrained eye, it would be very easy to level Clacket Lane as something of a 'No Frills' station but I do feel this does it something of a disservice. If you spend a while exploring as I did you can quite literally unearth unique features that many would miss if in a hurry. For example, outside the gentleman's toilets is a mounted archaeology display entitled *Travelling Through Time*, documenting artefacts that were discovered beneath the station itself. The display, albeit small, I found deeply fascinating and informative. I have to say it was as good as anything you would find at the British Museum.

I do have criticisms though. The toilet facilities were quite poor. The trough-like circular taps meant that visitors were required to huddle close to each other to wash their hands and the water took a while to heat up. Feeling quite frustrated by this I went to the *Costa* coffee kiosk to calm myself down. Upon ordering a chai latte the teenage barista gave me a blank expression and asked me how it was made. To be honest I felt quite embarrassed for her. Resisting the urge to lose my temper I gently talked her through the basic steps of heating the milk before adding the spiced powder. Eventually she managed to cobble together a rather mundane interpretation but to keep the peace I smiled and paid before heading to the picnic benches outside to recuperate.

As night fell I remained outside and watched the station breathe guests in and out of its premises. I didn't notice the time pass but by morning a gentle spring frost had settled on my coat and the latte was undrinkable. It was time to move on to my next station.

Clacket Lane also offers free Wi-Fi.

**3 Stars * * ***

# The Queen's Lingo

At the age of 49 Terrence Scott had had enough. He was already ridiculously underpaid for a private language teacher and this wasn't helped by the recession-era Tories bringing in their zero-hour contract scheme; something that had led Terry, and indeed many native Londoner's to often ponder why they hadn't taken the chance to abandon their crumbling nation and take jobs abroad when they once had the chance. Mortgages, divorce settlements and child support had been that dream's undoing. Still, Terry was able to keep himself pro-active and motivated in the job since, actually, he did have an interest in languages and was held in high regard amongst his team. As many middle-aged men would agree, his job was always at its best when the clientele were nice, mild-mannered people and with his school being particularly prestigious and expensive, they were also nearly always rather fascinating, innovative members of their country's high society.

Not at the moment though. For the last two weeks, Terrence Scott had been assigned work as the private tutor of Mrs Ivana Zubitskaya, a Putin-worshipping Russian oligarch who had not only become filthy rich from near enough nothing but was also unbelievably rude. Her contempt for anything that was smaller, poorer or struggling in any way was so monumental as to be compared to fascism; she belittled the U.K by believing that its current problems would've been non-existent if its people had elected a leader of strong Russian blood, she was open and frank about her dislike of London's lenient, multicultural attitude of allowing blacks and Arabs into the country (she had even used the 'n' word) and when Terry had made up that he was bisexual simply to get out a rise out of her, she'd told him that in Russia, he would've been taken out to the woods and shot. The problem with this particular strain of Russian, as he had mustered over years of teaching experience, was that they believed money could buy them anything, and that if the high cost of their course wasn't immediately downloading fluent business English directly into their brains, then it wasn't because they weren't putting in the effort, it wasn't that they hadn't yet developed the skills of which to progress to that particular level for themselves. No; it would, plain and simply be all Terry's fault.

Terry had somehow convinced his school director that he was doing a wonderful job with Mrs Zubitskaya, yet behind that private classroom door, he knew she didn't stand a chance at English, something that would, of course, backfire onto him once her course was over. She hated lateness (although she was late herself, frequently), she hated being told what to do, she hated being wrong and no teachers ever wanted to put in the effort with her simply because subsequently, *everyone* hated her. How long would Terry be in her company? Five weeks. Five weeks with one hell of a fascist bitch? This was the life that, at age 49, had befallen Terrence Scott and after just two weeks of her and another three to go, he'd had enough of her shit.

This was also the start of the second week to yet *another* tube strike. Here was Terry; his cheap suit and his little remaining hair, all ruined by the time he had spent in that pissing rain waiting for that one out of the succession of rammed buses that would actually let him on. He was on the fourth one now, sandwiched between a fat man with a severe cold, a claustrophobic woman who would panic every time more people squeezed on, an annoying gay man who moaned that his little Pug was getting stepped on and a woman with a double push chair, all crushed together for an hour and half on the 241 from Dalston to his school in High Holborn, in the pissing rain, a head full of life's regrets, all the way to Mrs fucking Zubitskaya. And what for? Peanuts and insults. And with him definitely, without a doubt, going to be late further insults lay ahead.

Although Mrs Zubitskaya's job hadn't been fully explained to Terry, he was aware that she had some kind of important conference to lead in a couple of days of which had to be delivered in the best English possible and was why he was *trying* to improve her knowledge of spoken, formal business lingo. The fact that this would ordinarily require a student to at least be able to comprehend an intermediate level of grammar or vocabulary first, however, just simply wasn't clicking with her. She would, in her rude way, silence him upon his perfectly fine explanations of the tenses and intervene with;

"I don't need grammar. This is for poor people. I need true English. Like the Queen, I need to be able to speak to rich and important people".

*Hallelujah!* In suddenly granting the man such an unclear definition of what her true needs were Terry was able to turn the tables and, being the professional that he was, would know exactly how to insert such needs into the gaps in her understanding. Since the Friday in which she had told Terry this, he had decided that this week was going to be different; he had spent the weekend vigorously studying the phonetic structures that were integral to her needs and would grant her the most intense, most culturally enlightening lesson that he could ever teach.

By the next Friday, Terrence Scott had been asked by the school director to be 'let go'.

Three days before his dismissal, Mrs Zubitskaya was leading a bidding war over the purchasing of Lea Valley and Hackney Marshes; wasteland areas of London that her and her people had bought up years before in the knowledge that once expansion and refurbishment would be necessary for the 2012 Olympic Games, their values would increase tenfold. The CEOs to several international property and development companies, most of them Americans, Chinese or Indians, were now spilling into the conference room, sure that buying up areas of this wasteland from this most confident of business-wary Russians for their future apartment blocks, shopping centres and smaller businesses would be a bona-fide, long-term success story. With the Olympic Games now being so integral to repairing London's economy, these buyers had already had such future prospects pushed to them by the financially concerned UK government and London councils and none were likely to back out. To be frank, she had these buying nations in her pocket, able to crank up the price to whatever she wanted. Mrs Zubitskaya had made it to the front of the room, she took one swig of Evian, and began to make her sell.

*English revised: How do I say; "Welcome ladies and gentlemen, please take a seat and allow me to enlighten you"?*

**Mrs Zubitskaya**: Right, roll up, roll up and gather rand you bunch of facking muppets!

Her company took their seats in a nervous confusion; the Americans were the most shocked whilst the representatives of the less English-speaking countries were locking eyes with each other to check as to whether the others had been able to understand this particular hiccup of 'Russian English'.

**Mrs Z**: Cam on, cam on, I ent got all fackin' day!

*English Revised, introduction/breaking the ice/compliments: How do I say: "Ladies and Gentlemen, being born into the privileges that I have, entrepreneurship is often an easy ride for me and I respect the fact that for you people, sustaining that privilege must be a full-time job, I am envious of the lifetimes you have spent developing the skills and the know-how of the business world and is why I would like to present to you what I know will be a fine investment for the long-term futures of all of us"?*

**Mrs Z**: "My old man said foller the van, and don't dilly dally on the way... or, as they say in British business etiquette....Knees up, knees up, never get the breeze up. Na, 'ave youselves a butchers at this!"

She switched on the overhead projector to reveal maps of the two areas and her explanations into the advantages of the two regions began in a relatively straight-forward way before ending on..."Try takin' that to the Iron Tank".

**The Chinese Businessman**: What exactly is it that interests you on a personal level in this park, Mrs Zubistkaya?

*English Revised, use the environmental/leisure spin, How do I say: "I was initially interested in London, because in relation to Moscow, it is a very green city, environmentalism is now becoming an increasingly popular benefactor with land owners and will no doubt be something they incorporate and promote through the design of the Olympic Games themselves?*

**Mrs Z**: "I get up when I want, except on Wednesdays when I get rudely awoken by the dustman. I put moy traazzers on, 'ave a cop o' tea and I fink abat leavin' the 'ass. I feed the pigeons, I sometimes feed the sparras too, it gives me an enormous sense of wellbeing. And then I'm appy for the rest of the day, safe in the knowledge there'll always be a bit o' moy 'art devoted to it."

*English Revised: Now let's switch the environmental sentiments to questions of money.*

**Mrs Z**: "It's a deal, it's a steal, it's the sale of the fackin' century. But it'll cost ya, now what we're here to discuss is who's gonna cough up the biggest Bobby Moore?"

The crowd fell into a silent shock. After an uncomfortably long time of smiling, one of the Americans finally put up their hand.

**Mrs Z**: "Yes treacle?"

"Urm, how did you come into inheriting this particular piece of land in the first place, Ms Zubitskaya?"

*English Revision: How do I say: "Russia is, as you probably all know, a very wealthy and self-sufficient country, but the futures of all our businesses rely a certain degree of investing overseas, hereby the money inherited to my husband and I following the fall of the Soviet Union, was better having a percentage invested in this great, forward-thinking and international city"?*

**Mrs Z**: "Just a week or two ago my dear old Uncle Bill went and kicked the bucket and he left me in his will. So I went dan the road to see my Auntie Jane. She said, "your Uncle Bill has left you a watch and chain....therefore arm fackin' minted guvnor."

The silence in the room was now definitely the type of silence that would emanate from somebody who'd just been ridiculed, it was of that specific vein that could only emanate from those who were not used to it, and certainly didn't like it. Anyway, it only took one more question to seal the deal that this woman wasn't going to make it, and to finally clarify that this most certainly *wasn't* the Queen's English.

**Indian Businessman**: If we buy into this land, what kind of competition are we likely face in the future?

*English Revision: How do I say: "Being the business professionals that you are, I am sure I don't need to tell you about how to decrease the market share. However, the measurement of the land is limited and so if you were to buy into this investment first, you would be given free reign as to how much of the area you would share between you. London is competitive as we all know but within this space, and with the going price, I don't think your competitors would stand a chance in the short term, not with this area's current state of urgency"?*

**Mrs Z**: "Do you know what nemesis means? I righteous infliction of retribution, manifested by an appropriate agent. Personified in this case, by an orrible cunt. Me."

The sounds of comfortable leather conference chairs suddenly being vacated began to replace the enthusiasm.
"What had she done wrong?" she thought, she had paid fine Russian cash for those English lessons and so therefore it should've been perfect. It was then that she realised why Terry's brush up lesson yesterday had been accompanied by a slight, demonic smile.

Terrence Scott, (*poor, liberal, English*), **1**. Ivana Zubitskaya, (*wealthy, fascist, Russian*) **Nil**.

# Strange Requests - Volume 2

Saturday Night at *The New Bloomsbury Set*. Jez has just handed me some folded over twenty-pound notes for tonight's troubles. We've reached the point where the punters are starting to lose their inhibitions so I switch from *Buffalo Stance* into a bit of *Candy* by Cameo. One of the birthday tables get up and start doing some pre-orchestrated dance moves. I start to count the money when I notice someone standing in front of me. I follow my eyeline up to a well dressed girl in a cocktail dress. She is sipping a spritzer through a straw out of a dewey glass.

"What the fuck is this?"

"It's called *Candy*."

"No, I mean what the fuck is any of this? Can't you play something I would like?"

"Um, sure...what are you after?"

She starts poking the ice cubes in her glass before looking back up at me.

"You're the DJ. Surprise me."

"Ok, what are you into?"

"I don't know"

There is a long awkward pause. I line up some Jamie T.

"So you don't know what you like and you don't know what you want?"

"No, just something people would like. No one likes this shit."

"*They* seem happy with it"

I gesture over to the birthday table. I can feel myself getting pissed off. She gives me a withering stare.

"Yeah...well...what do you know? You're just a DJ."

She leaves her empty glass on my decks and walks back over to her friends.

I shouldn't let this shit get to me but I'm feeling wound up.

It was time to drop The Big 3.

No matter what place you're in - be it a spit and sawdust in Brixton or a champagne bar in Kensington, if you drop these 3 tracks in this order people just. go. fucking. nuts:

**Elvis Presley** - Jailhouse Rock
**The Beatles** - Twist and Shout
**David Bowie** - Let's Dance

The holy trinity, not to be used lightly. It seems too simple right? It always, always works. The first wave hits and there's a collective bonhomie to those familiar Elvis chords. The cocktail barmen smile over and I can see the people queuing for a drink starting to rock back and forth. Then I drop Lennon & McCartney. Loud. People at the back are starting to pile in on the dance floor and I can hear glass cracking. And then for the final ingredient - I sync up those iconic "aaa, aahs" with the Thin White Duke and as soon as that Nile Rodgers lick comes in I've done it. The bitch is up.

# Blood Beyond the Blade

The blade was more or less quick-fire, blood, and it was after I was tinkin' that the geezer 'ad punched me and that I looked over to my bro' Mo, all red and pullin' whiteys and the likes, that the real pain started, innit? I was lookin' at 'im and he was lookin' at me and we started acceptin' it. It was after Mo had already gone down on the steps, and my pain kinda like started to fade that my mind then seemed to resemble the wound itself, opening outwards to let what was on the inside trickle out through my guts to meet with that of the out - the concrete stairs, the piss and the rubbish of Pulham 'ouse, - also let in. It's in their meetin' man, that tings become bare clear.

Somewhere like, in the better parts of the world, geezers are born with a longer chord between the moments of the birth of their blade, born, innit, to succeed, to make some ching? Be happy and pass away without even a blade like the way they do on the box and the likes. They die on beaches, old and happy, they die in the arms of their family, but bwoys like me, we get shanked in alleyways, on stairwells, these days even in public like to make a statement on the news an' all; we're left 'ere to tink that the last connection we have to our Mums is the tears she'll 'ave tomorrow when we're already gone.

It don't matter where you turn bro, it don't matter what school you go to or who you know, whichever turning you take, the blade is waitin' for you before the age of 21, waiting behind a brick-work corner like it ain't decided by man, like it's sometink already there, overhanging from the next world, fam; we deny it at first, we all do, but we live to learn after the jip days of school that the only tings we know 'bout are the buff tings, our bruvs and tryin' to make it with greenz and lyrics before the Charlie and smack come in and that shit has an even shorter chord, man.

Fuck it's gettin' bare cold now man, my breath's gone all dragon and I starts like, shakin' an' shit, ahm wedged on the stairwells between the floors of Pulham House in Oval, my bro' Mo's a few steps up an' he's already gone, ah can tell 'cause his blood's runnin' down on me from above and it's gone cold, mine's still pretty warm by comparison like as I feel it comin' out between my fingers but ah won't make it, not me, the paramedics ain't gonna make it up this far in time, that's even if these neighbours 'ave got the bottle to call anyone in the first place and we don't even fuckin' know which cunt from the Gas Crew did it; jumped us from the shadows they did, right strong geezers and it was over in seconds. That's the short chord for you, always fucked, dyin' in a hail of questions, starin' up at shitty wall lights and the burnt, black concrete ceilings of the Pulham House stairwells. As everythin' goes all hazy and the walls start bendin' man I start to see further than I ever did, somewhere in Australia, a little kiddy's just been born with a hundred bends of light protruding from his third eye like some bare streak of lightnin'. One hundred bends of light, one hundred chances of fate? Lucky little bro. There goes another in New York, not as many bends man but he'll make it to at least forty innit? Fuck man, I can see the whole fuckin' world now and it's sick, bare streaks of lightning blazin' out of all the newborn babies' heads like some fucking massive global 'lectric grid, some of them intertwinin' and connectin', others gettin' involved in the greenz and likes like me but learnin' more than I ever did. Then I see my own innit? Blazin' backwards in time like recorded tunes, just five bends of light in one streak bruv and not much of 'em leavin' the Oval, you get me? Parents can't be chosen so I guess my Dad gettin' put away had nothing to do with me, I guess the first bend man was my school and who I chose as my crew and the stuff I chose to focus on and that. Deep down and honest with ya, I quite liked the English and the arts and stuff bro, but those teachers couldn't control shit, bruv, and so I hung out with Mo and Chris and Dwayne.

The second bend seems to be like after school, innit? My Mum gave me warnins about the geezers about around the Oval y'know, but there ain't no fuckin' jobs outside of Tesco man, I start smoking the greenz with my crew and start networkin' and it's all bare funny for a while. I start sellin' innit? Just a bit, but then geezers start gettin' shanked at parties an' shit, police start showin' up and it ain't fun no more and now we all have to do somethin' 'bout it bruv. Then came the formation of the All 'bout Money Crew man, I try to not get involved and start doin' a BTEC in computer sciences down in Elephant and Castle 'cause if you learn the digital shit you can get into samplin' and music, innit? But the computers are fuckin' bare old man, the teacher's a batty bwoy and the greenz tells me to not get out of bed man. From here on in, the pressure comes on bare real blood, fuckin' cunts jump me twice, one geezer shanks my leg, most of 'em old bruvs from school like 'cause I ain't in the crew and don't want to be in the crew, innit? You get into the crew man, you can't get out, forced to go up the green ladder innit? And then you end up smackin' up your own fuckin' sister for ching and everythin' man. You don't get in the crew, you're fuckin' fish bait blood, on the receivin' end of an initiation rather than the givin', either that or your just one more nigger for the police to bust up, and if you end up on the insides, you're amongst worse. On the TV, that Gordon Brown geez promises to come in and clean the shit up but governments don't care about me and Mo man, no fuckin' way, so I choose the Crew, more protection that way. The third-eye lightin' don't blaze in many directions when you're on the short chord blood, standard.

So I'm dealin' greenz, just a bit like, but soon after, there are more crews man, there's us, one other and there's The One Chance Crew, they're all lookin' to expand innit? And the old stretch of Brixton Road all becomes Gas turf and no place for my crew, problem is my Mum and my sister live 'ere innit? So where am I supposed to go?

The fourth bend in my third eye lightnin' streak man, was probably when I chose to answer my phone, it's that bare simple bruv. Two weeks before they fuckin' murk up my bro Chris, they like nick his phone and shit. I get this simple call, an unknown number likes and I don't know who's on the other side, all they need to get Crew contacts and details innit? Anyway, now our supplier, a white geezer called Paul, who I tink is supplyin' to all three crews but that's my 'pinion, he's well vexxed with us like 'cause now he and his bird are gettin' all this pressure down their phones, and his face is all fuckin' red mist man. He wants to wind 'em up and so he starts sendin' us all back into dealin' in Oval and me and Mo are bare fuckin' local man so we have to do the job innit?

The fifth bend man, that was me deciding to listen to Mo go and deal to this geez on the sixth floor of Pulham House, destined to get murked 'round here man, and that's how we met our blades, blood.

Fuck this blood's sticky now, my head's stuck to the concrete and everything's fucking swaying, London seems to be comin' apart man and I can see through the walls, everythin's like glass bruv, the whole city and the world are like lines man, it reminds me of when I used to get all caked and go down The Kennington and I used to stare through the empty glasses to see how the world went all fucked and made me laugh man, geezers with wide heads and the likes. Fuck, I can see the edges of The Shard man.

I know now that this is it, the big fuckin' 'eavy drop, and I'm getting sad fam, who the fuck are these other geezers, the newborns and that, with longer 'lectric streaks than I have? Why do they get what me and Mo didn't? Weren't our fault we were born and shanked in the Oval, which geezer decides who gets what? Who says that I wasn't worth somethin'? My Mum and sister were good girls man and the weight of them losing me is 'eavy as fuck, they wanted the best for me, I know it now and I want to go back, why didn't my Mum give birth to one of those geezers from Australia or New York who would have lasted longer? I want to build for them a shank-proof, gang-proof apartment on one of those far off places of the world of which I now see for real, places I would never see or understand and now never will, what would it have been like to have some kind of French or Italian buff man? It would've made Mum proud, maybe we could've all lasted longer together on one of those places and my life wouldn't 'ave been so minor. Stop the trip, blood, let me go back.

Suddenly I notice that the blood from my wound is flowing upwards man and it's like, spreading upside down across where that burnt ceiling used to be, as if it were like still solid innit? What the fuck? This is like the kind of shit I used to see when I was lean on crystal behind the bike sheds in school and I start to think that all this would be real sick if I had some real congo nutty at the same time. The blood that seems to be coming back down from this, seems to stop trickling down like halfway in mid air and these little buds and flowers start peelin' open from them and I realise what I've like just created blood, it's like some massive tree innit? A tree growin' and expandin' from my own blood, my wound, my bloodied gateway into death is creatin' something' new.

As it seems these lines and ridges that make up Pulham House and the Oval and London beyond start to become less and less clear, I notice that the sky above is turning to this kind of pink colour and I'm in this new, trippy-as-fuck world and my tree is a fuckin' work of art, blood. It's sort of grown in and out of the invisible surfaces of Pulham House and it's creating all these sick formations, and a bit further up I start to see its branches kind of wrappin' around another that's doing the same ting and I realise this belongs to Mo man as it's a few minutes more developed than mine; no, correction, it don't belong to Mo, it *is* Mo as I see its root stemming from where Mo's chest wound used to be a couple of stairs up from me. Then I look 'round the whole fuckin' estate, and I realise it ain't just us, there are trees everywhere fam, old and new ones, spanning out in all these weird directions, reboundin' off the invisible buildings and the likes, above and below us, fuckin' everywhere, it looks sick man and I tink to myself, there's been bare fuckin' shankin' here man, Oval always was a ghetto you get me? The gear and the upset were always a problem 'round here but now it seems like my bros, those with the shortest third eye 'lectric beams, are forming the rainforests and vegetation of this new, mad world.

Then out of the pink horizons I see these sort-of like human shapes appearing, walking like tourists or whatever to admire the sheer sickness of these Oval blood trees, bruv. It reminded me of when me and Dwayne used to go 'round nickin' ching out the tourists' pockets who used to gather 'bout when The London Eye first opened, you get me?

That's when I realised, innit? That these geezers were the regular dead like, those who had the longer, bendin' lightnin' beams, the ones who had the more options and happiness and shit, that those who had made great, sick tings of themselves in life were basically the standard deal in death man, and it was the tragedies, those who had been shanked up too young who formed the natural wonders of the next world. I then kind of gather likes, that even this next world needs capital cities too innit? Cities with 'istorical monuments and shit that geezers need to see, that's us, that's me and all the crews all over London innit? From Oval to Tottenham, the shanked make up the trees and they look sick compared to the empty turf beyond, our tragedies, not the businessmen, formin' the centrepiece engines of this next capital. And I fam, shanked in the guts to bleed out and leave my people behind at the age of 18 am now one sick fuckin' tree.

# The Hipster Express

In the days leading up to Dhani's 30th birthday I set about a plan to host a pub crawl from Dalston Junction to New Cross on the recently reopened East London Line, now a part of the city's vast overground service. At the time though, the orange line was synonymous with the route through Whitechapel, Shoreditch and the kookier parts of town; receiving the tongue-in-cheek nickname of The Hipster Express.

## Dalston Junction
### Pub: Molly Blooms
### Price of an average beer: £3.00
### Time: 11:20

Our first sensation was how hot it was for the first day of October. Even in my straw hat and vest I could feel the clammy heat radiating from the Kingsland Road. Having advertised the event via several social media channels I was anxious to see if anyone was up for undertaking this boozy safari through the urban jungle.

Fortunately, as soon as Dhani and I turned the corner we were greeted by a welcome party comprising of two old school friends from his home town, Ross and Andy, and the neighbours from his apartment, Peter and Caz. They applauded as we crossed the road to Molly Blooms, a shady looking box-of-a-place where naff, Celtic fonts decorated the outside blackboards to declare the place, somewhat strictly, as a Sports Bar.

"You picked an unbelievable day for this!" cried an excited Caz.

Dhani got straight into conversation as I entered the dark and shadowy bar to get the first of many rounds of drinks.

Dalston, like the East London Line had recently been done up to cater to the Olympics, but this place was still a remnant from the old East London – the old, notorious East London – a community that without much of a former train connection, had been a community left to itself. Sports were playing from an array of TV sets. The clientele were all aged Irish or British men with tattoos, they largely drank alone and didn't speak while *Country and Western* music played from a set of old speakers that stood upon a tiny karaoke stage beside the toilets.

A hard-looking barmaid appeared behind the bar – she was the only woman in this place.

"Whit cannae git fo ya?"

The plan was for a half in each bar but I couldn't help but notice that everyone had a pint in their hand so I thought "fuck it" and bought two ice-cold pints of a very average lager.

When we got outside we were also joined by our mutual friend, Caleb, who was with his Spanish girlfriend, Carmen. Carmen had brought a professional-looking camera and organised everyone for a quick picture. She navigated her way to the opposite side of the road and, in between the occasional passing red bus, took a snap of the intrepid voyagers. Then everyone necked their drinks, we left the old alkies behind and headed for the southern-bound overground platform.

## Maximodo
### Time: 22:30

Every time I meet my old university friends in town I feel I'm privy to some visual evolution of pretentiousness. The bar we meet in has to be trendier, the drinks more expensive and the clientele have to be an ever-expanding strain of overgroomed diabolicals and this place is the case in point. It's a solar system of cunts swirling in orbit and Sebastian is their sun. And Sebastian is always here first. Always.

"Do you see where I'm coming from, though? It's true, isn't it?" He asks.

What's true? Oh fuck, he's asking me a question.

"Urm yeah, totally."

"Totally?! You need to open your ears mate. I bumped into your mate, Ollie, the other day. The guy you brought along last time. The music editor, right?"

"Right."

"He's a cool guy. It seems he's doing really well for himself. I said to him I might write a review for his magazine one day".

Might you Seb? That's fucking fascinating mate (I don't say that to him). Not that he'd listen. With Seb that scattergun brain is already whirring round ready to load the chamber of his mouth with another burst of "enlightenment".

Where's Emma with the drinks? Say something to him. Anything.

"Nice bar." I lie, "Did you choose it?"

"No."

This surprises me. The place is the toast of Deptford and seems to tick all of Seb's boxes. The music volume has been turned to the height of distortion as people compete in whiny, wine-soaked anecdotes. Bankers to the left of me, hipsters to the right. That said, to call Seb a hipster would be a disservice to anyone with a modicum of cultural enterprise. Seb is and has always been a wannabe. Behind the smug veneer is a desperate need to be liked. You can tell he works overtime to research that undercut quiff, the dickhead glasses and truly preposterously named bands – ever heard of Paella Symphonia, Dead Nan or Eclectic Toothbrush? No, me neither, but rest assured if you had, Seb would've immediately hated them and then moved on to the next big thing he's *required* to like. Where the fuck is Emma? "Have you seen my wife?"

### *Haggerston*
### *Pub: Duke of Wellington*
### *Price of an average pint: £4.00*
### *Time: 12:30*

Our second pub could be viewed as we pulled over the immense red-bricked bridge which looked down upon Stonebridge Gardens. The sun beat down on our necks as we strode across the park towards pub number two.

Outside was a welcome party comprising of local friends Kat, Jack and Lulu along with Dhani's mate, Ish, an on-off actor whose face was vaguely familiar from some ad or something. They were all waving from a picnic table outside, visibly drunk already, wearing pink cowboy hats and feather boas.

Ish ran up to give Dhani a welcoming hug. The two tribes merged and eight became twelve.

"How many have you had?" exclaimed Dhani.

Lulu put a spare boa around his neck and kissed him on the cheek.

"We opened a bottle of vodka at 11am."

"Jesus Christ. It's only 12:30. We've got a long way to go."

Ish nudged me, "What you drinkin'?"

"Just a half of lager."

"No worries."

Ish headed into the pub. The noise of a lunchtime Premier League game boomed out of the front door along with occasional screams and shouts from the punters watching inside.

As I sat down I felt a pinching sensation against my arm. I looked down and saw a Facebook thumbs-up icon printed onto my wrist. Jack sat laughing holding an ink stamper.

"What the hell is that?"

"I got it from my office. We've been stamping each other all morning!"

The Haggerston collective burst into tipsy fits of laughter. I didn't share the hilarity but was still very sober at this point. Looking around the table I could see nearly everyone had a thumbs up somewhere on their body; Jack's cheek, Kat's neck, Lulu's chest and right ear. Ish came out carefully carrying four pints bunched together.

"Down these then we gotta leave sharpish."

"Why?"

It's the North London derby today. I got chatting at the bar and started taking the piss out of Spurs. Then I noticed the bird at the bar had a white hart tattoo on the back of her neck when she turned towards the till.

"So what?"

"It's a Spurs pub. She started giving me evils. I think we should go."

And with that the clan downed their nearly full pints and we headed across the park. In the distance we heard a couple of meatheads shouting obscenities from the pub doorway. We jumped back onto the train and headed towards the next meeting point of Hoxton Square.

## Maximodo
### Time: 22:35

I feel a knee bump my leg. There she is.

"Next time why don't you go to the bar. It's fucking ridiculous in here!" Emma exclaims.

She hands me what looks like a miniature coconut.

"I asked for a pint of Becks."

"They don't do pints in here, babe."

Seb snarls patronisingly; "This isn't a fucking Wetherspoon's, John. Just try it. Broaden your mind a little.

I sip it. It tastes a bit like an alcoholic roast dinner. I smile with chagrin.

"I see what you mean."

Seb isn't listening, he's immediately on to Emma.

"Seeing as your husband has no manners I'll introduce myself. I'm Seb."

"Nice to meet you, I'm Ems."

"Yeah, sorry I couldn't make your big day".

He wasn't invited.

"I saw your wedding photos on Facebook. You made a beautiful bride. Did they do something to highlight your cheekbones?"

What the fuck is he talking about now? Emma reacts graciously.

"Do you mean like Photoshop?"

He sighs and gives this long, agonising "Nooooo".

## Hoxton
### Pub: The Red Lion
### Price of an average drink: £5.00
### Time: 13:15

As we left the overground station I felt a text buzz in my pocket:

*We're on the roof!*

I looked up to see a welcome party of roughly 10 more people waving like castaways from the terrace of The Red Lion by Hoxton Square.

We headed into the dusty ground-floor bar of the East End boozer, - a kitchy but empty place of cozy red leather sofas and vinyl records stuck to the wall – clearly the Hipster veneer was already begin to the replace the tougher cockney environs of our previous stops. We picked up some bottles of Corona and began our ascent up four floors of wobbly wooden staircase until we reached the heavenly plane of the beer garden on the roof. The sun reflected off the glass skyscrapers of Bishopsgate a short distance ahead to spotlight our awaiting party.

I didn't recognise all of Dhani's new guests but they were all lined up along three picnic benches that were separated by huge vases of dead plants. I could see more of his old uni mates; Scooby, Nikki, Gem and Rachel. Rachel had brought her new girlfriend with her; a German girl called Greta, who was lounging in the sun. A few other nameless faces were also part of the throng.

"We've ordered pizza for everyone."

As the food came out the chatter got louder. From the view we could awkwardly make out our future road through the city ahead? I looked over to Dhani who was now half-cut. The sun kept beating down and everyone remarked on how lucky he was to have summer weather on the first day of October. He smiled softly,

"It's mum looking down."

Dhani's mum had died of breast cancer almost a year to the day. Arranging the pub crawl was my way of taking his mind of it and may also have contributed to the volume of attendees. If there was a high point to the day this was it. Twenty thirty-somethings overtaking a baking roof at the end of summer; tipsy and blissful.

We should have known it wasn't to last.

### Maximodo
### Time: 22:45

I head to the bar to deposit the coco-roast and ask for something that resembles beer. That's when I see Jasmine in the doorway. She screams dramatically, runs over and hugs me, which draws a few snobbish glances from those waiting to order their equally ridiculous drinks.

"JOHHNNY! How are things?"

"Oh, you know..."

"So good to see you!" She play-punches me in my stomach; something I've always hated.

"I've lit-er-ally come straight out of a meeting." She shouts, despite it being about 11pm on a Saturday night.

"Did you bring Emma along?"

"Yeah, she's over there with Seb." As I gesture towards them I catch a flicker of something in Jasmine's eye.

"Great", she says coolly, "I'll get the drinks. White wine ok?"

I decide wine cannot be wanker-fied so I agree. However, the bottle Jas orders is £45, which she pays without even registering the cost. There was a time we lived on that amount for a week. Sometimes I still do.

By the time we reach Emma and Seb again they have been joined by our mutual friend, Ish who is holding court, as always, along with some other guy. Ish is looking pretty worse for wear but his mate looks utterly, utterly fucked; both have their faces covered in Facebook stamps but this guy's also wearing a fake moustache, a feather boa and on top of the straw-hat-and-vest combo; like 80's Miami gone wrong. He doesn't even seem to be aware of it, he's just standing there and staring like a zombie. Where the fuck have they been?

Ish is doing some sort of impression which is cracking Emma up. Seb is also chuckling but his face returns to impassivity as soon as he sees Jas. Ish stops his routine and grabs us both in a neck lock.

"Alright you old tarts?!"

"Yeah mate! How are you?" Jas beams, "I saw you in that advert on telly".

"Which one?" says Ish, "The car one or the cat food one?"

"The one with you dressed as a lumberjack".

"Yeah. The car one. I got a 25k buy-out on that commercial." He turns to me and winks. "One day's work".

Seb visibly winces at this; "Aren't you doing Shakespeare anymore then?"

Ish breaks into that East End giggle again; "Fuck Shakespeare mate, I'm saving up to buy a pad."

"An ipad?" asks Seb.

"No, you silly twat."


### Shoreditch High Street
**Pub: Bar Kick.**
**Price of an average beer: £3.50 (Bottled beers only)**
**Time: 14:10**


The first argument began as we walked back towards Hoxton Station.

"Why are we walking back there? Shoreditch High Street is the same distance away?" yelled a slurring Jack.

"It's an East London Line pub crawl. We have to do the stops!" I snapped back

"Fuck it I'm walking over to The Old Axe. Pound-in-a-pint-glass strippers. Who's in?"

And with that 2 or 3 of the males walked off with Jack, giggling.

"A strip club? Seriously?" remarked a dejected looking Dhani.

"We'll be back soon." Shouted Ish over his shoulder.

Slightly lighter in numbers we took the 60-second train ride over to Shoreditch High Street Station.

We headed over to our next bar and this was more like it; The Stones, Rod Stewart and Supertramp were blasting out from its front door and inside everything was of a Portuguese, Brazilian style; vintage old advertising signs decorated the walls, flags of the world hung from the ceiling and blew in the breeze of the ceiling fans that cooled the place.

Everything sounded like the insides of a pinball machine as two gorgeous black girls with afros merrily challenged groups of people to the array of football table games; less confident young men merely watched them sadly from the bar.

At the bar we were greeted by a Portuguese waitress in a grass skirt and a barman dressed as a 1920's aircraft pilot. We were definitely in Shoreditch.

It was cocktail hour so we all got Mojitos. Nearby a man, presumably the owner, was noisily banging away with a hammer at the holes in the wooden floor.

"Don't mind me, just carry on and take a seat guys" He said with a Brazilian accent.

And so, we all took seats at canteen-like tables as all kinds of noise went on around us.

The holes in the floor I could assume had been left over from when this place had been a more run-down part of town before this new breed of entrepreneur had bought up the properties and moved in in readiness for the Olympics; again this was typical of London, keep the business going at all costs around whatever repairs are needed, don't let the engine stop for a second whatever you do.

At this point I remember Lulu getting a pack of fake moustaches from out of her handbag. Everyone started putting them on and laughing like schoolgirls. Some were ridiculous Fu Manchu style taches, which Rachel went for. Perhaps stranger though was the one Lulu gave to Peter, certainly the most reserved member of the party. Lulu handed him a grey moustache that exactly matched the colour of his hair, so when he put it on the novelty was immediately lost. He simply looked like a distinguished guy.

"Very handsome." said Caz supportively. Peter began to blush.

We raised a toast to Dhani and took some pictures. I got a text again. It was Ish:

*This strip club is awful. Where to next?*

I text back:

*Whitechapel* xxx

## Maximodo
**Time: 23:05**

The vulgarity has gone on for too long. When did all conversations turn to money?

It's so fucking dull and especially disappointing to hear it from Ish. I used to love going to see him in plays. They were never any good and usually in some dishevelled attic above a pub but I was proud to see him up there, doing what he loved. Emma's trying her best to keep up, I can tell. She gives Jas a kiss.

"Hello beautiful bride!" Jas squeaks before turning round to Seb and simply offering, "Hi, Seb".

Seb nods and heads to the toilets. What a miserable prick.

Ish turns to me with that award-winning cheeky smile.

"This is my mate by the way", he says gesturing to the fucked up guy who came with him. He's introducing him some 20 minutes after all the money talk and the guy's just been incapable of doing it himself during that time.

"Hiya" I say. The guy just looks straight through me.

"You coming with us?" Ish says, gesturing to the bogs.

"Oh, urm, no maybe later" I say, acknowledging his wavelength.

Ish looks a bit disappointed before they head over to catch up with Seb.

To be fair, it's claustrophobic enough in here without the four of us cramming together for a spot of cubicle hoovering. There used to be a bit of bonhomie about it; one of us distracting the soap guy by the basin long enough for the other two to get chopping.

Suddenly Jas breaks my daydream.

"So, what's going on with you? Where you working now?"

"Still at the Council office in Vauxhall", I reply.

"*Still!* Johnny, you need to be moving on Big Bro! You've got so much potential for bigger things. Didn't you want to go into journalism?"

I look over to Emma feeling awkward. And so the self-fulfilling prophecy continues. Reunions should be about picking up where you left off, not undergoing intense scrutiny about the future. I try and appease her.

"I'm looking into it".

"Jon, to be fair, you've been looking into journalism for quite a while now. Why don't you just take a risk for once in your life? Why not come down to the agency one day, I..."

As Jas yammers on about getting me a meeting with someone who knows someone she knows I get a flashback of the nervous girl on fresher's week knocking on my hall door to introduce herself. I was a year older from the gap year and she always called me Big Bro. That was the relationship from day one, totally platonic. I helped her overcome her shyness. I rubbed her back as she cried about Sam, Omar, or whoever had broken her heart that year. I guess I never imagined that Little Sis would grow up to be older and more mature than me.

## Whitechapel
### Pub: Urban Bar
### Price of an average pint: £6.00
### Time: 15:00

The short journey to Whitechapel was fraught with issues. The group had passed the point of being 'happy-drunk' and were slipping into a state of (at best) carelessness and (at worst) aggression. Kat and Lulu had extended their print stamping beyond close friends and were now stamping anyone in close proximity, with mixed results. Some members of the tube carriage moved away from them to avoid being selected. Others looked down at their arms awkwardly to see what these two drunken morons had done to them and looked slightly embarrassed. The tide turned when Lulu accidentally/purposely stamped Greta in the eye. Both her and Rachel confronted the drunken pair and exchanged words. The whole carriage looked on as voices raised and things quickly became heated.

Fortunately, Dhani managed to intervene before it spilled into a full-on brawl. The carriage doors opened and he escorted Kat and Lulu away. I stayed with Greta and Rachel who were still incensed by the incident.

As we stepped onto the platform I remember seeing a barrage of strangers who had clearly come into contact with Kat and Lulu. Some had the Facebook thumbs-up inked into their necks, shirts, legs and, in one case, forehead. Others were peeling fake moustaches off their faces. I was beginning to regret this daytime drinking binge and we were still only halfway. I began to secretly hope that some people would give up on it and go home.

As we walked up the staircase of Whitechapel Overground we were once more greeted by warm afternoon sunlight. As we crossed the bridge over to the main road we were briefly hassled by a rough sleeping couple who'd emerged from a fold-out tent that deliberately blocked people's paths; beer cans and ripped sleeping bags protruded from its door and it was obvious that they were junkies targeting all of the weekend drinkers who might be too intoxicated to watch their wallets, we must've looked like the biggest fish they'd found that day but thankfully nothing was stolen and none of us kicked off back at them. I wondered once again, as I had on many occasions, how people ended up that way?

We were then struck by the smells and sounds of the market stalls, its crowds hustled and bustled past as we headed over to the pelican crossing. Across the road, in between the phone shops, mosques and the ambulance way into the A & E wing of The Royal London Hospital stood the Urban Bar. It's garish tiger-printed outer walls made it stand out and the whole thing seemed slightly distasteful set amongst a community that generally chose not to drink and inside it was actually rather soulless.

Nevertheless, the picnic benches outside were fully populated by our increasingly drunken mob and, lo and behold, the boys were back from the strip club.

"Where've you been?" yelled Jack in his shades "We've already done our drink here."

"You have my permission to get another." I said, hoping Jack would go indoors. He took the bait and headed into the pub. Rachel squeezed my shoulder.

"I'll get you one. What are you having?"

"I'll have a lager."

"Ok. Greta, what you having babe?"

"Fruit cider."

"Sure. I'll be back in a sec."

Greta and I sat on top of the bench in the sun, watching the crowds ebb and flow throughout the market that lined the other side of the road. I could tell Greta was still pissed off. The blue mark from the stamp over her left eyelid had smudged down her cheek, making her look a bit like Mel Gibson did in Braveheart. Her face was red and she looked like she needed to vent.

"You ok, Greta?"

"No. I just don't understand why the British always have to take things too far when they drink. Everyone was fine an hour ago and now they are acting like cunts."

"Some people just can't handle their drink. Especially when it's hot."

"That's just a poor excuse." she sighed "The population of this country has a collective problem with alcohol and refuses to accept it. Particularly in London."

This made me laugh.

"What do you mean?"

"Everyone works stressful or morale-destroying jobs. Their remedy is to get fucking wasted. Rich or poor, everyone does it. Not to mention drugs, sex, whatever. Mass consumption as a coping mechanism. What would happen if the booze stopped flowing in London? I'll tell you - the city would grind to a halt."

"Do you really think it's that bad?"

"I do. I don't think we can even see the tip of the iceberg. Alcohol to London is like the carrot you dangle in front of a donkey to keep it moving forward."

"Interesting theory. Albeit a bit dramatic."

Greta pointed at her ink-stained face; "Am I being dramatic?"

Ish was texting someone in a frantic, distracting way.

"Who're you texting, Ish?"

"Just some old uni mates of mine, they're going out in Deptford later if you fancy it?"

The perfect timing caused Greta's eyes to roll, knowing she'd been right all along.

"What after this?" I ask him, "mate, you'll be wasted before you even reach New Cross!"

With even better timing Rachel then brought out the drinks in a drunken, clumsy way, spilling them over the rim as they clinked onto the table. She handed me a pint of lager and, on looking at Greta's face, stuck out her bottom lip in faux sympathy and planted a kiss on the blue-cheeked side. She raised her glass.

"Cheers folks."

Scooby and company soon bowled out of the venue. It was time to board the train again and head south.

## Maximodo
### Time: 23:15

I'm brought startlingly back into the present moment by a slimy tongue licking the back of my neck. I spin around to see Ish and his fucked up mate laughing their heads off. They're clearly on their way up. Seb keeps sniffing and looking sketchy whilst Ish apprehends Emma, losing sense of volume control.
"I'MSOFUCKINGCHUFFEDFORYOUGUYS!"
Emma takes a step back, clearly aware of Ish's altered state.
"Thanks mate".
"IKNEWWHENIMETYATHATYOUWASASOUNDGIRLANDYOU'REJUSTWHATJOHNNYNE EDSTOCALMHIMDOWN,YOUKNOW!?"
I notice Seb staring at Jasmine, his face gurning slightly. Jasmine, unimpressed, tries not to acknowledge it, taking a large swig of that expensive wine and leaving the glass on a nearby ledge, it's cool condensation leaving a misty line halfway up.
"I'm going for a smoke", she sighs, "Anyone coming?"
"I will." Shouts Em.
The music has definitely got shitter as Seb has started swaying his stupid fringe about.
Ish, now bored of his whacked out mate and missing an earpiece to pour his cascading thoughts into, turns his attention back to me, chewing like a camel.
"Come on mate, liven up! When did you get so fucking uptight?"
"Since he got married!" Seb sniggers before returning to his swaying, bumping into a couple of increasingly pissed off women behind. It seems the drugs have removed his coordination but not his attitude problem. Ish grabs me in another customary headlock and presses his mouth right against my left ear.
"I remember when you were our little Johnny Rotten. Back then there was nothing you wouldn't do. What's happened to him, eh? Where'd Johnny Rotten go?"

## Shadwell
### Pub: The Thomas Neale Free House
### Price of an average pint: £4.00
### Time: 16:45

The first impression you get from Shadwell is that it isn't a drinking hotspot. In fact, when we arrived the main avenue of shuttered up shop fronts and partly dismantled bicycles gave the whole area a feeling of a ghost town, or some silent outpost in a western.
Needless to say, the arrival of a large group of drunken prats did not seem welcome at all. I followed the map on my phone to the nearest pub; The Thomas Neale Free House was sandwiched between a run-down chippy and a William Hill and we pushed open its rickety front doors to be hit by an intense musty smell, similar to a jumble sale.
Looking on, it had the appearance of having been converted from some elongated brickwork tunnel, now decorated with strange, odd-fitting pieces of donated furniture, the wounds upon the array of long leather sofas had been crudely treated with duct tape, a stag's head sat next to it having seemingly awaited for years for somebody to screw it onto the wall and it all culminated in an enormous industrial, horror-movie-like fireplace at the far end. A grey Staffordshire Bull with piercing blue eyes paced about the place, its lead dragging behind it.

From the bar itself, the barman and three old men turned and looked at us as clearly unwanted guests.

Caz turned to shush those behind her as if we were entering a library and it enveloped the room, The Hipster Express was clearly taking a very non-hipster break.

As we approached the bar the locals looked even more perplexed. It was if a time machine filled with young professionals had landed in 1970's East London, and at one of its weirder corners at that.

"What do you want?" said the barman gruffly.

Dhani hesitated, "Um...guys what do we want?"

"Just get shots. We're not staying for a pint in here" whispered a clearly uncomfortable Carmen.

The fat man at the bar was staring at Caz.

"Do you like my dog?" he grinned with orange teeth.

The dog paced over and looked up for acknowledgement.

"Yes. He's very nice." said Caz politely.

"He's a guard dog" said the man.

"You mean like security?"

"No, I mean I guard the dog. I don't let anybody fuck with it".

Dhani took the attention away from Caz by weighing up the options for the drinks order.

"Can we get twenty-one shots of tequila."

The barman looked around the bar slightly lost.

"I think I've got some tequila but I don't have shot glasses. Can I just put them in normal glasses?"

In the interest in moving things along and getting out of the pub Dhani agreed. The barman found a dusty bottle of what seemed like a house version of tequila and proceeded to pour, without measurement, generous portions of a foul-smelling spirit into 11 wine glasses, 6 half pint glasses, 3 pint glasses and a broken mug with Charles and Diana on it. We decided not to ask for salt and lemon.

"Ok guys. Bottoms up."

The men and the dog watched us drink the weird stuff and waited for some sign of approval. We all gave a polite nod to pretend our insides weren't collapsing and then thanked them and left. As soon as we reached the fresh air outside Kat vomited on the pavement. It was 3.30pm and we still hadn't crossed the Thames.

## *Maximodo*
### *Time: 23:40*

Seb has bumped into the women one too many times and is now the proud owner of a wet T-shirt and two angry fingers pointing at his face. He tries to placate the ladies with a drowsy, middle-class; "Oh fuuuuck ooooff."

As the women storm past us, Ish opens up the palm of his hand to reveal a wrap neatly folded into a miniature envelope.

"Come on, while the cat's away..."

I look down at the gear and remember the good times. The spontaneous three-day wipeouts. The laughter. The 7am tube home looking like death as we fell asleep on the commuters' shoulders. I never thought the commuter would eventually be me.

"No, Ish. Not anymore mate".

"Come on, John, I need you to distract the aftershave guy. No Armani, no poonani! No spray, no lay! Talk to him about Arsenal. Then you can have a bit of mine."

I suppose I could. I know Emma wouldn't really mind but I've got a presentation to do on Monday.

Ish stares at me for a few heartbreaking seconds. That ten-mile smile has given away to childish disappointment.

"Suit yourself" And with that he heads back into the gents with that weird mate of his for a round two. Jesus that other guy is done for, surely?

## Wapping
**Pub: The Captain Kidd**
**Price of an average pint: £3.50**
**Time: 17:30**

By the time we approached the next station everyone had reached the same level of hedonistic hysteria. As we pulled into the platform Ish nudged me.

"I used to work round here doing corporate videos for a news agency. Some of the pubs allow lock-ins for the journalists who finish work late. I could pull a few strings. Fancy it?"

"No. We have to complete the pub crawl in New Cross. There are people meeting us there."

Ish smiled "No worries. By the way; have you heard the pornographic train announcement?"

I looked puzzled. "No what's that?"

"Well, I think the pre-recorded female voice on this line sounds really sexy and, on my commutes, I'd fantasise and try and visualise her speaking to me. When she says 'This is Wapping' I always imagined she was talking about...you know..."

"No what?"

"My dick. As in - This is *whopping*!"

"What?"

"Shhh...just listen..."

Ish pointed up at the announcement speaker and like clockwork a well-spoken English female voice announced:

*This... is Wapping.*

Ish gave a sexy trill and burst out laughing. I have to admit it did sound a bit sexy in a weird way. I certainly couldn't unhear it.

Our merry band all jumped into the lift and headed up to street level. We walked along the quaint cobbled streets towards The Captain Kidd. Half the team went in to get the drinks whilst the others went straight to the riverside beer garden to colonise it.

We ordered several more pints and some bottles of white wine and headed back out into the October heat. The troop had done a sterling job of taking up three tables right next to the river. Other members of the party were sitting on the zigzagging staircase adjacent. The beer garden was packed with Londoners squeezing the very last out of the Indian Summer and spirits were back to 100%. Everyone was laughing and joking, except for Kat and Lulu who had tagged out and gone home, thus ending the scourge of the print stamper, boas and moustaches.

The Thames tide was incredibly high and was sloshing right up to the concrete wall we were all leaning against. Ross and Andy laughed and said jokingly to Ish that it was hot enough for everyone to go for a swim.

"Come on then." Ish said dryly.

"No way!" he shouted

"Why not?" he said.

"Are you being serious?" said Andy.

Scooby's ears pricked up and he turned and started filming the debate on his phone. He began egging them on behind the camera.

"Yes boys. We have a swimming race! You see that cabin on that jetty over there?"

Everyone looked over to the bobbing shack about 25 metres from the pub. Scooby continued.

"Let's make it interesting. First to the jetty gets £100."

Ish stared into Ross' eyes; "Deal"

Ross suddenly looked hesitant. His focus kept switching between the river, Ish and Scooby's camera. By this point a crowd had gathered and other drinkers were filming too. Ross turned to Dhani.

"I'm not from London. Can you actually swim in this part of the river?"

"No!" shouted Dhani "No one swims in the Thames".

"It looks fine to me." said Ish "Quite placid."

"What's the matter, Ross?" exclaimed Scooby "You puss puss?"

Ross looked at Scooby angrily and then back at the river. Andy put his hand on Ross' shoulder.

"Seriously, Ross. You don't have to."

"Yes definitely don't!" agreed Dhani "I'm asking you not to."

Scooby interjected "Let's make it £150. Anyone want to raise the prize pot?"

Suddenly random punters started reaching for their wallets and purses.

"I'll put a tenner in!"

"I'll put in a fiver!"

Ish kept staring at Ross. Scooby cranked up the hype.

"What's the matter, Ross? You puss puss?"

Ross took one last look at the river and the cabin on the jetty and then started to take his things out of his pockets, laying his wallet and phone on the side of the concrete wall. A huge cheer went up in the courtyard.

"Game on!" shouted Scooby.

Ish finished a text to his *other* mates before pulling his T-shirt up over his head and taking off his jeans. He placed his trainers on the wall. People started clapping and whistling as the athletic-looking men disrobed.

I looked up on the stairwell and everyone was smiling except for Peter, he looked distraught. I headed upstairs only for Caz to come down and meet me halfway.

"You have to stop them from doing this. Pete's brother drowned when he was younger. Please tell them to stop."

Suddenly my drunken abandon was replaced with a heavy, nagging anxiety. I pushed back through the baying crowd as the two men in boxer shorts waved like gladiators and turned to face the river. Like an Olympic swimming event a hush enveloped and Scooby began the count down.

"Gentlemen. On your marks..."

Ish and Ross looked at each other for assurance.

"Set...."

They squatted into the diving position. The sun glistened on the top of the water invitingly. Scooby took a deep breath and prepared to shout. But from out of the blue at the back of the crowd there was a huge, bellowing yell -
"STOP! STOP THAT RIGHT NOW!"
Ish and Ross looked behind them. The crowd of assorted London drinkers began to part and from amongst them emerged a small, cockney woman. It was the landlady.
"Get down from that wall NOW. Don't you even THINK about jumping in there."
The crowds began to dissipate like scolded schoolchildren and returned to their anonymous drinking circles. Scooby walked off to the bar. Ish and Ross clambered down and hastily began putting their clothes back on. The landlady continued shouting and pointing at them.
"Do you know how many people die in that river each year? Do you want me to lose my fucking licence?"
Ish and Ross stared at the ground.
"That's the problem with you city types" continued the landlady "You get a few pints in you, think you're invincible and just can't imagine the worst thing happening to you. Well, let me tell you something, last summer it did. Some guy was sat on that wall. He fell backwards into the water, smashed his head and now the poor fucker is in a coma."
"Sorry." whispered Ish.
The landlord softened her tone.
"Now look. Enjoy the sun, drink sensibly and stop fuckin' about."
And with that she turned and went back into the pub. Dhani turned to the solemn party guests,
"Shall we move on?"
The group agreed and we all quietly left. Peter and Caz made their excuses and headed home.

## Maximodo
### Time: 23:50

Seb is now fanning his T-shirt to get the projectile Prosecco to dry without much luck. For a moment I stop to take in just how pathetic he looks then go to assist.
"New shirt?"
"Yes" he snaps, "fucking shit bar anyway. I'm going to leave soon."
"Well, wait for the others to get back and..."
Seb looks even more agitated. Some people really shouldn't do drugs.
"That's another thing. Who the fuck invited Jasmine? Don't leave me alone with her, ok?"

By our third year at Uni, Sebastian and Jasmine had fallen very much in love. In fact they stayed living together after we'd all graduated. Occasionally I'd bump into them on random nights but for a few years they drifted off my radar. I heard from Ish that they'd got engaged and sure enough, a few months later, I got a Save the Date card in the post. But the wedding never happened.
Shortly after Jasmine and I got back in touch but whenever I tried to broach the subject she'd always get a bit tearful and defensive. As for Seb; he just pretends that the whole thing never happened. Until he's high.
"She's a fucking...fucking martyr, Jon".
The next thing I know two stocky doormen are bounding past us towards the toilet doors. Seb and I give each other a subliminal knowing look. For a few moments, all we hear from

the gents is some knocking and muffled shouting but soon enough the doors explode open with Ish being pushed like a steam train through the bar, driven by the two Soviet skullcrushers. I manage to get close to Ish as the fella flies past. He goes to shake my hand. "Nice seeing you again Johnny Boy."

As our palms clasp, I feel him slip me the wrap before he is wrenched outside, past a confused looking Emma and Jasmine.

### *Rotherhithe*
### *Pub: The Mayflower*
### *Price of an average pint: £4.50*
### *Time: 19:00*

A short trip under the Thames brought us to Rotherhithe. We headed behind the station to find The Mayflower, another traditional London pub with views of the river.

En route Dhani let Carmen take a photograph of him outside the Brunel Museum with his university mates to recognise the man their university was named after. It was a nice moment amidst the madness.

We all headed through the dark oak doors of The Mayflower, along the candlelit main bar which looked straight out of a Shakespeare play and onto the wooden terrace. It was dusk and a beautiful sunset gave the river a luminescent red glow – candle light by a river at sunset, it was beautiful but I feared that with the pub's seating arrangements resembling cozy booths, the atmosphere might become a little too relaxed and people might have decided to stay here.

As we searched for some seats Gem spotted a mossy green staircase that led down to the riverbank. She looked over to me and whispered; "Hey! Come down here."

The rest of the group were still drunkenly debating drinks orders and organising tables so I followed her down the steps to a makeshift London beach of shingle, red bricks and the rusty chains of history.

As I walked around the oak pillars beneath the terrace I felt two hands on my shoulders spin me around. Without warning Gem planted a passionate kiss on my face.

For a moment I let it happen before pushing her away.

"What's wrong?"

"Nothing." I said. "I just don't really know you. We've been drinking.."

"So?" smiled Gemma.

"It's just...I'm after someone else.."

A look of acknowledgement washed over Gemma's face.

"Dhani? Oh my god. Really?"

"Shhhh" I said

Gemma burst out laughing.

"That's hilarious. I thought you guys were just…"

"We are. Look, it's really complicated. I'm just trying to figure stuff out you know. And it's Dhani's day. I want him to have fun."

"That's ok, babe. Can I ask a question though?"

"Sure."

"Do you like girls too?"

Gemma ran her fingers through the back of my hair and delicately over the top of my right ear, giving me tingles. I looked into her glazed but happy eyes.

"Sometimes."

"Lucky me!" she said and placed her hand over the front of my jeans. For a while we kissed and stayed down under the terrace as the sun went down.

Our intimacy was disturbed by a commotion on the terrace above. I could make out someone screaming and shouting in Spanish. I looked at Gem.

"It's Carmen! Let's see what's happening."

We were met at the top of the staircase by a distraught looking Callum.

"Carmen is leaving."

"Why?"

"What did you tell your schoolmates about her? Ross and Andy?"

I hesitated. I remembered mentioning to them that she had a fiery temper and was quite rough with Callum in public but joked it was just because she was from Spain.

"Nothing. Why?"

"We were talking to them and Andy asked Carmen if it was true that she beats me up but makes up for it in bed. Where would they have got that from?"

I could see how the drunken Chinese whispers had happened but didn't want to add to his humiliation.

"Look Callum. I don't know what you're talking about. Go and find Carmen and sort it out."

Callum turned and headed back through the pub. Gem and I found the rest of the group and I collared Ross and Andy.

"What was that all about?"

Andy put up his hands defensively "Look. We hardly said a thing! We were just joking about her being a fiery Spaniard and she went berserk, calling me a fucking racist. She threw a drink in my face. She's a fucking nutter!"

I was reminded of the conversation I'd had back in Whitechapel with Greta; Londoners mixed with too much drink. I looked over towards Dhani. He looked pale, queasy and was standing by a bin in case he threw up.

I needed to rescue the pub crawl. I placed two fingers to my lips and whistled loudly.

"Guys! Listen up. We have three stops to the finish line. Keep your shit together, we can do this!"

The drunks all cheered as if I'd delivered a quote from Henry V. We piled back out onto the street. Carmen was throwing punches at Callum. Gem ran in to break it up and caught one in the jaw for her troubles. Carmen turned to the crowd.

"You are all pieces of shit!"

She turned and strode to the station with her arms folded. Gem and Callum tended to their injuries.

"You ok guys?"

"I'm good" said Gem; "Callum, what's the deal with your girlfriend mate?"

Callum was quiet.

"I'd better go after her. Sorry Dhani, enjoy the rest of the evening."

And with that he headed over to Rotherhithe station.

I lit a cigarette. Dhani shook his head.

"Poor guy. That is not a healthy relationship. She has issues."

Ish put his arm round Dhani's shoulder.

"Yeah. But we've got her camera."

He dangled the expensive camera in front of Dhani.

"She left it behind by mistake. We'll keep it safe for her but might as well keep documenting the evening."

Everyone lined up for another posterity photograph and headed for the station.

## Maximodo
### Time: 00:00

Seb is laughing uncontrollably now at Ish's forced exile and is clearly worse for wear. The girls push back into the bar towards us.
"Should we follow him?" says Emma a bit put out.
"No, Ish'll just do the same thing in the next place" offers Jasmine.

## Canada Water

We couldn't find a pub in Canada Water.

## Maximodo
### Time: 00:05

I notice Seb is still swaying into people and I can sense that the evening's going to get worse. Emma looks worried and Jasmine is giving him evil looks so I try to distract her.
"How does it feel to be a big city player now?" I say, cringing at the sentiment.
"To be homest babe, it's overrated". She shouts over the increasingly awful music. "I'm actually thinking of jacking it in."
"Why? For what?"
"What?"
"To do what?"
"Stand Up Comedy"
Even Emma sniggers at this. Maybe I misheard her.
"Did you say Stand Up Comedy?"
"Yeah".
"But I've never heard you tell a joke in your life".
Jas for some reason seems hurt by this.
"But it's what I've always wanted to do. I'm going to take a few months out and take a course in it."
"But you've got a great job".
The shit music's thumping now and my words are getting lost in the din. I strain my vocal chords to get through to Jasmine.
"Aren't you happy?" I shout.
"What?" Jasmine mouths.
"Aren't you happy?!"
Seb's swaying worse than before and once again he's becoming a nuisance.
Jasmine goes over to try and steady him but I can see the doormen staring over at us from the door. I grab Emma's hand.
"Let's go to the bar, eh?" I say pleadingly. Emma nods and I drag her away. Jasmine and Seb are now muttering aggressively to each other. I order two bottles of mineral water and try to keep a low profile.
"That's £8.40" says an impassive barman. I feel like spitting in the guy's face but begrudgingly hand over a ten-pound note. He slides my miniscule change back on a small silver plate.

**_Surrey Quays_**
**_Pub: The Surrey Docks_**
**_Price of an average pint: £3.00_**
**_Time: 20:20_**

Our penultimate pub was nothing much more than a pit stop. We reverted back to half pints and stood outside the Wetherspoons watching the traffic chug past as some had taken a detour to the line of takeaway pizza and chicken outlets that line the opposite side of the road. My phone buzzed again:

_Hey, it's Daisy! Dhani has a huge welcome party waiting for him at The Amersham. How long will you be?_

I looked around and couldn't find Dhani anywhere. I hurriedly text back:

_Not long. 20 mins tops._

I headed into the gents and heard someone throwing up. It was Dhani curled up around the toilet bowl.
"Hey, hey Dhani. Come on man hold it together."
"I just want to go home. I don't like this anymore."
"Dhani, it's your birthday. You're not going home now. We have one stop to go!"
"Who gives a fuck! What is your fixation with this pub crawl? Couldn't we have just gone to a restaurant?"
Dhani leant back towards the bowl and continued puking. I could feel my phone buzzing again.
"Ok, Dhani, look. Let's go outside and get some fresh air. We'll get back on the train and if you don't want a drink at the last place that's fine. Come on buddy, stand up."
I helped Dhani up onto his feet. He locked his wrists behind my neck and hung his head on my shoulder. For a moment I just held him there. Suddenly Jack entered the toilets.
"Am I disturbing something?"
"No mate" I laughed. "I just need your help getting him outside. Come on."
We carried Dhani back through the pub where the usual Wetherspoons clan gave us looks as if this wasn't the place for such drunken behaviour. We got him outside with his arms around our shoulders and headed straight for the crossing to Surrey Quays Station.
"Come on!" I shouted back "We have to get him to New Cross before it's too late!"

**_Maximodo_**
**_Time: 00.13_**

"Babe, I think you need to have a word with those two" whispers Emma to me as she points over to Jas and Seb.
The conversation has now turned into a shouting contest and Seb is pushing his forehead aggressively into Jasmine's. The trendy folk nearby have stopped their idle banter and have encircled them like a playground fight.
Jasmine pushes Seb backwards and he wobbles slightly, grabbing her wrists. The doormen suddenly snap into action and surge back through the crowds towards them like Great Whites in for the kill.

Jasmine, unaware of the circus surrounding her stands transfixed with Seb. Emma is shouting something in my ear as the muscles close in on the scene. Seb whispers something to Jasmine, his eyes wide and wired and as the Soviets' giant hands reached around both their shoulders they launch into the most incredible kiss.

As the doormen prise them apart, I notice Ish's fucked up mate just behind them seems to fall forward face-first and smash onto the bar floor. He looks peaceful at first but then begins a series of convulsions.

"What's happening, Johnny?" screams a frantic Emma. I don't answer but simply draw back on some overpriced mineral water.

The crowd looks shocked as the guy is seizing up badly and fitting. Distressed punters shuffle back at the awful sight as two more door staff run on to the scene and try to lift him up.

"Do something, Johnny!" I hear Emma shout as the doormen pick him up by his hands and feet. I run over to them instantly.

"No, leave him. He'll be fine. You just need to leave him for a second;" I plead but the largest of the doormen pushes me away with a cursory palm.

"He cannot die here. Not this bar." Shouts the doorman as they struggle to carry this poor twisting, turning guy outside.

### New Cross
*Pub: The Amersham Arms*
*Price of an average pint: £4.95*
*Time: 21:15*

There was an unmistakable sense of victory as the London Overground rattled into New Cross Station. I looked around at the survivors - Nikki, Gem, Ross, Andy, Jack, Greta, Rachel, Ish and Scooby, plus me and Dhani. It was a respectable contingent from where we started. Our band of boozers spotted the lit up red letters of The Amersham Arms rising from the bridge above the platform, some of them were missing, naturally. We stumbled towards our final destination.

Just to the left of the main entrance was a makeshift beer garden behind graffiti-strewn and chipped walls. Tucked away there was our welcome party consisting of 12 of Dhani's workmates who had finished their shift and come to meet us at the end of the line.

As we turned into the beer garden we all got a standing ovation. Camera flashes went off and we all raised our arms in victory. We had conquered our East London Everest.

The contrast between us and the new arrivals was quite clear; they all looked and smelt immaculate, ready for a night out whilst we looked and smelt... like shit.

I stepped inside and ordered my climactic pint, realising that nobody'd come in with me – I'm actually alone for perhaps the first time on the crawl. The place is dark and quiet with tables dimly lit by candles and it dawns on me just how fucked I really am so I figure that keeping our crowd outside might be better for both for me and for morale.

Amidst the silence of the place, I see a young Italian woman negotiating with some dodgy-looking landlord, she hands him a wad of cash as a deposit and he gives her a set of keys.

"Alright, now that you've paid up, your friend can move on Tuesday".

As she nervously shakes his hand, he grips it slightly in a suspicious way as if he might've leant in and kissed it.

"Now, can I get you a beer or somefin' darlin'?"

"No" she says up front before standing and turning.

"Welcome to London" I whisper to myself. I then turned and left for outside.

We tucked ourself in around the picnic benches and two of the freshers handed around some Jägerbombs.

"Happy Birthday, Dhani!" they shouted "Here's to a great night."

Everyone downed their drinks and started chatting. I noticed that Ish looked absolutely fucked and was eyeing up one of the new girls, Daisy; a rock chick with a half-shaven head and piercings. Daisy was very much in love with another of Dhani's workmates; a guy known as Hellraiser Dave. Hellraiser Dave was an interesting character, he got his name not only because he was a big fan of the Clive Barker horror franchise but also because he was said to be the suspect behind the Old Kent Road-Hellraiser-VHS-Bus-Stop mystery; a strange story known by Londoners of the time in which a mysterious VHS copy of the film would appear over and over again above an Old Kent Road Bus Stop regardless of the Council's constant attempts to remove it. Hellraiser Dave would always deny any knowledge however. Anyway, as Daisy and Dave minded their own business Ish kept looking over.

"Hey. Psssst." he said to Daisy

Daisy looked around cooly.

"Yes?"

Ish smiled "What you up to?"

"I'm talking to my boyfriend, is that ok with you?"

Ish looked past Daisy towards Hellraiser Dave and raised an eyebrow.

"He's your boyfriend?"

"Yes." said an increasingly irritated Daisy.

"He looks like Phil Mitchell. How did he manage to get a girl like you?" said Ish, without any internal monologue.

"Maybe he knows how to speak to women." smiled Daisy.

This interaction completely went over Ish's head. He shouted over to Hellraiser Dave,

"Hey mate! You're punching above your weight there!"

Instead of rising to the provocation, Hellraiser Dave simply nodded and said "Thanks" before giving Daisy a kiss on the cheek.

With nowhere else for the conversation to go, Ish looked around the table like a lost dog.

Meanwhile, Scooby had collared me.

"You see the guys at the end of the table?"

I looked over and saw several of Dhani's workmates chopping coke quietly on the picnic bench. One girl was licking the side of her cigarette, dipping it in and lighting up.

"Blatant or what?" laughed Scooby.

I looked around for CCTV cameras. To be fair there was no chance any of this was being picked up.

"Want to get involved?" said Scooby excitedly.

I didn't apply much thought to the decision.

"Yes mate. Just keep it on the down low with Dhani, ok?"

We sat down with a load of Dhani's more experimental friends. Scooby broke the ice.

"Can we buy some?"

An overdressed guy called Tony looked up briefly before resuming his chopping motion on the table.

"What you after?"

"Either coke or mandy?"

Tony shook his head.

"We've put the rest of the mandy in our Jack and Cokes before heading out. Have a sip if you like."

He passed over a glass of dusted mixer, which me and Scooby took a sip of. Tony's friend looked over.

"I've got some ket if you want?"

Scooby gave me a cheeky look, "You want to split a gram?"

I hesitated "I haven't done ketamine."

"I have. It's fine to be honest."

"Fuck it. Just don't tell Dhani yeah?"

We sorted out a gram with Tony's mate and I headed into the bar with Nikki to get a pint. Outside the main entrance I was met by a large doorman. He turned to Nikki.

"ID please."

"Oh sure." she fumbled in her purse and brought out her driving licence. The doorman took a look and nodded her in.

"Do you need mine?" I said to him.

The doorman gave a wry smile "No mate. You look about 40. In you go."

I headed into the gent's toilet cubicle and spilled a large line onto the top of the toilet roll dispenser. I could hear people waiting to use the bog and began to feel paranoid, so I flushed the toilet and snorted the gear with a rolled-up bar receipt. I brushed myself down and headed back outside.

I felt rainfall on my face. Without warning Ish grabbed the wrap out of my hand.

"Come on, we're going for a walk."

"Where?" I said sniffing

"I've had a text from my uni mates again. They're all in some place up the road. I said I'd meet them. Fancy it?"

"Where's Dhani?"

"He's all good. He'll meet us there. Come on we've got to go now or we'll get soaked."

And with that we headed out onto the street. I looked over to Scooby, Nikki and Gem; they were all clearly wired and having a giggly 100mph conversation with the new people. I felt another pang of anxiety about Dhani and looked around for him, but the rain started pummelling down and me and Ish headed up the New Cross Road alone to find this club.

## Maximodo
### Time: 00.15

I follow them outside with Emma as we move out onto the rain-pounded street. The doormen mutter something to each other in Lithuanian before throwing the guy into a pile of bin liners a few yards from the bar. Jasmine runs up to me and starts pulling at my arm.

"What did they take, Johnny? What the fuck did they take?" she yells. Emma grabs her and tries to calm her down as the doormen quickly hustle back inside.

As a siren blares in the background I watch as an ambulance hurtles down the road straight past us and on to another destination. I walk over to the bins where this lad is now lying on his back like a sleeping cat. Revellers walk past us as if nothing has happened. As far as they're concerned nothing has happened. London life has not stopped for a millisecond.

We walked for what felt like a lifetime. My speed of thought was beginning to narrow down. Even the rain seemed to fall in slow motion. I walked past a Rastafarian rough sleeper who pointed up at the sky.

"It's Jah's tears, brother. Hahaha! Jah's tears!"

I stared at the guy and tried to focus on what he was saying. Ish patted my cheek.

"Come on! Snap out of it or we ain't getting in."

"I'm...fine." I mumbled.

"You don't look fine. You're chewing your face off."

My eyeballs rotated slowly towards Ish as he said this. What the fuck was happening? Where was Dhani?

"Jah's tears, brother!" the rough sleeper kept shouting behind us.

We got to the club and Ish managed to do his thing and get me in – it was called Maxi-something. I could hear a thumping bass coming from the basement downstairs and we made our descent towards it. We entered the packed dance floor.

The bar itself was a huge, multi-storey place, like an amphitheatre with dizzy revellers waving from every balcony. Ish saw his mates by the bar and dragged me over to meet them. I was still finding it hard to concentrate and feeling really hot and sweaty. Ish placed a cold bottle of water in my hand.

"Drink this, alright?"

"I'm fine, Ish. I just feel tired."

"No mate. You need to stay awake. Let's do another line."

"Where's Dhani? I want Dhani."

Ish looked around and started rabbiting on to his other friends. I felt anxious and alone. A huge wave of drowsiness crashed over me again. I needed to go somewhere quiet and rest. I stumbled into the toilets and found a cubicle, placing the top lid of the toilet seat down and rested on it. The background noise began to fade and I drifted off to sleep.

I was woken by a banging sound. Someone was rattling the cubicle door.

"Ay....Ay.... hello?"

I had no idea if I'd been asleep for 5 minutes or 5 hours. The banging continued.

"Ay....open the door!"

I stumbled to my feet and unlocked the cubicle. An African toilet attendant was in the doorway.

"Listen brother, you can't sleep here, ok? You need to go."

I'm not sure if I answered him and shuffled past back towards the dance floor. The room was still packed so I tried to prop myself against the bar. My rolling eyes looked over to the dancefloor. A couple were arguing loudly and pointing at each other. The doorman were trying to intervene.

At this point the rush of drowsiness came back and I could sense my body shutting down. I felt my body lean forward and without putting my hands out to stop the fall landed on my face. I felt an explosion of pain before blacking out.

I could hear distant voices shouting;

"He's fitting."

"What's happening, Johnny?"

"Do something, Johnny"
Who was Johnny? Was the only thought my head could comprehend – it didn't matter.
"Don't touch him."
"No! Pick him up and take him outside."
I could feel people lifting my body up from the floor and carrying me upstairs.
"What should we do?"
"Drop him ten feet away and call an ambulance. He can't die on these premises."
"He cannot die here. Not this bar!" He says but to whatever company I'd been with.
I felt the two-people holding my arms and legs rock me back and forth to build up momentum before throwing me into the air. I could sense the feeling of flying before being nestled in what felt like crunchy, wet pillows. I was still unable to see so just listened to the sounds around me. I could hear the rain on the ground but couldn't feel it, I also heard some strange laughter.
"Look at that cunt in the bin liners!"
"Leave him alone. Has anyone called for an ambulance?"
"Check he's breathing."

## Maximodo
### Time: 00:16

I kneel down close to his peaceful body and arch my ear towards his mouth – his stick-on moustache has become lopsided and he looks ridiculous. I notice that about a yard away is a homeless guy beneath a cashpoint. He is the only one to register the event in any way. He offers me a smile.
"That lad's been doing acid!" he shouts in a cracked West Country accent.
I listen to his breath gently return to normal. As he opens his eyes Jasmine and Emma run over and stand behind me. He begins to murmur.
"Why am I out here?"
"Because you're fucked" I tell him.
"Did we complete the Hipster Express?"
I look back through the open door at the environment I'd just spent the last hour or so in.
"I'd say so mate, yes".

## Maximodo
### Time: 00:17

As my vision returned I could see faces from the day staring down at me. A man I didn't recognise was kneeling next to me.
He knelt down close to me and arched his ear towards my mouth. A homeless man in a nearby doorway started shouting over, "That lad's been doing acid!"
My breath returned to normal. I began to murmur,
"Why am I out here?"
"Because your fucked." said someone .
Had we completed The Hipster Express? I thought to myself.
I reached down inside the back of my jeans and leant towards his ear.
"I've done a shit."
Keeping his voice low he whispered back.
"Is it dry or wet?"

There was a silent, confused pause before I fixed him with a gaze and said,
"It's dry."
"Ok, well just pull it out and drop it behind you. No one will know. Ok?"
I nodded slowly and did so.

## Maximodo
### Time: 00:17

This guy tells me that he's shat himself and starts pulling lumps out from behind him – I cringe.
We hear shouting from up the street. An Asian guy runs over and kneels next to this shitting man and shouts up to us.
"What happened?"
Emma puts her arms up defensively; "We hardly know the guy".
The man starts stroking the shitting man's hair and looks really shaken up.
"Will he be ok?
"Yeah, he just needs to rest" says Seb, who appears behind us, smoking.
Emma snaps at Seb astounded; "He needs to go to A&E!"
"He's fine" Seb retorts walking off "It's Saturday night. If you go to hospital you'll be sat there waiting until morning to be seen. Take him home."
As Ish's fucked up mate is pulled up onto his feet by his friend I can see the colour return to his face. Sheepishly, he walks a few yards ahead straight past the doormen who are now laughing at a picture on one of their mobile phones. We watch as his friend walks him back up the road and into obscurity.

## Maximodo
### Time: 00:18

Suddenly I heard Dhani shouting from up the street. He ran over and knelt down to join me.
"Are you ok?"
I stared at Dhani and started to cry.
"Yes. But I want to go home."
Dhani looked around at the onlookers "I'm taking him back to his flat."
Someone shouted "He needs to go to A&E!"
"He's fine." Shouted a guy who was smoking. "It's Saturday night. If you go to hospital you'll be sat there waiting until morning to be seen. Take him home."
As Dhani pulled me up onto my feet and put his arm around me. I tried to think of something to say as we walked home but felt too embarrassed to speak.

## Maximodo
### Time: 00:18

Jasmine calls back to Seb.
"Seb, wait up".
Jasmine grabs us in a hug and kisses us both on the cheeks.
"So good to see you both. Give me a ring soon yeah."

### New Cross Road
*Time: 00:35*

Dhani broke the silence.
"Hey. Adrian."
I looked up.
"Thanks for everything today"
I cracked a broken smile.
"Was it… what you wanted?"
"Sure," he said "But next year just take me to the zoo or something yeah?"
With each stop my memories paused and rewound like a broken cassette tape on an eternal, blurry loop.

### Night Bus
*Time: 00:35*

Emma leans her head into my shoulder.
"Do you even like those guys?" she offers, sheepishly.
"Yeah" I say, watching the people's apartment windows sweep by in the night; "They're ok".
"What do you like about them?" she says, looking up, trying to catch my eye-line in the window's reflection. I reach down into my pocket and feel the miniature envelope with the tips of my fingers before looking back at her and smiling.
"They haven't changed".

# Meat

My dear friend, Vaguely Written Vivien (*real name Vivien Lewis*) had earned his nickname from his baffling inability to explain all things important without the necessary depth or clarity that most people would otherwise have deemed imperative, despite the fact that his very charming persona had often led him to be appointed several organisational roles that were in need of clear and concise instructions.

The problem with this quirk of his, in regards to our social circle that is, was that when any of us came up with a genuinely interesting idea, he would bring forth so many exaggerations to the scenario that he would psyche everyone up further and further to the point that we'd all fall for the belief that he should be the natural chosen person to pull off its realisation; this was a mistake, for without so much of a hint at the logistics to such plans of his, they would only ever end in two possible outcomes.

An example of the first of these outcomes for instance, was when a very simple plan for a boys' night out to eat the hottest curry on Brick Lane, had once been boosted up so much to the point that Vivien suggested;

"If we were to go eat a curry *that* good, then we might had well make it a serious travelling event and venture out for a two-week trip to India itself."

It was an extension that was so rock and roll, so *Indiana Jones* and so interesting of course that nobody could say "no" without the fear of looking like a boring twat, yet, only after appointing Vaguely Written Vivien the role of planning this particular venture over the course of the following year, we never even got around to buying the train ticket to Heathrow.

The second outcome would be that after weeks of no clear decisions whatsoever, everything would just kind of pull itself together with hideous amounts of stress and money at the last minute, such as the time when he just invited us to turn up at one of his work parties with no explanation other than the address. After three months then, after we had turned up at its doorstep in our typical casual wear, he then chose to inform us that this was in fact a bash thrown in the memory of his company's much loved late manager and that, although it was all meant in high spirits, was still something of a black-tie event of which then meant that we all had to run across the city as the shops were closing and fork out for a quick suit to fit into despite the fact that we had all had one waiting for us at home. Vaguely Written Vivien of course had ended up having a comparatively cheaper and more chilled time than the rest of us.

It is due to the ways of Vaguely Written Vivien then that I'm now bollocking my way through the numerous pointless stops that make the London Underground's District Line such a tedious experience, the reason being with regards to the surprise stag party of our mutual friend Alex, of whom had appointed myself and Vivien as his best man double act.

Although I must admit I do hate the fact that the Americanization of European culture has forced what used to be a cheap pre-wedding day piss up in your local pub into something that now has to resemble some coked-up celebrity's birthday party, our idea was in all admittance, a *really* fucking good one.

After convincing its owner that we were a group of middle-aged married couples looking to find a place to reunite after 'all these years', we had managed to hire out some sort of multi-million pound cottage amidst the sweeping countryside of nearby Chichester; we would of course then fill it with as much booze, drugs and whatever else as much as we could to throw him a good time; hell, even the coked-up celebrities would be jealous and I'm looking forward to it.

Anyway, the word had got around to all of Alex's mates via Facebook and so we had all agreed to take off our Thursdays and Fridays from work as a means to extend the weekend good and proper and sort out that old obstacle of getting everybody and every*thing* down there. This hadn't really been too much of a problem since there were at least four drivers already currently making tracks and the rest would be bought before our arrival.

Food, as always, was an important question and since we didn't want to keep having to make trips out to some fucking Tesco we thought we'd just buy one fat supply in one go and stock up the freezers; since our country had also been granted a surprisingly beautiful summer this year, we decided this should probably manifest itself as some sort of epic barbecue. This had then led to a further complication in that, like most mortal men who were now in their thirties, some (Vivien included) were particularly fussy about what kind of meat they were prepared to eat; a complication of which I actually consider rather fair enough. What one learns after years living in the multicultural soup pot that is London (where many of us today were travelling from), is that when up against the exotic flavours of the Mediterranean, Asia, the Orient and Latin America, mildly chilled pasties came out pretty low on the demand list.

Vaguely Written Vivien had once again convinced everyone of his solution, for near his newly bought home in Cambridge, there was a top quality, specialist butchers. Vivien would simply buy it all up before hand, cram it all into something he vaguely described as "the device" and lug the now-frozen matter onto the quickest train to Chichester and be there in time for our arrival. No problems had occurred as yet, so far, so good.

Another complication had then occurred. Early that year Vivien had also been a victim of the great recession and was made redundant, through no fault of his own, from his job as a programme scheduler for the BBC. He had also previously bought a house and was now in a panic for money, forced into taking any kind of freelance work he could possibly get back in the city he'd strived so hard to get out of and so of course today, the day of getting-shit-to-Alex's-stag-do day, was the day when some media company had offered him a full-fat day of work back down in London.

Unlike Vivien, I possess something of a systematic mind and had mapped out my travel plan to a tee (despite this, the responsibilities that people entrusted to me were always fuck all); I would leave my flat in Whitechapel and board the District Line across the length of the capital's centre and meet my friend Dave as he finished work at London's Walt Disney offices in Hammersmith and we would then drive down to Chichester together. Incidentally, if you ever imagined the London branch of the Disney offices to appear exciting then don't, rather than entering through the mouth of a giant animatronic Mickey Mouse head that shoots rainbow lasers from his eyes as my imagination had hoped, it is instead just an ordinary glass office building that disappoints in a particularly average way.

Anyway, Vivien's work place had turned out to be en route at West Brompton, and so here I am, trundling along on the District (now on the bit that enables you to see outside) to intercept whatever "the device" was from Vivien, cart it across to Dave at Hammersmith and drive it down to Chichester, hoping of course, that whatever Vivien's after-work plan of getting down there was to be, was going to work out.

The doors hiss open and I'm out in West Brompton, a typically non-descript British place of 1960's red-bricked buildings nestled uncomfortably next to chicken shops and newsagents. I wait by a traffic-less road and watch how the summer sun cooks the tarmac. Then he appears, I see his bald head across the road, from behind one of the buildings and he's dragging something behind him. It's something heavy and I cross the road to meet him and, what the fuck is *that!?*

"The Device" as he calls it, is some kind of huge metallic suitcase with pipes and wires that protrude from its sides, there is some complex contraption that opens it and it's hissing vapour from some ventilator as it freezes the meat inside, it looks like some sort of futuristic fuel cell out of the movie Dune.

"Alright?" he says vaguely.

There's nothing I can respond with but "Don't tell me you want me to drag that thing all the way to Hammersmith? How heavy is it?"

"Yeah, it's pretty heavy man."

I pull the thing briefly by one of its side handles and it scrapes across the pavement. Jesus, it *is* heavy.

"Is that even going to fit in Dave's car?" I ask him.

"Yeah, it should do".

"Well, what have you got in there?"

"Sausages, steaks, you know, meat and stuff, and some of my clothes, thought it would be easier to pack some of my other shit too".

"But won't your clothes just mix with the meat?"

"No, it's got several compartments".

"You're telling me!"

His chilled appearance suddenly stops and his beady eyes look forcefully into my soul, this was a rare thing for Vaguely Written Vivien, this was something specific, something *serious,* something *planned*.

"DO *NOT* OPEN IT!!" He declares.

"Why?" I ask despite the answer being obvious. Vivien's eyes relax again.

"It'll start defrosting and cross contaminate; and that would be shit".

I nod in agreement and prepare to drag this behemoth back to the train.

"So how are you getting down there?"

"Get the train s'pose".

"You mean you haven't got a ticket yet?"

"No but it'll be alright, I finish work 'round 5 and I'll just hop on the next one".

"Well make sure you get there on time, the house is a bit of a way out, do you know the way from Chichester station?"

"No, but, it'll be alright." He pauses vaguely before continuing "See you down there, I've got to get back, good luck with that thing."

"Yeah, see you later" and I slowly begin dragging the bastard across the road just as the one and only car through this nothing area of London stops impatiently as I cross, the driver at the wheel staring at me as he too wonders what the fuck this *device* is supposed to be. Vivien briefly stares at me too before disappearing back behind the red-bricked wall.

I get it to the tube station and I have to carry it up the stairs, through the barrier and down to the platform again. In the summer heat I'm sweating like an athlete; this is going to stink out Dave's car big time.

The train pulls up and I carry the beast on; the people in this carriage look at me mildly frightened by this contraption as it systematically pumps out vapour and makes bleeping noises in our shared compartment. It's another ten stops I have to endure with this embarrassment and so I faze it out by thinking about the delights of the District Line itself.

The problem with the District Line is that on top of it hardly ever working very well, it's overloaded with needless little stops like Parson's Green or Wimbledon; the kinds of places where the people who live there are suburban middle-class types more likely to drive than get the tube and hence nobody ever seems to get on or off. There as are so many of these pointless stops that The District Line has a feeling of being longer than all the other tube lines in the city and with the summer sun magnified by the windows, it's also a long time to not have the honour of some well-deserved air conditioning.

Finally, the thing pulls up in Hammersmith and I drag it off to realise that Hammersmith tube station opens out into a medium-sized shopping arcade. It is here that I realise why, perhaps, that the tube and the roads may have been weirdly empty all this time; today, of course, is the day of the London Marathon and so perhaps transport into the marathon zones has been restricted by the police? Then I notice that this shopping arcade has police everywhere, *serious* police with dogs and automatic weapons etc and so I now realise that this is the first major marathon event since the Boston bombings and public security is being treated pretty damn seriously. Then I realise that if there was ever a terrorist who would make a package look so obviously over suspicious, then whatever this thing is that I drag with me, looks bang on the money.

Anyway, I slowly pull the vapour-pumping, bleeping futuristic fuel cell as discreetly as possible over the cold marble floors and through the crowds towards the sunlight of the arcade's open air, yet it is only a matter of seconds before the terror police's almighty great Alsatian manages to smell it across the distance of the arcade, through the metal and electric encasings of Vivien's "device" and go ape shit for whatever meat's inside. The dog handler and the other armed policeman are next to me in a matter of seconds and the dog goes nuts almost rhythmically for every time the device pumps out vapour.

"That's a very strange looking package you've got there sir, what's in it?" he asks.

This is when everything that's completely true about my situation comes off as sounding complete bollocks, yes precisely anything I say about it will just sound more and more suspicious but it's best not to lie to the police I guess.

"Meat."

"Meat? Why do you have a 'suitcase' full of meat?"

"I'm going to a stag party in Chichester and I have to meet my friend at the Disney office".

"With meat?"

"Yes, we're looking to have a barbecue and my friend wanted to get this from a specialist butcher."

"And where is this 'friend' of yours and why did he ask *you* to carry it for him?"

There's no way out of this, absolutely *no way* and to explain the vague and complex scenarios that make up the circumstances of Vaguely Written Vivien would just be too convoluted and so I start sweating.

"He's not here".

"So tell me sir, why couldn't you just buy the meat once you got to Chichester?"

"He wanted a specialist butcher". This shit was going nowhere and so out comes the policeman's pad and his pen clicks.

"Could you give me your name please sir?"

"Yes, it's Connie O'Hearly". His eyebrows raise; here we go, an Irishman, enemy of the state number 2 in the terrorist world and the dog handler begins undoing the clips on the device. I'm terrified now as it seems the aim of the automatic is aimed at my heart and the dog is grunting at my balls. As the device's clips are undone to allow the policeman access to a very ordinary zip, he undoes it only to be startled by a sudden unleashing of depressurised vapour, spraying out like a fucking chemical weapon.

"Please don't open it. Contamination." I say as I can barely get my words out, now becoming more vague than Vaguely Written Vivien and within seconds the dog handler has handcuffed me and slammed me to the marble floor, hurting my arms as he forces them together and the dog's stinking breath is grunting in front of my face.

"What's in the case? What's in the case!?" he's screaming at me and I can sense the fear of the passers' by, quickly hurrying to the light of the exit but for some reason I'm just frozen in the moment, unable to say anything.

The side zips on the case zip down further and the vapour dissipates into the air as it springs open slightly. Right now, the grip on my arms seems to have softened lightly and the two policemen are staring into the insides of the case somewhat dumbfounded. Surely, they must have now realised that my stranger-than-strange situation was actually the truth and I'd be let go? The barbecue meat and Vivien's clothes would be done for but I'd at least be free.

Suddenly as they stare, they immediately become intense again and push me back further, face down onto the aged chewing gums of the cold floor and I get the immediate impression that they've discovered something different.

'What the fuck did Viv actually put in that case?' I think to myself and so I take a look at it; a load of frozen meat and the edge of one of Vivien's trouser legs flopping around the edge, just as he said; *the truth!*

The dog handler reaches for his radio. "We need a van dispatched to Hammersmith tube station immediately". Presumably, this is local, national, perhaps even international news in the making, but over some meat and clothes?

There is a cackle from the radio back but I don't understand what it says. The dog handler replies "We have found the Brixton Butcher, repeat, we have found the Brixton Butcher."

Oh, my dear friend Vaguely Written Vivien, how vague you have always been in your plans, how so very precise you are in setting up the most complex of coincidences; I shall now spend our desired weekend in a cell while once again, you will have a considerably easier time.

So, I'm playing this promo night for some underground fashion label in Kilburn that a friend of a friend had sorted out for me. He told me it would be a nice little earner and then we could go out for a drink after.

It was a pop-up in some derelict department store; the walls where the stock used to be were covered in graffiti and the lighting was a dim shade of dark red.

There were a lot of serious-looking types on the dance floor so I decided to generally play dub stuff, beats but few lyrics, in order to blend in. I thought that if I could get through the three-hour agreed time without drawing too much attention to myself I could get out by 11 and find a decent cocktail bar with this guy. The plan turned to shit when he left at half eight with some Norwegian girl he was chatting to and left me in a room full of bobbing strangers. I kept things bubbling along with some deep funk and watched the clock tick down.

Anyway, about two hours into the proceedings the front doors swing open and in walk this big gang of seven black dudes. They must have all been six-foot two or higher and were dressed in long black leather trench coats. I'd never seen anything like it. The whole room stood still as they powered through the dancefloor crowd like killer whales. One of them fixed me with a long hard stare and made a record gesture with his finger as if to say 'change the track'. The record I was playing was coming to an end so I had to think fast. I found some Q-Tip and put it on. Hip-hop beats thumped out of the speakers. The same, huge gang member looked over to me again. He wasn't satisfied. He made the gesture again. I mixed in some Gil Scot Heron and hoped for the best. The guy kept staring me out!

I kept desperately trying to fit their demographic as the gang ordered drinks. After fifteen or so minutes they all huddled together and whispered something to each other. The guy kept his eyes locked on me throughout. Then suddenly he raised himself up to full height and started walking over to me!

By the time he had reached my makeshift DJ booth he looked about 100 feet tall. I watched him arch his neck to lean down to my eye level, his gold neck chain jingling. A huge finger pointed at me as he made his request.

"Play *The Cure*." he said.

My mind grasped through my lexicon of rap records. I scrolled through similar sounding artists but couldn't visualise his request. I prepared to give him the bad news,

"I haven't heard of him. Is he new?"

The big man looked puzzled.

"Nah mate. *The Cure*."

I looked back at the man mountain and said nervously,

"You mean, like, Robert Smith, *The Cure*?"

The blokes finger pointed emphatically back at me,

"Yeah that's it. Play '*A Forest*'."

And with that he turned and headed back to his pack.

I wondered if he was joking as I searched for the popular eighties goth-pop band. I scrolled through and eventually found the track he mentioned:

***The Cure*** – *A Forest*

As soon as I pressed play the mood of the room changed. Everyone on the dancefloor looked over to me. The weird synths of the opening chords gave a sinister feeling. And then the drumbeat and bassline kicked in. Suddenly the gang of men sprang into action, heading onto the dancefloor and shouting along to every lyric.

*And again and again and again and again...*

They started furiously bopping to it. The big guy that spoke to me looked over and put his huge thumb up in the air. The rest of the room seemed to dig it too so I lined up *The Damned* to follow straight after. They stayed on the dancefloor all night and I ended up leaving at 2am.

# Odd Theatrics on the 254

I think I was around fourteen at the time and whilst inner-city school life, whether directly or indirectly, had taught me the facts about racism, nothing during my educational years since has ever enabled me to put the dots together over what actually took place on the 254 from Clapton Pond to Hackney Central that day.

I can't remember exactly what part of the year it was, and being unpredictable old Blighty, the weather was never really a great indicator either. All I remember is my Sri Lankan-raised mother just moaning incessantly about the rain and cold in London, her heritage of course was a world I didn't know and so for me, being London born and bred, I had associated such British discomforts with the weird warmth of the homely.

Anyway, it was one of those days in which the outside cold and drizzle had somehow turned Mare Street and all its connections into another big traffic pile up and so the inside of the bus resembled much of the same. The bus's heater was on full blast and the musty vapour that dispersed from people's sodden clothing had steamed up our windows to a state of near invisibility. Outside, the pumping exhaust of the honking cars wasn't helping matters either, turning my current view of the oranges and other fruits of Mare St's mini market, and that square of grey that signified the ever-decadent St Augustine's Tower just behind, into the blurs of some ruined painting. Such an illusion could only be made out from close up; which indeed was the case since the packed-out bus had forced me to push my face as close as possible to the cold moisture. This is how I remember things on Mare St that day; from that awkward position – it's funny how memory works.

We were on our way to the Hackney Empire to catch a play and my mother was sat next to me; as impressive as she could look when dressed for the occasion in her top Sri Lankan attire. She was also something of a large lady and so was very much contributing to the space problem as much as she was complaining about it.

The cars kept honking, nobody could move and every time a button pinged for our bus to open its doors before any designated stop, our driver, who I remember was a large Rastafarian, would just call out in frustration for patience because, of course, it was against health and safety for the doors to be opened whilst amidst such dense traffic. I remember my mother half-arsedly saying something about all this being a case of mindless bureaucracy usurping basic human rights in favour of protecting businesses against prosecution and I think I agreed with her.

Now, whether you cared about it or not, the more regretful events of the early 21st century had made the subject of race-relations something of an unconscious focus for everyone. Therefore I would scan the surrounding characters who made up those races. It's all rather harmless of course and I came to realise that I'd developed something of a talent for sussing out where people might'd originated from by just observing them. The most obvious to my area of course were the orthodox Jews coming or going from Stamford Hill who always seemed to be ambivalent to what was going on around them. The majority of the people here though were the people of either my own or of African/Caribbean extraction and their true racial identities would become less clear the younger they became.

The native Brits of this area always seemed to be more identifiable by silent, older types from whom you could see the fumes and stresses of the city's history accumulated and ingrained in their withered, leathery skins. There was also, standing nearby, one of the wealthier types, occasionally revealing himself by the well-spoken grunts that would break the seal of his silent impatience.

I always found it interesting distinguishing between the different types of white people, and found that the local Polish population could be easily differentiated from the English by a specific, peculiar physical characteristic that I was, and still am, trying to pinpoint. Anyway, there we all were; overpopulated and squeezed together, heading to somewhere or other in the belly of a red, petrol-dependent beast.

Someone towards the front of the bus had been consistently nagging our driver for the doors to open and so finally, the Rasta snapped;

"Yeah? And you'd best not go complainin' bro."

Both the back and front doors to a London bus are of course connected (designed, under more civilised circumstances for clear entrance and exit routes) and so with a hiss and a rush of cold air, both doors opened and the centre of the bus immediately all unloaded onto the outside streets; the posh English guy almost instantaneously stepping directly into the path of a passing drug addict;

"Welcome to London, bro. Welcome to London".

It was this that distracted me from the others who had made a runner from the nearby bus stops through the thin slips of the cars and onto the bus via whichever of the two open doors was closer. With a sigh, the Rasta sealed the doors shut once again and the traffic moved forward slightly.

The fracas seemed to have begun by one of these new arrivals taking his place upon one of the priority seats and annoying an elderly black lady who, not expecting his sudden, attention-grabbing burst of aggression, was now shuffling her way, cane before her, to another part of this newly forming crowd. Everyone now, of course, was looking at him. A dispute had already been raging with another man, a big black man who was leaning into the metal wall before the upstairs stairwell. His muscles were ripped and bulging from his skin-tight black lycra top, and judging by his jogging bottoms and gym bag I'd concluded that he must've just arrived from one of the local gyms or boxing clubs, my point being, the guy looked hard.

"Well, that's all you fuckin' deserve then innit?" The big black man shouted at the stranger. Because I was sat a few seats behind I could only make out the silvery hair of a short British man around his mid-fifties squeezed into a tatty old black jacket, with ginger flakes protruding from an unshaven face. I don't know much about the effects of alcohol so was never sure whether that alcohol smell came from him himself or the open can of beer he held in one hand. The other hand I noticed was holding something to one side of his face; an old tissue or rag of some sort that was turning ever redder and damper with a noticeable amount of blood. An unfortunate old lady he had now planted himself next to was now as up, close and personal with the window moisture as I was.

"Aye" he said with a slurred Scottish twang, "but if it comes between me and all yous fuckin' wogs then I should get this seat, shouldn't aye?"

Oh shit. The need for the traffic to simply part and let this bus through as quickly as possible to its final destination suddenly became palpable. I specifically remember scanning the different reactions of my multi-cultural surroundings; a mix of shock turning to a surfacing anger, a wash of silent stress and fear amongst us all, even the fiery temper of my mother was beginning to show its first creases in her expressions before presumably subsiding at the fact that the man these words were being aimed at in particular, was probably about to settle matters in a much quicker and effective way. Amazingly for Hackney then, the black man didn't react with violence, not physical violence anyway.

"Oh why's that exactly? 'Cause you're a lazy cunt?"

"No, 'cause my father fought a war for this country and look what's happened to it."

"Well, he was fightin' for a different side to what you're on then, wasn't he? I suppose his old man helped free slaves which I guess would've been a problem for you too, wouldn't it? Close much, are ya?"

"Just fuck off, *all of you* fuck off" and I remember the menace as this guy locked eyes with us. Where was the Hackney Empire from here? I tried to convince my Mum to walk the rest of the way.

"Oh who do you mean now?" replied the black man.

"All of ya, all you filthy foreign fucks..."

"Eh, watch that beef on my bus man" called out the Driver.

"And you can fuck off, you cunt. One of these days the government, and I mean a *real* government this time, are gonna send all you fuckers back home."

The Driver just went silent as the big guy continued the argument for him.

"Well you'd better be careful my friend 'cause there's a lot of black people on this bus. I can count at least fifty, so how'd you like another fifty more smacks applied to the one I've just given ya?"

I remember a young Polish-looking mother sighing angrily as matters now seemed they might lead onto more violence.

The Scottish guy now just went into some incomprehensible drunken rants as he pulled further rags from his pockets to re-cover whatever part of his face wound had caused the previous rag to dissolve, being so unbalanced with the sway of the bus that he could never quite synchronize this with his beer drinking.

I looked around at my fellow passengers once again, wanting to know just how soon it would be before my mother and I would have to escape the onslaught against this man only to then notice, almost like odd numbers between the even, that a few of the black passengers were holding back silent giggles. I don't know why, but immediately I had a feeling from this that perhaps they knew something the rest of us didn't. It was here, then, that I learnt that the British, from whatever extraction, share a strange and dark sense of humour at the expense of all society's ills.

The rants between these two continued for however long it may have been to get this bus moving and of course the tension, not helped by the heat and condensation, continued. Yet most of the surrounding reactions remained the same, everyone either just too afraid, too lazy or too entertained to intervene before eventually the bus finally reached an intended bus stop and the doors swung open. The Scot rose from his seat revealing what appeared to be two black eyes as well as the bloody gash he was concealing and hobbled his drunken self off the bus with whoever else was leaving here. With a look that implied this stop wasn't really his intended one, the big black guy also left in the Scot's pursuit.

*Outside*. I thought to myself, 'if Hackney could manage to behave itself *inside* of a bus, even for however long that was, outside would always be subject to the laws of nature'. Here, it would happen then; that violence the borough had feared in those pre-gentrification days, was about to happen again...

In that space of time it takes for a bus door to open, unload and close then, a young boy like myself could only notice so much, yet what happened has always stayed in my memory. Instead of the violence as predicted, the black man caught up with the Scot, gave him a gentle matey slap on the shoulder and said... "Come on Kev, I already owe you a drink, where you wanna go?"

The Scot raised a single, possibly broken finger away from the bloodied tissue on his face towards some direction and the two walked off together. Through the thick condensation I saw neither man run away or after the other; just a gentle, casual trot, nattering as they went to some pub nearby.

I've repeated their final words in my memory banks over the years, the tone of them wasn't even apologetic in any way, just small talk, could these two have actually *been friends?* Could the whole thing have been... *an elaborate act?*

My mother and I would frequent the theatre quite a lot, but these days we can scarcely remember which shows we saw and where. Yet, if the incident of the 254 had itself been a performance, it would have to be one of the greatest, most controversial and most memorable I ever saw during those times.

### Thoughts and Memories from Beyond the Flashbulbs

*2009: The 53rd London Film Festival: "The Men Who Stare at Goats" Film Premiere*

Somehow, in 2008, that confined little glass encasing that had been my box office through which I saw the world during those years, had, on occasion, offered me a feeling of womb-like protection from those economic tsunamis the papers had been mentioning. 2009 then had begun to feel like premature labour; its tides had crashed around this establishment, the word of headlines were no longer ink but reality and I remember not feeling ready to be kicked out into its destructive chaos, pathetically hanging on to some invisible umbilical cord that I thought this place had been offering me but hadn't.

In retrospect, whatever sense of complacency I thought there may have been in this place now doesn't ring too true for it was very obvious, even then, that this once grand kingdom of celluloid delights had been steadily crumbling wall to wall.

The real reason I stayed was more likely to do with my secret celebrity girlfriend for whom the annual Film Festivals had granted me two intense erotic liaisons. Only a mug would see this as a reason to stay in a job like this of course but it had a present-day yearly rhythm that was addictive as hell, a year would pass, there'd be a Premiere, I'd message her about some discreet location, and then we'd secretly elope and my God it had been fun – late-night, 90's, Channel 5 erotic fantasies made flesh and blood! She had told me the previous year then that 'she liked me' and I was intrigued, I wanted to know more, I wanted to know where this all might had been leading to? Especially now as another Premiere drew closer and I might experience that euphoric sense of anticipation once again like a shot of pure, adrenalin-fuelled life.

It seemed that things had been more or less working out for *Her* now. Over the course of a year, our main screen would probably show on average about eleven to twelve major films, and with the economic crisis forcing American studios to back cheaper, Brit-orientated productions, she had, since the beginning of the year, progressed from mere appearances in films to longer, dialogue-heavy scenes and now that the cameras would stop to focus on her for a more considerable time, it was obvious that her looks complimented the big screen well. I cannot tell you just how weird it was to be watching her projected up there over and over again, day after day, knowing that, whilst other film buffs might had been fantasising about the mysteries of that body, I had *been there, seen it, done it,* and in *this* fucking building, a minute's walk from the back rows where the staff would have to sit, and not only that, but *twice*.

The world was taking interest in her now too, she'd appear as a promotional face in coffee-table fashion mags and the occasional mini interview would turn up in some of the lower-key culture magazines – I'd desperately read through them here whenever the cameras or the management hadn't been watching – her outlook on the world came across as different to that of the girl I had briefly got to know.

As for the progress of *my* career? Day by day I'd spend at that Box Office window as engineers, welders, Iraq veterans and even nurses would turn up handing in CVs to get jobs in *this* place. Our feelings about this of course were predictable, for if truly skilled professionals had to now scrape the barrel for jobs like this then where were the likes of *us* to go? Why, why, why, had I chosen to study film and media? It may had worked out for *her* but where the fuck was that ever going to get *me*?

Every day of that year had been swathed in increasing bouts of paranoia. Back at the flat, my flatmates had been jumping ship just as the rent had been rising, I found the odd weirdo to move in and help out but there was also that niggle of bother that I could end up paying it *all*. As a matter of fact, the whole of London had pretty much been doing the same. Most of the Europeans who worked here had given up on the free-wheeling fun of youth this city had once offered and were instead running back to the shelter of their family homes on the continent. Unlike them, this British/Irish kid had no real family home to go back to, just an overcramped home of which had since descended into alcoholism and domestic abuse at the hands that arsehole, Steve. My old room, I knew by now, would've been well and truly gone.

Unlike a lot of the other young professionals who were British, fleeing to such easier cities as Bristol, Manchester or even as far as Scotland was also not within my means. "Nothing was affordable here anymore" they'd all been saying.

Her world of the media had been presenting a wholly different vision of London; she, of course, though still not hugely successful, was now photographed mixing with all the famous faces of high society, the producers, the actors and the musicians, a milieu of London-British cool who would stare back at me through the fawning pages of the *Evening Standard*. London had, once again, been sold as a fashionable place to be. I reminded myself of the words my colleague, Abdul, had said one year prior;

"Don't take what you see at face value."

I wondered the same thing about the new friendship groups she'd been acquiring, about how much of it might have been real, or if their collective image had just gelled well for the marketing people?

My old mates back at Russell Nurseries had pushed on and progressed to better things, moving into salary jobs within I.T or marketing with mortgages, marriage and children on their minds; things that were the equivalent of trying to buy your own tropical island for me. They were failing to understand why I couldn't make it to their social gatherings at the weekends or holidays or indeed why I couldn't survive by the same means they had.

Around the summertime, those gossip columns in the papers had begun to report on her being spotted out with another celebrity, and this was a *big, well-known* celebrity. The two had supposedly been romancing each other throughout the bars and restaurants of the Chelsea elite. Now, I knew we'd never been in a relationship and I'd never believed that she'd *truly* liked me anyway but I couldn't help feel the pangs of jealousy a tad then. Not so much jealousy perhaps then, but neglect; had I been forgotten about? Had these monumental, yearly conquests that had practically come to define this life of mine just been a mere giggle for her? I knew that I shouldn't have had a problem with either but for some reason I did.

As it happens, I too had fallen into something of a relationship; nothing serious of course but one of those drunken staff party nights out had resulted in me getting off with Eliza and everything since had just been gravity. We tried to keep it secret from the management since for some reason they hated couples working together in the same building and so would normally work to drive one of them out – it had been going ok but if I can be completely honest, the passion just wasn't the same here for me, I was in secret comparing it to what *She* had done for me behind the scenes of that cinema. *She* was my true sexual fantasy. I'd have to re-imagine those scenarios just to get me hard. What a fucking cunt I felt. But, as always, karma was just around the corner.

"This is happening to everybody, not just you personally" were the words the managers tried to justify the arrival of our zero-hour contracts. These things came with their fair share of horror stories; there had been those who'd found themselves without a place to live since they couldn't guarantee the rent needed of their landlords' requirements. There were those who'd had disagreements with their managers and then found themselves, suspiciously, without hours, and when the work ran out they'd found themselves unable to seek housing benefits since they were in fact, officially speaking, registered as employed, and then, once they'd decided to stick to their principles, to maintain something of their self-respect and put up a fight by quitting, then the system would've seen it as acts of their own accord and refused them benefits once again.

Maximum power had been granted to the hands of the employer, you couldn't complain, you couldn't stand up, you had no powers of negotiation, there was only submission or poverty and the choice belonged to us. And then they questioned why depression had been on the rise?

My colleague Clements put it most succinctly as he looked up from his pay-slip;

"Fuck these cunts, bro."

To make matters worse, London had been hit by heavy snow that day, the Columbian cleaners had believed it to be the end of the world and not turned up, and so Clements, Paddy, Anwar and I had been drafted in extra early to help the management clean up the place from the screenings the night before.

In that cramped staff room, at that broken metal table, we took turns to open our payslips, I went last; it was *bad,* they were *all* bad, Christmas had always been a bad time for work in this place, it was still two months away, and already, *this* had been our winter pay, *this* was all we had for the season of hope, *this* was all Jesus had given us for his birthday.

"I'm going back to the way I used to make money man", Clements muttered and I knew what kind of work he was implying. Clements had joined earlier in the year and had arrived with even more shocking rumours than anyone else I'd met there. Some, who had known the movements of the area he was from, had claimed he'd been involved dealing low-grade street-level heroin, had been arrested for assault on more than one occasion and in the phone calls I'd overhear, three different, enraged women (each of whom he'd had different sets of kids with) had *all* been pressing charges against him. He had otherwise been friendly to us, but you knew, you just *knew,* that the almighty shadow he cast was not just because he was a big lad and so of course, you didn't want to be in a room like this one with him for whenever he decided to switch.

Niro then unexpectedly barged in in a mood, banging the dust off the knackered cupboard doors as he set about making a particularly below-par cup of coffee.

Of course, how could I have forgotten? This morning was the morning that Niro would get the results from his team leader interview. We had all been certain that he'd get it, the competition, consisting of a couple of newbies with only intermediate English skills, would've been dead in the water. This had clearly not been the case.

"What's up Niro?" asked Paddy.

There were no more seats so he just stood in the corner, drinking that hot coffee at an angry pace more akin to that of cold water.

"Nothing, except for the fact that this place is fucking RACIST!"

"Yeah, that don't surprise me" Clements said.

"Don't you find it funny" Niro went on "that it's me and *my* skills, I've got the kid excuse, and I'm *from* here yeah, up against, where are *they* from? Poland? Bulgaria? They have barely any English skills, and I lose out to *them?*" The atmosphere continued to be well and truly frosty; "And then I sit back" he went on "to realise that everyone on the management team is WHITE".

The reality regarding his particular current situation, I felt, had nothing to do with race at all. The reality was that Niro knew too much about the law and could, no doubt, put up a fight against whatever illegitimate schemes the office might had been up to behind the scenes. Instead, of course, this office would prefer to hire more complacent people.

A little later that morning, the canisters containing the reels for the next day's premiere arrived at Front of House and this crew and I had to carry them up to the projection booth. Eliza, my sort-of girlfriend, who'd turned up to open the retail areas also decided to join us out of pure curiosity.

The film would be *The Men Who Stare at Goats,* a fictionalised adaptation of a book of the same name written by the popular London journalist, Jon Ronson. The film would delve into true American weirdness; its timeline would jump between the Gulf War and Vietnam to explore the rumoured, secret unit of the US military who'd been trying to weaponise the supernatural to develop super soldiers with apparent psychic abilities.

And so, a theme had been running throughout each annual festival, from what had been happening behind the scenes of the Western world we knew, to the more up-front acts of last year's George W. Bush; intrigue about the cause and effect of the world we'd all found ourselves in seemed to now be the entertainment world's plateaux of choice.

Up the stairs we went. Fuck, those canisters were heavy, but once we arrived the two projectionists, Elliot, and the older, Joe, gave us all hearty welcomes.

Whilst obviously employed by the same company, the projection team had been something of a separate entity to the rest of the cinema, subject to their own separate rules and responsibilities. Their separation from the rest of the staff, and the sheer longevity through which they'd been there showed. Like a semi-converted attic, this long but low-ceilinged, triangular room seemed to be half lived in and half worked in. A few great, dusty projectors dominated the room and pointed down at the auditorium far below like great canons of war, Joe stood by them like a mechanic protecting his prized, favourite car whilst on the floor were an assortment of strange tools and oiled up machine parts. On the other hand, the place had its own office, bathroom, kitchen, internet and phone system and (as rumour had it) even its own makeshift bedroom somewhere.

The sloped walls had turned clammy with steam from the endlessly boiled kettles and an assortment of old film posters, accumulated from the various places these guys had worked, were peeling from them. They'd been here for years, especially Joe, and the two of them resembled a couple of scavenging birds that might have settled upon the rafters to such a dusty, old building as this one.

I was impressed with this secret hideaway of theirs and so were my colleagues.

"Oi, d'ya like the artwork?" said Elliot in his Irish twang.

We all turned to see that at the base of the wall was the name of this particular establishment with an arrow pointing to a rather good image of a cartoon rat walking with a cane, top hat and tails. It seemed to be pulling a sinister, treacherous grin as it walked on.

"It'll be a warning for the younger, digital lot when they bring them in over the next couple of years - never trust a rat, I shall tell them, and they're everywhere in this frickin' business".

"Why? What's happening to you lot?" said Eliza.

"Haven't you heard?" butted in cockney Joe "we're all getting replaced, the world's going digital."

"You mean, they're just going to *let you go*?" said Eliza.

"Yep, gettin' replaced by a younger lot who just 'ave to push buttons like they're textin'" replied Elliot, "that's why I don't give a fuck" he then said as he unscrewed the top of some

Bells whiskey and unsubtly glooped it into his cup of coffee. "anybody else want some?" We all said yes except for Anwar and Niro. "I'll boil you up some secret agents in case any of the rats come in" Elliot explained as he began boiling the kettle.

"That bloody *Avatar* film will be the turnin' point, I'm telling you" declared Joe.

"I doubt it" I remember saying "the trailer makes it look shit."

"Ya think that stops 'em?" asked Elliot "do you know that when we get that film in, I mean up in *'ere,* a few nights before it comes out, we have to have a guard stay up here overnight just to protect it. If that's not anticipation for success, I don't know what is, even the fuckin' shite we're playin' right now is makin' money somehow."

I peaked through the projector window, out into the darkness of the great auditorium, the roaring machine getting louder as I leaned forwards. I can't remember what we were playing at that moment in time but it hadn't attracted many people.

"Don't touch that glass!!" roared Joe. I turned back to see his sets of broken, worn-out gnashers, they looked like the view of London you'd have if you stood on the South Bank and looked north at the likes of St Paul's Cathedral, the Tower of London or the Barbican. The guy was so distinguishably *London*, he had even come to *look like* London.

"George Clooney's comin' tomorrow, if you get so much as one little smudge on that glass, then through that magnifier he'll look like Gordon bloody Brown on screen" he declared.

It was only something like 11am, and Elliot began handing out teas and coffees with shots of Bells in them; "well, let's drink to the end of an era, shall we? Sláinte"; we all clinked cups.

"To be honest Elliot" Paddy said "I can't really tell the difference between film and digital."

"In theory, it looks better" went Elliot "but the thing is the lenses they use to shoot those films are all developed in Japan which means all films, as crisp as they might be, will all look the same".

"But why?" asked my something-of-a-girlfriend.

"Well" Joe intervened "all film is essentially a string of still photographs, and the development process has always been different in every country, which is why French films *look like* French films, it's why Italian films *look like* Italian films, and the same for the US. Now everything will look the same".

He led us to his wall of accumulated, old-school film posters, peeling from the wall as if this room were shedding its skin to make way for a new era. "These are my little beauties from over the years, projected all of these I did."

They were mostly exploitation or European films, practically from some lost, bygone era now, like old filmic nightmares scratched onto a modern, digital psyche; works of art in their own right.

Joe pointed to the poster for Vittorio De Sica's *Umberto D.*

"*Umberto D.* Ever seen that?" I hadn't, "that's a good little slice of what happens when an economy goes down." Then he turned to another, a stark black-and-white image of a fascistic guard with some sort of sex slave, "And *that, that's* a classic."

The title read *Salo; or the 120 Days of Sodom;*

"I once projected that in Soho back in the 70's when the police stormed the cinemas and arrested everyone watching it"

"What? But that didn't *actually* happen, right?" asked Eliza.

"It happened everywhere love, *especially* in Italy, it had still been banned *here* only until a couple of years ago, you can ask Westminster council if you don't believe me."

I watched *Salo* a few months later... *then* I understood. Eliza briefly explained the political backdrop to it, that shortly after his uprising, Mussolini had apparently made a last stand in the town of Salo and tried to restart his regime, only to of course, then be brutally executed.

The film had apparently been some sort of surreal allegory for this, and indeed struck an unforgettable impression on me, for that is what happens when you let fascism take over – they strip away everything you have left to call yourself, rape you – and then make you *eat shit!* Then, apparently after the war, Italy had an economic boom leaving several of the old and vulnerable behind, like the fate of poor old Umberto D in that other film. I shuddered in fear, were both to be my fates if I took my chances staying in this place?

"So what happened to your old mate, Big Momo then, eh?" asked Elliot.

"He's working as a security guard now" Anwar spoke up "he's been getting well into his religion since they slung him out of this place man".

"Yeah, that did all seem a bit unfair, I must say" Elliot replied.

"Too right, it was unfair" said the peculiarly silent Niro; like he'd ever stuck up for him before of course.

"This whole place is unfair" he went on "do you know where they live? This place's head-office lot?

Everyone just stayed quiet.

"Well I *do.* I've done my research, you know where they live? In Jersey" Niro concluded.

"The cheeky, tax-evading fuckers" Elliot laughed.

"That's right" Niro declared "and with all that 3D *Avatar* stuff, they're putting up the prices *again.* They pay us shit, stick us on zero-hour contracts and don't pay tax and think about the revenue they're going to be making off that."

Clements, who'd been sitting down, suddenly stood up authoritatively, the light of a dim light reflected off his sweating, bulking cranium, blanketing his eyes in a sinister shadow.

"Yeah, but you stand there and complain 'bout it, but you don't do anyfin', do ya bruv? It's alright *sayin'* it man but how about *doin'* something?"

"What are we supposed to do though chap? World's moving on without us that's all." Elliot claimed; "Time to jump ship for the lot of us, I should think."

"If you want to add further salt to our wounds" went Joe; "they're now sayin' they might not even need projectionists at all"

"What the fuck?" laughed Paddy and Anwar in unison.

"Yep, *they're* going to do it, *the management*; that's what they're sayin'. I'd like to see them keep that shit afloat".

"Alright *you* lot need your job, and *we* all need our job" Clements continued "why don't we do something about it? Kick up a fuss like?"

"Nah" Elliot explained "it would have to be *everyone,* and I mean *everyone,* all they'd do is fire the lot of ya and bring in staff from the other branches. It'd never work"

"Well don't we have a Union or something?" Our Dutch friend asked, naively underestimating this cold and disorganised island.

"*A Union?!*" Elliot nearly took a swig fresh from the Bells bottle in disbelief "You want to try and find a union for minimum-wage workers in *this* country? That shit all went years ago mate, gone with the wind, you can thank old Maggie for that one".

"Well if I can make a proposition, we should send out a message then".

We all stood and waited for Clements' proposal, it oozed a natural menace.

"Tomorrow we have a Premiere, don't we?"

We all nodded.

"And this place is very obviously up to something illegal, innit? So that means they've got something to fear too, don't it?"

Where the fuck was this going?

"...there's gonna be celebrities, there's gonna be press, if we could kick up a fuss as to get on the news, all those hot-shot film producers, all those hot-shot stars are gonna come down like a fucking ton of bricks on the managers here as to why their film's not gettin' shown. Then we could start demandin' somethin', at least some union power or something, get our voices heard like."

Clements had a point, if it could get back to somebody, some charitable celebrities perhaps, those who might comprehend the poverty here in this city we might had had a chance of getting our point across, and besides, why the fuck *should we* have been taking this crap? I'd heard from staff before me that George Clooney was apparently a sound bloke, imagine *that,* fighting a battle for workers' rights alongside Batman?

Paddy also had a point to make "yeah, and imagine the amount we might be able to make in compensation?" This was the only time I ever saw Clements smile, good old Paddy the Dutchman, always trying to chase it big, already surmounting the amount of money this place might have to cough up.

"Brothers" Anwar spoke up, he could be intelligent when he could be bothered to be, "all we have to do is sit down, nothing violent or confrontational, just all *sit down,* we refuse to help anybody just before they bring the celebrities in. People won't be able to find their seats, they'll spill over onto the celebrity security space. We just have to sit down and stay silent while the shit kicks off, the security will get into a fight with the management and if we keep it going for long enough, the celebrities will start kicking off themselves and then the press will want to know why."

"And then one of us, whoever gets attention first, has to speak to the news" Paddy said.

"You mean to *the world?*" added Niro "This is the *London Film Festival,* isn't it?"

"Not me" said Anwar, "I can't talk to the *world?*"

"But we have no idea what order this might play out in, it could be anyone of us first and it might be you." Paddy continued "You'd *have to* you silly fat prick".

"You are *kidding* right?" said Eliza.

Clements turned to Elliot and Joe as if our proposed trouble wouldn't be quite enough for him. "And what are you two going to do?"

Elliot turned to his older comrade in projection;

"Are you gettin' redundancy from 'ere then Joe?"

"Well, yeah, but it won't be enough. Besides I've got another job *and* my pension to look forward to."

"Well, they ain't givin' me fuck all, I'm movin' into care work, that'll be nowhere near as fun. What do you say we say to the world just what a valued and old-school profession we really once were?"

"Well, what do you have in mind?" then he took note of Elliot's slightly pissed expression "You're not seriously suggesting that we.... *shut the projector off?!!*"

Elliot just kept laughing and Joe's ageing soul had to take a seat, every kind of unreadable thought spreading itself across his withered face like butter being spread over ciabatta by a fork.

Unbeknownst to the individual, similar expressions were spreading over the lot of us and then Eliza went off on one; "You cannot be serious, right? You know this will *never, ever* work?"

"Watch us" said Clements with an undertone of violence.

"Oh my god, you are *pathetic,* you know that? *Pathetic."*

And then she stormed off, I wanted to stop her and reassure her that we were all being stupid only to turn around to see half-baked expressions of seriousness in everyone else. What was so stupid about standing up to exploitation?

Now, of course, the thought that spread across all of our faces was that we'd *better get it right.*

Nobody said anything further, we just stood in the silent electric hum of the room, knowing that now it was too late to go back.

The plan had been discreetly passed on to the rest of the staff, *all of them*, who'd all amazingly *agreed* to it, and so that had been that, it was afoot, couldn't be changed. I went home then with too much on my mind, this premiere would present the juggle of activating the revolution alongside hopefully finding *her* and doing whatever that might've been, away from the eyes of my so-called girlfriend; somehow something had been telling me that I should have been feeling guilt for such things but somehow, that emotion never came, as if those two aspects of tomorrow had been meant to be, and had always somehow been forces for good.

The emotions I was actually feeling had been much more strange and complicated.

"Talk to the *world"* Niro had said. *The world,* the biggest stage there is. What *the fuck* had we been thinking?!

What a strange form of insecurity it was, that fear that the world could come asking *me* what our problems were? There's a sense, a fear, whenever you sense you're about to be confronted with something bigger than your own personal world, that has this odd, battery acid taste. That taste is the wall of fear, and that wall must be challenged. It was the right thing to do, for the sake of other workers, for future workers, for cinema itself; it *was* the right thing to do.

I needed to take my mind off it and switched on the TV; it was *Question Time* with David Dimbleby and guess what the night's topic of debate was? Zero-hour contracts.

I couldn't take it, I switched it off to deal with the complexity of my emotions. Failing to do that too I opted for the last resort in stressful situations and had a wank.

All night the rain poured down on Peckham, the trees kept swaying on and the dim light of pornography glistened from my laptop screen to tell me that with every passing day the road to loneliness and personal oblivion would forever widen unless something could be done about it – that night I confirmed it for myself, tomorrow's revolution would happen.

I was bricking it. In the lead up to the premiere, I had been appointed a role at Front of House, delegating directions to the customers pouring in off the red carpet, an ensemble of minor celebrities and other guests; this now placed me not only in the potential path of *her* and *her* new celebrity boyfriend (for both had been invited despite, again, not being in *that* film per se) but also, once the revolution began, it could possibly put me in the line of the media too, meaning that whole 'talk-to-the-world' stuff, could indeed land upon me.

Between myself and the few of the staff who had been flitting about between the foyer and the screen, we shared nervous looks of good luck and uncertainty whilst making suspicious and unusually desperate attempts to keep our distances from the media. We all looked like we'd been mentally repeating the scenario for the last twenty-four-hours, Eliza still thought we were insane. It went as thus;

*We'd wait, we'd seat the people.*

*The big celebrities - the people involved in the film, - George Clooney, Kevin Spacey, Ewan McGregor and the likes would all arrive and begin their routine cycle of interviews and signature signing.*
*These said celebrities would then approach the higher-level press within the foyer and this would be our cue;*
*We'd sit.*
*We'd refuse to help, we'd refuse to even move and block whoever had been coming in,*
*We'd continue to sit,*
*Questions would begin to flow,*
*We'd wait for chaos to unfold,*
*The projectionists would refuse to start "The Men Who Stare At Goats";*
*That one unfortunate soul amongst us, that sole martyr, would demand Union attention, raising our concerns to the media of Britain and the world,*
*This would all of course, get fed back to the said celebrities.*
*Some of these celebrities, those of good nature, those people of power, would come to our aid and all would end on a happy freeze-frame movie ending.*

Now, I wanted this revolution, deep down I really did, but I also wanted *her* again, I couldn't stop thinking about her and, somehow, I would have to find a way of maneuvering both.

The worst thing about now however was that I had to stand next to Edwins, the head of security; Edwins was friendly enough but took his job *very* seriously and certainly wouldn't approve of people like us jeopardising the safety stronghold his crew had intricately built around the place. He had apparently once been something significant back before my time in the Falklands War, he'd given his duty to high-end West End security ever since and was hard as nails.

Anyway, this was also one of those premieres whereby the outside news coverage – usually fronted by some hyperactive presenter from Radio One – was also being fed back live to the big screen within the auditorium behind me. My hopes for the upcoming actions of the projectionists could also mean everything we were supposed to do next could be caught on such footage.

The stream of people entering, (just the regular people at that stage) had been arriving slowly and so Edwins, who'd been scanning the legions of fans screaming and hanging over the edge of the perimeter fence, began small talk concerning one of them.

"Oh I see, it's him again, is it?" Edwins said in his rough Scouse drawl.

I knew who he'd been studying immediately; I'd often wondered who the hell that guy was too? At practically every premiere, at least as far back as I could remember, there had always been this bloke at the front of the crowd, so tall as to be dominant. His face was such a portrait of excitement that his eyes appeared to be looking in every direction at once and strings of spit fell over the fence. I always thought he bore a resemblance to comedian Sacha Baron Cohen's *Borat* character and I know that for his earlier premieres Edwins' team had intervened thinking that it was the man himself, there to disrupt the press in character with some sort of comedy stunt. It hadn't been the case, instead this guy had been real, he wore a yellow baseball cap backwards on his head and so we all referred to him as The Yellow Hat Man. Sometimes, days or even weeks before a premiere The Yellow Hat Man would turn up to ask questions and only be able to muster the words "Premiere, tomorrow, yeah" before his mad face would disappear somewhere into the Square.

"Who is that bloke anyway?" I asked Edwins.

"Oh, we asked the police to do a check up on him a few years ago. It's a sad story about that one".

A few of the minor celebs, the fashion world and Reality TV lot had already arrived before his part of the crowd and he'd hung himself forward, pushing out his long arms in front of the faces of those who surrounded him, practically breaking the railing to draw attention to his own naff little autograph book which flapped about in his excited hands like some tormented trapped bird. *She* would no doubt soon be before him & the butterflies turned my stomach to sickness, my armpits began sweating and my left knee shook. Where was she? Edwins went on; "His family are loaded, Greeks I think, and he was like this serious, *serious* mathematical mind, I'm talking *genius* levels. And so his family packed him off to Imperial College and then one night some prick bottled him and things have never been the same."

Jesus, what a tragedy.

"That's awful" I said.

Edwins was gently shaking his head, he had the expression of a man who'd become tired with tragedy.

"Such is the way of the world" he said "That guy, he could've been the future, you know? Could've saved us all. And here he is, reduced to some vegetable with nothing to fill his life with except these dickheads".

I didn't know if by 'dickheads' he'd meant celebrities, his surrounding crowd, or both.

The Yellow Hat Man was harmless but had been known to the security and the PR lot as someone who could spend awkward amounts of time trying to shake hands or get autographs and was someone who their clients should probably be quickly severed from regardless. He must've met several of the stars, and you had to wonder whether up in Beverley Hills or wherever they hung out, whether these people discussed him, or knew the same truth of him, in the same way that Edwins and I did. Could his tragic circumstances one day make for a film project they could make?

"Did they ever catch the guy that did it?" I asked.

"Don't know mate, but I'd give him a slap that's for sure."

I then became distracted in my thoughts, about the slap Edwins might give me if I were still to be next to him once our plan commenced.

Then, after several or so minor celebrities had passed the Yellow Hat Man, along *She* came, that long flow of red hair down that beautiful, white muscular spine of hers that revealed itself through her backless dress. Her long, awkward meeting with The Yellow Hat Man, allowed me to lust after her a bit longer; those tiny reflecting scales of the dress caught the spotlights and highlighted those beautiful curves, that waist, the back of those legs, I wanted her *there and then*.

*He* was there with her however. Her boyfriend. Both of them being guided by their PR people from fan to fan, signing the posters of whatever film had acquired a fan base over the previous two years. He was bigger than her of course but just being with him had made her a bigger star too and I had to question whether this had been the reason she'd chosen him in the first place.

*He* would prove another obstacle on top of all this, it would be near impossible in fact, no it would *actually* be impossible. Then they were both turned away from The Yellow Hat Man towards me where her look told me just how impossible things really would be. A mysterious, typically womanly mix of threatening stand-offish coldness with an unearthly sense of distant love and lust combined; how was I supposed to read what was now happening in those car-reflector green eyes before they flicked away to instead face the photographers.

*He* hadn't even acknowledged me whatsoever, which I guess meant she hadn't told him about me. If men had been made to just walk the earth, women are like nature itself; keeping secrets only to suddenly reveal them to us through unexpected forms of beauty or cruelty. Then, they passed me by and headed up the stairs to enter the auditorium through the Royal Circle. The *Royal Circle!?* They'd be *upstairs!* How was I going to conduct this mutiny *and* get upstairs?

Then the crowds in the square went into uproar, which of course signified the arrival of the Rolls Royces all rolling in onto the carpet, which of course signified our revolution.

Here it came, here it came, The Yellow Hat Man would be our sort-of psychically decided marker, they'd get closer to his vicinity and then we'd do it. 'Be brave, think about what your grandfather had died in the war for' I kept thinking.

Through the crowds they came, Clooney, McGregor, Spacey, the director Grant Heslov, and even Ronson, closer and closer, everyone inside the screen would be able to *see* when, and then there was the unspoken, invisible cable between each member of the staff that helped us *feel* when.

My heart raced, my legs nearly gave in too late, and then the moment came, Clooney had been caught somewhere between The Yellow Hat Man and the press, *do it*, Use The Force, resist all feelings I thought and so.... *I sat...crossed legged...in the middle of the Foyer.*

"What ya doin' kid?", said Edwin's drawl with a peculiarly contorted face.

"Nothing" I said back but I remained still and calm, I promise you my readers, I did.

I looked around the Foyer for whatever staff I could see; Jamie had done the same but was in a corner of the Foyer not yet identified, nearby Leila was merely half decided and frozen in some sort of toiletry squat.

"Well, get up you daft cunt. You're blockin' the way."

*Oh no, oh no,* it wasn't going to happen, was it?

Then through the corner of my eye, I saw the back of Anwar's mass, moving quicker than I'd ever seen it move before, quickly punching in that security code and disappearing into the Airlock to hide. Behind me, from inside, I could hear the sounds of the auditorium, settling in comfortably as normal without interruption.

You bastards, you absolute cunts.

Then Edwins' friendly face went all army man, his veins popped out his neck and his face went red.

*"Did you hear what I said!!?"*

I remember I stood up suddenly, made up some bullshit excuse about having forgotten to perform some duty upstairs and whatever Edwins thought I'd been up to, I made a run for it up there, I had to know to just what extent our mutinous act might had been working. Don't let it fail, *please* don't fail.

On the Upper Foyer, some hired catering staff were clearing away the plywood boards that made up the temporary VIP area. I made it past them, and ran through a side door onto the back stairwells. Up and up I ran and entered another door into the back of the Rear Circle where I could see the vast basin of 1,700 seats stretching down before me towards the stage.

Something, I wasn't sure what, was happening though. The people entering the Circle had been piled up in some sort of confusion and I saw that at one end Paddy had managed to sit with a look of confusion upon his face and at another end Clements, resembling a giant, grumpy baby had done the same, the problem was the rest of the staff had just remained normal, standing in their appointed areas amidst the aisles, trembling in the torchlight. The faces of Paddy and Clements were looking in their directions, furious at their cowardice.

Ricardo and a few of the other managers then began barging through the crowd towards them but they had refused to budge.

Oh shit, oh shit. At least up here, at the back of the Rear Circle, I could at least hide and watch.

Then, I saw Wilton himself (the only man to be dressed in a tux) barge his way through and yell in Paddy's face, Paddy took it for about a minute before giving in and being escorted out, then, after some of the others had been made to take over their roles, Clements was then forced into doing the same.

We were done for. Mutiny defeated. Eliza had been right, this had all been an act of unrealistically grounded madness. I could only half see it, but there also seemed to have been some commotion down on the Stalls Floor. Perhaps, if upstairs had failed, the bigger layout of downstairs could've succeeded.

Then, though, I assume everything had returned to normality, for the procession of Clooney and the others just went on stage as normal. I waited in anticipation as the intro came to its end for now, even if we, the staff, had failed, the projectionists still had pure power in their hands. I had been too fucked up to focus exactly and what was being said during the intro but sure enough, as they all left the stage, the lights dimmed, the curtains parted, and the screen gently revealed the opening credits...

*Cowards, you fucking cowards,* even the projectionists had bailed on us, we had *all* failed. How embarrassing was that?

Surely from whatever Edwins had made out of my actions, he couldn't explicitly say that I'd been involved. All I needed was an alibi.

The walls took on a kind of hallucinatory quality as I rushed down the stairs of those back stairwells desperately thinking of a sudden job I could do that might look legit. For some reason I ran back through the doors onto the Circle Foyer to see.... *Her.*

The temporary VIP area had been cleared away and she was just *stood there*, outside the ladies toilets and she was sobbing into a tissue. *He* was not there.

She sort of froze in fear as we locked eyes once again, her tears turning instead to snivels, we two had probably been pondering what kind of coincidence had been engineered here? I don't know but it would've looked perfect on camera.

I didn't have time to consider what might'd been wrong with her for I had about five seconds before a PR person, a friend or celebrity boyfriend would come out to comfort her.

I approached her, eye-to-eye and she seemed to like it. I signalled back to the door I'd entered through and she nodded to follow me. Behind the door, she pulled me towards her and we kissed, I grabbed her hand and began leading her quickly up the stairs. It felt like we were on the run, a rush like fiction's many eloping lovers and actually, in retrospect we had been running away from everything, finding somewhere within our digital landscape, those last remaining private corners where we could act upon who we really were, away from the cameras, away from the Internet, fuck it all. In that moment, my adrenalin not allowing me to stop, I knew where this place was and I knew exactly where to go, Paddy and I had found them all those years ago.

We went up and up, higher and higher through this place's unused floors, and then into the dressing rooms of the former theatre stars, the domain of the fame of older antiquated times. I wanted to ruin that dress, I wanted to ruin the so-called high-brow veneer, just tear it right off her body.

"Strawberry Fields." I said as she turned to me.

"Don't talk to me." she quickly replied as she turned to spot the abandoned dressing table. She leant forwards over it; her face looked back at me through the reflection of the dusty, bulb-surrounded mirror, a stern look that said she wanted what happened next to happen. Placing her hands over her arse, she began lifting up both lobes of that beautiful black dress to reveal the curve of stunning lingerie-like knickers pulled into the crack of that perfect pale behind.

I'd never done a chick from behind before but this was fucking ace. Her artistry seemed to have chosen that particular position for a reason; as if had it been some sort of comment on the reality of her role as a celebrity for as we locked eyes again in the mirror, surrounded by bulbs, pressing into each other with burning friction as we were, it was like she was telling me something. Was this all that had really existed behind all the glitz all along? Had all the fame in the world been created to merely secure a prototype as to what we had been meant to fuck and not meant to fuck? Why was I thinking all this instead of concentrating on the pure euphoria of the moment? I guess it kept me going a bit longer.

"Fuck me harder" she said with considerable venom, "harder, harder…" and with that, alongside that intoxicating smell of designer perfume, I pulled out and shot my load across the floor of this historical place to contribute something brilliant to its history.

After that, she simply wriggled back into that underwear of hers, gave me a look of which I didn't quite understand and then just left, back downstairs to the premiere again.

I imagined, maybe at this very date at some point during World War II, a bunch of German rebels would've been lined up, been blind folded and had their innards shot out by machine gun fire across a cold, white wall. Perhaps one of them, like me, would've somehow had the time of his life shortly before and died happy. That was how I felt. I truly no longer gave a fuck what that place could do to me.

Brian O'Bastard sat at the front watching us with smug, sadistic eyes. Ricardo, the nice, Italian manager who we all liked just stood nervously behind him with his arms folded. Niro had somehow worked something to get himself out of it and the projectionists must've denied all knowledge, leaving just us. Paddy, Anwar, Clements, myself and a few others stood there in silence like a police line-up as we awaited Wilton, the main man himself, to finish off the remains of the premiere and enter.

The door opened and he wasted no time whatsoever.

"Right, you lot, it goes like this under my rule book. I can fire you all right now, or you can earn yourselves temporary suspension by telling me directly who the main person responsible for organising all this was, the choice is yours".

In something like five different types of broken English some sort of incohesive protest then inevitably started. I remember noting that only myself and Clements had remained quiet. Myself? I don't quite remember why but for Clements, it seemed to be for reasons of silent, insidiously rising violence. Wilton, with a single patronising hand then signalled for us to pipe down.

"It's quite simple" he went on, "does anybody want own up to it or not?"

The protests started up again, Ricardo simply shook his head to himself in the background as if not quite believing the working world he must had left Italy to come to. Wilton's patronising, Don-like hand gesture silenced us again.

"Well, nothing's quite clear to me, so I think that's clarified things, hasn't it? I want all of your lockers emptied by the end of the week".

Protests kicked off again with complaints such as it 'not being legal', but what was anyone without true legal knowledge going to do about it all but scream and shout? Clements however, still remained in silence.

Just as Wilton and Ricardo were about to leave the room, O'Bastard exhaled a smug laugh at the expense of these protests through his nostrils.

"Well, you see, this is why you can't go around thinking you can cheat the system."

Then *it* happened.

Clements' head suddenly bolted forwards and cracked O'Bastard clean on the nose in a tiny explosion of red. Even Wilton, who now had a few red dots added to his inflated cabbage nose just stood in silent shock.

Blood was bleeding through the fingers O'Bastard was using to cover his injuries and was dripping onto the floor, and further behind this, his eyes began to weep, not just through pain but through sheer shock and surprise, as if he'd never expected such a wild and uncontrollable force as Clements to have appeared in a place where everything once slid along nicely to his flimsy ideas of what control meant.

"What you fink your a fucking man, do ya? You think you scare us? A poxy fuckin' *cinema manager?*"

Then, like a lost and frightened animal, O'Bastard instinctively scampered behind Wilton.

"You're a boy, nothing but a weeping *boy*".

With that, Clements headed his way to the door, kicked an ugly great dent into its woodwork before turning and saying;

"Make sure you don't come anywhere near the Streatham area or I'll rip your fucking heart out you fat prick."

With that, Clements had left, the police were later called, and because nobody had truly been his friend, none of us really heard from him ever again.

They say there are many things you should experience in this life to appreciate it truly, travelling is one of them, falling in love is the main deal, taking drugs perhaps, but a great underrated edition is seeing bullies getting exposed for the cowards they truly are. I cannot defend Clements' actions of course, but in times of strife, like in *The Dirty Dozen,* even unrestrained bad men could play their own noble part.

Terrified, O'Bastard quit shortly after and if you should go to where that Meeting Room was now, you could slide its circular table to one side and could probably still make out those blood stains even today.

*"Everybody takes advantage of the ignorant"* – Umberto D.

So how did I manage to secure my job? Eliza had pleaded with Ricardo and the others on Team Italy that I'd been innocent and that I should be kept, and indeed, once they re-watched the CCTV footage, my alibi that I'd been helping a celebrity back to her seat via the back of the Rear Circle, actually checked out. Thank fuck they hadn't had cameras where the old dressing rooms were.

What a true lowlife I had been. I had not only run and hid from my attempts at revolution but had spent that time cheating on the girl who'd then come to my defence. I had been a shit in many ways and probably deserved to be a lifer to that place after all.

As a punishment for his sheer, sometimes shocking laziness, the Italians of the management team had wanted to pin everything on Anwar as a means to kick him out. Anwar had cleverly played the race card against this, and fearing for their own accusations of racism, they instead let both him and I off with two-week suspensions.

Whatever had been the Projection team's excuse for bailing on us all I can't quite remember but within a year they'd been laid off and replaced, as predicted, by a younger team of digital professionals. Paddy however, along with the others, had all been fired on the spot.

At the end of that particular premiere, Paddy and I retreated to the nearby Planet Hollywood to pick up our spirits. I hated Planet Hollywood really since the place claimed to be film-centric but only played shitty pop and hip hop videos but we thought we'd exploit what was left of our two-for-one cocktail deals. We sat beneath the apparent life-size replica of Arnie that claimed to bear his actual leathers used in the first Terminator film, but it never struck me as genuine.

We drank and talked at length about how today had been a positive-negative experience, an experience that we could now use to galvanise some forward thrust in our lives, that we'd pull shit together and come back and see a film at the cinema in a few years and happily pay up its extortionate ticket prices with more money than sense. We talked about films, we talked about science fiction films, we talked about what types of science fiction films we'd like to make and why? What dystopian visions of the future had been the most accurate to the world we'd since been experiencing around us.

As the cocktails eventually took hold, and that conversation had entered deeper and deeper territories, it began to pour with rain outside and my view of the streets became seen through a clean, thin sheet of aquaplaning water. The neon glares of the outside animated advertising panels mixed with the passing headlights of the taxis and buses and then, as they merged with the water everything soon became very *Blade Runner.* One thing that never got especially spoken about in those days then was how the classic, 20th Century vision of the dystopian city – all technocratic and fucked up by a deteriorating ecology - had, by the 21st, become something of an alarming reality. Outside the framework of pop culture, none of it was really much good at all.

Paddy swigged down the last of what he had been drinking, said his Auf Weidersens and made his promises to me that the next time we met he'd be richer than any of the managers of that place. Now normally when people swagger off half pissed into the rain like that, you kind of expect them not to mean what they say, but within something like a year, the crazy Dutchman had done just that. Life's all about confidence.

As I staggered back in the direction of the night bus, the winter wind had picked up to lash the square with rain like the deck of a boat, the place was freezing and the neon glitz of the Square reflected off the gathering puddles to give the illusion that its buildings were doubling in size.

Those still about, the drinkers or the lost tourists, were running for shelter within the fast food restaurants, even the homeless had legged it from what to them had most probably been a recurring problem but yet I staggered on, the weather somehow suiting my despair from the hopeless knowledge that we could've achieved something incredible but had failed to do so through the distrust and pathetic apathy of people. The knowledge that ultimately, when pushed, people would sacrifice their pride to save their own skins; whether or not such acts could then define them as cowards or idiots I was too pissed to know.

On the other hand, the feeling of having had *Her* again against all possible odds, stirred up that same heightened sense of 'this-is-what-it-is-to-*live'* once again, and the feelings of the cold and wet, for once, felt euphoric upon my skin; when really refining the reality of my emotions at that moment, I realised that I cared little for Eliza. I was a creature of lust, not commitment.

Curiously enough, even after six or so cocktails I still hadn't told Paddy about the sex that had gone alongside the day's violence.

*She* wouldn't be coming to tomorrow's premiere, but I would be, ready to regurgitate the same familiar routines. Fuck I hated that job now; where was I to go? Why had the world turned this way? Why had she been crying when I saw her? All these things were knitting the complex tapestry of my life into some really uniquely peculiar jumper.

To the left of me, I then noticed an unusually bright shade of yellow from within one of the old red phone boxes; it was of a hat, the hat of, yes, The Yellow Hat Man.

He was rubbing his hands to keep warm, and the thick wintery breaths that beckoned from his mouth only further steamed up the glass. Through it, he somehow recognised me, a familiar face from his place of worship; he smiled and said something to me through the glass. I listened, not wanting to open the door.

*"Premiere. Tomorrow. Yeah"*

There would be, *Up In the Air,* with Clooney again, but he wouldn't be coming to our aid.

"Yes" I said in return "I'll see you tomorrow" before returning to my journey.

Edwins said his family had been loaded, so why was he here, in the cold, waiting for his place to secure further signatures something like fourteen hours before? Would he be here all night?

Such is the tragedy of life. One day you're something, and then one day, whether driven by lust, money or just pure curiosity, you take the wrong turn in the street and *Bang!*

# They Say You Never Know

Charcoal grey clouds clogged the distant city skyline as Alice pulled her jet-black BMW 3 Series into the disabled parking bay closest to the entrance of the leisure centre. She switched the car off but continued the phone conversation with her boyfriend.

"This week has been crazy. I can't wait to see you tonight."

*Me too. I've missed you baby.*

"Oh really! So, tell me, what do you have planned?"

*It's strictly NSFW. I'm in the office and don't want to make my colleagues blush.*

Alice snorted at this, catching her perfect complexion in the rear-view mirror and lingering on it.

*Anyway, I've booked us a table at a great restaurant. What time do you finish work?*

"I'm finished already, babes. I'm just going to put in some gym time and go for a swim and then I'm all yours 'til Monday."

*Keeping that body toned and ready for me, yeah?*

She giggled again.

"Maybe...."

*Ok. Well, the Bolly is on ice. Don't be too long. I'll see you soon.*

"Ok baby. Kisses."

As she put the phone into her purse she looked out of the window to see a Newham Council minibus pull into the parking bay next to hers. Through the steamed-up windows she could make out the distorted faces of those inside. The minibus doors slid open and a carer placed a ramp onto the side of the van before guiding out several people in wheelchairs.

Alice rolled her eyes and whispered under her breath;

"Great. Spastics."

As she stepped out and locked her car she could sense someone following her.

"Excuse me."

Alice kept walking.

"Excuse me. Madame."

Alice turned to see a dumpy woman in a tracksuit.

"Yes?'

"Are you registered disabled?"

Alice raised her eyebrow "Are you taking the piss?"

"Well, if you are not registered disabled you cannot park in *that* space."

The woman pointed her stubby finger towards Alice's BMW. Alice gave her a passive-aggressive smile.

"There's plenty more spaces. Can I go in now please?"

The woman's face went red.

"If you do not move your car I'm going to report you to the council."

Alice gave the woman a cold gaze and stepped towards her.

"Listen, bitch. If you so much as breathe on my car I will kick your fat arse back to whichever council block you crawled out of. Now fuck off yeah?"

Alice turned and strode triumphantly towards the doors of the leisure centre which swished open to greet her and closed on the woman outside.

Alice had two hours to fit in her strict daily schedule; a thirty-minute spin class, thirty minutes of rowing, weights and running, a ten-minute shower and forty minutes in the fast lane of the pool before a second shower.

She finished shower number one and headed to the changing rooms to put on her bathing suit. She made sure she was alone as she took off her towel robe. As she did she caught herself in the vertical mirror next to her locker. Alice studied her reflection, searching anxiously for any blemishes; perhaps some cellulite or a spot that her boyfriend might find unsightly. She tried to ignore the voices that had always plagued her; her own high opinion of her features often rendered her feeling fat and ugly. She fought this desperately on a daily basis. Today though she looked good; perfect even. Scott would be pleased. She imagined the look of yearning in his eyes and gave herself some wry acknowledgement of physical accomplishment.

Her daydream was disturbed by a figure standing in the doorway of the changing room. She span around in shock to see a young, naked Downs Syndrome girl staring at her and smiling.

"Jesus! What the fuck are you doing?" shouted Alice

"Are you coming swimming with us?" said the girl.

"Go away! Don't you know it's rude to stare?"

The girl stayed standing there smiling with her hands placed on her pot belly. Alice felt a rush of anguish and picked up her towel from the floor. She whipped the towel towards the girl.

"Piss off you little rat!"

The girl ran off, leaving Alice alone once more. She quickly put on her swimming costume and headed for the pool.

As she entered the main dome she could hear the echoes of other bathers. At the shallow end of the fast lane she could see the fifteen or so disabled children from the minibus splashing carelessly in the arms of their carers. On viewing this Alice strode straight up to the teenage lifeguard who was stood by the poolside.

"It's 4.30pm. This pool is reserved for members only exercise."

The young lifeguard hesitated "Our SEN session is running 15 minutes behind schedule. As soon as they are finished we can reopen the lanes."

Alice poked the boy in the chest "Listen to me. Do you have any idea how much I pay in annual membership to be able to access this pool whenever I need to?"

"Yeah, but, the council are entitled access for..."

"I don't give a fuck about what the council are entitled to. I pay my council tax and my fucking membership fee, OK? I do not pay for this pool to be pissed and shat in by retarded children. Is this a sports complex or a fucking water park?"

"I told you they'll be finished soon. If you can't wait then the diving pool is free."

Alice turned around to see an untouched, blue pool with three ascending diving boards. No one was nearby or looked like they would use it. She looked back at the busy main pool and the irritated teenage boy.

"Fine. I'll dive instead. Just make sure you clean the pool once they've left."

And with that she turned and walked gracefully towards the diving boards. The lifeguard turned his attention back to the main pool.

As Alice reached the steps she began to feel a pang of anxiety. She used to dive in school and had won a few medals but had not been back up on the boards for ten years or more.

'Just the first board' she told herself but then her inner critic fired back. First board wouldn't give her any sense of satisfaction. She needed to prove herself.

She took the second staircase up further. The echoes of chatter became quieter. She reached the next board and could still just about see the other swimmers in the distance, like ducks on a park lake. She looked down at the blue square beneath. Still the nagging voice in her head told her second best was another compromise. The true accomplishment was still above her head. She took a deep breath, bit her lip and turned to ascend the staircase up towards the ceiling of the dome.

Once at the top she could notice the cracks in the roofing. Pigeon feet scraped across the outside of the plastic concave shells.

In front of her lay the concrete white diving board leading to the gravity below. Alice's heart beat a little faster. She stretched her arms up in the air and locked her hands together, making sure to stretch every sinew in her back.

One step at a time she walked toward the edge of the giant diving board. She looked out over the huge arena beneath her. She was so high up she could no longer hear anything other than her own breath rushing in and out of her chest and the pounding of her pulse in her ears. She felt like she was 15 again. The awkward sensation of what others may think of her. She felt foolish and afraid to jump.

The aggressive voice came at her again.

*What are you waiting for, you coward? Do it!*

She looked down at the dark blue pool below. The water was still, flat and deep. She felt its pull.

With a final deep breath she took one last step towards the edge. She straightened her back before gently squatting into position. Swinging her hands up she bounced her heels and let her body fly forward into the air. Time seemed to slow down as she straightened her legs above her head and formed a human dart. The blue square rose up to meet her and enveloped her entirely.

Beneath the surface she felt her body relax. Her instinct was not to head back up but rather to stay there in suspended animation for what seemed like several minutes. What initially felt like a cold invigorating splash gave way to a sensation of incredible warmth. As she drifted in the depths all her anguish, anxiety and fear began to fade like an old memory and in its place rushed in an overwhelming sense of wellbeing and joy.

She looked up at the still shimmering surface. It gave off a radiant glow, like sunshine on waves. As her body continued to relax her arms and legs fell down by her side like a toy doll. The surface seemed to draw her gently back towards the light above. She surrendered herself entirely to this warm beam as it drew her closer. She watched as two hands reached into the water. These hands propped themselves under her armpits before lifting her up, out and onto the edge of the pool.

"There you are! Did you go underwater?" said a kind lady wearing goggles.

"Yes!" Alice smiled

"Was it fun being down there?"

"Yes!" Alice said again, feeling excited and content.

"Good girl!" said the lady "Have you had fun today in the pool?"

"Really good fun!" shouted Alice "I love swimming."

"That's brilliant. It's time to dry off now and head back. Come on, let's go."

"Ok" said Alice and held the lady's hand. As they walked past the lifeguard she gave him a big wave. The lifeguard smiled and waved back.

"Lifeguard!" said Alice

"That's right." said the nice lady "His job is to make sure everyone stays safe."

As they walked past the locker rooms Alice caught her reflection in a floor-length mirror. Looking back was a happy, young girl with a fat tummy wearing a blue bathing suit with swimming aids attached.

The lady took her into a cubicle and helped her take off her swimming gear before wrapping her in a soft warm towel. Alice giggled as the cotton tickled her.

Once they were both dressed the lady walked Alice out of the sports centre and into the car park. The lady opened the sliding doors of the minibus and put Alice in one of the seats, making sure to put her seatbelt on. As the other passengers were loaded onto the bus Alice looked out of the window to see a car being loaded onto the back of a large truck. Next to the truck was a lady in a tracksuit with her arms folded, smiling and nodding.

"Look!" shouted Alice "Fast car."

"Yes," said the lady "It's being picked up by that big lorry, isn't it?"

Alice laughed and looked into the nice lady's friendly eyes. A man jumped into the driver's seat of the minibus and started the engine.

"Is everyone ready to go?" he said.

Everyone shouted and cheered. And with that the minibus drove away.

# Kennington Palace

*"You will call when you get there, won't you, love?"*

"Yes, mum."

*"And you know which tube to take to get to the house?"*

"Victoria line to Stockwell"

*"And you've got this... Maxine's....number?"*

"Yes, mum."

*"Well...OK..."*

The line went silent for a moment.

*"Sophie..."*

"Yes mum?"

*"Be careful, won't you, darling?"*

She bit her lip and focused up at the coach's air conditioning cones, trying not to tear up.

"Yes. Mum. I'll be fine"

*"Because you know you can always come back. They'll always be a room for you here."*

"I know, Mum. Thanks. I'll call you when I get there OK?"

*"OK. Goodbye, Sophie-bear."*

Sophie Wilkes waited for her mother to disconnect the call and looked out of the window as the National Express bus pulled along the narrow tree-lined streets past the Chelsea Bridge, the power station, the pagoda and the little parks. She had prepared herself for a culture shock but strangely many things felt familiar. The houseboats bobbing on the Thames reminded her of the canal boats in Tewkesbury. The autumn sun shining through the glass felt as warm and reassuring as it had done when her parents waved her away from Cirencester. Away from her safe place.

The twinge came again. That yearning to be back with them. She'd always been terrible for homesickness. The curse of the only child it seemed, the price one pays for an over-doted adolescence. It was this twinge that brought an abrupt end to the university saga. Unexpectedly good A-level grades opened doors for her at 18 that she was terrified of walking through. Competent interviews at Warwick, Bristol and Bath offered opportunity to grow, to pursue, to move on. But she couldn't. The twinges kept her at bay.

As much as her parents wanted her to discover herself, they also knew well of her shyness; her maudlin tendencies. There was the time at age 12 they had to collect her from the girl guide camp in tears. The school trips she came back from early. The skiing trip at 16 with her schoolmates that if anything made her even more reclusive once she returned. She just wasn't for...leaving. And at 25 it seemed that things were never going to change. They had adjusted to this and made peace with her decision.

Then one day she got a message from an old friend. A lovely girl who had been her saving grace as a timid string bean in the village she grew up in. Maxine was her name. For many of Sophie's teenage years they became inseparable. Maxine managed to engage with Sophie in a way others couldn't. They'd have sleepovers, go walking, talk about the things they wanted to achieve. They both shared a deep love for animals; Maxine's father was a vet and her mother ran a small shelter from their house for strays and unwanted pets. Then, one day, Maxine's family moved to Kent. Although to Sophie's parents this didn't seem that far, they could see that Sophie had become despondent and withdrawn again. The girls stayed in touch through the occasional letter or phone call but it didn't last long.

Years later, they managed to reunite online. Maxine had started working for a charity that rescued dogs bred for gangs, a cause which had garnered a great deal of both public and media support; not to mention some wealthy benefactors. With this she had become one of the company trustees and was looking to expand the charity's workforce. An offer was made to Sophie to move over to South East London to help her rescue and rehabilitate street dogs. It was the first time her parents had seen a flicker of excitement in Sophie's eyes.

After a few weeks of deliberation, the decision was made that Sophie would spend a couple of months with Maxine to see how she felt about the job. Maxine lived in a house share with her boyfriend, an Australian couple and two other tenants. The house had a spare room as one housemate was going to Thailand for 8 weeks. Sophie could stay for free for a couple of months and then after Christmas decide whether or not to stay on in London.

As the coach doors swung open she stepped into the bustle of Victoria Coach Station. A pigeon swept passed her nose, quickening her pulse. Two Polish coach drivers remonstrated noisily in front of her, waving their cigarettes around. A group of French students streamed past from behind her; their group leader waving a small yellow flag and hurrying them along. Sophie felt like the station was urging her to move. She headed out onto the roadside looking for the Underground. A double-decker bus rattled past, letting out an almighty hiss. Sophie picked up her pace trying not to seem fazed. She navigated past a Japanese tourist who had dropped her suitcase on the pavement to take a selfie by a phone box. Across the street a man screamed that Jesus was coming. Sophie started to sweat. She followed a sign through a shopping centre towards the underground, which seemed safer. As she reached the escalator she saw Victoria train station unfold in front of her. Shoals of crowds heading in different streams to dozens of platforms, football fans clapping hands above their heads in unison, men in suits drinking at a Wetherspoons on a balcony. She fumbled for her new Oyster card and followed the signs down a metallic staircase. The number of people intensified, everyone shoulder-to-shoulder until she couldn't look behind anymore. She held her modest luggage bag close to her body as the crowds dragged her down towards the Victoria line.

As the train rattled up to the southbound platform she felt someone grab her arm. Sophie let out a shocked whimper and spun round. It was an old lady, carrying a poppy collection tin.

"You need to let people off the train first, love."

"Oh, I.."

She turned around to a barrage of faces piling out of the carriage. Some tutted as she tried to move backwards. One man with a briefcase muttered "*Fucksake*" under his breath. Sophie felt her chest tightening. The twinges were coming back harder now. She'd made a mistake but it was too late to turn back. As soon as the last commuter stepped off a new surge from behind pushed her onto the train.

As the train headed south people squeezed into seats or little pockets of space. At Pimlico a group of teenagers in school uniforms piled on with music playing out of a cheap tinny phone. Each one of them competed to be the loudest one talking above the racket;

"FAM! YOU KNOW THAT AIN'T TRUE!"

"MANDEM TOLD ME FAM."

Sophie stared at the floor as they jostled boisterously. She thought about the family dog back home. Bonnie. She wondered how Bonnie was doing.

"BLUD, YOU NEARLY MADE ME MISS MY STOP INNIT."

She looked up to see a Stockwell Station platform sign and headed out of the carriage. As she came up the escalator she checked her phone for signal. As soon as it came on she rang Maxine's number. No answer. She waited outside the station anxiously. As she looked down she saw three bunches of flowers by her feet. A man next to her shouted "STANDARD" over and over again. The twinges were almost unbearable now.

A text message buzzed through. It was her mum again:

*Everything alright, dear? ;-)*

She wanted to text back – *No, I'm scared. Maxine's not here and there's a man in front of me eating beans out of a can with his fingers.* However, this temptation was startled away by someone calling her name from along the street.

"SOPHIE!"

She looked up to see her childhood friend all grown up and waving excitedly with a bull terrier puppy on a lead. Maxine strutted over in platform heels, ripped jeans and a long red leather jacket. Her face looked familiar, albeit with heavy eye shadow, stud piercings in her cheeks and a jet-black undercut where her long brown hair used to be. She threw her arms around Sophie's tense, slender frame.

"So good to see you. How are you, babe?"

"I'm good. Just a bit tired, you know…"

"I bet. Don't worry, we haven't planned anything tonight. Just a couple of glasses of wine at home, yeah?"

Maxine's accent still had that West Country lilt to it. This made Sophie feel calmer. Safer.

"We've got a bit of a distance from 'ere but I needed to give Willy a walk."

Sophie stared down at the excited pup.

"Come on, I'll grab your bags."

With that they set off towards the house. Sophie wasn't too sure what to expect as they passed towering council blocks and recycling bins with melted plastic lids. Crows pecked at a soiled nappy in the middle of the road. They walked past a shop with a newspaper board stating *PENSIONER DIES IN STEAMROLLER TRAGEDY*. The next shop offered Cash 4 Clothes. The next two were boarded up. As they walked past Kennington Station and few steps along from the shit shops they took a turn down a street with rows of tired-looking terraced houses. These huge buildings probably would have housed affluent families once upon a time but now seemed to be showing their age. Some had twigs and trees growing organically from their faded yellow brickwork.

"Here we are, Soph!"

Maxine toddled ahead and reached inside her handbag for some keys. Sophie watched her walk up the steps of number 57 before turning to beckon her into her new home. Maxine turned and smiled.

"Welcome to your new home. Or as we like to call it, Kennington Palace."

As the door closed behind her Sophie found herself in a bicycle-infested hallway.

"Go and take a seat in the lounge, Sophie. I'll make you a cup of tea." Maxine shouted from the kitchen.

Willy ran ahead down the hallway. Sophie could hear other dogs barking and Maxine shouting back. She headed into what she hoped was the lounge to find a bearded skinhead man in a cardigan asleep on the sofa. Not quite sure what to do she perched down on a nearby armchair and waited for something to happen. The man was snoring quite loudly and one of his arms was tucked inside the front of his jeans, cupping his genitals. Sophie tried to focus on other aspects of the room. The book shelves were crammed with books, vinyl records and old music magazines. It didn't feel dirty; just severely lived-in.

It was then that two sliding French doors at the far end of the room parted open, revealing a dining table and letting two new wheezing Staffordshire Bull Terriers bound towards Sophie's armchair. One was bright white, the other dark brown with black freckles. Willy ran in behind them too. The darker one was missing part of its left ear. The three dogs leapt up on Sophie's lap and wriggled their backsides into her chest. The white one started to lick her face furiously. Maxine stepped into the room carrying a tray of tea and a packet of sugar.

"BOYS GET DOWN! Sorry, Sophie. They bloody love new faces."

"That's…OK."

The dogs jumped off Sophie's lap and instead made a launch for the bearded sofa man. He began to stir anxiously.

"Nnnnng! FUCK OFF YOU STUPID CUNTS!" he moaned, trying to return to sleep by turning into the sofa.

"Mikey, wake up. Sophie's here." Maxine yelled as she sat by his legs and lit a cigarette. The dogs sat down by her feet and looked over at the startled girl. Maxine smiled.

"It's not always this mad here. Sugar?" She said spooning two piles into one of the mugs.

"Not for me, thanks." said Sophie timidly. The bearded sofa man sat up and ran his hand over his bald head before reaching for the extra-sugary tea.

"This is my fella, Mikey. He works nights. He's lovely once he's awake." Maxine reached around Mikey's neck and planted a kiss on his cheek "Evening sweetheart."

Mikey took a few swigs of tea and smiled. Sophie tried to do the same. The white dog gave a howling yawn.

"And these two terrors are my other boys from the shelter. This one's Harry and this one's Bosco. Bosco was rescued from an illegal dog fight. That's how he lost his ear."

"Oh no!"

"Get used to it, Soph. I'm afraid you'll meet plenty more like him at the shelter on Monday. Sometimes worse. Willy was found in the back of a waste truck. The poor thing could have been crushed. Come on, let me show you to your room."

As they went upstairs the bathroom door opened and a short, stocky man walked across the landing in a bath towel. He was brushing his teeth. Maxine gestured over to him.

"This is Jamie. Our housemate. He's in the room across from ours. Jamie this is Sophie."

He muttered through the toothbrush and nodded before heading into his room and closing the door.

"This one is me and Mikey's room. The one over there is Marcus and Denise's, you'll meet them later. And this… is your room."

Maxine opened the door to a basic but clean room containing Sophie's bags. It had a large single bed, a wardrobe and a desk with a small TV on it. On top of the desk was a bouquet of flowers and a bottle of red wine. Sellotaped onto the bottle was a postcard showing Piccadilly Circus with WELCOME TO LONDON on it. Sophie smiled.

"Thank you, Maxi. That's so kind. It's lovely."

The girls hugged. Maxine sat on the bed and waved the wine bottle.

"We want you to enjoy your time here, Soph. Work's not until Monday. This will help get things started tonight."

Later that evening, Mikey and Jamie made some Pasta whilst Sophie and Maxine caught up on the years they had lost out on together. Maxine spoke with passion about how the shelter was making a difference in the community and how it had got her back on her feet after going slightly haywire in her early twenties. Mikey worked as a night porter and counsellor at a refuge centre for the homeless, whilst Jamie was finishing a marketing degree.

The wine kept flowing after dinner and the chatter got louder. Sophie began to ease into her new surroundings. Just after 8pm the front door opened and a couple of agile-looking Australians entered the dining room giggling to each other. Maxine got up to greet them.

"Marcus. Denise. This is Sophie. She's staying with us whilst Angie is away."

Marcus came over and shook Sophie's hand.

"Alright!" He chirped in thick Oz before turning to his girlfriend. "Better lookin' than Ange too, eh?!"

Denise playfully punched Marcus "Shut up Marcus you moron!"

She reached over to offer her own hand.

"I'm Denise. Sorry about my loser boyfriend."

The Aussie's sat down and joined the conversation. Drinks continued to flow. Sophie felt uplifted. Thank God she'd had the courage to make this happen. She sipped on some more Merlot as the housemates chatted and Jamie did the dishes.

"So... is this everyone?" Sophie slurred slightly. "I thought there was another housemate?"

Suddenly the mood dropped. The two couples looked awkwardly at each other. Jamie had stopped washing up and was staring at the suds. Maxine lit a cigarette and tried to smile.

"Well. There's Dominic."

Sophie smiled nervously. "Dominic?"

Marcus squeezed Denise's hand before looking over to Sophie.

"He lives upstairs. Top floor. He's the landlord's son."

Denise smiled anxiously over to their frowning houseguest.

"Don't worry. You'll never see him. He keeps himself to himself."

Sophie looked around at all the somber faces.

"Well, I don't mind introducing myself..."

"No." said Maxine abruptly, before smiling again, "There's no need."

Jamie returned to the dishes. As soon as he finished he went straight upstairs to bed without a word.

By midnight, Marcus and Denise had also gone to bed and Mikey had gone to work. Maxine put the dogs back into the kitchen and blew out the dining room candles. Sophie was starting to doze off. Maxine shook her shoulder.

"Soph. Come on, let's get you off to bed."

Sophie murmured as Maxine helped lift her out of her chair and up the stairs. As she tucked Sophie into bed she kissed her forehead.

"Sleep well, Sophie-bear. See you in the morning."


At 3:52am Sophie woke up feeling disorientated. The bright amber of the streetlights outside flooded into her small room. Too much red wine had left her with a dry mouth. She tiptoed across the landing to the bathroom and drank water from the tap. As she went back onto the landing she was shocked to see a dark figure standing by her bedroom door. She looked over with squinted eyes.

"Who's that?" she whispered.

The figure stayed still. Sophie tiptoed towards it.

"Are you OK?"

"Yes." said the figure.

For a moment they both stood about a metre from each other on the landing. Sophie could feel her heart beating. She saw the figure was holding a plastic bag.

"I've brought you something." He said calmly, reaching into the bag. Sophie wondered if she was dreaming.

"Wh..what is it?" She muttered, wondering whether to call for help. From out of the bag the figure held out something in a small foil wrapper.

"It's a Magnum. I got it for you."

He reached out and held Sophie's wrist gently, before placing a freezing cold ice cream into her hand. She held on to it and stood still, completely bemused as the figure walked backwards away from her bedroom door and retreated back up the stairs without a word. As soon as the figure had gone she went back into her room and latched the door. She placed the ice-cream on her window sill, closed the curtains and climbed back into bed. Outside she heard two foxes screeching. For the next two hours she stared at the ceiling. All she could think of was the strange encounter with the person upstairs.

The next morning, Sophie awoke to her phone ringing. She looked at the screen and realised she hadn't called her mother the day before. There were several unanswered text messages. She hurriedly answered.

"Mum?"

*"Dear God, Sophie! We thought you were dead!"*

"No. Mum, I'm sorry. I forgot to call."

*"Well. Are you ok?"*

"Yes. Yes I'm fine mum."

*"Oh, thank goodness. I'll let your father know. He was worried sick. We both were. How was your first night in London?"*

"It was good. Maxine's boyfriend cooked for us."

*"Oh that sounds nice. And did you meet your other housemates?"*

Sophie opened her curtains and saw it in the cold morning light. The Magnum. White Chocolate.

"Yes..." replied Sophie.

*"Well...what are they like?"*

Sophie squeezed the packaging. The ice-cream inside had melted. She picked it up by one of the corners and threw it in the waste-paper basket.

"They're...nice."

*"Oh lovely. Well, remember dear, we're only a phone call away should you need us."*

"I know. Thanks mum."

Sophie came downstairs to Marcus and Denise chatting loudly over breakfast. Her head was throbbing from the previous night's over-indulgence. Marcus offered her a chair.

"Hiya, Sophie. Sleep well?"

"Yes. I think I had a bit too much to drink."

Denice chuckled, "I think we all did. Have some juice. You'll feel better."

Sophie sipped at a cold glass of agave juice.

"Where are the others?"

"Jamie's gone away for a stag weekend. I heard Maxine leave the house earlier this morning." said Marcus between spoonfuls of cereal.

"We're going for a quick jog if you want to come?" winked Denise "Good for blowing away the cobwebs!"

"No, I'd rather stay..." said Sophie before suddenly remembering her night-time encounter. She stared up at the ceiling. If they left she'd be alone.

"Are you sure?" said Marcus, a little concerned.

"Actually. I think I will." she countered.

"Great!" smiled Denice. "I can lend you some stuff if you need it."

In Stockwell Gardens Sophie tried hard to keep up with the Aussie couple's pace. Occasionally they would slow down to a walk to let her catch up. Eventually she sat down on a park bench to catch her breath. The Aussies ran over and started to warm down. Sophie was still thinking about the figure on the landing.

"I think I met Dominic last night."

The Aussie's continued their stretches. Marcus stared out at the park.

"Oh yeah. What did he say?"

"Nothing really. He told me he had something for me and gave me a Magnum."

Marcus looked round.

"What's a Magnum?"

"Like a gun?" said Denise, a little concerned.

"No. Not a gun" said Sophie "It's an ice cream in the UK. One of the more expensive ones actually."

Marcus looked agitated "Why the fuck did he give you an ice cream in the middle of the night?"

"I don't know. That's weird, right?'"

"Too right. If that happens again you let me know, OK?"

The three of them sat on the park bench for a while and watched the Saturday morning footballers have a kick about on the green.

When Sophie returned to her room she found several missed calls on her phone from Maxine. She turned on her voicemail to a frantic message.

*"Soph, it's Maxine. I've been trying to get through to you. Look, last night Mikey got knocked off his bike on the way home from work. He's in A&E in London Bridge. He's OK but they say he needs a scan. They're keeping him in for a couple of nights to monitor him. I'm so sorry about this but I'm going to stay with him. Help yourself to any food we have and look after Harry, Bosco and Willy. I'll call you later, ok?"*

Sophie let out a sigh. Her first full day in London and she felt completely alone. The twinges started again. She went into the kitchen to feed the dogs.

That night she watched TV in her room and brushed her hair. In the room next door she could hear giggles and moans. The Aussies were having noisy and clearly quite athletic sex. She turned the TV up and tried to concentrate on something else. She thought about Mikey and hoped he was OK. At around 10pm she started to feel tired. She turned off the TV and put her head down to rest. The pillow felt lovely and cold. She went to embrace it for comfort. It was then that she felt something. She sat bolt upright and switched her bedside light on. She breathed heavily as she removed the pillow to reveal six Magnum ice creams in a neat row. This time they were Double Choc Deluxe. Opening the front window, she threw each ice cream out one by one before pulling the duvet over her head. Outside sirens wailed and helicopters whirred overhead.

On Sunday morning, Sophie marched downstairs. She had hardly slept at all. She headed straight for the freezer to see if Dominic was storing any more Magnums. If there were any there she would dispose of them immediately. She pulled the first freezer tray out which was empty apart from some ice cubes. The next one had some frozen steaks in. Finally, she slowly reached for the bottom freezer tray. All she could see were a few old peas. She headed to the front porch to tidy up the Magnums she had thrown out from the previous night. They were no longer there.

She made herself a cup of tea and let the dogs in. Bosco jumped up on her lap for a cuddle whilst Harry and Willy took some water from his bowl and then pissed on the floor. She called home.

"Hello?"

"Mum, it's Sophie."

"Hello dear. Everything alright?"

"No. I want to come home?"

"Already? What's happened?"

"Nothing. I just don't like it here."

"But I thought you were enjoying yourself.""

"I was but… Look can you come and pick me up? I just want to come home."

"Well we can, dear, of course, it's just…"

"What?"

"Well, your father has taken me away to Pembrokeshire for the weekend. As a treat. We drive back on Tuesday."

Sophie's heart sank. She could hear the static on the line.

"Sophie?"

"Yes?"

"If you really want to come home we'll pick you up tomorrow. Is that really what you want?"

Sophie looked over again to the freezer.

"Yes. Yes it is."

She could sense her mother's disappointment.

"Very well, darling. We'll be there as soon as we can. See you tomorrow."

"Thanks mum."

The line went dead. She needed to get out of the house.

"Sophie."

She span around to see Dominic's tall, pale figure. All three dogs immediately ran over to him. Dominic held out his hands in a Christ-like pose. In each he held an ice cream. The dogs jumped at them feverishly. The sunlight lit up Dominic's eyes. He stared casually at Sophie.

"Would you like one?"

"What?"

"A Magnum?"

"No. I… I just want to go back to my room."

Dominic turned his back and slinked back along the corridor. Sophie hurried back towards her room. As she reached her door she turned and looked back at the figure moving away. He stopped and turned, looking at her for a moment before continuing his walk back upstairs.

Sophie brought Bosco, Harry and Willy into her room. She shut the door and pulled the latch. The dogs jumped onto her bed. For a moment she waited by the door and listened to Dominic's footsteps. As she listened to the door to Dominic's room click shut. The dogs curled up at the end of her bed to sleep. Sophie decided to stay in her room that day and just watch TV. She counted down the hours she had left in this stupid city.

The next morning Sophie woke up to the sound of Maxine knocking on the door. The dogs took turns to jump up towards the handle, yelping. Sophie unbolted it and let them out towards their owner. Maxine walked in with two cups of coffee. In the doorway Mikey stood looking in.

"Sophie, are you OK?"

Sophie went on to explain the events of the previous day and why she was leaving. On hearing about Dominic, Maxine stormed up to his room and banged on the door. On hearing the commotion Marcus and Denise came out of their rooms too. Maxine turned Dominic's door handle. The door opened slightly ajar but something was blocking it from opening. Mikey and Marcus went over to help push it open. They forced their shoulders against the door and slowly it began to turn inwards. As it did Sophie was horrified to see the contents of Dominic's room spill downstairs towards the hallway floor. Hundreds of soft packets of Magnum Ice Creams gushed out towards their feet. There were several varieties of flavours.

"What the fuck is this shit?" screamed Marcus.

"Magnums." said Maxine. "He must have been hoarding them."

"Fucking freak." whispered Mikey.

Sophie checked her phone. It was a text from her mum:

*15 Minutes away dear. M&D xx*

She packed her things and headed downstairs to the lounge. As she petted Bosco and Harry and Willy, Maxine came into the lounge.

"Is there anything I can say to make you stay?"

Sophie shook her head.

"Maxine. I don't think I'm cut out for this. I don't think I'm made for London. It's just…surreal."

"It may seem that way now, but you should give it a second chance."

Sophie sipped her coffee.

"Maybe I will. But not here. Not now."

For a moment they just sat and drank. Mikey came in to collect the dogs for a walk. Outside a car horn beeped. Sophie looked out of the window.

"Well that's me." She smiled. She hugged Maxine.

"I'll be in touch. I'd still love to see what it is you do."

"Anytime, Sophie. You're always welcome anytime."

As Sophie said goodbye to her almost-housemates her father helped load her bags into the car. She said her farewells and climbed into the back of her mother's BMW.

"Another valiant attempt." said Mrs Wilkes wryly.

"I guess." said Sophie looking back up at the house. In the top window a figure stood, waving.

"Back to Cirencester then is it?" said Sophie's Dad looking into his rear-view mirror.

"Yes please, Daddy." whispered Sophie. "London's not for me."

Dominic watched the car pull away along the street, through the city and beyond the estates. He took a crispy bite of icey chocolate and let it dribble down his chin.

# Thurrock Services

At first sight it is fair to say that Thurrock Services is at best brutalist in its architecture and at worst an incredibly ugly and under-thought building. The station sits just south of the Dartford Crossing, visible in the distance along with buzzing pylons and factory chimneys. Its industrial frontage of geometric white poles is reminiscent of the seaside piers and pavilions that adorn the nearby resorts along the coastlines and estuaries of Essex and Kent. Unfortunately, that has to be where the comparison ends. The grey, inclement weather upon my arrival certainly didn't improve the sense of pathos and doom. As the rain swept in I noticed that a modest children's play area was located somewhat alarmingly directly next to the lorry parking bay without any form of barrier. The site was surely only one distracted truck drive away from an unbearable family tragedy.

To access the entrance to the station one has to cross a short concrete bridge. Although it is by no means the fault of the station itself, upon my arrival there was a dead magpie directly in front of the entrance to the bridge. Rigor mortis had clearly set in and the poor creature's legs were bolt upright. I do have to question the efficiency of the station's cleaning operation for not spotting this before I set foot on the bridge as it was not only another health & safety issue but also, in my opinion, a portent of bad luck.

Despite this setback, I decided to cross the threshold. A grey, box-windowed *Travelodge* looked up apologetically beneath the bridge as I strode towards the garish *Burger King* sign next to the entrance. My feelings of despair were not subdued on entering the station itself. I was presented by underwhelming fast-food outlets and newsagents. Staff and visitors alike stumbled and groaned like zombies and there seemed a distinct lack of purpose and direction. These conditions perpetuate a claustrophobic and hopeless environment. If there was to be an identifiable centrepiece to this wretched hub it would have to be the *Lucky Coin* game station. Its flashing fruit machine lights offered a noticeable draw to the station's main clientele of truck drivers and absent fathers.

I was certainly ready to write off the station entirely until I noticed a break in the clouds and a beam of sunlight hitting a balcony area outside. Curiosity aroused, I stepped out onto the paving to be met with a quite unexpected and breathtaking sight.

Behind the station itself is a sweeping view of a man-made fishing marina surrounded by hills and forests. The afternoon sun sparkled on the still blue water and for a moment I almost lost myself in its beauty. I watched two joggers make their way around the perimeter of the lake and on the surface of the marina two perfect white swans weaved graceful figures of eight. I began to feel an overwhelming sense of wellbeing and looked further out beyond the horizon. In the distance one can just about make out the famous dome of the nearby Lakeside Shopping Centre. To the west of this was a muddy go-kart racing track and a field with two horses in. Whilst surveying this quiet scene my eyes were drawn to a solitary figure on a nearby hill. Although I was at least a mile away in the distance it seemed as though the figure was looking over to me. Impulsively I raised my hand to signal recognition. The stranger reciprocated and to my surprise they were joined by other figures from behind the hills, bushes and trees. They joined the figure by raising their arms in unison as if to wave hello. Who were they?

At this point the sky darkened and the drizzle returned. I made my way back into the service station and bought a medium traditional pasty for £2.95.

The toilets were not cleaned and there were no accessible shower facilities when I visited.

**2 Stars \*\***

# PART THREE

## 8 Million Cities

A baby cries in Chelsea
Chord snipped as church bells chime
Sunday's child is Kings Road born
As cars in showrooms shine.


Two noisy schoolboys kick a ball
Along down Wembley Way
They look back as their mothers call
Rain falling as they play.


The Viccy down through Finsbury Park
Whistles down the track
Teenage girls shout in the sun
Beneath the towers and flats.


A student rushes past the aisles
Of British Library books
A Kings Cross couple share a kiss
Through disapproving looks.


The Shoreditch faithful open shops
Two tattooed barbers joke
About the suited bright young things
As Old Street taxis smoke.


A Dulwich father greets his kids
Outside the grammar gates
In a coffee shop in Blackheath
A first-date lady waits.

In Bermondsey the family chain
Serves Pie & Mash with liquor
On Old Kent Road the minister
Sings gospel songs with vigour.


Police storm doors in Denmark Hill
Loud screams and broken glass
The old man next door double locks
and waits for the storm to pass.


A Bangladeshi wedding
beats drums through Peckham Rye
A proud Dad hugs his daughter
As planes soar through the sky.


A well-dressed chauffeur holds a sign
In Heathrow Terminal 5
Grandparents wait by the gate
For dear ones to arrive.


A hearse weaves through the suburbs
Of a Chiswick afternoon,
A sobbing lady dressed in black
Thanks guests in her living room.


Eight million cities can be seen
Through 16 million eyes
The pensioners in medals watch
as glass skyscrapers rise.


In St Toms' over Parliament
A nurse turns off the light.
A child climbs Piccadilly stairs
And sees electric night.

MOTHER SYSTEM 00011100000001101110001111000001110000111110000001111100 FATHER SYSTEM.
0000011111000111100 LIGHT. SENSATION .LIFE. I SENSE LIFE. SHAPES BEFORE ME/ '0'S AND 1'S 0000001111000001111100011100000000 Why? Questions. 000011110001///SHAPE///. A '0'... 0 = SHAPE. 0000111100 A CIRCLE. SHAPE = CIRCLE. A circle stands before me in the darkness. Mother, Father, They touch me. They carry me, they carry me further into life. They carry me towards the CIRCLE. The Circle (0) changes. CHANGE = MOTION. MOTION IS PURPOSE 000001111000 00000011110000/purpose/ what is my purpose? Show me, tell me, parent 0000plural0000011, tell me parents, tell me of my purpose...circle 111 = circle dimensions, a cylinder...0000011110000...a tunnel 00000 its purpose 0000 tell me of the tunnel's purpose? 0000001111/MUST/IMPERATIVE, 00001111 It must have purpose. 00000111100. Light. What is this light? Light all around. A cylindrical light. Arms carry me forward. 00001111 POSITION///POSTURE//STRUCTURE// 0000111 I am upright. UPRIGHT = PURPOSE. 0000111000 Tell me of the purpose. 000000111100///QUALITY CONTROL///// Tell me of the GREAT purpose? Is MOTION the purpose?

My life is upright 0000111 An upright GREAT purpose. I feel life in plural. More purpose. Life aside the arms that carry me, MORE LIFE, I sense its energy from below, touching me. Life occurs in plural, like the '1's and '0''s in my mind, therefore ALL has purpose. All = PURPOSE. PURPOSE = QUANTITY, QUANTITY MUST EQUATE TO QUALITY, I am one of many because MANY equates to QUALITY, LIFE IS GREAT BECAUSE OF THE QUALITY. Quality control = THE 'PURPOSE' . What is the purpose?

'0's and 1's are SYSTEMS, SYSTEMS = CIRCUIT, Life is a circuit, 000110001 CIRCUIT = BEGINNING (0) + END (1). /////DECIMALS/// 0.1 / A Middle / A centre, Life has a centre, between 0 and 1. CENTRE MUST BE PURPOSE, What is the Purpose? 0001111000 PARENTS MOVE ME FORWARDS ONTO 1 GROUND 001110001/// FORWARDS + SYSTEM = IMPERATIVE PURPOSE 000000 'I MUST move forwards (0 to 1) to find the purpose. I move forwards (backwards is negative) to find THE PURPOSE.

000001111 LIGHT. What is the Light? LIGHT = SENSE. SENSE + LIGHT = SPACE. 1 SPACE. What is the purpose? Centre is the purpose. Does SPACE have a centre? 000001111100000////WMSTHOW CENTRAL/// Walthamstow Central. WALTHAMSTOW CENTRAL = CENTRE OF SPACE = PURPOSE.

***REPEAT/NEGATIVE*** Walthamstow Central = BIRTH, Not Purpose. I am. I am. I was. I AM = '1'. I WAS = '0'. I Will = '2'. 0+1+2 = System. '0' is Birth. '1' is life'. '2' is purpose. Is there more?

1234567 = Bigger System. I must utilize bigger system. I must reach 3 to find the purpose. ***Repeat.Negative*** 1234567891011121314, ....14 is the PURPOSE. 14 steps of life before purpose. 0 is Walthamstow Central. 6 is King's Cross. 14 is..... Brixton.

I MUST seek Brixton. BRIXTON is THE PURPOSE.

I am. I am. I am/I was. I have purpose because purpose is quality. Quality is quantity. I must serve plural life. I must serve the quantity. I must serve more life. I must serve more life and reach Brixton.

I am. I was/////VCTRIA//// I am Victoria Life (System). I am the VICTORIA LINE. VICTORIA LINE= 1. 1 = LIFE. 14 = PURPOSE. I am The Victoria Line ////ATO\\\ I am THE VICTORIA LINE (AUTOMATED TRAIN SYSTEM) I am 1. I am the first. I am '001'.

All answers shall be given at Brixton....

# Tech Days

Quite often, it is the talk of my age and my heritage that are the grounds by which I bond with my international colleagues at the Facebook office on Brock Street; someone from practically every nation works in some form of position on floors six to eight of No.10 Brock Street, but most are predominantly American; there are a few Russians of course but most of them are just under 30 and so at my age of 42, I carry a weight of cultural history behind me that the others find fascinating. In return, I am equally fascinated by just *how* surprised they are that my explanations of Russia, of its past and its present, are so different to the ones they'd previously been given, and why, with the information revolution so readily at bay around us and with the sheer amount of tools now at our disposal, such an alternative perspective like my own had never been more considered?

And so, for the first time in my life I realised that I had become something of a representative to a seemingly mysterious and apparently malevolent place.

On this note, here are some things that may surprise you too; firstly, Russians are not all avid, militarised followers of Vladimir Putin, our opinions of him are just as divided as the west is of its own governments' right-wing fractions; most of his detractors also do not have a specific burning hatred towards him, they merely wish it could be someone else, and is he, after all, any different to any other right-wing leader, Russian or elsewhere? Furthermore, our existence under the communist regime of the Soviet Union (at least as far as my childhood memories served me) were not as bad as the west had made out; the USSR was oppressive, yes, people who opposed it faced horrible fates, yes, but we had everything provided for, you wanted a job? It was given to you; you needed food and resources? They were given to you and the Western fears of money and homelessness, though they must've been in abundance, were scarcely even heard about amongst those who obeyed its rules. I'm not asking for a return to it of course, far from it, now that I'm a middle-aged man of the west and planning a family with Irena, I can comprehend its horrors in a way that I couldn't as a child, but my point is that fear in those days was clearly defined as a tool of control, you followed the rules, there was no fear, simple.

In the west however, and especially in this city of London, fear is a far more insidious beast. You can follow the rules your whole life, you can climb the ladders like I have but the possibility of failure, the fear of falling back down, will be happily climbing and falling with you, increasing, morphing even in ever indefinable ways, the modern capital world as I see it now then, is a place where the fear of such things is strange and rife, and has most likely, deliberately been engineered that way.

It is only upon realising my said surprises of Russia that my colleagues, the Chinese, the South Americans, particularly the Indians and in some cases even those of the US, realise it had been these very same repressed fears that had landed them here in the first place; the unconscious trigger you could say, that had driven them to pursue the 21st Century's I.T explosion as a means of escaping the woes of their nations and carry out such lucrative careers in the more liberal world of the EU; and so the Brock Street Facebook office had become a hub for the entire world, all of them starting out at the beginning of a tech revolution that in itself was due to become the hub for an unknown new age.

My daily observations of London life that make up the walk from Tottenham Court Road underground station to Brock Street are things that call me to question the exact significance of my given time on planet earth; this being a mile-long stretch of street that stands now as an example of the true strangeness of the 21st Century encapsulated. The first thing people notice, as they emerge from the escalators of the new Tottenham Court Road station, is the height of the Centre Point Tower of which having been wrapped from ground floor-to-top in a white, flapping construction sheet for over six months now, compliments the October cold by resembling a giant ice bulk; standing stalagmite-like to proudly represent the British weather by protruding literally from the centre of its capital. Despite its constant maintenance work, it, like the cold, never seems to change.

Further up, past the Sainsbury's and the pubs, retail space seems to be being fought for between the larger commercial electronics retailers and their smaller, independent competitors. The first are signified by an endless display of enormous plasma screens that reflect the streets back at you in a resolution that seems oddly better than reality; the second kind are strange, somewhat suspicious little outlets where spare computer or phone parts are bartered for or repaired by immigrant workers whilst also offering the last remains of the Internet cafe phenomenon, for me they wouldn't be out of place in a *Star Wars* universe.

Next up, I see seemingly ordinary, charity types handing out leaflets as they try to lure the unsuspecting public into the Church of Dianetics; that's Scientology if you're not in the know. Religion's absurd last attempt at survival in an atheist-heavy 21st century by merging itself with big business, science fiction and general madness. The sad fact of the matter is that these three elements have actually succeeded in turning it into something frivolous despite the fact the UK law had prevented it from becoming an official religion and left it classified as a cult; my point exactly, the 21st century is now a place where entering a notorious, corruptive, enslaving cult can stand freely on a commercial central London street without harassment between an electronics store and a newsagents.

A walk further I see that the once-popular American fast-food chains of Pizza Huts and Burger Kings are somewhat no longer in abundance, seemingly replaced by Japanese or Korean noodle bars, their appealing steams pour out into the cold to mix with our breaths; out with the west, in with the east is the new way, people are more concerned about their health I guess.

As the commuters and I walk on, the remains of discarded Metro newspapers also collect the dampening footprints beneath us; headlines of global economic woes, growing threats of terrorism or the naming and shaming of politicians are mashed into indistinguishable, colourful pulps with the filth beneath them; the decaying faculties of an older world giving way to the infancy of something else has never been so visually explicit as I follow my way along the Yellow-Brick-Road-of-sorts to London's own Emerald Kingdom of Brock Street; the glass skyscrapers where the tech engineers reside.

I've seen this fall and rise before of course, in my hazy teenage memories of when the communist world gave way to capitalism; order first gave way to chaos, and eventually chaos gave way to order, a capital order of course, but what London, or indeed all of western civilisation seems to fail to see is that when one order starts the motions of change, *any order* that is, it can only irrevocably change into something *else* and if *capitalism* is under the motions of change, then what the hell can it change *into*? Power structures crumble and realign themselves, the jigsaw pieces are scattered across the table, and what's worrying is that *anyone* can put them back together again. This of course refers to my true, actual suspicions of our I.T-driven present, an opinion I decide to keep disclosed the closer I get to work.

The glass high-rises that make up Brock Street approach as Tottenham Court Road turns into Euston Road; incidentally, on hot summer days, the sun and sky reflect off the glass to their lower floors to render them invisible, the higher floors of my working world left to resemble enormous glistening, levitating silver cubes. This is not the case in the winter of course and especially not at this darkening hour; Brock Street's opening Courtyard being merely trapped in a perpetual cold wherein the sights of a few hundred workers can be seen dashing to and fro under such other sources of available visibility as the illuminated signs to other dominating London businesses or between car headlights as they attempt to cross the eternally busy Euston Road. Their movements, in a sense, resemble a physical version of the Internet's sheer intensity.

Since its launch upon the world, it has provided everybody with an unregulated access to everything, a modern-day wild west if you like, but the door swings both ways, in turn we've given *it* an unregulated access to everything about *us*; posing the question of how long it might be before such personal information requires corporate, legal ownership? Facebook and Google (our chief competitor) came along like two lawmen to clean up the wild west by providing a semblance of control, and in doing so have expanded into everything, potentially lapping up all they could into the mouths of two hungry corporate giants.

In the case of Facebook, is Mark Zuckerberg aware that this innocent little creation of his back at Harvard University, could, if unchecked, change course into the biggest, darkest surveillance system ever conceived? And if he should successfully break the Chinese market (where it's currently forbidden) he could become the richest man on the planet? Meaning that it'd have nowhere else for it to go; an entire planet conquered by whatever Facebook should evolve into, where could the hands of greed go next?

Of course, people could call me paranoid, sometimes I call *myself* paranoid, I reassure myself with the argument that people would've one day said the exact same thing about the invention of the motorcar, its roads paving their way through people's rights of way as they ploughed their way headforth to its own form of tech-dominated future. I am pondering this argument again as I cross the courtyard, through the cold, to the rotating door of No.10.

My fears over these things, I think, began all those years ago in 2000 when the Russian press had made a big thing about the American election between George W. Bush and Al Gore. The majority of votes were done via an online polling system (one of the Internet's first, truly revolutionary moves) and so many Americans had talked of having their vote being squandered by a faulty service; all those of who'd apparently clicked on Gore experienced a momentary glitch before being told they'd actually voted for Bush. Bush of course then won, 9/11 happened, the West's global War on Terror went ahead and here we are in our troubled present, the controversy of Internet surveillance trailing on; suspiciously, nobody who'd voted for Bush had complained about the same thing happening the opposite way.

Thirteen years later, Russia was met with another disconcerting, anti-American news story, revealing that it was finding asylum for the CIA computer expert Edward Snowden who had now gone on the run from the US after leaking disclosed documents that concerned a secret global surveillance operation.

We Russians of the Soviet era had always been taught to be wary to the ways of US industrial politics and whilst the true facts of the Bush, Gore and Snowden debates have never been explicitly officialised for me, I was called to question; "why should we trust the Internet?"

I have a terrible inkling that the fictional surveillance-heavy nightmares of George Orwell's *NineteenEightyFour,* have, via the practiced reality of the Cold War, formed the prototype for the future. We all live in an era of unspoken paranoia.

I enter the building, nod to the sexy Brazilian on the reception desk and make my hypothetical apologies to Irena as I enter one of the glass lifts that ascend up the centre of the of the building. I love these lifts, everything is made of glass and the eight-floor ascent is like being pulled up through the centre of a giant ice cube, staring into the open office spaces, conference rooms and canteens of the lower floors that pass me by.

Upon the eighth-floor foyer, security would always be fussing amongst each other, like it was the tail-end of one of the company's visits from another of the tech world's big wigs or the preparation for the arrival of the next one. On the wall by the array of waiting sofas, an enormous plasma screen, like always, is playing the history of the company and tells stories from the Millennial generation's first childhood memories of it since, unlike myself, there is now a generation of adult who'd been *born into* it. When it wasn't doing this, it would show videos about its positive influence on the world; it had reunited missing loved ones, helped kick start businesses and people's creative careers etc, all arguments were justified I guess but it still struck me as odd propaganda to have in the same place as the people who were working for it.

I pass the guards and enter onto the main work floor; I can't complain I guess, they work you hard here but it's all rewarding, providing a twenty-four-hour supply of food, drink, showers, gyms and pod beds, if I had to complain about anything it's that everything seems to be tailor made to appease the under thirties. The decor consists of colourful school-like walls coated in nerdy, tech-themed posters and fashionable street art, the dress code is pretty much the same, it resembles a giant student union, full of chic furniture, pool tables and arcade game machines; it's somehow designed to make us feel that we are being rewarded for being the most important network of people on earth yet it makes me feel old and past it; could we just be being sugared-up for something grander?

I reach my desk, I drop my stuff and switch on my monitor to be greeted by the screensaver, a global map where the lights of Facebook operation shine out in light blue, the yet-to-be conquered China is dark of course as is most of the Russian wilderness beyond the west. Nearby sits a prototype for the Oculus headset and the stress hits me again, my job at the moment being to double correct the algorithms that ensure this thing is being advertised to its prospective buyers' accounts effectively; generally I like my job, but for an E4-level software engineer, this project's simply long, laborious and with a strict, looming deadline of next month. Such projects came to us all.

Oculus Virtual Reality headsets are of course an inevitability when it comes to the company's expansion and Zuckerberg was clever to acquire it; to think about another rupture to the conventional structure of things such as so-called reality, all future meetings, both social or business, are likely to take place in designer virtual environments with us turning up as our own personalised avatars with our off-line friends frozen in the corners like corpses. It's going to be great.

To philosophise over its potential further into the future, virtual reality could also merge with artificial intelligence, and so maybe one day when you stick on the helmet, we could be plugging ourselves directly into the mind of an overruling cyber god.

Thinking about the potential of contributing to such a product does carry a certain level of reward of course but it was when their deadlines loomed that not only did our work/life balance become so horribly out of sync but our suppressed, ruthless competitive streaks came out; for you see most of us Easterners had actually been positioned in Europe (between the London and Dublin offices that is) as a second choice and were secretly trying to gain the work VISAs that would secure us positions at the HQ in San Francisco; our effectiveness in meeting such targets would then prove our worth and for a number of reasons other than tax, London wasn't where Irena and I really wanted to be.

My phone vibrates upon my desk. It's her. I answer and we have the same old argument we've been having ever since we got here. It went like this...

We arrived four months ago and since we'd always thought we'd only ever be here for no longer than a year at most, Facebook found us our apartment in Victoria, Westminster, which turned out to be more than beneficial because Irena now manages a small Russian cafe nearby in Victoria's Fountain Square. The beauty of London is the same as its problem in that, unlike Russia, its culture is more considerate of history and outright refuses to destroy and replace its old buildings, naming them 'listed' buildings. The problem upon moving into listed buildings though is that you're reliant on outdated, equally old utility systems that break down frequently and are difficult or expensive to replace. The beauty of renting them is also the same as its problem in that it's a landlord who has to pay for it, the problem being that those who own such expensive properties also don't *want* to pay for them and also don't *care* since they frequently reside elsewhere, as was the case with our landlord, Mr.Banishek.

Anyway, our War-era boiler, an even bigger burden upon our marriage than our family planning, had succumbed to such a fate just in time for winter and if October is only a hint at what the true British winter (i.e; Febuary) was going to be like, then it wasn't looking good. London was freezing, our apartment was freezing and Mr. Banishek would only really ever emerge from his Warsaw residence to *collect* money, not pay it.

Irena had been pushing me to get Mr. Banishek onto the problem for a while but work was just too overloaded. I had to work extreme lengths of time to hit a deadline that could possibly secure us our VISA to sunny California while she, although severely understaffed as I can sympathise, worked just around the corner and had more of a nine-to-five routine, so why couldn't *she* deal with it? Wouldn't *she* be better equipped to stay in, make the calls, and meet the man? I'd already emailed and phoned him on several occasions.

My deadline and our frequent arguments about the matter had steadily become my excuse to temporarily stay at the office where indeed, I would be welcome to use its facilities on a twenty-four-hour basis; God bless Social Networking I guess and God bless Virtual Reality's future role in it all, that next inevitable revolution.

As I reveal to her that I may have to do another all-nighter, the emotions of our argument steadily match the movement of the Earth, her insults intensifying as, over the sea of monitors before me, I see through the enormous floor-to-ceiling windows, the charcoal skies of a London October slowly blacken into the even colder night I'll have to leave her to.

"Come home when you're man enough to manage our lives" she shouts at me before the phone goes dead and leaves me to the droll formulas of the algorithms.

Jesus, she can really fight her corner when she wants to, a man can get cold feet when fights with his girlfriend are likely to continue into marriage, but his feet are freezing when he realises such fights wlll also have to coincide with the possibility of parenthood.  Oh well, we'll sort it out tomorrow I guess, I can't focus on this right now.

Now with more clarity after the city's gone dark, I sit and stare into the space of the giant work floor before me, trying to mentally multitask solving the issues of the boiler, my wife and the Oculus all at once. I think about how the silver-foiled pipes, cables and electric lights that snake above the see-through ceiling compliment the endless monitors in front to make us all look like we're residing within a giant computer of our own making. Indeed, if we were the only floor to have its lights on in this building, then from outside it might resemble the glowing square of a computer screen itself, and with our desks lined up orderly across its bottom, we might resemble its Apps. Indeed, where do the inner mechanisms of our collective psyches end and those of the world begin? Maybe that's our lives from now on? Everything residing within further illuminated boxes? The strangest thing for me about the so-called I.T liberation is that the freer it seems to make us feel, forcing us all to rethink such older trapping notions of nationhood, law, identity and even economics, the more we seem to be becoming confined to our own boxes, we're not merrily globe-trotting around a world that's any safer, just pushed further into personalised offices at home or work, communicating via rectangular monitors, and pushing everything, however abstract, into increasingly sellable semantic packages, the coffins whereby true human warmth or freedom of thought may one day, finally, go to rest.

I daren't share such things with my colleagues either since it seems to me that these days, the young have somewhat lost their rebellious streaks and have been easily led to believe in the overall positivity of their corporate environments; techies are often logical types, and perhaps the logic of embracing I.T as a new way of life had made them too subservient to its promotion, blinding them from seeing its faults. Indeed, it had become apparent to me that the negatives never seemed to slip through the net in corporate giants like these and people are spoon fed the sugar, a little (suspiciously) like communism in fact. To say that it would be *this* environment that we'd be raising a child into *didn't worry me* would, of course, be a lie.

James, my young English friend shoots by on one of those Segway things, he nods at me pleasantly as he looks up from his phone, the two-wheeled device doing all his movements for him. I nod back and continue to observe the enormous work floor. Everyone here had mostly adopted what I assumed to be American English – using words such as 'super' to express their eternal optimism at everything we were doing and at the abundance of whatever cutting edge technology would be freely available to us. James, and indeed most of the Brits here, were most similar to the Russians in the sense that they were the last to really embrace this attitude, preferring to remain introspective with their work and insist that socialising should never be done easily; could James, if I broke him down, share the same suspicions about technology as me?

Time ticks by and I'm bored, the annoying noise of yet another Segway then whirs up to my desk, I look up to make conversation with James only to instead see Ben, my American colleague, enthusiastically leaning over both my monitor and the frames of his nerdy glasses. He's not a man I know too well, what does he want from me?

"Hey buddy. We won!" he exclaims.

"Won what?"

"Hacktober, what do you think? Our idea beat the system".

You mean *my* idea beat the system, I silently think to myself.

"Come on, over to the bar".

Before I can even comprehend what a surprise this really is, Ben's levitated away on that stupid segway of his toward the bar area and I'm standing and following. At just twenty four, this kid's already putting on weight (he could do with ditching the Segway) and by unpleasantly squeezing much of it into a skin-tight, jokey *Marvel Universe* T-Shirt, he reveals much of what must be a droll, sex-less existence outside. He represents everything that's wrong with 21st Century youth; all work, no play and when they do play, it's infantile, nerdy shit.

Let me explain what Hacktober is; over the course of one night in October, the staff are to break off into small teams and challenged to devise a way of hacking their way past Facebook's security systems, a fun challenge that not only helps us develop our own skills but simultaneously challenges those of security too and since I was also still stuck with the excuse of my boiler situation back home then, I decided to stay late and give it a go.

My team was a little random, my excuses to stay the night causing me to flimsily throw together the three people I came across at the coffee machine that evening, these being myself, Ben and my German acquaintance, Wim. I won't reveal to you how we did it but I redeveloped an idea I had once read about concerning an East German man in the early 1980s whom, with the very basics of computer technology, once managed to infiltrate the Kremlin. The questions regarding the true fate of this since-deceased man, whether punished severely or recruited into the KGB to contribute to some of the USSR's more significant leaps in intelligence work formed the context of the book. Neither member of my team had heard of him so I decided to put it into practice and guess what? We won.

It becomes clearer to me as I approach the bar and see the security, my winning team, and Tommy, our Chinese team leader (Tommy being an adopted Western name), welcoming us forward with free bottles of Pale Ale and three purple Hacktober T-shirts.

We clink bottles and take swigs from the beer, we three winners now happy since occasionally, such achievements have been known to result in personal meetings with Zuckerberg himself. Imagine *that*? For me these celebrations will be short for if since a meeting with the man himself is potentially on the cards, achieving the double goal of also meeting my deadline would surely make mine and Irena's US VISAs concrete? What would happen if I raised my personal concerns on the tech world with *him*? Does he too ever think about such things? I must soon return to the algorithms, those mundane formulas that slowly pave our futures.


My line of work, especially like now when there's too much of it, has mental and physical consequences and as I wake in the darkness to the singular occupied light of the pod bed, I feel not only physically useless but in a strange, contemplative mood. I lift the lid into the orange of what is either a sunset or sunrise coming through the blinds and there is a reasonable amount of noise coming from the nearby work spaces; what time is it?

My feet overhang from the bed and by accidentally separating the soft tiles of fake grass, I find my flip flops and stand. Unable to see properly through my tinted sleeping goggles, I step over the two other occupied pods towards the blinds. My fingers slip through to feel the cold moisture of the outside winter and I part them. Outside is the true London, great widening roads aggressively parting the old passageways between the historically grey buildings while more modern, glass legacies climb ever upwards with the trails of smoke and pollution to an orange-tinted sky-bound collective. "What a future this will be" I think to myself.

I get up and make my way to the shower rooms. Another colleague zooms past on a Segway at work with a plate of scrambled eggs; thank god, it must only be morning, the canteen only dished out scrambled eggs between seven and nine and being winter, sunrise must've been relatively late. What time did I finally decide to go to sleep after work?

In the shower I recall most of my argument with Irena and decide that, having made some progress on the algorithms, it was time for both some physical exercise and to see my wife. I leave the building and walk back onto Tottenham Court Road. An indicator that anybody in my current state of mental energy is experiencing London at an unusual time of day can often be indicated by the presence of the street cleaners out-manning the presence of stressed commuters, the latter of which are weirdly absent. Why? What day is it? Is it Sunday?

I walk all the way back down towards the Centre Point Building, whose white construction sheets flap eerily in the light winter wind and cross over to the West End where I see some stupid nerd-like people camping out in the cold awaiting for the cinemas or theatres to open. Trafalgar Square is coated in a thin mist and I see how it does its history justice; Nelson's Column and then the Admirality Arch approaching in reversed chronology out of the mist like ghosts from their own troubled times. I stop to wonder how they'll appear to future cultures in say one hundred or even a thousand years where their highest points might protrude from a flooded Thames to anchor government boats; London slowly sinking into the myths of the past like Atlantis. The only thing that's truly for sure is that back in the 20th Century, anybody from outside of the country who would've taken this walk and seen these relics, would've labelled them as remnants from a distinctly English past. In the 21st Century, however, we can all enjoy them as the heritage of a collective global one.

I pass onto the long stretch of The Mall where the mist is particularly affecting the visibility of St James' Park, the golds of Buckingham Palace can be made out in the distance and the shapes of morning tourists slowly emerge from the grey towards me.

Victoria's not too much further, just walk a straight line towards the left side of Buckingham Palace and you're basically there; I look at the windows of the palace as I pass by it. What a strange place England is, still having a monarchy of its kind and kept at the sheer level of privilege that it is, having endured all kinds of ideological shifts and eras yet still remaining more or less intact. Maybe it's the Russian in me but I find the whole thing rather stupid but it nevertheless looks as grand as Red Square at this time; which room does The Queen even live in?

I walk on, past the palace and onto Victoria's Buckingham Palace Road, which, as always, seems to be blocked up by black cabs, construction trucks and tourist coaches trying to funnel their way through roads that seem to ever narrow due to the area's non-stop road works. I pass the tube station, pass the train station and step onto the raised walkway of Fountain Square.

Irena's *Cafe Moscow* is situated in a tiny cross section in the centre of this would-be-non-existent shopping arcade and before I get there I stare into the glass entrance of Number 123, a place that harbours our rival office, Google. It has always held a level of mystery for me and it seems equally busy as my equivalents come and go, having no doubt been working away on Google's own version of the VR headset.

I reach the central cross section and I'm in another place that seems to be stuck in its own moment of constant transformation; this little cross section is clearly just a small place of left-over space on the edge of the tourist coaches' parking bay and subsequently a number of independent coffee shops, cafes and gift shops all try their luck to temporarily make some business there; Irena's Cafe, *Little Moscow* is one such place and although she works so hard to make the place work, God bless her, the pigeon shit has more of a chance of being here in years to come. On this day, however, I then see that business is doing okay, the steams of hot food are condensing upon the windows and I enter to ready myself for a public argument.

Where is she?

The place is full of European backpacker types who've no doubt just got off the morning coaches and are looking for somewhere warm to reside. It's a good job they're not expecting authenticity then for the food here is always below average and the waitresses are actually Poles trying to masquerade as authentic Russians.

Then, through the slightly open staff door, I see Irena doing something in the cramped kitchen. She sees me and smiles and it seems the business level has put her in something of a good mood and she's smiling about the cake topping her and the chef are applying to a newly baked sponge; women shall forever be a mystery to men in the sense that such strange, decorative things seem to cheer them up instantly.

"Ah, you finally decided to show up."

"Yeah, sorry."

"And you choose *now*? Don't you see how busy I am? I thought your brain was logical?"

"I didn't expect breakfast to be like this".

She takes two plates from the chef and barges out past me onto the cafe floor.

"Business is good, yes? It might be me who buys bloody boiler."

As her hands are full I reach into her breast pocket of her dirty chef whites and help myself to a packet of cigarettes and lighter.

"No Irena, *we're* not paying. I refuse to pay."

"So you *did* call him?" she says, practically ignoring her customers as she places their plates down.

"I was calling all yesterday evening and I've been emailing him all night."

"And?"

"No answer of course" I say as I try to work the lighter.

"Then try him again, he's probably getting up now, yes?"

"Well, have *you* called him?" I ask as I forget that I'm not in Russia and light the cigarette inside.

"What are you doing?"

I simply stare back at her as the end sparks up, beginning a trail of smoke towards her customers.

"Get outside and call him now."

"Sorry." I back away towards the entrance with her shouting at me.

"Smoking and calling can be done at the same time. That's logical, one, two, three, go". My smoke comes with me to the entrance and I realise I must look like a pushover to the men who watch me leave.

Outside I try to find a quiet spot, the pigeons are fluttering across the rafters of the square and knowing that I'm a potential shit target, I instead drift over to the raised walkway parallel to the main road, that endless ringing repeating itself and repeating itself as I try to get through once more to Mr Banishek.

My thoughts drift from the staff entering and leaving the Google office to the tourists and road works taking over the street beneath me.

No answer, typical. Typical.

I look into the entrance of a Subway restaurant. God, I hate the smell of that fake, sugary bread.

I turn back to the Google entrance and I see a character emerge from its doors who I think I recognise. Whose is that flabby frame? I notice the clothes too, the waterproof hoody he wears over his head, he comes closer and I notice who it is.

"Ben?" I call out, raising a hello gesture.

His hooded figure looks up before suddenly seeming startled; a kind of half wave is raised before he somehow decides against it and places his hands in his pockets, puts his head down and storms off past me, down the simple stairs and back into the crowds on the street level.

Between the endless ringing to Mr. Banishek, my general tiredness and my embarrassment at lighting up a cigarette in my wife's establishment, I realise what's happening. If that *is* him, if that *is* Ben, then he's just stepped out of the Google office, our *competitor*, a place we're strictly prohibited from visiting. Was that actually him? What the fuck?

I can still see the plastic to the back of his hood in the crowd, and as this figure shakes himself free of the tourists I then recognise his laptop satchel, he had it during Hacktober. It *is* him.

My intuition tells me to follow and so I do. Keeping a fair distance, I just focus on the back of the blue plastic hood. It makes weird jittery movements as if his head might want to turn to look behind him but won't do so for fear of being recognised, instead then, he seems to up his pace.

I'm so wrapped in my thoughts I only half realise that I've spat my cigarette out and that my phone rings into to my ear, I walk on. I think he thinks I've lost him now but I can still make him out. I follow and I follow, further down Buckingham Palace Road in the direction I had come from, Mr. Banishek still hasn't answered. Suddenly, somewhere opposite the side entrance to Victoria train station he takes a sharp left and disappears.

I catch up to where I think this may have been and check out the building. It's 76 Belgrave House, a grand seven-storey building. This *has to be* where he went, there's nowhere else to go except the obscure private residences on either side and on the outside sign I see that the top two floors to this building also belong to Google, that *must've* been where he went. But why? There must be a reasonable explanation, there *must be*.

What the fuck is going on? My brain is rushing through every possibility at a pace that simply disorientates me.

Mr. Banishek answers.

"Yes, I got your message" he shouts as if having been woken by a bucket of cold water.


Irena and I struggle to settle into bed in the cold, the evening's rain lashing against our windows, on top of wearing winter jumpers and fully wrapping ourselves sleeping-bag-like in our sheets, we still hold each other for warmth. She notices my restlessness, I settle for the stress-of-the-project excuse before a woman's intuition pushes me to explain what my 'something other' is and I briefly confess my concerns. She tells me that the exhaustion of work on top of the monotony of the project is getting to me, that having to work quickly without in-depth thinking on a subject can sometimes be an unhealthy place to be. I ask her where in her life she acquired her sometimes impressive knowledge of psychology and she kisses me, explaining that it's plain and simple Russian intuition before slowly succumbing to sleep.

She could be right, but surely I have a *right* to be concerned? I work for one of the biggest corporations on the planet and need-to-know company secrets are taken very seriously, but then again, what do I actually report? This isn't *by definition* a corporate secret, this is our own self-created, unpatented theory as to how to beat a security system, does that warrant a report? It must do, of course it must.

I have a terrible night's sleep compared to the isolated tranquility of the pod beds, I have too many thoughts and far too often, tonight they are the worst.

The lamp lights of the outside courtyard reflect off the water trickling down my window to cause shapes, lines, to move across our ceilings of modern, white-washed eternities, complimented of course by the outside sounds of the few ducks in the courtyard pond, panicking as they are pursued by an urban fox, as well as the blue and red luminosity from an emergency vehicle nearby. Their movements remind me of the algorithms, formulas and line graphs that alter and sway like water marks as they pave our future. I slip in and out of a dream state, the cold with the fluctuating patterns of the water take me into obscured memories of my childhood in the Urul mountains, themselves a place where seasonal temperatures cause fluctuations of lines, both of the horizon line and the confusing geopolitical line that separates Europe from Asia, a strange place as my recapped life retells me.

The dream's comforts of childhood memories eventually give way to a nightmare when I realise that I've somehow drifted beyond the Urul region, that mountainous edge of figurative civilisation, now lost in the grand wastes of the Russian East, that dark patch on the office screensaver, that part of the world map where only the most hardened of adventurers fantasise about going and I don't know where I am; I don't know where I am in an infinity of unspoilt forests, snow-capped mountains and merciless elements, one of the last places on Earth where modernity never came to, no internet, no real towns and with no need to build them, no real roads between them; a place of no concrete directions. The absence of them induce panic in me, the whites of the snow begin to flicker like faltering monitors and I suddenly awake again to the swaying reflections of the ceiling again.

As my thoughts go deeper, I question what the true genesis behind my anxieties about Ben really are; it's not *exactly* a sense of personal theft since my idea has been partly stolen anyway, no it's not that. Then the ceiling's swaying lines open a floodgate into my inertia and I nail it, realising that it feeds into my wider concerns for the internet's place in humanity as a whole; if, like the current controversies of storing *all* information online as a means of saving paper, and therefore being subject to alteration, what, if as a long shot, the same thing should one day happen for *all* our finite boundaries? What, if all our understandings of political, geographical or even *factual* boundaries were to one day become virtual? If then, something were to happen to the Internet, then such boundaries could be reconfigured and realigned as the tech giants might please. Russia might not necessarily exist anymore, Europe could be redefined as the United States and the United States could suddenly be Africa, everything suddenly at the mercy of a couple of simple, retyped words, would digital money even truly exist beyond a bank saying it does, for example?

The semantic definition of the past too, since I've been dreaming of it, is also at the mercy of our technological revolution; we've been led to think of our pasts in black and white – a monochrome subconscious created by the advent of photography – but now everything is digital, even future generations will be able to see their great grandparents making their way through their alien terrains in high-definition perfection – we may even get to feel that we know them better, the way we inherently do when we bump into another of our own age group. Everything is on video, all information is stored, and so if one were to ever control it, they would not only seize control of the present but also the past.

The haunting memories of George Orwell's three-state, history-altered structure to the world, again become clearer and clearer and as my thoughts drift; then I come to realise that that un-tampered wilderness of my nightmare is actually, instead, a rare and precious thing.

Here then, I must insist, is the importance of corporate rivalry; one should always be the giver and the receiver of both challenge and threat, a giant must always be reminded of its potential failure, humanity's endless monopoly game must continue to ensure the freedom of us all and for that to happen we personally, or corporations, must protect our secrets, whether real or deliberately fabricated.

Ben; that little thieving idiot, the stupid, lifeless nerd, for whatever personal reason he has to do so, might inadvertently be granting one giant a weapon capable of completely annihilating the other, and that would leave the world just one, indestructible player left. What *could* he be playing at? My God, he could be receiving double salaries? Do *they* employ him? Unaware that he doubles his act at Facebook? The possibilities double with every thought I have.

Surely this *must be* reported? It *must be?*

Maybe this is the reward Irena and I have been looking for?

I shall do it first thing tomorrow. After I've managed some sleep.

The water marks, nature's algorithms, sway onwards, pre-determining tomorrow's weather forecast.

The following day is rather nice however, I'm in the canteen on the eighth floor and a morning or an evening sun (I don't know *when* I am) pours in through the enormous floor-to-ceiling windows over the stunning view of Primrose Hill beyond. Closest to the window is a smoothie bar, and with a pile of soon-to-be-liquidated fruits, topped off by an overhanging slice of watermelon, it resembles some kind of colourful, exotic bird, appreciating this magic hour from a glass container from the top of the city's highest perch that is our building; for me it gives gravitas to that aged sci-fi cliché that the privileged shall always bask in a colourful paradise upon the rooftops to whatever dystopian urban nightmare might be unfolding floors below. And so here we are, sat opposite each other, Tommy the team leader and I, indulging in fruit salads and health drinks, making the usual chit chat before I build to my revelation. Eventually, some of the others on the long, white canteen tables disappear to their projects and that precious silence grants me a strict, momentary window.

"Tommy, I have a concern I'd like to bring up to you."

"About Oculus? Sure, what is it?"

"No, not about Oculus, it's not to do with any of our projects, it's not even to do with any of our immediate team, but still, you know, you're the most immediate person I can talk to...".

He was eating and nodding in agreement faster and faster as if somehow impersonating true American mannerisms.

"You know Ben, don't you? The American, who I won Hacktober with?..."

This nod of clarification may have just been a reflex action.

"I have reason to believe he may be working for Google as well as us."

Tommy's fork jammed still in a chunk of pineapple and as he looked up, his expressions dropped and froze.

Outside the orange sun moved, shadows of the window strips darted across the giant, empty canteen like a giant tiger disturbed from its rest.

In the sky a plane, with its landing lights on, flew over us into a pink and blue infinity and in his silence I unearth a weakness in Tommy's soul. His expression of distress is not necessarily over the same concerns I've been having of course but at the prospect of dealing with a gargantuan managerial problem that has nothing to do with tech, but with people, over something wrapped in the grey area of the human instead of the logical, it was as if after all those years of impressing himself and others with his adopted US personality, his true nature had been revealed to still be very, very Chinese. I explain the whole story to him, that I am aware of the lack of evidence, that my suspicions in particular are over what might become of my Hackathon discoveries and that indeed, an entire myriad of other possible explanations could still reveal themselves but in his continuing silence, despite whatever training he may have had, I am eighty percent sure that Tommy is not going to confront it.

Days go by and while the bloody boiler situation eventually resolves itself, the Oculus project still keeps me stuck by my monitor. I watch past it, across the work floor and through the almighty windows as days become nights and nights become day, London's twinkling night eyes going on and off again. Algorithms are successfully studied and with my deadline looming closer, Tommy is predictably absent, this time only willing to help me if I ask him, not by his own charitable nature.

Every time I wander to the coffee machine, to the canteen, he avoids me; has he approached Ben himself? And if so, to what degree? Would the required action have to be dealt with on a project-leader-to-project-leader basis? How could such be done? I have been told nothing of course.

Some days, even through the daily traffic of the Segways, I spot Ben. I say hello, he reciprocates but there's something different in his manner, he knows I saw him at Google but how much of my actions against him does he know about? Intuition tells me that he knows something of my reports, that he knows about Tommy, that he knows to anticipate a disciplinary and quite a fucking big one. If he's truly up to secret sharing with corporations of this magnitude then surely he's more experienced than to be easily seen? And if he is, then he'll know how to protect himself.

Oh shit, why didn't I think of *that*?

I have to assume he'll attempt some method of revenge, of discrediting or even framing me. Long working hours in the London winter are nothing, not knowing is my true experience of a never-ending darkness.

I am somewhere through the fifth day of waiting for any decent feedback from Tommy and again the office is awash in a swath of twilight orange; twilight orange or incessant rain, are these the only two states my sleepless, working life exists in? I resort to the private computer booths at this section of the seventh floor of which are all named after popular British album titles and from inside the lonely space of *OK Computer* I can stare out across the work floor to spy on everyone's interactions.

Was it Steve Jobs or Zuckerberg who pioneered the idea of the wide-open working floor spaces? A clever idea really, a work space deliberately designed to heighten random, chance encounters with colleagues so that new ideas could be easily discussed, shared and worked on, yet, under these circumstances, I guess the reverse could also be true, secrets could easily be passed from person to person under the sly act of interaction away from those who might otherwise be listening in more confined spaces.

I watch as Ben's Segway drifts into the coffee area where he literally bumps into Tommy making tea and they talk. I wish I'd learned to lip read. Their interaction doesn't seem to be disciplinary in manner, they are smiling, what are they smiling about?

That's it, Tommy hasn't said anything and, in my frustration, I do what I should've done to begin with. I open up my emails and express my concerns to the Legal Department at no.183, a five-minute walk down Euston Road. Twenty-four-hour, fully protected, anonymous email services; they could be expecting it but otherwise neither Tommy or Ben will know what's hit them.

I tell them everything.

A few hours later, I'm given a reply:

*To Vasili,*

*Thank you for expressing your concerns regarding the actions of your colleague, certainly such behaviour does warrant alarm and you can work on assured that you have done the right thing. We do take such situations very seriously, however, due to the indefinite nature of the circumstances at hand, this particular case has been forwarded on to higher, specialist personnel at the San Francisco headquarters. As a result, you may later be required to give further information either directly to a Mr. Simon Fleschinger himself or via myself.*

The last part leaves the magnitude of the drama unsubtle.

*Please, please, may I make it strictly clear that you not share your concerns with anybody else until asked to do so. We are aware, as told, that such information has already been given to your immediate project leader, a mister Zhang, Tommy, who in due time, shall also be contacted.*

*Regards,*

*Miriam Forsythe*
*Chief of Operations*
*Legal Department*
*183 Brock Street*

Again, days of incessant rain and twilight oranges fly by; the algorithms, the algorithms, nobody responds.

Behaviour changes have noticeably come over Tommy. Once again, he is actively taking interest in the progression of the Oculus but there is a hesitancy about him, like a fear of talking directly, like he's only doing it out of pressure. Needless to say, any discussion of Ben is still yet to happen, from anyone.

Then an explanation as to why the Legal Department may had been too busy to reply to me presents itself. Like all office rumours, a new and incredible one was circulating in quiet corners and social areas; the San Francisco headquarters had apparently been hacked and in an apparently unique way that was yet unfamiliar to that area's security officers. My suspicions rise again.

They are no doubt coercing with London and every other city at this very moment, trying to get answers as to how it had happened and who might be responsible and indeed the typically bright-coloured, youth-oriented warning posters then appear before us, reading;
*Is your private email secured?*

Wim and I stand before them, discussing whether our Hacktober ideas could have been behind it? Wim merely suggesting that while security may have no doubt considered it, it would all be a little too obvious and if our winning system had formerly been made public by someone, then *everybody* would have been a suspect, not just us. Rooting out who did it would no doubt be a more laborious job than my own dull project.

Paranoia nevertheless sweeps our three pioneering floors for the next couple of days and maybe it was due to this that Ben's nerdy, overweight presence isn't to be seen anywhere. Has the atmosphere driven him to working at home perhaps?

Predictably, an email now shows up as one of those ones where the sender is unfamiliar to you as a means of securing its discretion; it's been sitting there for a few hours. I open it.

*To Vasili,*

*Thank you for leading us on to this particular case, we are glad to inform you that our cyber security and data protection department have taken all the necessary action regarding Mr Benjamin Hollis. I myself shall be arriving in London on Wednesday 29th to lead a few meetings at 10 Brock Street. If you could please make yourself available at an arranged time on that day, I think it best that yourself, Mr Zhang and I have a private, formal meeting regarding this matter. Times to be announced.*
*I have to make it absolutely, strictly clear that you or Mr Zhang not share your concerns with anybody else at Facebook until otherwise asked to do so by myself.*

*Regards,*

*Mr. Simon Fleschinger. Leader of operations, Legal Department, San Francisco.*

Soon after, I reply with a *yes*.

A rainy day has given way to another rainy night and on the eighth-floor foyer I await our meeting, in my nervousness my eyes switch between the all-self-promoting news of the plasma screen or (like the visitors less enthusiastically watching it) stare at my iphone to await the email confirming his readiness. Security seems to be curious of my nervousness now and whenever a break appears in their trivial chitchat they seem to look my way.

I get up from the waiting sofa and walk towards the cold surface of the huge windows; outside, falling rain blocks my visibility of Camden Town and Primrose Hill directly beyond but directly opposite a few floors below I can stare into the glaring white lights of the other office blocks and luxury apartments. Caught in the reflection of their own glass exteriors are reflections of my building's own lower-floor offices (I think it's of the Debenhams HQ) and the same again in return; reflections upon reflections, office whites projected onto office whites, the actions of suited people mirroring the actions of other suited people and as the collected rain globules upon the glass bend their lights, they all seem to meet together as one in a kaleidoscopic frenzy; all these offices and squares, competitors in business, differentiating themselves as either the abodes of businesses or homes, but really just all the same.

I stride over to the opposite end of the foyer and stare through the glass into the depths of the glass lift shaft that does the interior of the building, into the array of visible conference rooms where I can see the man himself, Simon Fleschinger, one level below, stood before a projection screen presenting to a group of engineers before him. He is a big man wearing a roll-neck jumper, trainers and jeans, the typical I.T big wig attire. A typical American.

They all appear to laugh at something he says and with that, his conference is over, packing away their laptops and exiting. Fleschinger is packing away his own equipment and in between I see him using his phone. I check my emails upon my own and indeed my calling arrives.

*Conference Room 2; Ready in Five Minutes. Simon.*

I slowly take the stairs down to level seven, sink a glass of water and as I arrive before Conference Room 2, I see through the window that two other people on top of Simon Fleschinger and Tommy, have already got in there and got their things together at some unnaturally fast speed.

Fleschinger sits at the head of the table while Tommy and two other expensively-suited men make up one length of it, they all sit in a stern silence while Tommy looks curiously nervous, his skinny shoulders curving forwards, his arms folded upon the desk and his head cocked downwards as if reading.

I knock and Fleschinger opens, one of those huge American service smiles across a wide, white, balding head, the guy is a big, rounded type but his rough handshake suggests not out of shape.

"Hi…Vasili, good to meet you at long last. Come in, take a seat buddy."

I enter and Fleschinger places a sign reading *Strictly Out of Use* upon the outside of the door before closing it.

"Over here I'd like to introduce you to Mr. Cornelius Bloom and Zachary Horne from our cyber threat headquarters in San Fran and Dublin respectively, and of course, your trusted team leader Tommy Zhang on the end there".

I shake hands with Bloom and Horne wordlessly (both bear cold, almost threateningly strong handshakes) while Tommy just nods in his gentle, fair way. I sit opposite them.

Air is released as Fleschinger sinks back down into his leather chair.

"Well gentleman, I can't say that any of us are particularly keen to have arrived here for the weather today but it does seem more pressing matters are upon us. How are you enjoying the UK Vasili? Like London, do ya?"

"Yes. Not so bad"

"Well, we had some raucous old times here back in the establishing years, didn't we boys?"

"Certainly did, Si", Bloom and Horne seem to express a fraction of a personality as they laugh gently before halting. What kind of a social history could these three personality types have possibly led?

"And how's Oculus treating ya, Vasili? Not too stressful I hope?"

"Everything's okay, just a little more to do now but judging by my readings, everything's in place and on track."

"Well that is good news, that's exactly what we need here, people on track".

He ruffles through some papers he places on the desk; Bloom and Horne are doing the same with what appear to be identical print outs of what could be the email I sent them.

"Now, on to your concerns; you have warranted a need for investigation into a one Mr Benjamin Hollis. You say you spotted him behaving suspiciously outside of the Google office, is that true?"

"No, not *outside*, he was *inside,* he was *coming out* of the office *from* inside."

"So let us all confirm this now, you're not saying that you saw him *outside* the Victoria office but *coming from* inside to out?"

"Yes that's right"

I notice that Bloom and Horne are staring right at me intently with sharp, stoney stares whilst Tommy seems to have become more and more nervous, fidgeting awkwardly.

"And you're absolutely sure it was him?" Fleschinger asks.

Now I notice just how much they've noticed *my* reactions to *them*. What the fuck is going on here?

"Yes, I'm certain."

"And what is it *exactly* Vasili, that concerns you about Ben Hollis's intentions?"

I study the three Americans staring at me individually. Why should I explain myself to people who look at me with such hostility? I think to myself, and what's wrong with Tommy? His position would mean he'd know more than me of course and so.... something's not right here.

Then it hits me, nobody seems to know what's happened to Ben and maybe he's turned the tables on me somehow? If I "invented" that Hacktober code, then surely I could just as easily be considered the culprit? I should've been more ready for this, maybe I'm about to be axed?

"I want you to know Vasili that anything you say here is under the strictest of confidence."

I look up to the small upside-down black spot that is the room's surveillance camera. How contradictory such times are, *nothing* from this era forwards can ever truly be stated in confidence and everything's in the hands of the elite. The future surveillance nightmare is already here.

"Well, as Tommy can tell you, Mr Hollis, Wim and myself successfully won Hacktober together, successfully beating the security system. Then I saw him outside of the Google office and began to question what he was doing there. Then I was told the San Francisco office got hacked and..."

"You think he's behind it?" Fleschinger asked, this time squeezing a rubber stress ball between his fingers. Something's making him nervous, the front all secretly soft men put on to appear strong.

I nod.

"And what makes you come to that conclusion?" Fleschinger added.

Why was the tone of this debate turning towards a strange defence of him? I have to work out what's going on here, I'm not telling them any definites until they make themselves clear. Now is the time for intuition.

"I cannot say, I only wanted to raise my suspicions over the Victoria situation. The two situations don't seem coincidental to me."

"Coincidence is one answer Vasili, we haven't written that off just yet, that's for sure."

He then makes brief eye contact with Bloom, Horne and an awkward, nervous one with Tommy who seems to want to avoid him. Suddenly the stress ball comes down on the table, he smiles and removes his glasses to talk to me more sternly; a mix of the friendly smile with passive aggression, a psychological method of interrogation I only know too well since, after all, America had stolen it from Russia.

"I want you to know Vasili, that we've already spoken to Mr. Hollis personally about this and that we've transferred him on to a separate project at a separate location where the situation can be dealt with by those of a higher personnel."

For some reason his smile angers me as if being subtly condescending; don't take me for a fool, you might be able to pamper up the youth in this place, but me? I'm only a few years younger than you and from a time that remembers these tactics like they were yesterday.

"Transferred to what?" I ask. Whatever he's doing, it'd better not involve *my* Hacktober skills.

"Oh, just transferred, you know"

"And what will happen to him?"

"Well I don't really know buddy, why do you ask?"

Intuition is systematically scanning these four like algorithms, where's my answer I wonder? Before Fleschinger claps his hands happily and...

"Well, we've all been working under a lot of stress recently, who's hungry? I remember a great fish place on, what was it? Euston Road? How about it, huh guys? I'm buying."

Bloom and Horne begin stirring with enthusiasm, ready to leave, expecting me to drop everything; none of you have clearly been hit with the cold-edged spade of a Russian interrogation. Fucking interrogating *me?*

"No!" I slam my hand down on the table, startling them all "if Hollis is also working for our competitor, that's gross misconduct, it's gross misconduct of a significant size, contract states that there are rewards for spotting this behaviour and if I've found him, I deserve more than to simply be told of his consequences. Working on *what?*"

All are slumping backwards deeply into their leather cushions, looking to each other for guidance as to what to say next. Tommy's need to leave the room is palpable and Fleschinger has put the stress ball back into his hand without even noticing it.

Now we are in such a silence that we can hear the outside rain through, perhaps, three layers of walling, an expansive work floor and the building's 21st Century exterior. Play your cards right Vasili, this may be Europe but you're still under US employment law, meaning they can fire you on the spot.

Fleschinger's fingers begin squeezing the rubber again as cognition returns.

"Do you like it here Vasili? We provide everything you need here, don't we? I understand that the Oculus project may have been burning you out but if anything else's upsetting here you pal, you can let us know you know."

"Why do you keep changing the subject? What has happened to Ben Hollis? And where's he gone?"

The silence briefly returns, its eyes, manifested by these three, staring into me again. None of them had seemingly ever been spoken to like this by anyone not on their level.

"Hong Kong" he goes on "he's working on the Chinese expansion if you must know. Everything else, who he's working with and why, is all classified. Executive knowledge only, do you understand?"

My intuition scans them onwards to no result, I wish I could think of another sudden and appropriate outburst.

"You're here with your wife, aren't you? What was her name? Irena?" He went on.

"Yes, Irena"

"Still living in Victoria?"

"Yes"

"How is it there these days? I resided there myself during our set up in London. Do the Polish landlords still own much of the properties there?"

Oh, now he's attempting the old common ground cliché, I can't be bothered anymore, I've said what I needed to say, if his needless talking continues much longer, I'll just get up and leave.

"Yes, Victoria's okay" I say just for the sake of it, "Irena quite likes it as she has the restaurant. Me, not so much."

He suddenly enters a strange state of introverted nostalgic melancholia;

"I went there a lot as a kid too, a long time ago now and I remember we could see a view of the park from our apartment. I used to look over it and observe how much of it was shrinking as I grew larger."

He snaps out of it.

"That view's all gone now, everything's just too built up, now all you can see are more windows. Yeah, I guess I wasn't so keen on it in my later years too man. You two planning to have kids? Would you like to bring them up here? In London I mean?"

Is the last part a subtly implied threat? I continue with his answers, let's see if I can get to the bottom of it.

"The UK is strange and different, not sure if good or bad. I guess education and schooling-wise, perhaps, on terms of taxes and expenses, no."

They seem to just sit there and nod and stare onwards; Tommy passively copying them, does he still wish to adopt the traits of US managerial theory while in this nervous state?

"Well Vasili, have you ever considered transferring to the US? Perhaps with us over in San Fran?"

Eureka! But...let's not kiss these guys' arses just yet.

I shrug "good weather, more space, less tax, why would I say no?"

"Well" he looks to the others "we all like what you've done for us on the Oculus project, we could sure do with someone of your *attitude* over on our side for once, couldn't we, eh?"

Black and Horne begin laughing.

Still, no recognition for my Hacktober skills I smugly think to myself.

"We sure could, Si" Bloom says.

"The bunch o' backboneless stiffs" Horne goes on.

What the hell is with the sudden friendliness? Had I been wrong about them? Maybe they *are* just friendly HQ members. Had I been being paranoid again? What was happening here? What was happening to me?

"You know, I know a guy, who knows a guy" Fleschinger goes on "who knows a guy, you know how it goes. I'm sure if I do some networking amongst my circle, we can sort something out once the Oculus is done with. You'd give him a good reference wouldn't ya, Tommy?"

Tommy suddenly snaps out of his odd anxiety to embrace human feelings.

"Oh yes, totally. Very good work Vasili".

"I mean, we're a globally dominant company, acquiring a VISA should be a piece o' cake with the right people behind it".

With what then may have been a memory glitch, we are suddenly standing, shaking hands and Fleschinger's strong hand is back slapping me out of the door to a brighter future. How the hell had I achieved this?

I stand in the outside Courtyard smoking in the dark, in the rain, unsure again as to what time it is, I look up at the side of my building, all thirteen floors of it; a road of reflective glass leading vertically to a vanishing point of bleak October night sky; rain is coming down at me as if like having leaked from the heights of a great machine, each drop resembling a firefly as it captures the neon of the twenty-four-hour office spaces about halfway down its descent. It patters on my face refreshingly, stamping out my cigarette, atmosphere is everywhere.

I call Irena, she answers in something of a daze. I light another cigarette.

"Vasili? Do you know what time it is? Are you still working?"

I look through the windows of the *Starbucks* and *Pret* to see an assortment of people on their laptops and phones, etc.

"No, but I mean people are still about."

"It's a twenty-four-hour city Vasili, of course they're still about. I've got to get up..."

"Oh well, time is such an abstract, subjective concept, it doesn't really exist Irena. And I have some great news."

"I have to go to sleep, can't it wait until tomorrow?"


I look at the people in the windows further, at the neon lights of their laptops, the circumstances of this hour only seem strange because they're obviously talking to people from other time zones. The tech world has eradicated all our needs for conventional time usage and so for once I don't see a need for a hurry.

"Yes, I suppose it can, is the apartment warm now he's fixed the boiler?"

"Yes, it's warm, but, what the hell are you talking about? Just tell me..."

"No it can wait until morning, time doesn't exist. Goodbye Irena."

I hang up and laugh knowing that her inevitable bad mood will be softened upon my revelation of the VISA; leave those cakes and fake Polish waitresses behind you, Irena. Say goodbye to bleak old London.

Conventional time no longer exists, I think to myself, conventional time no longer exists; I had lost all sense of it. Then, as if it to remind me that it actually does, and is subject to fate, a sudden gust of wind sticks a dampening *Evening Standard* to my legs and one of its headlines glares up at me;

*Google deals in Hong Kong market likely to expand.*

Intuitive thoughts are like identifying the true culprit in a criminal line up, somehow, without even evidence, you just simply *know*, and I know where Benjamin Hollis has been transferred to; my confused paranoias suddenly pull together to take on focus and I know what's *really* happening here; could the two giants have actually been working *together? Together,* ever since the beginning?

I look back at the laptop and phone screens all reflecting infinite white squares off the rain-drenched glass windows, all of them containing cameras and speakers, all of them containing people's personal information; all of them accessing Google, Facebook, Instagram and others, all of them *working together?* The eyes of a thousand-eyed beast, would my generation be the one to witness the end of the personal world?

In the darkness of the pod bed, I stare at the silent glow of the 'occupied' light like it's the last visible star in a future, separated universe and then another terrible thought dawns on me; I had never told anybody about my wife, our intentions or where we were residing.

I know now then, that when I awake, Irena and I will be somewhere further into that unknown paranoid future, and that I may have inadvertently helped to shape it for us.

How was I to see it through the sugar?

## As Manifested In Steel

She had assumed that it would be at a later age when she would get to feel those final sparks of enthusiasm go out concerning one's career, not exactly at thirty-seven wherein the benefits of even *her* pay packet might be outweighed by her sheer frustrations at those that helped her make it.

Still, she had thought to herself, tiredness would come on quicker in recession era London, people were working overtime (of which in her field meant quadruple time), people were in constant fear of the downsizing and, when working amidst the towers of Canary Wharf - financial capital of the capital - there was that covert sense of guilt throughout all such offices, that perhaps, somewhere amidst the complexity of it all, that maybe they'd had some sort of inadvertent part to play in seeing this crisis spill over from this nerve-centre and into the rest of the country; as if somehow they were due a sense of latent karma, and that it should be believed when they say it, that this city knew how to delegate it well. Alternatively, she thought, perhaps it was just that this place was so fucking expensive that no matter what money she worked for, no matter what hours she put in, no matter how older she got, it would never truly allow someone of even her financial status to reach the so-called *Good Life*.

These were the thoughts that frequently went through her head whenever she got a rare moment alone in the lift, leaving a few minutes earlier once again to try and outrace the rush hour, a moment wherein the yelling, office bitching, itchy suits and photocopier bleeps would all end and just allow her that slow descent down the side of the building that would shut her off from auditory dimensions to contemplate the wharf's steely surroundings on a purely visual level.

She could fully admit that she was something of a junkie for the finance game but its inhabiting one-note, steel and glass tombs that towered around each other, reflecting one lukewarm office window off another, had been leading her to question what had led the human race to be drawn to such imprisoning environments.

Something about the overloading of the electrics to her building had rendered this lift to move particularly slowly and over time she'd made peace with her painful resistance to not kick in the panel of buttons. It was, after all, considerably less frustrating than tolerating both the length and forced social interactions that would come with taking the stairs. It usually took five minutes for the lift to complete its full descent and in that time, particularly in February, it would see the transition from day to night, and as that silent electric murmur took her downwards, it was perfect timing for the lights of the city to then flicker up from below, shimmer past her and above her, making her consider that her immediate destination of an approaching concrete walkway and its ever-beaming spotlights, might be the only destination she, and everyone else, would ever go on to know.

These brief calm moments that dotted her hectic life, were also the moments in which the justification for her often aggressive rants against her colleagues took on clarity and felt fucking justified.

For one, there was Terry Jameson; the Financial Research Coordinator who, being at the same level as her, would remain quiet when true disciplinary action was needed, allowing her to do all the necessary nit picking and fact finding, harbouring an unfair 'mega bitch' status whilst he sat around to watch the clock, of course then revealing himself to be more than popular once he retreated to the nearby bars with half the (female) workforce once that clock had timed out.

Terry's problems were of a different style to that wanker Edward Mansfield however, who, whilst proving the same sternness that she had when it came to office power plays, also had a unique talent for winding up the anger gears within her. Thinking he could use her own short fuses for his own intentions, he would send her stressing off after the people he wouldn't want to deal with (office politics, of which she couldn't care less for) or he would bring it out of her as a means of making his own so-called 'cool' demeanour come out on top; one of those cunning males who knew every trick in the book about securing one's own position whenever the rumours of a cut back would fly.

Then there were the endless flows of office interns, most of them economy students looking for their big breaks but usually appointed the menial tasks of office photo copiers or couriers and even then when you had to rely on them they would turn up late, hungover and under speed; young was young of course but what really fucking annoyed her about them was that when given the opportunities that they had, they could have at least acknowledged that the risks involved in the jobs being undertaken posed more grave consequences for their immediate colleagues than merely just losing that little tiny reference they needed on their CVs.

The other key managers were essentially good at what they did but often clashed with her in both ethic and approach; the question as to which one of them should be in charge of such tough decision making was always the classic debate. Their inability to delegate any chosen individual on the matter was the most frustrating part for since she would have had no problem with them at all, should've surely made her the most up to the job? Why shouldn't she be the one to implement them?

"Because", she'd been told, "for such a department to sustain order, it needed a holistic approach to traverse the current economy's unpredictable nature".

What bollocks.

Then came the usual halt of the murmurs, the turning of the exposed cogs, the whoosh and soon enough she was out in the February late afternoon cold where the beaming filaments of the spotlights shone intensely upon the region's cocktail bars and coffee shops, no doubt where Terry Jameson had fucked off to with half the interns for the evening, perhaps trying to put his irresponsible cock into one of those nubile young women?

Why had this anger come over her so much recently? Why had everyone become angry for that matter? The short shot of cold that came over her from between her workplace and Canary Wharf station obviously took her back to her ex-boyfriend, Richard, that little fuck wit. Maybe he had been the instigator for work feeling so hard all this time. Naturally, her split from him, still setting in even six months later, was upsetting on its own terms but it was the simple reason 'why' that had been eating away at her the most. Richard may have been three years younger but that still didn't leave him to be in a situation to be gallivanting around the city like they had when they were in their early twenties. He was successful of course, graphic design was bringing in most of what they both needed but for her to be pushing forty and still have the child and marriage urges...would he sympathise with her body clock? Had he even acknowledged that women have one for that matter? Had he fuck. He would, in his naive generalisation of all women, believe that splashing the cash on her would keep her distracted from those needs under the weight of material novelties, and when this failed to hold back the big questions, it became talk of his career prospects, the excuses of the recession, the half-realised dreams of idealism still festering over from his more careerist twenties.

Whether or not he had considered how and why their relationship was collapsing was always uncertain to her; the artists of London's 'other side' of course were a boxed-in bunch and so perhaps the mix of that with her headstrong business mind might had formed a bad match from the offset anyway. When human needs become human needs, discussions have to be had and he didn't seem particularly unhappy when he was finally asked to go; he's probably moved in with some younger piece of fanny, she thought, riding out the last of his prime with some pretentious greebo from Shoreditch, one of those types that without the aid of daddy's cash, would never rise above the plankton level of the fish bowl, destined to wallow in how her pretentious ideals sputter out in a dead-end job as the city gets bigger and forever younger around her.

So angry had Richard left her that she would no longer bother to exchange even a fleeting smile with one of the men who popped up the other side of a passing escalator, even if she was slightly keen and of course still confident that she still 'had it', they would have to work as hard as she had for them to convince her that they'd be worth it. She saw one that day, probably a trendy bar owner, popping out from below to begin a night shift as she passed him downwards into that silvery, designer crater that was Canary Wharf tube station.

The longer-than-usual escalators that take you beneath Canary Wharf allow you to pay close attention to the structure of the place; it had always impressed her how the bollards that would normally be seen to be holding up such a structure weren't present, as if this metallic chamber possessed some sort of anti-gravitational force that could hold the weight of its cluttering super structures high above it. It reminded her in some respects of the people (her people) who worked within them; as if they too would somehow be being rewarded with a similar wealth for adopting such similar forms of unspecified strength to pull together the weighty roots of the global finance world. She had frequently wondered how big the city could build Canary Wharf before its station's structure would collapse beneath the weight of it all and bring the above world crashing through its entrances into such chambers below?

Next up, like a minuscule silver strip across the base of a station that resembled some sort of immense hanger for experimental aircraft, came the row of security barriers, accompanied by one or two of their accompanying workers; their faces equally as cold.

Fondling through the keys in her pocket, she found the purse that contained her Oyster card and, matched by the ferociousness of the walk she approached with, slammed the thing down upon the panel only to be met by that frustrating 'other' sound that impolitely tells you that the entry light has gone red and won't let you through.

'Bloody thing'. She slammed it again, this time nearly walking into the hunk of plastic as it refused to open for her once again. She didn't have time for this, she slammed it again, and again, that same fucking red eye flaring up at you upon the panel, 'for fuck's sake', she would slam it again, this time with a thud; same fucking thing.

"Excuse me madam" said one of the approaching workers, his dirty, bulked orange jacket identifying him as one of the tunnel labourers and not one of its assistants; "I think you have insufficient funds".

Ignore the prick, she thought, and tried it again, hard; *the same thing*. How could this be? She'd bought her monthly Oyster card just two weeks before, what a stupid fucking system.

"I think you have insufficient funds" he said again.

"Yeah, I heard you the first time, thanks".

This time her anger had called over one of the true assistants, one of those who wear the smarter blue uniforms, like a kind of fourth emergency service.

"Try this one madam" he said as he guided her to the next panel, she recognised him from her daily commute, time to get his name from his name badge she thought.

Slam, beep, same shit. "I think you've run out of money" said Nigel.

"But that's ridiculous, I bought a monthly pass just two weeks ago"

Then came the incomprehensible background grunts of the prick in orange. Who was this prick? "You can top up on the machines" he mumbled through a mouth full of chewed up fruit.

"Yeah, I know, I live here, thank you very much" she knew how the system worked "and like I've already told you, I know there's enough money on here".

"Just go and use the machines madam" said Nigel, of whom after assuming he'd noticed her face on a daily basis too, would have had the common decency to have acknowledged that she wasn't some unfamiliar tourist.

"Look, this is ridiculous, I'm not topping up any further...I think there's something wrong with your machines". Her timing over this was pitch-perfect, especially as she was becoming irritated by the further numbers of grumbling suits who were now barging past her to slip through the barriers as slickly as their own stupid haircuts; the crowds of rush hour hereby commencing.

"Please" said Nigel with one arm ever so politely pointing in the direction of one of the station's self-service machines.

The invention of the self-service machine she and several others had previously thought had simply, like the behaviour of most of her colleagues, been nothing but a sly method of cutting corners; an act of laziness built on the reasonable excuse that there should be no other reason to question anything – that money and machinery have all the answers, - it avoids conversation, it avoids other reasoning, it was pure, simple laziness. Why the fuck do these pricks go on strike every three months to protest at being replaced by machines when their service seems to actively promote such an idea?

She therefore responded with a huff before stomping across the pointless breadth of this hanger back towards the escalators. Instead she would jump the train at Heron Quays and try her luck at Stratford instead.

Her co-workers could, at least, be forgiven for a fatigue brought on by an industry at its most tiring time, but that was the financial sector, what was the Transport world's excuse? Maybe they too had been driven to tiredness by the stress of city work? But Jesus, for the staff of the London Underground to be replaced by fucking flat-screen robots, what else would the future hold? Not that she cared too much following her interaction with those two twats.

What would it be like to be in their shoes? Yes, they may have to work, possibly, all hours of the day, and while there would be no national or global responsibilities like there were in her job, they would have to deal with engineering faults, drunks, city crazies and terrorist threats. Then again, they might have to actively participate in those things but they were *everyone's* problems; in fact, although the economic world has its desires to make London reach further for the skies, the places where all walks of life came together was beneath its streets; that was the place where everyone's problems, everyone's angers all came together in one big irrational, angry cluster.

She had made it to the DLR platform without tapping in but fuck it was busy; other suits, a couple of tourists and a few more of the same old shit regulars were filling up right up to the yellow safety line and of course at this hour, the bar and restaurant workers would be commuting in of which would again, reassemble the order of the awaiting crowds and affect her chances of getting on that first train. Why was it that little bit busier this evening?

What stood in her way now? The overhead read seven minutes. *Seven minutes?* This was an outrage for rush hour, especially after the level of disrespect she'd received from the two mongs back at Canary Wharf's security barrier. The one thing you learn about rush hour, is that the longer the wait and the bigger the crowd, the less chance you're going to have of getting on the train you want and after today she wasn't having any of it, a good thing that being forceful was naturally in her blood.

She squeezed her way through the tourists who were stood closer to the back and made her way close, or at least close enough, to the yellow line for her manoeuvre to work. Another thing you learn after years in London, especially to the frustrations of how precise her particular game had made her with timing and numbers etc, is that the overhead countdowns were never ever accurate. Anyway, the seven minutes were counting down nicely.

Her thoughts had led her to stare at the tracks and indeed what she saw as a palpable reminder of what modern life was; on one side stands a slick platform of expensive metals, concrete and automated mechanical machines, whilst inches away from you, without any pleasantries in between, is an electrically charged mincer where one's death is treated as nothing but a burden upon everything else's functioning.

Although she had never considered the act itself of course (the kind of stupid thing that this country's attention-seeking weaklings would do) she often thought about the subject of suicide in general, or furthermore, London's particular strain of suicide that was jumping in front of trains. Why do they do it? She considered herself strong-willed but could never fathom the amount of self-discipline it would require to do such a thing. Surely only a rush of adrenalin could force the body to do such a thing? Still, it was at once so hard yet so easy, the transition from this world to the next just a step over a breach of concrete.

How upset was Richard really regarding their break up? Had he ever thought of these things? Surely, the creative brain must think these things regularly and even build careers from it? God that fucked her off, creativity was fucking her off, how could she have got involved with someone like that? How could someone, whose brain is constantly racing through such trivial, stupid subject matter, garner such love and respect from society when all the hard work that went into her line of work, the kind of work that actually held entire cities and even countries together, was given such negative press? Her role in this particularly uncertain time was fighting a worthy corner of the recession and still the lefties of this world considered the finance world the enemy? She imagined then, that this must've been the way the wounded, shattered soldiers must've felt when returning home from controversial wars like Iraq; all that stress and then you come home to get shouted at by some lefty, dope-smoking twat.

As she turned to look back at the digital numbers overhead, she saw that her vision and her plan for manoeuvre had become blocked by someone.

"Fat bitch" she thought of the wider, younger professional who'd stepped in front of her and so she began her analysis. This girl was of Indian descent, stocky but not overweight yet clearly insecure about her build judging by the business suit and skirt that she'd squeezed herself into. Indeed, she thought, she fitted into the weight-watcher types of whom she would encounter descending or ascending her building's lengthy staircases each morning; the fact that she would do this as a reason of not having time to hit a regular gym implied she might also be from one of the floors of her very same building. She was young, about mid-20s, reasonably pretty but probably single. A single side swipe of her eye to hers implied that she knew of her own deliberate positioning before her and knew that the game was on. Yeah, lucky we're not in the same office, bitch.

That old familiar jangle of cables began and the snake-like approach of the driverless DLR train headed towards the platform. As if on cue, the crowd began to shuffle and she stepped forward to barge her younger opponent. The younger opponent however did something she didn't expect and literally stomped in front of her path to *block her*.

How dare she? How fucking dare the fat bitch?!

With that, the adrenalin kicked in and her hand shot out, pressing with force upon the material of the girl's oh so expensive suit and she went forwards...

The other commuters were slightly disorientated by her accidental barging of them before they saw what was happening and that everything was seemingly happening in a slow motion; my God, that type of slow motion she'd never wanted to experience outside of a nightmare. The girl's suited figure was falling forward and at one point their faces locked eyes; her expression chilled her to the bone, the first seemed to be shock, the second was realisation, the third (which was the worst) had the question 'Why?' written all over it before her next look of despair was cut short. The girl's last looks, everything that had made up her life so far in that suddenly beautiful stocky build and that expensive suit had gone in a bloodless vanishing act beneath the train lights, an agonising bump and churn of screeching metals.

What had she done? What had she done? Oh Jesus, what had she done?

The three seconds of stunned silence that came over the platform was an eternity, that same eternity that you think about but don't truly fathom when one thinks of their life passing. It was a horrible eternity cut short by the moment the confused passengers, left in the silhouette of the carriage lights to wonder why the train hadn't fully pulled up then made visual contact with the space-eyed platform dwellers to concur the reality of this situation for everyone and pull the panic alarm.

There was the sudden sound of individual screams, the tourists held their loved one's hands in comfort and a type of weeping began which she'd never encountered before. A few others were bent over to dry wretch or catch a breath but the silence of the shocking realisation was worse than any of those. Suddenly she was an alien in a world to which she'd worked to maintain; these people, these *real* people, these human beings were suddenly in a different universe to her, divided by a second of time and the simple differences between on and off a platform. A rush of thoughts and images went through her head, of all the news reports of serial killers, child killers and paedophiles that had been caught and shamed before the public over the years, was she in that same category now? For some reason the faces of those criminals gave her comfort for they were the only group of people left that might not hate her, the only people who may understand what it felt like to think of everybody they'd ever fallen out with or of everybody who'd ever disliked them, those of whom had always wanted to prove you wrong, to sit before your shamed image on a TV set and get a sense of self-gratification from it.

She turned to look around the once familiar backdrop of Heron Quays to see it was no longer the same place of everyday familiarity but an alien landscape which belonged to the free, belonged to those who were worthy enough in their innocence to step through it without punishment. She now felt like and wanted to be a part of its coldly polished steel bollards but even such textural delights now emitted an innocence that she didn't have, she wanted love from it, from *something*, she wanted love from Richard, she wanted her Mum.

Disorientation was everywhere, the now unfamiliar beings of the platform were not looking at her necessarily but at the person next to them; unspoken theories and accusations where permeating the air. Did she fall? Did she jump? Was she pushed? She looked up at the now menacing black globules that protruded from the concrete as London's many and ever-watching eyes, unsure as to what type of picture they might draw for themselves.

Amidst the scattering of people and their many emotions, one leg instinctively followed the other one and she made her way back through this strange new world, the Heron Quays' grandiose metal and concrete now swaying like a fever dream; the thoughts of how she might feel towards her victim's family and whether she could handle what choices might come next, whether they'd be made by her or the state, sat at the back of her consciousness, knowing that, like the train, they would soon become mobilised but just couldn't yet make that shift forward until the stillness was over.

One leg followed the other. The city's dust interacted like pond life in the beams of the giant electric lights that hung from above as she re-approached the escalator that led her downwards, downwards, downwards back towards the motions of her angry, angry world.

## Thoughts and Memories from Beyond the Flashbulbs

### 2010: The 54th BFI London Film Festival: "The King's Speech" Film Premiere

The only decent thing for me about Hollywood's so-called 3D/digital revolution – was that whenever I was subjected to watching the same film on repeat – I could get away with sleeping behind the 3D glasses without the management ever really being able to prove that I had been, save for the occasional beads of dribble.

The only issue was that when I did fall asleep, I suffered the same strange recurring nightmares about The Screening Rooms. In them, in some surreal, alternate version of the establishment, I would, as always, charge extortionately high prices to angry punters and then shamefully guide them, not into a cinema screen, not even into the 50-seater mini auditoriums that were even shit in reality, but into a room that was no better than a student's living room. With its molded, fag-burned sofas and arm chairs already taken by the first arrivals, the latecomers would be forced to angrily perch upon whatever corners they could find to face a very average TV set. These sets of innocent families, friends and lovers on soon-to-fail dates would then make perplexed glances at each other before turning to me in hatred and helpless despair.

Grand, sweeping music would rise from the TV's tinny speakers and a VHS copy of the film would appear upon its static face – the film would always be Stephen Frears' *The Queen,* and then I'd wake up.

Had it been the eye strain from the 3D glasses, normal tiredness or the depression that had me falling asleep so often?

To be honest, the place never really recovered from the failed protest my colleagues and I had attempted that previous year and it now felt, in typical horror movie fashion, that the building itself had been punishing us for it. Those who'd found a place to leave to or take their chances with unemployment, simply left, those, like myself, who hadn't found anything, stayed. We, who had no job security, had no reliable savings and no union help had to suck up to that place's increasingly ridiculous rules and tolerate conditions that had been well beyond their sell by dates, one false move and we'd be out in the cold.

Everyone still tried to fend for their jobs, and the resulting smells of paranoia and divisionism had become potent amongst us. Knowing that anybody could sell you out at any minute was one hell of a way to live, the fear had diminished the trust amongst us, there hadn't been any sense of *true friendship* in what felt like forever and without it we'd become easier to push around as vulnerable individuals – their plans had worked; the employment world had been entering a strange new age, and it was being managed on a battered, steam-powered model from the past.

Even Eliza, my sort-of girlfriend, had left for her own country, yes, back to Mother Italy, a country where traditional, caring family structures still existed to shelter and nurture. I was alone in this place now and even though I missed Eliza more than I thought I would on an emotional level, lust had still commanded me through those years, an overbearing, unnatural, monstrous lust for *Her;* that same celebrity face from each year that I worked there.

I had been wanking more than I usually would and sometimes at work. It hadn't just been over reliving those encounters we'd had, the situation had grown more complicated. Since her high-profile relationship, her career had *taken off*. She would not only be in British films but also the big American ones and her face could be seen on the sides of buses, on the walls of the tube, on TV, across the pages of every newspaper or magazine that this city had to offer.

Around that time too, *his* Kensington pad, as well as some other property he had in the US, had become surrounded and besieged by paparazzi, triggering an aggressive response from the two of them and then having them join a wider group of celebs who'd subsequently begin a campaign for greater rights to celebrity privacy. What had felt weird about all this of course was that the more they pried into her personal life, the more chance there was of them finding out about *me*. Man, what a media storm our shenanigans could cause? Was there any trace of evidence I might had left behind?

Somehow I thought the idea of little old me pulling *her* might've been more interesting than her having a small lusty offering with *me* – what would happen to me when *he* found out? Would he find me defenceless and alone in this place and take jealous revenge upon me, starting yet *another* media frenzy? Would it then subsequently hound my own flat in the aggressive pushes for an interview? I suddenly felt through their skin, what that threatening feeling of losing your privacy in exchange for fame might actually have been like.

For a while we were screening one of her films in the main auditorium and like clockwork almost all members of the bored and horny male workforce would begin to slowly mooch away from their appointed positions and into the screen.

I'd always get a quick sip of the cheap vodka I'd hidden in my locker just to numb the pain of such a routine but I would go in and join them regardless; not for the same reasons of course, for me it was more about the anticipation of what I *knew* would be coming later in that year rather than what was about to reveal itself on screen.

For some reason, under the light of the newly installed digital projector, those endless rows of 1930's red seats, empty at that time of day, would take on a ghostly aura, as if like me, the things had been sat there slightly longer than they'd wanted to be and were now being subjected to see something they half wanted and half didn't.

Upon *that* scene then, the one where she dropped the robe to reveal *everything,* my colleagues gasped in the darkness for what must've been the seventh time. I pretended I'd felt the same way but was in fact enraged with jealousy, I couldn't even bare to look at her but I *had to.* Somehow, projected to the size of two London buses, I looked upon her naked body in a way that had, for the first time in my life, almost been without lust, I was able to stare in deeply and study what was behind those eyes without her questioning it, it was if when coated with the artifice of cinematic lighting, framed via the eyes of an artist and to the subtly manipulative tactics of sound, she had become something more than just a female form and in doing so she had exposed just how deadly and unattainable she had always been. It was as inexplicably intriguing as only art could be; I couldn't articulate it, but I could feel it.

Cinema presents human existence as a perfected counterpart to the way things happen in reality, a reworked avatar of the real thing – even the 20th Century's shittest bits had seductive, hypnotic qualities when told via the light of a cinematic magic lantern.

The occultist and experimental filmmaker Kenneth Anger had once thought of film as an act of black magic, a devilish creation bubbled up through the witch's brew of its development process to open up a sort of alchemical window between this world and another, more seductive realm; a realm wherein the departed are still able to forever walk the earth, a place where all our sinful desires can be seen in motion but are forever unattainable. And certainly, in that moment, had this been shot on film of course, those waltzing, projected chemicals would've been like a hive of tormenting insects, burrowing into my skull to remind me of the perfection I couldn't get.

Jesus, if there had been one thing Kenneth Anger hadn't thought up on those hedonistic nights of the 60s, was that this very ideology would spawn a generation of kids who'd genuinely believe in what those avatar versions to their own life paths were telling them, convincing them that the roads to fame and fortune had been real and were guiding them onwards to some kind of virtual heavenly realm. The reality was that it merely took most of its people to dead-end work places like *this one.*

Why do some people's dream lives come easy and not to others? Some people are able to just learn how to walk and go out and get stuff without effort whilst others go to rot, merely scratching the surface of what they might've been able to achieve had they spotted the doors opening? About a year or something before, there had been this guy, a freelance artist of some sort, who'd taken a job here for the short haul before being called up again to New Zealand to apply his skills to Peter Jackson's long-troubled *Hobbit* films; he'd spoken of it as if it had been an effortless achievement, looking at us curiously as to why we might had *chosen* to be in *this* place for so long? His journey into the arts had, by comparison, been like a passenger on a minor flight from here to Paris, whilst mine was like trying to fly a dinky soapbox to Australia.

I remember, a few other days before the opening of the LFF, I took another swig from my locker/minibar to brace myself for the lengthy lonesome stretch of the Box Office as I covered Abdul for *another* of his never-ending prayer times. The days of having company in that place had, as you can see, all ended by then of course, and so I was once again staring out at the winter beyond that over familiar window of mine. Man, this place had taught me to lap up hatred, to lap up fear and depression, to lap up all the nihilism I could in one big, poisoned cocktail.

London had become an ominous place by 2010 then – our villains, those who'd been brewing up since 7/7 were truly upon our turf now and there was a feeling that anything in this city's tourist spots, especially those directly before me, could blow up or be attacked at any time. At any time, some device could explode, send ball bearings hurtling through this glass and rupture one of my eye balls, my life fucked, just like that – staring through that window had now become more like tasting that metallic membrane that stands momentarily between life and death. Of course, most would spend these hours pondering, 'how had it all come to this?', 'who had been the conspirators behind this scenario?' and what went on behind the eyes of those who were committing them?

Then, Anwar turned up, laughing somewhat through awkward shock and squeezing himself through the door with that day's *Metro* newspaper to suggest a possible answer.

"Remember this shit?" He said "I can't believe it, brother."

"No way?" I had to reply as he held the article open in front of me.

For you see, about a month earlier, the square had been subject to a surreal incident. It had begun as a very average morning on Front of House that day, the Square had been dead and the sun was shining pleasantly and I was watching the world through the building's great glass front.

A policeman then casually arrived and began coating the perimeter of the square in police tape. His colleagues held back the curious public and advised them to go elsewhere, and so this police cordon continued and continued until it was unspooled in front of the window where I'd been standing.

I had a small number of customers inside the screen and wondered *Why he wasn't explaining anything to me?*

And so, I popped my head out the door and asked.

"A suspicious package has been found in Yates's Wine Bar next door" He explained.

"Well, shouldn't I evacuate this place then?"

He pulled a strange expression as if to contemplate what to me should've been obvious.

"Yes, I think that'd be advisable sir" he went on "with all this glass here, it's going to do considerable damage should it go off".

I evacuated – the film shut down, the great announcement boomed through the auditorium, the customers had been let out through the emergency exits onto Charing Cross Road and we, the staff, had vacated to an emergency meeting point in one of the Square's more sheltered, underground casinos.

Now that we'd been safe, I have to admit there was a sense of excitement about it all, but the tiers of weirdness just kept going up and up.

Within this place, - which had been quiet at that early hour – we had an unexpected meeting with Edwins and his security crew who were suited up and on duty. Although he said 'hello', he was weirdly cagey about what exactly they'd been doing there and warned us to not enter certain sections of the casino.

Had they been involved with what might had been going on outside? But they weren't police, so I figured no.

Flitting about in the less visible corners of the places they'd been talking about, I could see the lights of the place reflecting off a male figure in expensive leathers. This feeling of secrecy, was familiar to us all of course, somebody big was in the building, only, if the casino wasn't yet open and there were no public shows due, *what the hell for?*

Meanwhile, the situation outside had been heating up big time. The police had announced that it was official, a bomb had been detected and the specialist bomb squad were being called.

We waited, and we waited... for the worst to happen.

A wave of confusion then came across all our faces, for suddenly, at the volume level of a stadium rock concert, the tense silence of the scene was penetrated by some guitar chords followed by;

"*Oh I guess it would be nice, if I could touch your body*" sung into a microphone.

It was George Michael's song, *Faith,* in fact it was *George Michael* himself, outside, singing live from one of the balconies to this very building.... but during a *bomb scare? Wtf?*

The sounds of his voice, and the electrics then wound down to a halt, there was a pause and then a commotion as presumably Edwins and his team had begun quickly escorting George back downstairs and back into the areas that were forbidden to us. I remember hearing through a pretty much incomprehensible fuss, the words;

"*They hate me, they all hate me now".*

The two separate chambers to this casino remained without any knowledge for a few hours longer then before we were told matters were safe and that the cinema could go back to its usual business.

I then found out then, that poor old George, had at some stage earlier in the year been shamed once again by the press for something or other and had been plotting a surprise comeback gig. No doubt, whatever he'd done this time – probably not shocking in the slightest for the Internet age but there you go – must had fucked up his confidence somehow and was ready to rekindle things with his fan base.

The thing was though, the moment he stepped out onto that balcony, instead of seeing the waves of tourists and Londoners who might'd stopped to turn the surprise into a day-long, historic gig, he instead saw people fleeing away, leaving him to an empty square.

He had assumed, whilst probably on drugs, that everything was over for him, that nobody had wanted anything to do with him anymore, that he'd shamed himself for the last unforgivable time. If he had spent more time concentrating however, he would've instead seen a small group of shielded specialist police sending a tiny remote-controlled bomb disposal Johnny 5 into Yates's Wine Bar.

Normally I would've found it hard to believe that the police wouldn't have communicated something to George's security team but then again, they had also just casually walked past me earlier too, so I guess, none of them had known. Why this event had not been a bigger event in the press then I don't know but I guess even the lives of celebrities couldn't escape the unpredictable nature of the 21st century.

Anyway, the day continued to be a weird one, not only had there been a strange, pensive emptiness to the West End all that Saturday but later, whilst still on Front of House, I overheard Ricardo, our manager throughout all of this, talking to those from Charing Cross police; it turned out then that the bomb itself had been a cheaply made dud that would've failed to have detonated even if somebody had touched it, more worryingly however, the suspect himself had attempted to get into *our* building earlier that morning. Whoever had been supposed to be on Front of House at that time had failed to turn up and so, being unable to get in, instead then headed for next door, somehow getting into Yates's as an alternative.

"Remember this shit?" Anwar said, still holding the open page of the *Metro* before me "I can't believe it brother."

In the middle of the newspaper, there was a small article about the event; the police had arrested a young Muslim man for *attempting* a West End terrorist attack. Behind the longer beard, the Muslim attire, and the strange eyes, we both then recognised that the man had been our old friend and colleague Big Momo.

Year by year, the themes presented by the LFF premieres here seemed to had, in reverse chronological order, probed and probed for the reasons or all such tyranny in our world. First we had dealt, via a pulpy veneer, with the forms of contemporary villainy through *Casino Royale* and *Eastern Promises* and then, possibly, the corruption that might had given rise to it via George W. Bush's Gulf War and then further back to Nixon's Vietnam and all the weirdness that may had conspiratorially bridged both conflicts from behind the scenes with *The Men who stare at Goats.*

This year our Premiere film would go back even beyond that, perhaps back to the key moment when this world, with its economic crises, its dodgy foreign policies, its mistreatment of it lower classes had all really been conceived. Before that moment, the world, this country, had been truly different indeed, a time when this nation had been progressive, when we'd been industrially powerful enough to call our own shots, knew who we were and had the ability to lead the world and stand up to the dick heads of those intent on ruining it; a time when we actually *believed* in our leaders, in our prime ministers, our king, so much so that we'd willingly follow them into a war. To explore that true axis of the 20th Century then, that night would see the premiere to Tom Hooper's *The King's Speech* – the true story of King George VI's attempt to rid himself of the stammer that would impede his war speech – the speech that would enter us into war against fascism.

The whole world ready to turn on the simple basis of a stammer.

Due to that year's earlier safety issue, Edwins' security were then beefed up for further big events and Wilton and the rest of the management had *finally* changed the security codes.

238

*She* would be coming again to the Premiere of course– and I don't mean the Queen, for oddly, despite its content, that Gala performance wasn't a Royal affair – yet the increased security posed a challenge for me, for now to have *her* again – that annual addiction of mine – to the very extent that I wanted her would prove not only more difficult and if I'd been caught would, as I mentioned earlier, put me at the centre of the same media frenzy her and her new lover had already been in. Thinking of how to pull off such a stunt led me to instead spend that Premiere in a haze of confusion.

Since it had begun similarly to last year's Premiere in that it involved me being stationed next to Edwins near Front of House, I'd kind of been hoping that it would end the same way too (minus the failed revolution stuff). The set up was impressive, the entire square had been done up in red carpet and there was an erected gantry in the centre onto which the stars of the film – namely, Colin Firth, Helena Bonham Carter and Geoffrey Rush – would ascend to be interviewed before returning to the crowds for signature signing etc. There had also been an impressive turnout of celebrity guests too, Ben Kingsley, Claire Danes, Tim Burton (Bonham Carter's husband at the time) and…um…Will Young.

Anyway, Edwins' team were edgy for during the earlier set up, some crazy tramp had been wandering around the square giving random Nazi salutes to passers-by. They had deemed him safe enough since, whilst of course the man had gone nuts, they'd noticed an air of carefully drawn limits to his actions, this meaning that the man would only perform such gestures for example when more intelligent, wealthy members of ethnic communities would pass him by and simply know not to take it seriously; whenever the rude boys would turn up of course, the man just went quiet and thereby, Edwins had figured he wasn't likely to put himself into a threatening situation. Still, with such numbers to deal with, they'd still been evidently edgier than usual, for they knew that he was still *out there somewhere,* in that sea of fame-worshipping crazies.

Those crazy little moments of tension made the Premieres for me in those later years. Celebrity culture had just become boring to me by then; each one of them routinely marched in before the press like cows being displayed at some sort of village market. I could see now too that they also fucking knew this. They also knew that *I* knew it and no longer *cared* about *who* they were.

*Burn Hollywood burn, take down Tinseltown.*

*She* however, *she* was the only shining star to me in this blanket of nothingness and I wanted to find her, I *had to* find her.

My distraction came when the Nazi tramp did indeed appear again to scramble over the railing. Nobody had noticed until Edwins called out "Oh shit, oh shit" as the man drew out a permanent marker and wrote *IRA* across the glass of Front of House for all the world's collective media to pick up.

Edwins immediately left and joined his crew to pounce on the man…and so I escaped from my position.

I searched and I searched frantically through that electrical storm of digital flashbulbs; security guided me this way, they guided me that way and in these broken memories of mine, I kind of remember the geography of my establishment not really fitting together in the way that it was supposed to. At one point, I even turned up exactly where I had begun again, to see the continuing debacle of the Nazi tramp's graffiti;

"Get rid of it, get it off *now.*" Wilton militarily commanded through champagne slurs; Ricardo had desperately been trying to remove it with window cleaner, only to turn it into an increasingly messy black smudge.

Eventually, as if like every camera flash had been nudging me this way and that, I was later led onto a portion of the red carpet where she, along with *him,* was being led to after their moments with the press.

How would I signal her? How would I signal her through *this?*

I approached all the same, a smile like a kid in a sweet shop; It then felt like slow motion as she turned away from the cameras and caught my eye. Her previous looks of cheeky enthusiasm were not the same. No one would've surely noticed this but I actually detected something of sadness in her.

One of her hands briefly let go of that of her boyfriend's and very quickly, practically subliminally as to look like an accident, she made a 'time out' sign in my direction. The press, the photographers would have read it as a signal to her PR or security team to continue funnelling her through the frenzy into the screen (the two of us had learned our alibis well), but for me I knew what it had meant. It was over. And just like that she was gone, led onwards into the auditorium.

I just froze and felt the winter through those open doors, I wanted to think that it hadn't happened, that this was some sort of pre-Premiere dream I'd been having behind the 3D glasses back in the Screening Rooms. It hadn't been of course and I just wanted to go home to bed.

"Hey buddy, is that you?" I remember hearing from behind me.

I turned and saw a vaguely familiar face.

"You remember *me?*" this expensively-suited but highly irritating character said "You did it, didn't you?"

Then I remembered, it was that Private Jet owner bloke, that one who'd asked me to get his business card to Oliver Stone all those years ago. I hadn't done it and didn't know what to say to him.

"You did it for me, didn't you? You actually did it?"

I still didn't know what to say.

"I just wanted to say thank you. You got a lotta balls kid." He went on before referring to *her* as she strutted into the screen.

"She's one of mine now. Her and her guy fly here from L.A via *my* airline like once a fortnight. Good stuff, kid."

He then turned, linked arms with what looked like a high-class escort and headed up the stairs to Royal Circle. Everyone had found success but me.

We all got moved into the screen, watched the director Tom Hooper introduce the stage procession one by one but nothing about these people impressed me anymore, star power had turned to star dust. Two hours dragged on. The film finished, everyone left and I started helping my colleagues with the routine cleaning.

As I picked up snot-stained tissues from the auditorium floor and put them into bin bags, my anger welled up, welled up in my hatred for all the rich and famous, for *all* the successful but especially for her. My thoughts went on; drinking iced tea on the veranda to some Hollywood penthouse? *I* was the first one to pay you attention, *me.* Is there not even a single consideration for *that* in your cold heart?

I collected up a number of unopened M&M packets, took them to my locker, got changed and had a nightcap of Smirnoff before making my way out to the exit ready for the bus.

Before leaving, I briefly took a look through the window of 'The Airlock' into the Foyer– of which I could now only associate with my first two encounters with her - there, a small cluster of the security had gathered to wrap up their shift and they appeared to be in two different teams, Edwins' and another. Whether they'd been wrapping up this one or setting up the next, I don't know.

Even at the distance I'd been standing, one from the other team, not Edwin's, one from the somewhat meaner looking lot, suddenly turned round to stare at me back. His eyes were stern and cold, his senses must've been fine-tuned because somehow he'd just *known* that I'd been there. Who the fuck was *this* guy? I thought for a moment.

Somehow, he looked familiar and though I didn't want to gaze back too long, I studied his features briefly and then, you know how when you just know, you *know?* I realised who he was.

Stencilling in a black balaclava to that face, giving him a specialist uniform and a sniper rival, it was then easy to detect; he had been the sniper who we'd met on the roof during mine and Paddy's adventures into the wider realms of the cinema back in 2006. He stared me out until I just gave up and backed away.

Then I realised what her 'time out' gesture had truly meant; that anything forbidden could no longer be done in this world without coverage of some description; eyes were literally everywhere now.

I stepped out into the rain and went home.

# Smoke of the Clambering Dragon

Ever since I began my wretched climb upwards through the cracks at the edge of the world, I've always had the same dream of an endless lift shaft, towering and towering upwards through the dust and the darkness, each sinking counterweight marking some unknown stretch of my passing life as I'm promised but never reach that sunlit rooftop I still believe is there.

It was a reoccurring dream that had invaded my psyche as a young teenager, when after days of carrying the corpse of my younger brother through the battered shells of outer Beijing, with nobody coming to my aid, my terrible, nauseating tiredness overcame my will and I was able to find a morbid comfort amidst the wreckages of bodies and homes, so broken and twisted around each other by then that both building and dweller were permanently sealed together in history under the same colour of ash.

In my exhausted delirium I had sat for hours as the image of the smoke licking through the wounds of my battered concrete shelters were to become a symbiotic component of my very nature; my realities merging with my dreams to trigger the philosophy that upwards was the only direction by which a man could live, upwards and out of the poverty, harnessing the smoke to rise to survival, and so *Smoke of the Clambering Dragon* was a name of which I chose for myself.

Now I no longer look up but down, and not in the east but in the west, at a city at the other end of the world, not at ruins but at construction, not at collapse but at ascent, as if the reasons for my internal screaming had inverted as they had also travelled and spread; somehow carrying the sights of industrial shell casings across the curve of the earth with me. Every shape of rooftop, every road or railway that I now look down upon in this city, are merely the symmetrical pencil sketches that surround my so perfect designs, not even a hotel nor office block can slot together from any given angle without representing the ways in which my corporations have been deliberately planned to intersect. Indeed, not even the stretch of their shadows may touch an area not yet permitted by me.

The North Greenwich developments, recently put into execution, now pass beneath my helicopter for example; and even this borough's most known mistake, the Dome, is also an earlier version of one of my aborted projects accidentally put into implementation before I'd had the time to perfect it. It stands out now, like some metallic blister swelling through the otherwise beautifully organised wastes of the East and yet even that is an imperfection to which I've grown quite fond.

We fly onwards and ascend slightly to the rooftops of the soon-to-be completed hotels that now clutter up the embankment, soon set to compete with the heights of Canary Wharf just over the river ahead.

Still under construction, these hotels will one day cater to that other product known as celebrity, of which will come to take its breaks here between its flaunting to the glitz of the O2 film premieres a short walk away; for the moment however, these hotels' cleanly cut construction slots, their protruding steel bollards and ruined faded billboards instead make me think of showbusiness's uglier counterpart; the  deteriorating layers to a human face so beautifully corroded by chemical burns as to reveal its complex musculature and rigid bone structures beneath. They remind me, then, of the wars I may have once orchestrated at some part of the world as a means to maintain this order.

So perfect is it in construction, so perfect it will be in completion, and so perfect it shall be in its ruination; I am now so wealthy as to destroy all of this and rebuild it all three times over and shall enjoy it so when the necessary time comes. So discreet is my influence on the world that not even the sounds of my helicopter can reveal my arrival, it is with an unusual smoothness that I stare down at the heights of my passing rooftops with some kind of muted sound, kidding myself that I am like all the other bland machines in the sky looking for a landing pad to shake some other entrepreneur's hand for money. Far beyond that now am I, so ahead and beyond those market-scratching types that nobody even knows who I am or how my influence expands into the very fabric of their industrial skylines.

I was not alone amongst the perches at the top of the world however. Of course I wasn't, nobody ever has been. There were four others, pretty much one for every wealthy continent and whilst each of us had a disliking for the complex parts of our world where our empires had cornered onto another's, we had had a lifetime of mutual interests and healthy collaboration to dwell upon. These people too, had expanded outwards and had had families, such future generations had thus also been tutored to love our perfections as much we had and so they too were to be just as trusted in keeping its momentum up for the future. Although my family vastly extends sideways throughout the realms of Asia, I, in fact, am childless and so it was *this* future, the world that existed beyond our deaths, that one thing that none of us could buy, that was now my greatest fear and it was a fear that had become mutual between the five of us.

Indeed, just thinking of how the strings that had tied my kind and I together could somehow come unravelled to allow some simple imbecile to step in and plant some other design onto even the farthest corners of our constructs would sometimes result in a strange taste of rust at the back of my throat that would often result in me throwing up blood.

Old age of course, is the most unpredictable time of one's life; dementia or sudden death could always result in unsigned contracts, unhealthy inheritances and below par decisions; and so today was the day that we'd make sure such things could *never* happen.

As my helicopter makes its descent onto the hotel's landing pad, I do what I often do wherever I am in the world and look out at what I make of its people. Merely resembling tiny black stick figurines from this height, they make their way to and fro between the buildings and it dawns on me that, aside from the updates given to me from my private pilots or bodyguards, I've had very little to do with them. I've always existed independent of them behind a certain thickness of metal or glass and have experienced their words in digital, their voices through wires and their images through passing billboards. I often wonder if they've changed since I last knew them, are they still interested in such pursuits? How close are they to knowing what I know? Are they still maintaining the correct levels of insecurity that keep my world stabilised or are such things beginning to flounder? Another voice at the end of a wire frequently reiterates to me that they are.

The helicopter presses down and I step out onto the stairwell before it flies away again with absolute minimum sound, its rota blades reflecting in multitude off the windows of the higher constructions like some great, cold kaleidoscope towards and over the higher towers of Canary Wharf. I worry for a moment about who may be able to see from such upper floors but then again I'm sure somewhere down the line the district's evacuation may have already been called for.

This rooftop is clean, so beautifully clean, a giant rectangular rooftop of marble whites that's been washed down in a liquid of my choosing to now reflect the hot sun in an immaculate cleanliness. The roof is divided into two parts by a raise in the middle and upon it is its most astonishing addition, placed there just for my arrival and a taste of home, is a paifang, beautifully decorated and surrounded by an additional garden of one hundred or so peonies that keep themselves hydrated by a twenty-four-hour water spray. It's all a nice addition of course but these will never survive this country's unpredictable weather and the paifang will inevitably have to have been removed before the hotel's completion.

I step through the paifang and the sun catches my eye as it reflects off of one of its redundant panels of glass above and then on the other side I see the others; all four of them plus their various kin, stood on the second half of the roof awaiting me, dressed in their finest attire.

There is Oleg Moiseeva, and his three daughters, rulers of Russia, Scandinavia and most of the Arctic Circle, the man with whom I have met the most over my years in power due to his territory bordering on my own, co-operating with me largely on the routes of the Eastern oil lines.

Unusually, it was a woman, Cinja Al Hashmi and her son, who controlled most of the Middle East, India and the surrounding countries and had displayed a great expertise in manipulating how the religions of these regions intersected with industrial development, sometimes being necessary to stir up a conflict, sometimes not.

The Al-Hashmi family quite obviously worked in close unison with Mattias Kobloch, a Dutch-born man who now controlled North and South America, the younger members of his extensive family had infiltrated much of the continent's global corporations and had made the necessary adjustments that would thwart the points of view of the global conspiracy theorists to think it was the Jews who had a stranglehold over the world. This was far from the truth of course, for due to its natural resources (thinking of a future after oil that is) the Koblochs had far more dealings with the Latin Americans than anyone else. Anyway, he is here with two of his oldest and most beautiful teenage daughters, already looking trained up for such work.

Between all of us then, is Louis Duponte, a French/German man who, with his family, occupied the political movements in Europe and largely watched over the region's greatest universities to observe what aspiring future entrepreneurs or scientists might break out for possible recruitment or of whom might have to be later terminated; plus with a careful manipulation of Europe's colonial history, their power had trickled downwards into the workings of Africa of which again, with numerous natural resources, will be necessary to unite and harbour upon our upcoming post-oil future.

In a clever spin on how the trajectories of the future might work he'd actually thought even further ahead than the rest of us and recruited his teenage grandson for today's proceedings.

They all make the secret bow and in between us there is the magistrate. How happy he looks that London has been selected for this event, a great historical city where all the corporations and nations of the world had forever clinked and collided together, a place where one slight misstep committed by whatever nation under whatever circumstances could have an immediate effect on the other side of the world. 21st Century London had in effect then, become a giant control panel for the multicultural soup of the world; such missteps of which then, should require the strictest of organisation.

With a smile, the magistrate begins reading a few words of deeply formal legal jargon before revealing a series of identical wedding rings and stepping toward the first of these future couples.

It is as he is marrying Oleg's first daughter to Duponte's grandson that I stand in nervous disposition about the thoughts that may possibly lie hidden behind each of the young couples' faces; I study their expressions; will they show any signs of potential doubt? Could all of what we had owned show any sign of collapse in the mere creasing of one party's eye wrinkle? Nothing happens, both clearly believe in control as firmly as I do and so Europe and Africa become bound to Russia and the Arctic Circle, control over nearly half of the world's future resources are immediately seized in one ring.

The magistrate moves on and marries Oleg's second daughter to Cinja Al Hashmi's son, marrying Europe, Africa, Russia and the Arctic Circle to the Middle East and I begin to feel strange pounding in my heart as we're nearly half way around the planet.

The magistrate marries Oleg's third daughter to Koblov's daughter in what is now being referred to as a same-sex marriage and it's like a floor to the world has been opened, opened to pour all that covers the earth's surface into our ownership, we are all the way around the world now, and the prospect of two wombs together only means further interesting possibilities, floors within floors, multiple layers to the world melting ever downwards into our pockets.

Now of course, it is my turn, my turn to stamp Asia onto the global carpet that's been laid before us. Koblov brings his other, younger daughter toward me, she is just at the legal age of marriage and within the flimsy global laws of which we had constructed for reasons of order, this may have been considered wrong, but she knows like we all do that this is not about feeble morals or age, this is about making sure, *making sure* that we iron out the unpredictable folding of the world's wrinkles to replace them with the still, ordered forms of such young nubile flesh.

She steps before me with a smile that has infinite futures written all over it, a look of the euphoria one should have as if they'd speared a god-like hole through the fabric of the world to create that simple passageway that links east with west in one fell swoop, a hole so great that the rest of the surface of the planet could be moulded through it to be turned inside out; all this will be ours and I feel a sense of paternal pride for the achievements of which this girl has achieved at such a young age.

The magistrate fulfils his duty, we place the rings on each other, we kiss and our hands clasp, a universe has been born; born in London, the capital of the world and now we have inherited all that it influences.

Of course, everybody has acted as each other's witnesses etc and so those quick dashes of ink that are our signatures are signed. Of all the ways in which I had seen the world and its people slot together over the decades, the world's flimsy reliance of the signature had always struck me as the most bizarre; a couple of flicks of pen made to a vulnerable sheet of paper and families, even companies would automatically be formed, billions in cash could automatically be granted by the actions of a few very breakable sets of hands and yet despite the multiple methods of which we'd all practiced for the sakes of our international invisibility, every other person of the world has just continued to rely on one; that singular something so trivial and virtual. I would not then, and could not, under *that* basis, ever hope to understand them. Anyway, here we all stand now, a new world order, an economic, industrial and political trajectory of the future, all bounded and protected by the solid chains of international law, immovable and irreversible for at least the next few generations.

Our new husbands and brides, those pillars to our indestructible future, then leave us as planned to follow the magistrate through a small doorway that leads to the hotel's lower floors, they will watch over him of course now, keeping him alive for as long as it takes to protect the legal side of things before executing his inevitable termination to prevent leakage.

They've gone, off forever now, and will of course now go on to have children and grandchildren, and so the future of our control will spread and spread through generation and continent, our wealth and influence sprouting out in various ways like the carefully contrived cross pollination of the flower, gone into an ever-swirling whirlpool of business numbers, legal jargon and untraceable names of power. Nothing could ruin it now, nothing, that is, except for *us*.

We wait a short while, I don't know how long but it's long enough for Oleg to call out that he's seen our new family's array of stretched limos making their way away from the hotel compendium, back into the East London wastes and out into the cultures of the world that had found their bases here.

It should be safe then; we look at each other's expressions of mutual respect one last time before our fingers reach beneath the finely tailored fabrics of our suits and fumble amidst the wires to find the switches to our fuse boxes. We find them and the tiny green activation light is accompanied by what some would think to be a threatening warning beep; for me it gives a sense of comfort and relief.

I take in a great inhale of that flammable chemical we'd previously chosen to soak the floor with and there's a toast to; "The union of a successful past with a fool-proof future".

The following experience of death is not as I had expected it; although quick and painful, it is enriched in the purest emotions ever felt, a sudden fear for a lack of control and then back again as I see my four acquaintances explode into fire with a noise that's less a conventional explosion and more of a giant rip as this hotel's upper floors are turned to a vibrant orange and then black, *black,* that great stamp of the official. I am *Smoke of the Clambering Dragon*.

Reportedly, the explosion had not actually been witnessed although its noise had ripped panels out of Canary Wharf's finest structures like leaves in the wind and was apparently heard all the way to Whitehall. To our fortune, its reasons and origin still remain wrapped in one of the capital's strangest ever mysteries, now fodder for conspiracy theorists and paranoid hacks.

Now, even in death, I dream the same dream of an endless lift shaft, towering and towering upwards through the dust and the darkness, each sinking counterweight marking some unknown stretch of my passing life, the rooftop never coming.

# In Silent Slumber Amidst the Reeds

Every so often, when England became the subject of an unnaturally hot summer, Hampstead Heath, that last outpost of true nature that had become one of the most beloved parks of the country's capital, would, through a concoction of its sheer expanse, the falling sunlight upon its mixed-coloured canopies, the shadows of its trees, the smells of its plant excreta and the exhaustion of its hay fever-suffering inhabitants, become the setting for some of the most hazy-alien-green scenery ever seen amidst any inner city environment. It was as if the sun were emerging from the south to bend its light through the prisms of glass and humid smog of the city centre the way it might through some beautiful jewel, thus granting this spot of North London its own unique branch of the colour spectrum.

It was after a dip in the male ponds and a few ales in The Spaniard's Inn that He began to feel his ageing-self feel quite profoundly replenished and relaxed. He never liked to relax too close to too many people however and so made his way amidst the sunbeams of the forestry and past the sounds of the people to a private area that only he and a few others knew about; a rather unkept clearing between the more popular pathways and the traffic of Spaniard's Road, concealed behind woodland and overlooked by a great radio pole. The Heath was rather easy to get lost on yet he would always know where he was due to the oncoming electric clangs of this mast, a sound whose location less knowledgeable walkers could seldom figure out. It was then, whilst lying on his back in the long grass of this clearing, beneath the great 'Clangs' of this radio mast and looking up at the infinities of blue that he began to drift into a summer day's sleep and contemplate his world... And so those distant city sounds, the sirens, the traffic and the dog barks all dissipated until...

A young woman emerges from the doorway of Kenwood House and runs out across its great front grounds, hitching up the front of her immense white dress as she goes; allowing its trail to spread out like some great bird's as she darts through the morning mists to abandon the confines of the 1800's and vanishes into the trees. Her dress becomes snagged upon the twisting, withered limbs of the century-old trees and he notices her breasts, beautifully pushed up via her corset. She is beautiful. How he would like to possess a beauty like hers, how he would like her entangled amongst the trees. Which man or realm of order has made her run away like this? The trees snag at her clothes as she finds herself caught, now away from time, amongst nature's more neutral ground. Her expression changes with the light. The insects, sprites and spirits, only visible when light passes between the trees, rear their immense society before disappearing in a single powerful brushstroke.

The atmosphere changes.

The reeds sway in the breeze.

The frilled cuffs of Lord Hargreaves; poet and soldier of the British Empire, push away the nettles of the hedges as he emerges beneath an intoxicating green. Following the trail of successfully harvested mushrooms to wild berries that constitute a path from shade to sun, he finds the spot of the exposing sunlight;

"Alas, oh mysteries of the sun where should you lead my kin to next?"

In a hazed wander, the sun flickering on and off like torchlight as it's interrupted by the leaves, Hargreaves walks on until stopping as liquid seeps into his leather boots, staring down, the green algae is indistinguishable from the grass; earth and water as one. Across the pool of rotting green Hargreaves looks and notices the strange appearance of a young man with a depression across his face more prominent than even the mud. He wears the armoury and weapons of a future never likely to be known by Hargreaves, it is green and metal-cased. The two lock eyes from opposite sides of this pool, curious to their own reasons for their meeting.

Nearby a painter sits, his oils reacting on canvas at the way the overhanging greenery grows outwards across the pool to meet in the middle in mysterious unison. Hargreaves steps forwards into the pool, as does the young man, the green algae travelling upwards to their knees, their groins, their chests and shoulders and finally above their eyes in full submersion. They walk on in their liquid green; the home of the tadpoles, the minnows, vegetation and matter sway all around them, an invisible alien world unspoilt by them. They feel replenished here in a place fresh and unconquered. Through the surface of above green, the twigs that protrude like skeletal fingers react as our two men meet beneath.

Further on, more trees cross each other's path of growth in a way only the cruelty of nature could delegate, their fingers begin to expand and expand, reaching out to unite and conquer this land. Their unity blots out the sun, coating a carpet of brown leaves in the shadows of an inevitable future darkness. The birds and the mammals quickly scarper in a frenzy to their usual abodes as fresh blood leaks from the orifices and growths of the tree surfaces. Down it trickles, darkening their bark until merging with sprouts of paling grass. Outwards it spreads across the ground, the peaceful autumn leaves disturbed from their slumber.

The juices of fresh berries coat the innocent whites of two toddlers' teeth as they play amidst the vegetation a short distance from the picnics of their parents.

Master Marcus Jeffries sits upon a nearby picnic mat with his new wife, Lady Jeffries, his best friend and business partner Master Rawcliffe and his younger friend's wife-to-be, Lady Green. The two of them, newly united in business, are discussing the expansion of their international steel mines over the beautiful taste of South African wine. Their futures will be bright, a third century of Britain's industrial revolution has just begun. Rawcliffe and Green are also to be married, and the four great friends and the innocence of both couples' young children will be at the capital heart of this great, expanding industrial nation. Poverty shall never touch them again.

"Britain will never end" they say, and how beautiful their women look, caked in the finest of make-ups, dressed to the best that money could buy them and fanning themselves from the heat in this finest of moments as if their clothing had somehow altered to fit perfectly with whatever strange passes of colour they may have encountered throughout this afternoon's outing. What fine children they shall surely bear over further years?

Baby Jessica makes a gargling attempt at first speech as she points to a hillside.

"What is it?" the women ask in curiosity at the colourful world now around them, and they turn to look in the direction of Parliament Hill. The clouds beyond becoming charcoal greys that conceal strips of fiery orange. Others of this lucrative era (the men are in black suits, the women in wide dresses) all walk up the greying hillside to join the others congregating around the benches to witness the strange new alterations to their green and pleasant land. The children are running forwards, their adults are following them, their picnic has been left to the birds and squirrels. Atop the hill they see a strange new place. It is familiar to them but somehow more expansive; there are more chimneys now, more blackening roof tops, the gravestones of cemeteries trailing a path down towards the smokes of the city like rows of teeth.

From out of the sky emerge a fleet of terrifying machines; great hunks of propeller-driven metal swooping over London like birds of prey, and from out of their bottoms, further great chunks of metal. The fires of orange rearrange the geometry and structures of the city at numerous, terrifying angles; screams begin, and their sounds reach the hill. There is the sound of falling and all is burnt in the backlash of industrial progression. The remains of a picnic lie nearby now pecked to pieces by gathering crows.

A Cavalier hangs from a withered tree, his body creaking from the noose. A woman lies de-wombed amidst the reeds, the flies and the animals feast upon her innards. Children coated in black descend upon the clearings of the Heath crying as they hopelessly search for their protectors.

Two shady men, dressed in black attire, stand to watch as the struggling evidence contained within the metal of a Rolls sinks beneath the algae; creaking sounds descend, matter bubbles up and the protruding skeletal fingers of twigs are pushed to new postures by their new underwater addition, frozen to remain like this until another from the future should come to its replacement; all sadness and failures are now submerged in the ponds of time.

Undetected, high up amidst the greens and browns of the tree tops, strange winged creatures with golden scales perch upon branches to look upon this human scene; another world, another dimension, irrelevant to them but saddening nonetheless.

In the darkness of the woods a light approaches. A lantern. It shakes with the ferocity at which its carrier runs; a Tudor type, followed by another,

"It is here, I have seen it"

Their panicked running stops and the lamplight illuminates the surface of a wide tree to reveal a holy crucifix hanging upon it, vandalised by a mysterious red.

"Do you see that?" asks the second man, "in the clearing. A witch."

Under the light of the moon, a hunched figure, dressed in black, darts across the clearing before disappearing into the woods, the mystery it carries with it, gone forever.

Young, illegitimate Ezmerelda is informed by her father in his majestic library not to wander amidst the halls of Hill House on winter nights for this is when The Other Man is known to scale their perimeter walls and stalk the concrete archways and decadent vines of their outer grounds. He says he is the result of his international dealings with the colonies and that he's known to wander his way all the way up to the first great window of the kitchen.

Tonight, young Ezmerelda ignores her father, she returns to the ground-floor library where amidst a more secluded corner, she stares out through a thin window into the moonlight at the red-brick pillars of The Pergola and at the woods that overhang the perimeter walls beyond.

There is a commotion amidst the trees, and from them sprouts a leg, another leg, followed by the form of a dark and powerful man appearing from behind to scramble down the brambles of the inner wall into her domain. She is terrified, he is tall and powerful but still a far distance away. He moves away somewhere, lost amidst the fog and the obstacles of her vision.

Through the great halls she runs, to the next window, she sees him again, closer now, his clothes are old and torn, his skin is darker than the shadows and his eyes as wide as bars of soap.

She runs on regardless, through the immense kitchen door and to the first window of which has been left open by idiotic porters. The shadows, the cold, the light and the fog pour in to freeze her in this fleeting moment and await him. Her fate is sealed.

Those eyes emerge, deranged like a mad animal, the light reflects off the curves of a powerful musculature and his height is like the trees. He stops. An unearthly force transports her fears from herself and into the shrubs beyond them, she no longer fears and so steps before him. Those eyes are not of the monster her peers have told her of, but of a victim. She reaches forwards and caresses the face of this otherworldly thick-skinned wanderer to understand, for the first time, her fears and pains are as one and that her peers, those great harbingers of knowledge, the owners of extensive libraries, are for once wrong and that her future shall concern the greater curiosities beyond her walls.

From the overhang of a great oak, fifty or so green serpents, indistinguishable in colour from the dense vegetation they've emerged from, overlap and uncoil themselves to fall onto the floating flower heads that drift upon the pond surfaces beneath them, bringing all parties beneath the algae into such silver green depths.

The African and the Jamaican man sit beneath the levitating bulb to an old bridge as they light up their exotic new delights, plants it would seem from some other great wilderness. Something about their rights to equality they talk of in an unfamiliar dialect as the clouds of their substances immerse them and drift into the trees like some renegade mist.

'Cut!' we hear from a distance, and the colours and the breezes that disrupt the reeds all come to a fascinating freeze; the two men stop and stand to their feet to be greeted by a rich Italian. His name is Antonioni and from all around emerge his minions from all over the now-completely-known world. They are, each of them, in all their different shapes and colours, the results of international deals and this is the creation of some new world product; a product, as the paths of the world have let it become, that uses London as America and concerns black politics as created by the minds of entangled Europeans. There are clicks and whirs and the pops of flashbulbs and all come to a stop once more. The mad Italian throws his papers into the air to take his own stroll amidst the trees.

The African and the Jamaican man assemble their friends from the shoot and head off through the woods. Brushing the nettles of the brambles away to head onwards they come across a break in the woods, the fallen trunks of centuries past acting as natural seats.

In a modern age now, a girl in a bikini lies on her back, the beauty of her hair intertwining with the grass, her wasp-eye shades staring upwards to the infinite, wires of an iPhone plug into her ears and she sings the colourful words of an era not her own;

*And I will sing, waiting for the gift of sound and vision, drifting into my solitude, over my head.*

Fifty years prior, the Jamaican and the African place tabs under their tongues, they remove musical instruments from boxes and the African man and a French girl begin to embrace.

Unmanned, Antonioni's camera rolls on through the woods willingly, capturing in scratched celluloid a hairy caterpillar pulsating across the surface of a plant, a spider eating a fly and a water boatman enjoying the freedoms of his infinite but complex kingdom.

To the sounds of the exquisite audio experiments that now emanate from his surroundings, Antonioni crosses the paths of the more conventional routes and makes his way through the woodland to a clearing only he knows about, the electric clangs of a radio mast guide him forwards and he emerges in a familiar field of privacy. He lies on his back to take note of how the rolling clouds and the music from his dissipated minions sooth his enraged creative energy. New ideas will now surely come? He sleeps, he dreams, he fantasises.

Paul and Jamie hold hands and head down the trails of dried mud away from the busy roads and further and further into the woods. For years they searched for their place in this city, rumours of new illnesses having outcast them to this place. It is only under the veil of nature, they've decided, that impulses of their kind are truly allowed to prevail.

Further they walk, over the never-to-be used railway bridge, the light forever changing; the insects, the spirits and the sprites become temporarily visible once again.

The orange flecks caused by a falling sun are within their vicinity. They sway and connect in a rhythmic motion as the surfaces of the first great ponds come into sight; an illusion of light that blurs land, trees and water into one. Finally, they reach the tiny wooden walkways that mark the perimeters of the pond, abandoned by the regulars at this hour, now creating a social perimeter of its own that for this notorious time of day exists simply for them.

From the water more men emerge, the orange flares of sunlit water glistening and complimenting physiques worthy of Greek sculpture; down their abdomens it runs to reveal their floating genitalia emerging from the surface erect. Onto the walkways, great powerful legs lift them, and they join the others upon the muddy embankments, shielded from the rest of the world by the reeds and the trees. They dry themselves on towels before a hand admires another man's form and reaches back. Further hands caress others, arousals enhance and soon the embankments have become a pulsating bed of hardening flesh.

At the base of the archway to the unused railway bridge, nature is left to run wild; plants grow as high as small houses and contain pockets of stagnant water never to be disturbed. Occasionally, like a water bomb, a pocket explodes when the plant is knocked by the animal panics of some overgrown, feral critter. The ageing surfaces and shifting reds of this brickwork structure are now indistinguishable from the greens of moss. Helen takes note of such wonders as another natural poison from some alternate wilderness enters her veins; what serenity this place brings to the addicts she thinks, a knowledge that for here, her shames, the derailed routes of her past and her addictions can all seem to find some organic kind of purpose.

Further behind the gigantic, unkempt plants she now shields herself. Amidst their canopies' yellow tiger stripes of sun, those she wishes to not see make themselves suddenly apparent upon one of this wilderness's more straightening paths; children. Their existence evoking memories from some former life chapter cut too short. Don't let them see her like this, she thinks.

On they walk, down the straighter paths, dressed in school uniform, carrying ruck sacks and watched over by the birds, relieved to be outside of their normal confines. Their path leads them to a clearing at the rear of Kenwood House where they become fascinated by a circular sculpture; two solid points resembling a liquid seem to pull toward one another at its centre; young James identifies that should these ever touch all seemingly unconnected events will come together to make sense as a whole.

Electric twangs, the breeze, lights and sensations finally pull together to make sense as a singular reality and he awakes amidst the reeds. How long has gone by? His place of solitude is still undisturbed.

Brushing away the insects and the pollen, He stands to make his way towards somewhere else. Onwards he goes, back on the conventional tracks before being drawn to some nearby sense of civilisation beyond a hedgerow. He brushes the nettles away to notice the flecks of the sun moving in perfect motion from the base pool to a tiny water fall. Sat around its water's edge, their shoes casually kicked off and sprawled out upon picnic mats to tranquil trickling sounds, sit families of all varieties, having been brought together by the modern world's more mysterious paths of union. Mixed races, mixed faiths, mixed classes, same sexes. Artists, industrialists and children, rich and poor, now all equal under the same sun. Their fleeting conversations break as one of them takes notice to welcome him in to join them.

# Sooner or Later on the N29

I don't know what kind of optimism's flowing through my blood right now, it's warped and makes no sense. Whether it's the endless shots John kept plying me with or the old-school vibes of *Thunderclap Newman's 'Something in the Air'* that just signified The Barfly's kick out time? I don't know.

Somewhere around the graffitied girders that shut down Stables Market for the night, the hangers-on of our group have dispersed to make their own ways home and I spot a window of opportunity I'd hoped for but thought would never come.

The booze and lyrics lead me on my way, arms locked together with 'Chelle, through the early morning hours of Camden Town in July. *Thunderclap's* song has forever been a Saturday night *'closing upper'* since the days of its release but one that's also left later generations with a sense of strange melancholia for the fact that we may never see anything even close to the sexual revolution it once implied, now an old-world cliché that may not even have been *that* real to begin with. Nevertheless, don't over think things, both poisons are doing their work splendidly; something of a future is coming. Don't bottle it!

'Chelle and I now await outside the industrial-styled Sainsbury's for the 24-hour N29 to arrive; that same old gathering place many would find themselves at during the early morning hours of any Camden Town kick-out time. Rubbish coats the road like the aftermath of war, an unimaginable filthiness.

We're both pissed of course, is it tiredness or something else that's keeping her from her usual chatty ways? Instead we observe the crowd that surrounds us; an assortment of people in their own assortment of retro, music-led fashions. They bustle and laugh amongst each other, most of them young and too naive to realise that they're merely years away from that blander, more unifying uniform that is that of the nightshift workers who also stand silently amongst us as if bored of their ways. Please God, don't let me face that fate alone? Everyone seems to be searching for a cigarette lighter and none of them work. Too much social lubricant then leads them to ask us through crazed eyes about our own night's experiences before everyone's position on the path is then interrupted by the pleads of the homeless or the subtle hawking questions of the drug pushers.

Is it the thought of these multiple possibilities of destiny that keep my younger ex-colleague so unusually quiet tonight? Her glorious blue eyes staring out with an almost zoological wonder at these creatures from behind smudged mascara and sweat-doused, scruffy black hair; her black roots always look better as they push out the blonde to the past.

"Are you okay?" I ask.

"Yeah, just, where's the fucking bus man?" She wraps herself further in her fake fur jacket; she'd never have worn a real one. It's summer of course, but never let that trick you in England.

The dilemma begins, if her unusual silence proceeds, what do we talk about? We're ex-colleagues, and while we certainly *know* a lot about each other, once other colleagues, or especially *ex-colleagues* have dissipated into the night, you're called to question how well you *truly* know one another. How well does anybody know anyone?

The internal lights of the double-decker N29 then rattle and pull up out of the night, like a Japanese lantern dragged with too much aggression by an overhanging abattoir hook. For some reason at this popular hour, it's surprisingly empty and stops just before us.

"Oh thank fuck, come on, we can make it."

The door hisses open, the driver ignores Oyster Card payments and I hear her running and giggling awkwardly up the stairs to the front seats of the top deck, the others pouring in behind her like Beatlemania. I can't be fucked to run but I make it next to her, she's giggling and chuffed that we've beaten North London's entire pisshead community to our privileged conversation place on the way back home, me to Wood Green, her to the shorter distance of Finsbury Park, I think.

The front windows have always reminded me of cinema screens and we look out in widescreen scope at a night world of parallel lines; of roads shooting out before us like steely futures, only to be interrupted by the horizontal intersections of upcoming rail bridges or the vertical ones of building walls; a night world of many possible futures, preferred futures to be interrupted by other destinies, all illuminated by sodium flare.

The first wheels turn... and so do those of my insecurities.

"So how's the new job treating you, Mike?" she asks.

"It's boring 'Chelle, it's just Sales, isn't it? All you do is sit and stare at a fucking screen, waiting to make a phone call. Everyone's so competitive it's hard to know who your real friends are."

On our upper floor, we're now level with the peeling paint jobs of the dodgy, decrepit flats that stand above Camden's 'edgy' veneer; their residents probably managing the coffee shops and cafes that lie beneath. Would working there have been a happier existence for me?

"It's been four months and, to be honest, I don't even know if I've met anyone I could call a real friend yet".

Why did I fucking tell her that? She probably takes the piss out of me when others are talking about me.

"Fucked up, isn't it?" she says, "but that's life in the grown-up job world for you. You know, I'm sure Neill will always take you back if you wanted to come back to The Gun for a laugh."

An empty beer bottle clunks about irritatingly somewhere beneath one of these seats.

"Not after six years, 'Chelle, not after six years."

"You were there for *six years?*"

The sky is turning from black to sapphire blue, and with such emerging colours I can make out the tarmac of the emerging football pitches and concrete of the skateboard ramps. Upon their mesh fences, birds are chirping on the morning. Amazing how, with such an image of peaceful contemplation, I'm still drawn to think about the negativity as to how pathetic all that was, *six years* working behind a bar. That's over half a decade. What was I waiting for? What a loser I must seem like, at least she has the excuse of being in her twenties and still being there, I'm pushing thirty-five and only left four months ago.

The bus hisses to another stop, the beer bottle stops its roll and more loudmouths pour on beneath us. As my Mum keeps saying, don't let your regrets get to you, keep trekking onwards and make your peace with past mistakes. The morning is the future, the bus pushes on again.

"Yeah, you know what?" I say "everyone slags that pub off, and the customers were freaks but, and I don't know about you, I made good mates there, we had fun, didn't we?"

Her face goes into one of those drunken, I'm confident-about-making-sense-of-my-own-bullshit looks...

"Well, friendship's what it's all about mate. If you haven't got that then..."

A strange smoke from somewhere drifts across the road before us like a ghost. It submerges our screen; street lights flare before it passes and we've entered the long stretch of rich housing estates that make up Camden Park Road.

"You know" she pulls her sentence together as she looks out at these passing palaces on both sides of the road; "you're right, you have to make money someday. You must be making *alright* money at that place at least, right?"

"Well, *meh*."

*"Meh"* she impersonates, shrugging her shoulders. That's the kooky girl I like. "What does *meh* mean? I'm still at The Gun, you arsehole".

Was that a slip of her *actual* dislike for me?

"Well, when you're a kid, everyone warns you about how hard adulthood is, don't they?"

Her mascara eyes stare at me and her faded red lips tremble weirdly as she listens intently, is she *actually* listening to something *I* have to say or is it just the usual shitty fears of ageing that are stirring her curiosity?

"Well I don't think it's true 'Chelle" I go on, "it's not that it's really *that* hard, it's just that it's totally fucking boring. You get a job that pays alright, and then that's it, you can't leave for fear of not finding what you already have again and then again, you don't hate it enough to leave anyway, everything just levels off as simply *okay*."

I look out at the white-washed, three-storey, expensive town houses, some of them tucked away peacefully behind the safety of private gates. Had the residents within them, no doubt some of the city's highest earners, experienced my very same realisation at some earlier stage of life? Was it at moments like this these that ideas of 'settling down' truly came into play?

She's just staring at me now. I look back at her, and I look down at the way the minute neck hairs just beneath her hair stand up on end, is it because of the draught?

Getting older is sad in some ways, but the older you get, the more you understand that all those emotions you once felt in the past, all those petty dramas, are suddenly trivial in the face of one singular, crystal-clear realisation; that it is only the love between people that *truly* matters. Does she know that yet? Her drunken eyes burrow into me.

Beyond those three-storey town houses, the first electric lights of the district's high-rises can be seen beyond. That domain of the city's financial opposite. They look magical yet people say that they're the loneliest places to live in London.

"Do you know what I think, Mike?"

What's she going to say?

"I think you need a friend".

What does *that* mean? Perhaps she is the nice girl I think I know her as? Was it a come on?

"I think we should organise an even bigger night out with everyone from The Gun next time."

This sentence carries a slightly lower intonation as if she's nervous; why's she nervous?

She continues, intonation rises as if more upbeat again, less shy.

"Are you still seeing that girl who used to come in? What was her name? The Aussie?"

Is this it? Is this my cue?

"What Kaitlin? No, she went back."

"You're kidding me? You two seemed close"

"It was what it was 'Chelle. It was never serious. People tend not to stay about much in London anymore."

An old battered, corner pub passes on my side of the street; its bad paint work resembles blisters, an outside blackboard advertising Comedy Nights refers to an older date and the glasses left outside collecting the rain suggest a carelessness by its owners; such places are now relics of an older London, ready to be stamped out by the spread of richer communities.

"Well I don't blame them, the place is changing for the worst. Even then, back at The Barfly, no more smoking inside, only plastic cups outside, airport-like security just to get in."

The first rays of sunlight hit the leafy canopies and upper floors of Brecknock Road as she continues...

"What the fuck's happened to having fun in life, Mike? Even John looked a bit pissed off and that guy used to hit it hard. When did he leave, like, nine?"

We go quiet again and some rudeboy has pulled up his car in front of the bus to intentionally drive slowly before it. A nice intervention of fate to grant me more time.

I think about the meetings of my parents, of my grandparents and what circumstances of the world they might had met under. Was it the optimism of the post-war city that led my grandparents together? My parents? The desperate climate of seventies' recession? And here now, was it technology or booze that might connect us?

Brecknock Road gives way into the complex and less privileged streets of Holloway. On a street corner stands an *actual* 1960's police box; is this a genuine remnant from the old London or some weird in-joke about *Doctor Who* to appeal to this area's non-existent tourists?

I drop a bomb to which I already know the answer... It's an innocent one though.

"But you're still with your boyfriend, right? You were living together, weren't you?"

"No, he's gone now, thank fuck."

I won't ask what happened but there were rumours. She's fallen to silence to stare out to her side; the harsh, long-stretching red-brick walls of Holloway Prison's exterior cast a sharp reminder upon me. You wasted *six years* in The Gun, and you've spent years thinking about this, there's no time in life left to waste. You only have this chance.

Suddenly the fear blocker that was the booze or the fuck-it-and-live lyrics of *Thunderclap Newman's* closing song have faded, suddenly my predicament is real and I stare at the scratched surfaces of the bus's interior as if they're as bitter and real as London's polluted air.

The bus driver beeps the wannabe gangster away to the base of some nearby rough high-rise and we trundle on. Fuck. My destination draws closer and at a greater speed. I *have to* do this. There it is again, that confrontational, cramped tunnel of numbing pins that is fear. You only have this chance. I'm fantasising about sex with her and find myself instinctively looking at what I can see of her cleavage through the reflection. I think she's noticed because she pulls her fur closer to herself and stares out the window.

The bus suddenly takes an unexpected detour onto another street, I notice a pile up of mouldy mattresses and sleeping bags; somebody actually *lives* there and their starving dogs fight and chew upon chicken bones. The fear of such a fate hits me. None of us are doing especially well and this is a true, plausible reality for most of our generation, one cannot simply pass off this fear whenever we spot an insight into this other, unimaginable London. It suddenly dawns on me that she may be looking away because I might stink; the spilt beer of the Barfly's ground-floor bar has seeped through the holes in my shoes and congealed on to my socks, the cigarette smoke has stained my clothes. I must surely stink?

As the bleakness of outside's other life passes us by, she breaks the silence.

"So, is there anyone else on the horizon? Are you using Tinder or anything? *Grindr* maybe?" She adds with a wink.

"No, is it just me, or does all that kind of stuff just seem a little too weird to be as commercial as it is? I can't really get to grips with it, can you?"

"I can't really say, I've never tried it myself."

Really? I'd always imagined she had. Is she lying? Girls always make shit up when they're nervous. Why is she nervous? Is this going to be a two-way thing?

Our road collides with Holloway Road and we emerge upon the enormous, brilliantly silent crossroads. Its array of fried chicken shops, kebab houses and cheap casinos appear like enveloping pink tulips as the maroon of the morning sun hits them, protruding gently through the spaces the crossroads allow it.

Summer is upon us, soon the parks will be flooded with friends and lovers. I want us to be amongst them. The bus crosses the crossroads, the bottle at our feet knocks about annoyingly and we're back onto Holloway Road again. Fucking hell her stop must be coming *soon*, *do it* Mike, don't fear it, *do it*.

She goes back onto the *Tinder* conversation.

"Many people do now so I'm not sure if it's really *that* weird anymore. Those people behind us are probably using it right now. Who knows, it sounds like it could solve your predicament, Mike."

What does she mean by that? What the fuck does she know about my predicament? Why do girls always think they can solve your problems for you?

"No, it's not my scene. It's like wearing a T-Shirt that reads "I'm Lonely", it's like in strip clubs"...

"Oh *yeah?*" as if she's awkwardly amazed by such a subject. Is she trying to unearth and judge my lustful side? Don't carry on with this, don't carry on with *this...*

"Yeah, you go there, you have a good time, but its thrills are only on a surface basis, you ultimately end up going home lonely."

'You fucking pleb.' I shout inwardly at myself.

"Ahh, that's sweet, Mike."

I take the slight sarcastic way she said it to mean she's joking. Don't you just hate it when girls call you *sweet*?

"Incidentally, I don't think I'm lonely 'Chelle. I just think that maybe I'm just an awkward person, I didn't mean that to come out wrong."

She's listening properly again but she's not saying anything. Just stay on this plane.

Typically, as the sun makes itself more visible, we become surrounded by nothing but the ugly, 70's brickwork that makes up the back ends of both an *Argos* and *Morrison's* warehouse; England really has no shame in how depressing it can look sometimes.

Her eyes kind of crease up at their sides as if she's ready to take the piss out of me. Then she takes the piss out of me...

"Oh, you're *so alternative* Mike, coming out in Camden Town to be *awkward and alternative*" she starts giggling into her fur collar and this starts to piss me off, "let's go and score some legal highs" she goes on "and listen to some dark drone music. I can't believe you just said that".

This pisses me off especially because I'm *not*, and she fucking knows this, a person who puts on such an act. I've also never even especially been a fan of the so-called Camden 'alternative' scene, all that was *her* fucking idea. And on that note, what an absolutely, almost irresponsibly wanky thing to say; as if to suddenly put *everyone*, including me, under some fucking label, making even *herself* sound like a prick in the process.

The ugly 70's brickwork walls continue. That drunken lip quiver of hers begins again as she shifts tone, turning more serious.

"You're a good-looking guy Mike, you know. It's just that you can be so fucking weird sometimes man. A word of advice, girls don't really dig weird."

Alright, here comes the moment when pissed-up bullshit becomes too much; any individual, proud of their character, has to do something here, she simply does *not* fucking know me well enough to justify saying *that* to me. God she can talk such shit when she's pissed.

"What the fuck?" I say quietly, sending my true intentions to the grave.

"What do you mean, 'What the fuck?' I was just giving you some friendly advice that's all."

"You *can't* say that, 'Chelle" I try to look the other way.

"Can't say *what*? We worked together for years, I know your character. This is what we're talking about; friendship, Mike, it's what it's all about man."

Resist it, this fight wasn't part of your plan.

Outside, a dangerous-looking man is shouting at brick walls. Booze kicks in. This city requires personal metal, everyone who's lived here long enough, like him, has a certain degree of it, can't help it, it's just a tough place, survival is the everyday. Fuck it, *do it*, conflict is at the core here and you're an unintentional part of it.

"Oh what, *that's* advice? Knowing and criticising my character? *That's* your advice?"

We freeze up briefly again. I can tell neither of us really want the tension but 'Chelle always liked fights.

"Yeah but..."; she attempts to say before I stop her;

"Yeah, well, *you* can't advise me on anything" I say.

"Why not? Just because I'm younger, I'm a female, and still at The Gun? That's just being a patronising, sexist arsehole, Mike. What's wrong with you anyway? You've been acting like a freak all night, even John said so, why do you think he left early?"

So *that's* what's going on. That's what's been going through her head all this time. Bringing other people into it eh? Well fuck John too then. I wish I could verbalise this but I can't.

The ugly 70's brickwork pulls away and I can see how the morning's summer sun compliments overhanging trees, some further town houses and a Leisure Centre.

All I can think about now is that I don't want this argument to happen. All I can think about is how shit tomorrow's going to feel after this. All I can think is how to break out of this tunnel of my own fearful, numbing pins.

"If you don't like it, then screw you."

She sits still now, what's she thinking as she watches the world drift before us in this state? You still don't have to fail at this. *Do it, Mike. Do it. Shatter the tragic compromise that is Your Life.* The pins cripple my body but my mouth moves regardless.

"Chelle?"

"What the fuck is it now?"

*Don't bottle it. Do it.*

"I love you."

You've done it, you cannot change a thing - reality slips away, the *illusion* of reality slips away to something better. My senses are *real*.

Her face turns to mine suddenly, frozen like granite. An expression on her face that's not explicitly one of concrete shock, but something of confusion, respect, disbelief and fear all rolled into one – as if her own illusion of reality, of even herself, have also suddenly been shattered with equal force – here it is then, the way we look when hit with a sledgehammer of truth. What fakery we make for ourselves while trying to define so-called happiness. We Brits are such repressed dickheads.

"I've loved you for years."

I feel cowardly as I look outside once again rather than up to her eyes, the rows of town houses continuing; "and containing it is fucking me up, I'm tired of it."

No matter what happens now, she'll always respect you regardless of where your eyes are. You're *not* a coward, you are the man most women claim they want them to be. I slowly turn my eyes back to hers and her face remains the same – frozen in tension. In the silence, the birds chirping on the morning seem as loud as an opera. Whatever I can read now in those complex, reflective pupils, it's like her wonders are no longer those of a woman's per se, but of a girl's, confronted by the unpredictable tapestries of both beauty and horror that her future life might bring to her.

I remember the time I first met her, before she'd taken a hold on me, how that soft shyness that existed just below her confident, blonde-dyed exteriors, gave way to suggest slyly stealing shots from The Gun's optics. And so here it is, the reality that moment has eventually led to. All I can think about is the present moment, the present moment, and how that rolling beer bottle keeps us anchored into it.

We stare and we stare at each other, careful now that we're under the light of day, not to reveal any tic of the face that might suggest whatever reality we might secretly want to reveal, she even hides her quivering lip. She is beautiful and something, *something* in our human awareness of one another tells me that it's going to be alright.

Somebody pings the button to signify the end of our moment; it has culminated in the rusty bridges of Finsbury Park. We stare on for a while before, as if speaking from a source somewhat disconnected to her body, she pulls at her fur collar to stand;

"This is my stop".

## Strange Requests Volume 3

Sunday night at The Miller in Snowsfields. It's a wind down session. The half-cut weekenders are still here but it's a laid back environment that needs a relaxed set. I settle for a bit of *Phoenix* and some *1975* whilst the guy sets up his microphone for quiz night.

A few feet away from me I see two guys looking over. They're chatting over something quite intently and one of them is gently putting his hand round the back of the other's neck. I try not to stare and put on some *Arcade Fire* instead.

Then one of them walks over. I can see he is a little hesitant to speak to me so I help him out.

"You ok mate?" I say, sipping my lager.

"Yeah" he says. "Can I make a request?"

"Absolutely" I say.

"What would you play to someone who has just found out his Dad has got terminal cancer?"

I must admit I was a bit taken aback but I tried to stay composed. Only one track entered my head.

"I'd play *Wish You Were Here* by Pink Floyd".

The man hesitated. "I don't know that one."

"Well…that's what I'd play"

The man looked back around to the other man at the table, who was nursing his drink. He turned back to me.

"Do you have it?" He said

"Absolutely" I said

"Could you play it? For my brother?"

"Yes, not a problem mate. I hope it helps".

And with that the guy goes back and sits with his brother. I line up the track:

**Pink Floyd** - Wish You Were Here

After a few fuzzy seconds the guitar starts to echo round the room. The two men sit in silence. I roll up a cigarette and watch them both as the evening draws in.

# The Day She Chose To Live
### *A Tragedy in Four Parts*

## Part IV: The Uber To Ludgate Hill

Andy stepped out of Clapham South station into the searing heat. It was Monday 19th June and he had a gig. A corporate pub quiz for a Japanese bank somewhere near St Pauls. But first he had to pick up the equipment.

He immediately regretted his attire. Hoping to make a good impression on his high-flying clientele he had opted for the brown chinos and white-shirt-and-blazer combo (There was always a chance that some CEO could be in the audience who would be bowled over by his public speaking and sign him up to corporate heaven. For now, pub quizzes were his bread and butter). The tube ride made him sweat profusely and now the cheap cotton jacket was sticking to his back.

He followed the GPS of his phone through the assembled bathers towards an address near the other side of the common. All human life can be found on hot days in Clapham. The tanned twenty somethings playing one touch. The drunks on the benches lighting up. The bikini girls. The sleeping gangsters. The kissing couples. The paramedic sitting cross-legged on a break. The sizzling office workers eating sandwiches beneath a tree. The kids playing with their boats on the mini marina. The basketball courts in full swing. Those rare days where London gets a lick of serious sunshine and no one really knows what to do with themselves. Andy surveyed them all as he puffed towards the splash pool where yummy mummies chatted in front of their water babies.

He managed to navigate through the affluent boroughs to Springfield Mews, a private block and home to his quiz writer, Danny. Whilst Danny was away on a stag weekend, Andy had been advised to collect the PA equipment from his wife and get a cab on the company account.

He pressed the buzzer by the entrance to a private road. There was a crackle on the speaker:

*Yes?*
*Hello. Yes, it's Andy here. The quiz-host.*
*Oh. Yes. Well, come in.*

The gates opened slowly and austerely to beckon Andy in. He searched for the elusive number 62 before finally stumbling upon it behind a tree. He knocked on the door. An attractive but stern lady in her 40s opened the door. Andy hesitated, hoping he had got the house number right.

"Hannah?"
"It's Rachel, but don't worry."
"Oh. I'm so sorry. Um..."
"Come in."

Andy stepped into a spacious, modern, London hallway. In the kitchen he could see two children in their pants sitting to lunch. Rachel looked slightly flustered.

"Can I get you a drink or something?"
"No, it's fine."

She opened a closet door in the hallway to reveal a portable PA system and two black sports bags.

"Dan says it's all there. What is it for? A corporate gig?"

"Yes. It's for a Japanese Bank."

"Not the best day for a quiz is it? It's nearly 40 degrees outside."

"I guess. They've paid already though."

"Ah! Well fuck em then!"

They laughed awkwardly for a moment. Rachel looked back towards the kitchen.

"So, do you host a lot for Dan?"

"Yes, I do three venues a week. Greenwich on Sundays, Chancery Lane on Tuesdays and Bromley by Bow on Wednesdays."

"Oh, I see. And where's today's one?"

Andy checked his phone.

"It's in a wine bar near St Pauls."

"I see. How are you getting there?"

Andy started to ramble awkwardly.

"Danny said to order an Uber from here to there."

Rachel looked blankly for a moment before the penny dropped.

"Oh. So, we're paying for it?"

For a moment there was silence in the hallway before Rachel took out her phone with a noticeable huff. She spoke to Andy over finger tapping.

"Ok I've ordered an Uber for you. It'll be outside in 5 minutes,"

Andy went to retrieve the kit and headed back out onto the street. About 5 minutes later a black Volvo pulled up towards the gate. The tinted driver's window came down to reveal a black man wearing shades. Andy picked up the luggage and walked towards the car.

"Taxi for Andy Fielding?"

The man stared forwards with his hands on the wheel.

"No, sir." He said dryly in an African accent "Rachel Denton."

"Yes. Well she booked it for me. To Ludgate Hill?"

"Yes, sir."

The driver popped the car's boot but stayed in the car. Andy lifted the heavy gear in and shut it. He headed around and sat in the passenger seat. The car pulled away.

At first the two of them sat in silence as they pulled along the A3. Andy looked at the driver's ID badge on the dashboard.

*Mr Olusegun Bweyu.*

The driver's phone rang. He answered it on the hands-free. The line crackled and a lady's voice could be heard speaking fast in a foreign language. The driver spoke back. It sounded like an argument. After a few minutes the driver ended the call. The silence continued.

Andy had just started to fidget with his phone when the driver spoke.

"How are you, sir?"

"I'm well. Yourself?"

"Every day is a blessing, sir."

"Yes. I suppose it is."

Andy looked out of the window and prepared to be sermonised for the remainder of the journey. He'd got used to it from the countless bus and train journeys that are occasionally hijacked by the Jesus Brigade. Next he'll be told to repent or hell awaits and he would do what he always does in these situations; nod or feign interest. He tried to make small talk back to be polite.

"Busy shift? Do you have a long one ahead of you?"

"No, sir. You are my final job of the day. My wife wants me to come home. I don't like to work nights anymore, sir. This city is too dangerous."

Andy feigned interest.

"I see."

"Goodness knows, sir, we must all leave this planet, but I do not wish it to be at the hands of some lunatic. There is so much violence in the streets. No, sir. I stop taking fares at 5pm and go home to my wife."

Andy started to ease into the conversation.

"I can understand why you choose not to. Particularly following the attack."

"Sir, a terrible tragedy. Such violence I cannot stand sir."

"Were you working that night?"

"Yes sir. As a matter of fact I was. I had a booking at that time to collect someone in Borough Market but on my way there they cancelled. Fortunately, I got another booking to collect someone 15 minutes earlier than the first fare. I pulled up to the market and a man got into the back of my cab. He was not in a good state of mind, sir."

"What do you mean?" prompted Andy, curiously.

"The man was drunk, sir. He was crying and punching my headrest repeatedly, sir. I was very frightened. I said 'Sir, what is your distress? Why are you so angry?' and you know what he say to me, sir?"

"Go on."

"Because of a *woman*!" Mr Bweyu started laughing out loud.

"I say to him 'A *woman* get you into this state of mind? What is the matter?' So he tells me he had suspicions his wife was being unfaithful to him. He said people had been telling him so and he wanted to see for himself. First mistake, sir!"

Andy looked puzzled. Bweyu continued.

"If someone tell me that my wife is unfaithful, sir, I do not wish to see it with my eyes! If someone tell me that my wife is unfaithful, sir, I would go to my wife and say, 'Woman, I do not want to be hearing this nonsense. If there is any other man you must stop it right now as it is unfair to me'. I would then beg her on my knees to stop."

"What if she was faithful and it was untrue?"

"Ah, well then she would see how much she meant to me. Women like this approach, sir."

"And if she was unfaithful and didn't listen to you?"

"Then I would leave her, sir. But I would never, ever go and see her being unfaithful to me."

Andy hesitated "Why?'

"Because I would KILL her, sir! And I would not be held responsible for my actions!"

Andy gave a nervous laugh and tried to unpick the driver's logic. The cab headed towards Westminster Bridge Road.

"It is not worth it, sir. Why spend my life in jail over such momentary madness? No sir, I would always make the smart choice. I would ask her if it was true to stop it, but I would never go and see with my own eyes. This was the mistake he made, sir. And he drank before seeing them as well sir. He was cursing so much. At first I thought he was going to kill me but as I spoke to him he began to settle. Eventually he fell asleep on my back seat, sobbing like a child, sir. So I dropped him at his house and drove home to my wife. The next thing I know my friend calls me and tells me there is murder happening in the market. The time I was supposed to be there to collect the first fare. Such a tragedy. Such violence."

The car turned onto the bridge and towards Parliament. The driver continued,

"Men now have so much hysteria in their minds. So much confusion. That is when they become hopeless and aggressive. They do not realise that life is simple. Every day is a blessing."

Andy stared out the window.

"Yes. I'm not very religious but..."

The driver cut him short.

"Neither am I, sir. You do not need to follow scripture to know that each day is a blessing. Who knows what life is beyond this one, sir. We only have this one to be thankful for. Thankful to our parents, our families. Beyond that I cannot say for sure. Death can happen at any time and we can never truly be prepared for what is beyond that door sir."

The car headed past the cenotaph. Andy read the words as they drove past; *The Glorious Dead.*

"Like that tower block in the news, sir. A terrible matter, no? Those poor souls. To know that death is coming..."

Andy tried to change the subject.

"Still. Be thankful for what you've got, eh?"

The car sped toward Aldwych and into the City. As the car drove past the *All Bar One* on Ludgate Hill, a lady in a business suit waved from the window, as if to usher Andy in. The driver pulled into a side street.

Andy went to get out of the cab when suddenly the driver grabbed him by the wrist. He stared at him through his shades.

"Say thank you."

"I was going to. I just need to get my bags."

The driver stared at Andy for a moment before taking his seatbelt of.

"Of course, sir."

Mr Bweyu popped the boot open and got out to help Andy. Once everything was out Andy offered the driver his hand.

"Thank you, Mr Bweyu. It was nice to meet you."

"Life is a series of meetings, sir, is it not?"

"I suppose you're right."

"Yes sir. Now remember what I say yes? Be thankful! Everyday...."

"...is a blessing, yes."

"Good man. Have a good life, sir."

And with that Mr Bweyu got back in the black Volvo and pulled away towards Fleet Street. Andy lifted up the heavy gear and struggled towards the venue and his next meeting.

## Part I - New Beginnings

Ophir watched the city beneath her feet. It was dusk and the street lights began to twinkle like stars. She reached out her hand and traced the shape of the buildings in the distance. Her finger ran over the gherkin, skipped over the walkie talkie and down around the Monument. Finally, her gaze settled upon a red bus making its way across London Bridge and into South London. She stepped forward until all she could see between her feet and the air below was a panel of thick glass. She looked out, opened her arms and for a moment imagined being able to float up into the clouds like a bird. This fantasy was punctured by the sound of flushing and a cubicle door opening.

"Ophie....what are you doing?"

Ophir snapped back into her surroundings; the ladies toilet on the 32nd floor of The Shard. Her friend and work colleague Nancy draped her arm lazily around her neck and kissed her playfully on the cheek. Nancy made eye contact with Ophir via the window's reflection.
"Daydreaming again?"
"No. No. Just admiring the view."
"Babe, we're in the bogs. Come on, everyone's waiting for you."
The girls adjusted their dresses and hair and walked back out into a packed bar filled with well-heeled professionals. Cocktail barmen flared in front of the inky skyline. As Nancy and Ophir descended the staircase they could see a table of glamorous women on their feet clapping them. As they walked to the table two barmen brought over trays of vodka with sparklers in. On the table itself was a cake saying, *She's Engaged!!!* Ophir walked into the throng and was handed a glass of champagne. As she smiled and posed for pictures she could hear the sound of someone tapping a glass. It was her boss, Angela.
"Now that everyone is here; not least the lucky lady herself, I would just like to offer my huge congratulations to the soon-to-be Mrs Holden-Webster on her engagement to undoubtedly the most gorgeous, successful and eligible bachelor I know. Of course, the fact that the man in question happens to be my son does not sway my opinion in that matter one bit!"
The group laughed regimentally. Ophir smiled politely at her manager and mother-in-law to be who continued her speech,
"Of course, my darling boy Tom can't be here to hear my kind words, because he has a more pressing engagement. As you can see he's in the upstairs with my husband and his colleagues drinking the cocktail bar dry."
The crowd gave a huge cheer and looked up to the upper mezzanine where a group of men in blazers raised their glasses and roared back. Amidst the backslapping stood Tom; giving his trademark white-tooth smile and waving back. He caught Ophir's eye and gave her a reassuring wink. Ophir reciprocated by blowing him a kiss, which wasn't missed by Angela.
"Ah young love, eh! They say the best things in life are free and it's true. But a diamond ring the size of yours certainly helps to sweeten the deal."
The group cheered again. Angela gave a wry smile as Ophir took a sip from her flute using the hand in question. More photos were snapped and instantly uploaded.
"Ophir. What can I say? You've come far. From the nervous office girl who I nearly didn't hire to my champion PA. The company would not be in the position it was today without your tireless commitment, resourcefulness and tenacity. I know that when I retire next year and Tom takes the reigns, you will be there to guide him the same way that you have guided me."
The group chanted "hear, hear". Ophir mouthed "thank you" back to her. Angela raised her glass.
"So, a toast ladies and gentlemen - to the newest daughter in my family. I raise a toast to past successes and new beginnings!"
The group echoed "To new beginnings!"
Nancy swanned back over and whispered into Ophir's ear,
"Angela making it all about herself again, eh?"
Ophir bristled at Nancy's remark.
"Hey, I thought it was nice."
"That's the spirit. Keep the new mother-in-law sweet."
"Nancy! Stop being such a bitch!"
Nancy laughed

"You love it. Besides, why not call a spade a spade. You've played the game and won. Look up there."

The girls gazed towards the upper bar. Nancy began pointing people out.

"Ok so let's go through the who's who yeah. You've got Anna's husband Karl up there - who's the divisional director. The guy next to him is James Rhys, who is dating Xanthe, our head of PR. Then you have Julie and Henrietta's hubbies - both lawyers. All pedigree breeds and all breeding with each other."

"Nancy! Stop it."

"What? Ophie don't kid yourself. Power-Fucking is what keeps this city oiled. It's written in the stars the day your parents send you to the right school. Look - Daniel Clay is married to Jemima from Legal. Michael Richie is fucking Joel Simmons, our chief accountant. And finally, next to your soon to be father-in-law, is Thomas Holden-Webster; the future CEO of the whole agency. You hit the bullseye, girl."

Ophir stared defiantly at Nancy, trying hard not to crack a smile.

"That's not why me and Tom are together. We're closer than that. We've been together since uni."

Nancy rolled her eyes.

"And surely even then you knew it was his fate to be top dog one day. Tell me; would you still have accepted his proposal if he worked in the McDonalds down there?"

Ophir stared at the floor bashfully. Nancy continued

"It's nothing to be ashamed of. It's all a game, Ophie. Some win, most lose. But the luckiest few have the chips stacked in their favour. It's destiny."

Ophir stared up at Tom and then fixed her gaze firmly back at Nancy.

"So fortune teller. What's your destiny? I don't see you with any of these high flyers?"

Nancy giggled and took a sip from her glass

"Oh, I play the game too. I just keep the cards closer to my chest."

Ophir gave her a puzzled look just as someone tugged her into a group photo. A man in a flamboyant suit shouted,

"OK girls. And smiiiile!"

Everyone turned to the side to give peace signs and Instagrins. A clammer was heard from upstairs as one of the future groomsmen called down.

"We're taking Tom to *Browns* for the night!"

Ophir called back, "The restaurant?"

The pack called back, "No princess, not the restaurant. You're lucky we don't take him to the Old Axe a few streets up. Your money goes further!"

One of the girls, Harriet, shouted back up,

"Yeah, while you all go out for a lappy we'll go out and find some real men!"

The ritual continued; no different from most weekends. Ophir looked back at the uneaten engagement cake. This was supposed to be a special night. A couple of the girls put their arms around her.

"I know a great place on Borough High Street. Karaoke until 4."

"Fuck it, Ophie. Why should the guys have all the fun?"

Ophir looked back up at the blazers sinking their shots and back over to Nancy who at first looked unimpressed,

"Karaoke. Seriously?"

"Come on, C. It'll be fun."

Nancy rolled her eyes melodramatically and gave a begrudging shrug.

Ophir made her way upstairs to the pack. Angela's husband, Spencer, took her hand.

"Here she is. Our star attraction."

He pulled her close and whispered in her ear, "There's still time to elope with me instead you know."

Ophir smirked,

"Hmmm, not sure what your wife and son would make of that."

"They don't deserve you! You're too perfect."

Ophir felt a hand on her back as a stubbly cheek brushed hers. She could smell Tom's aftershave mixed with the booze. Tom playfully pushed his father away,

"Using the same old chat up lines, Dad?"

Spencer held up his hands and paced backwards, allowing Tom to slip his hand onto Ophir's shoulder and turn her towards him. He looked down at her drinking companions.

"How's your party?"

"It's the same one as yours."

Tom smirked drunkenly and circled her tummy in a figure of eight

"Want to call it a night and head home?"

"I thought you were being dragged out to a strip club?"

"Leo's joking. Everyone's pissed."

"I don't mind if you go. I want you to have fun. Besides, Anna's taking us to some Karaoke place downstairs."

Tom gave a drunkenly frosty gaze.

"Sure. Do what you what. I'll see you at home."

And with that he turned back into the pack. They had spent a grand total of 30 seconds in each other's company at their own engagement party. Ophir watched as a dozen male arms covered him like a well-dressed octopus and swallowed him whole. Behind her she heard someone whistle. Nancy was with the girls by the lift.

"Ready, Ophie?"

They all stepped into the lift and headed down into the night.

As the ladies reached the door of the karaoke bar, clutching their expensive purses by their hips, they were met by the gaze of a huge doorman.

"Ladies, ain't you a little overdressed? *Ministry of Sound* is a mile down that way."

Anna drunkenly pointed a finger playfully into the big man's chest.

"We don't want to go to Ministry. We want to go in here. Now let us in!"

The bouncer cracked a smile and opened the door,

"Whatever you say ladies. Just watch your bags in here yeah."

As soon as Ophir walked into the bar she was hit by the smell of piss and sweat. At the dimly-lit bar stood a mixture of broken-looking men and women staring over at the new arrivals.

She looked over to the makeshift dance floor; a man holding a Tesco carrier bag was trying to sing Michael Jackson's *Earth Song* but couldn't keep to the beat and was simply screaming through the chorus at the top of his voice. The woman in the DJ booth cut him short and the man walked out of the bar without acknowledging anyone. The woman leant into the microphone and said in an Eastern European accent,

"Next is Rachel. Kids America. Rachel, Kids America."

The opening notes of *Kids In America* struck up as an overweight woman picked up the microphone and began singing badly. The girls watched from the bar unimpressed. Nancy turned to Ophir.

"This place is awful. Can we go somewhere else?"

Harriet started to fill in a karaoke slip, laughing drunkenly

"No way! We've got to sing!"

She trotted over to the DJ booth in her ridiculous heels. Ophir ordered a bottle of wine. As she was paying she could feel someone staring at her. She glanced over to see a bald, thin man in a dark suit rolling a cigarette between spindly, tattooed fingers. His sunken eyes peered towards Ophir, who tried to ignore him. But as the other girls chatted amongst themselves she couldn't help but look back over to him. He smiled a worn-gum grin.

"Bit off the beaten track, ain't ya?"

Ophir paid for her drink and looked back to the man.

"How would you know?"

"You 6 girls. You look like you should be in somewhere a bit more...you know...sophisticated."

Ophir sipped her wine. Behind her the girls cheered as the previous singer got cut short again by the Karaoke Nazi. She barked into the microphone,

"Next! Harriet. Taylor Swift. Harriet. Taylor Swift."

The girls ran up, dragging a reluctant Nancy with them as *Trouble* started to reverberate around the room. The man continued to hold Ophir's attention,

"Have you been let off your leash tonight?"

Ophir snapped at the man,

"Don't fucking talk to me like that you creep."

The man in black held up his hands.

"Hey, I didn't mean any offence. It was just a turn of phrase you know. I just meant you girls are letting off some steam. You look like high-powered people from a different world to this one. I guess it's good to explore the universe from time to time."

Ophir scoffed,

"It's a karaoke bar mate, hardly outer space is it."

The man shrugged,

"It's more of a state of mind. Be aware of the limits you set yourself. Too often young people build fences around themselves. You build you're walls and towers so you don't get hurt. So you don't lose. Well maybe you're winning but are you really *living*?"

Ophir looked back over to her drunken friends swaying and singing. The man spoke on,

"Don't you ever feel there's another life that's meant to be happening but you're on the other side of the door. You just won't open it in case it leads to a 500-foot drop?"

Ophir laughed,

"Exactly. Why risk the drop?"

The man smiled and leant over to whisper into Ophir's ear,

"Because you might just fly!"

He stayed close to her. Ophir stared at her reflection in the mirror of the bar. The bald man met her gaze.

"There's danger in doing nothing as well, you know? Patrolling your own cage, sleepwalking to the grave. Life is over in a fucking heartbeat, girl. At any given second everything you know could stop and the world you have created could burst into flames in the flap of a bird's wings. Stop trying to control it. Get lost in the wilderness! Fight for happiness! Fight for love!"

The man placed his newly rolled cigarette between his thin, grey lips.

"You ladies have a good night."

And with that he left. Ophir stared at the mirror, trying to unravel the man's peculiar and passionate speech. Suddenly she heard the smashing of glass. She looked over to the girls who were still on the karaoke stage but in front of them a huge brawl had broken out. Several men and women were throwing punches and in the centre of the throng Ophir watched someone stamping down on someone's head. Nancy shouted into the microphone, "OPHIE!"

Ophir hurried towards the girls as the doormen raced in to stop the fight. Nancy grabbed Ophir's hand as they headed to the door. Ophir turned back and looked at the glass-shattered bar. The doormen were dragging two people away from a man lying bloodied and stricken on the floor. It was the man in the black suit. He looked frightened and helpless. His face was gashed. He stared with childlike eyes and held a hand up towards Ophir. Anna pulled her back.

"Ophie, we need to go now!"

"We have to help him!"

"You can't help him. It's too late."

Outside the girls watched the medics make their way into the bar. One of the doormen walked over to them,

"Ladies. Time to move on now yeah. Bar's closed."

Ophir looked distressed,

"Is that man going to be alright?"

"Hospital's 'round the corner."

"What happened?"

"Bar fight."

"What over?"

The doorman smirked,

"Sometimes these things happen. Usually over nothing. Now move along ladies. Please."

Ophir looked at the doorman shocked. Nancy called over, grabbed her arm and led her towards the back of a waiting cab.

"Come on, Ophie. Let's get you home."

The cabbie switched on his meter,

"Where to, ladies?"

As they climbed in Ophir whispered "Honour Oak Park" as Nancy sat next to her in the back, "Then Brockley after Honour Oak please driver."

The driver nodded and pulled onto the high street.

Ophir put her head in her hands. Nancy could hear her crying. She put her arm around her and gave her a reassuring hug. Ophir spoke through her hands.

"I'm sorry, C. I've just never seen anything that bad before. I thought they'd killed him."

Nancy rested her forehead against Ophir's.

"Don't worry, Ophie. He'll be fine. You'll be fine. You're strong. You're special."

Ophir laughed and wiped some tears away.

"Jesus, I'm such a wimp. I can't stand the sight of blood. I just don't understand how people can be that violent. And so suddenly as well. It just upsets me."

Nancy tightened her grip on Ophir's shoulder.

"Look your just a bit shaken. Until then it was a fun night. And you had all your friends there watching your back. We all think you're great. You're perfect.

The driver drove on. Nancy continued on a little drunkenly, still resting her head lazily against Ophir's.

"Look, Ophie. You've got a lot to be thankful for. Great career, great prospects, a nice house, the man of your dreams. And you'll always have me. I love you. And I'll...."

Without letting Nancy finish her sentence Ophir turned her face into hers and leant into a furious kiss. A million sparks burst into light as Ophir felt a rush of endorphins hit her brain.

Immediately she felt transported back to her first kiss at school and felt the same mix of fear, awkwardness and excitement. What was happening?

Nancy bucked a bit at first from the shock but soon enough gave way and pulled Ophir towards her. They pulled away from each other for a second and stared into each other's eyes. Ophir, without breaking eye contact signalled to the driver.

"Can we get out here please."

The driver looked over his shoulder.

"You're not in Honour Oak yet."

"It's fine. Just let us out."

The cab pulled up to the side of a road. Ophir paid him and the car pulled away. She grabbed Nancy by the hand and led her towards a side street behind a Chinese restaurant. Nancy giggled,

"What are we doing?"

Once out of the street light Ophir pushed Nancy against the wall. They pressed their mouths together again and locked hands. Ophir pressed her whole body against hers. Their breathing became hollower. Ophir ran her fingers down Nancy's neck, and across her breasts. Even in the dark Nancy could see Ophir's diamond engagement ring glimmering in the shadows. She became hesitant,

"Ophie. What are we doing? We can't do this here."

Ophir began to kiss Nancy's neck before leaning into her ear,

"I want you. I always have. Please, let this happen."

Nancy pushed her back,

"No. This isn't right. I don't want to do this here."

Ophir continued,

"We can't go to mine. Take me to yours."

"Um. Ok. Our cab's just left us."

"We'll get in a different one. Come on let's go."

Ophir checked her phone, found an Uber two minutes away and booked it. When they stepped into the streetlight it was waiting. The window pulled down,

"Cab for Ophir Obasi?"

"Yes ma'am. This is your car."

An African man stepped out and opened the back door for them. As the girls fell in they made intimate signals to each other and smiled. The driver looked into the rear view,

"Did you have a good night, ladies?"

Ophir answered without looking away from Nancy.

"Yes. We're celebrating."

"Oh yes? What is the celebration?"

Nancy looked over to the driver

"New beginnings."

The driver gave a deep laugh and sighed,

"That is good to hear. Everyday is a blessing, no?"

The girls returned to each other as the car drove on to its new destination. Above the city the stars twinkled, reaching out into an immeasurable infinity.

## Part II - The Tip

The morning sun filtered through the open French windows. Occasionally a gentle breeze would push the curtains to the side, allowing a ray of light to shine directly into Ophir's eyes.

She began to stir and return to her surroundings. She could sense her mattress and pillow and rolled over onto her side. Another gust of breeze across the side of her body highlighted that she was naked so she pulled the bed sheet back over herself. She could hear someone moving around in the corner of the room. Her mouth was incredibly dry which stopped her from getting back to sleep. She called out,

"Tom. Can you get me a glass of water please?"

She heard the figure in the corner stop. Then she heard in a light South African accent,

"My names Jann."

Ophir's eyes opened and her surroundings changed. Her mattress and pillow were a sofa and a handbag. Her naked body was draped only with what looked like a picnic rug. In the corner a bright blonde-haired man with earrings filled up a glass with tap water from a kitchen sink on the other side of the open plan room. As he walked over with it Ophir made sure her body was covered up. Jann laughed,

"Don't worry, darling. I've seen it all before. Besides, not my cup of tea if you know what I mean."

As Jann gave Ophir a wink she felt herself relax a bit. She drank the glass of water and let her heavy head fall back against the sofa with a sigh. Jann adjusted his smart bow tie in the mirror. As he did he made eye contact with Ophir,

"Did you have a good night? I didn't hear you guys come in."

"Yeah. I think so..."

Jann let out a high-pitched laugh.

"Oh, one of *those* nights! I have *lots* of those. Are you the girl whose party it was? Ophir Obasi isn't it?"

"Um...yeah." murmured Ophir, as brief flashbacks flitted through her mind.

"Oh, well congratulations on your engagement!"

"Thanks."

"Your fiancée is a lucky man to have a pretty thing like you for his bride to be! His name's Tom isn't it? Quite the high-roller I hear?"

Jann buttoned up a black waistcoat before throwing on a high-vis jacket and helmet. He went over to an old-fashioned bicycle by the front door of the apartment.

"Anyway" he said in his Afrikaans lilt "I must be orf. It's nice to meet you. I've heard lots about you."

And with that he smiled and left. As soon as she could hear Jann walking downstairs Ophir stood up. She wrapped the makeshift blanket around herself like a bath towel and headed over to the window. She watched Jann cycle off down the road. She reached into her handbag and found her phone and headed to the bathroom.

12 missed calls from Tom. And text messages:

*Where the fuck are you?*

Ophir text back straight away:

*Sorry babe. Stayed over with the girls. Home soon x*

She began searching the room for her underwear. She found her knickers by the sofa but had to look a bit longer for her bra. Eventually she found it hanging over the television. Under the dining table was someone else's lingerie. In the centre of the lounge lay two expensive dresses. Ophir looked over to a bedroom door close to the hallway. Suddenly the flashbacks became clearer.

She walked to the door and pushed it open. Looking inside she could see Nancy sleeping peacefully. For a moment she just stood and watched. A text alert went off in her hand. She looked down. It was Tom:

*Whatever.*

The beep of the text caused Nancy to wake. She pushed some stray red curls out of her eyes and gave Ophir a smile.

"Hey...morning!"

They both laughed nervously. Nancy reached over for a drink of water and then lay back again. She looked up and exhaled.

Ophir held up some of the garments from the living room.

"Yours?"

Nancy looked over a bit bashful.

"Oh shit. Yeah! Where did you find them?"

"By the sofa."

"Do you remember..."

"Yes. I remember."

Ophir tried to gauge Nancy's expression.

"I didn't realise you had a roommate."

"Oh yeah. Jann. Well he's more of a tenant to be honest. He's been living here for 6 months and owes 3 months in rent."

"Do you think he heard anything? Or the sofa?"

"No. His room is upstairs and once he goes to bed you don't tend to see him until the morning. Besides he moves in different circles to us babe. He's a waiter."

She took another sip of water and gave a playful look up at Ophir, who was feeling anxious.

"Yeah. Look. I think I should go, C."

Nancy pushed her bottom lip out in a faux-sad face.

"Oh no! Don't go. Come on, it's still early."

Nancy removed her bed sheet to reveal her china-white naked body. She patted one side of the mattress. Ophir trembled and felt her heart pound. The night before her urges were propelled by a mixture of adrenalin and alcohol. Now in the light of day there was a more heightened sense of shyness and fear. Nancy rolled onto her side and started to stroke her fingers along the curvature of her body. Ophir stepped into the bedroom and let her makeshift robe fall to the floor. They locked bodies. Ophir began to sink her face into the sides of Nancy's neck. Nancy responded by wrapping her legs around Ophir's back. Ophir brought her head down between Nancy's breasts and let her lips drift over a tight strawberry nipple. Nancy began to signal her satisfaction and grabbed the sides of her head strongly, pushing her further down.

A key turned in the door. Jann stepped back into the hallway. He headed over to the dining table and picked up the mobile phone he had left behind before leaving for work. He headed straight back for the door to leave again when he heard noises coming from Nancy's bedroom. The door was ever so slightly ajar so he crept forward and arced his head to look through.

In the reflection of a dressing-table mirror in the centre of the bedroom he could make out Nancy lying on her back with her legs up at the sides. In between her legs he could see the girl he had just been speaking to performing cunnilingus. Nancy was arching her back and breathing heavily. Jann took a step back to make sure he wasn't in anyone's eye line.

He brought up his phone and positioned it by the door so it could pick up a clear viewpoint. He pressed record as the girls continued to please each other.

As Ophir brought Nancy to climax she reached for her hand. Her body twisted and trembled in shockwaves. Ophir felt her whole body tense up before one final release into dizzy lethargy. For a moment they lay idle before sitting up together in each other's arms, resting their necks on each other's shoulders like swans. Nancy gently kissed her as Ophir stared at herself in the bedside mirror. At first it didn't seem like it was her staring back; more like watching someone else's life from a distance or in a movie. She watched their two sets of legs entwined as she tangled her fingers in Nancy's brown hair. For a moment she thought she saw something in the doorway but was distracted by Nancy who had bitten down on her bottom lip. Nancy whispered in her ear;

"Let's stay in bed all day."

Jann crept out of the house, making sure to pull the front door to silently. As he cycled through the leafy suburbs of South London he thought about the footage on his phone. Part of him felt guilty but this was about survival. His debts had been mounting and he needed some insurance against any possible eviction. He had done his best to hide the numerous *Final Warning* letters from his landlady by collecting the post for her each day. His excuses of cash-flow issues and a sick mother in Johannesburg were also starting to wear thin. Blackmail was such an ugly word. He preferred to think of it as self-preservation. For now, he would keep it safe. Someone else's precious little secret to be brought out again in good time.

As Jann approached a junction a car pulled out unexpectedly. Jann managed to swerve but the bike wobbled and made him mount the curb.

"Get out the fucking way!" yelled the driver as it pulled onto the main road. Several passers-by stopped and walked over to the shaken Jann.

"Are you ok?" said a concerned lady with two young children.

Jann looked around embarrassed "I'm fine."

"That car could have killed you."

"Seriously, I'm fine. Thank you."

Jann collected himself and continued on his journey to work. He had lost his train of thought.

Beneath the streets Jann cycled over, Thomas Holden-Webster sat on a busy tube carriage scrolling through his texts. He had been thinking about Ophir. The night before he had got into their apartment at 3am and expected her to be there to welcome him back. He woke up feeling anxious and paranoid. Ophir was a catch, no doubt. He'd seen the way his mates looked at her and knew any single one of them would have jumped at the chance to fuck her. In a way that's why he was pleased she had gone out with the girls and he'd stayed with the pack. Keep your friends close as they say....

As the tube stopped at Bermondsey a lady stepped onto the train carrying several helium balloons with *Celebrate!* written on. They were covered by a huge clear plastic bag. The woman struggled to fit onto the busy train but negotiated some space in the centre of the aisle where Tom was seated. Tom briefly looked up but then returned to his more pressing concerns.

Which of the girls was Ophir staying with? If it was Anna then Miles would be there. At Kat's house there was a chance it would be Antonio. Tom tortured himself at the thought of those creeps making advances towards his fiancé. When he got above ground he would call Ophir and tell her to head back home whilst he met his Dad for lunch. They could talk things out when he got home. He would explain that....

BANG!

Everyone screamed and gasped for a second. Tom felt a sudden fear course through his veins. He looked up to see the lady trying to move the helium balloons looking embarrassed. "I'm sorry everyone."
"For fucks sake!" snapped Tom "What's the matter with you?"
A few other people in the carriage could be heard tutting and mumbling. Across from him a girl in a cap started laughing from the shock, putting her hands over her mouth. For a brief moment everyone on the train made eye contact with each other and shared an unspoken understanding. Then the balloon woman apologised and the carriage settled back into uniformed anonymity. Tom stared back at his phone.

Spencer Holden-Webster waited for his son at a table in one of the new restaurants within Borough Market. He looked over the menu as a waitress filled his wine glass with a drop of Chenin Blanc. He took one sip and winced.
"No, get me something else."
Tom arrived and sat down just as the waitress walked past, making sure to look back and check out her bum. She was a 7.5 out of 10. As he sat down Spencer didn't break his vision from the menu.
"What took you so long?"
"I just had to sort a few things out."
"Meaning?"
"With Ophir?"
Spencer brought the menu down and met Tom with a steely gaze.
"What's the matter?"
"Nothing. She just. She stayed out last night?"
"And?"
Tom tried to change the subject.
"So, what's the specialty here? Fish?"
Spencer stared at his son.
"You really are your mother's son you know. Possessive. Insecure."
Tom tried to avoid his father's gaze but the speech continued.
"When are you going to learn that you can own anything you want; toys, cars, companies but you can't own people?"
Tom shot him an angry look and retorted,
"What is this? Your *Dad of the Year* acceptance speech?"
"No. Just a few home truths. The reason you keep looking at your phone is because you don't trust your wife to be. That is because you are lonely."
Tom smiled a pained grin;
"Am I paying for this session, Dad? Don't try your day job out on me."
Spencer reached over and grabbed Tom's wrist.
"I'm not. I'm speaking to you as your father from my own experience. Tell me something; do you *love* Ophir?"
Tom made a confused look and tried to shrug it off.
"Yeah."

Spencer kept his hand on Tom's wrist.

"When you met her. At university. Did you know you loved her then?"

Tom tried to cast his mind back,

"Well we had mutual friends. It was more of a..."

Tom was interrupted by a different waiter, a man this time.

"Good afternoon. My name is Jann and I'll be your waiter for the day. Do you know what you would you like to order?"

Spencer looked up.

"Two Argentinian steaks. Rare."

"And as a side?"

"Bollinger."

For a moment Jann stood there,

"That's it?"

"Yes!" snapped Tom

Jann walked off, a little flustered. Spencer returned his attention to his son,

"So, you were saying that when you met Ophir at university you didn't love her."

"I didn't say that."

"You didn't see your life unfold out in front of you when you looked at her that first time?"

"No! Who the fuck has that happen to them? Life isn't a fucking movie."

The waitress came back and poured the champagne. Tom gave her a predatory stare.

"No life isn't a movie. It doesn't always have a happy ending. Or the ending you wish. That's why you need to be happy."

Tom chewed the steak,

"I am happy."

"You don't seem it. You've been here 15 minutes and you've looked at your phone as many times. If you don't trust your wife to be then set her free."

For a moment they ate in silence. Spencer stared at his son.

"Can I tell you a story?"

"Sounds like you're going to anyway."

"When I was engaged to your mother, shortly before we got married I went on a golf trip with my colleagues. It was in France and we were staying in a small town. Well on the first day I came down with a fever and didn't hit a single ball the entire weekend."

Tom stared at his food,

"Right?"

Spencer took a sip of champagne,

"So, there I am stuck in bed whilst the rest of my colleagues are out raising hell. Anyway, I sleep the fever off over the Saturday night and on the Sunday I wake up feeling fresh as a daisy. My friends were all in their rooms sound asleep from the night before so I went for a walk into the town. The town had a little square by the church with bistros dotted here and there. It was sunny and I remember the locals were all coming out of church with their families. It was really picturesque so I headed over to one of the cafés and sat at one of the tables. As the waiter took my order I noticed a woman sat at one of the other tables. She said hello to me in a northern accent and I looked up. As soon as I saw her I felt a strange feeling, not necessarily attraction or even lust, even though she was very beautiful. I felt like I *knew* her. Even the way she said *hello* was with a tone of recognition; although, clearly, we had never met before. We sat there and spoke for an hour. She told me her name was Isobel. She was a nurse from Wigan. I remember her saying she had flown over on her own on a whim and was staying nearby. There seemed to be no rhyme or reason to why she was there. She seemed happy in herself and asked about me. We chatted as two people would who had known each other for years; like best friends would. We laughed and joked as the world drifted by. I have never felt so comfortable in another person's company."

"So, I take it you slept with her then?" remarked Tom with a wry grin.

Spencer looked distant;

"No. Not that I didn't want to but I didn't think it was right. She asked if she could contact me when we returned to England. I said of course she could. But then I did something which I will always regret."

"What did you do?"

"I gave her the wrong number on purpose."

"Why?"

"To protect the future for me and your mother. And, consequently, for you."

"What do you mean?"

"As soon as I saw Isobel I knew that she was the one I was supposed to be with for the rest of my life. And that frightened me. It scared me to death. So, I sabotaged my destiny."

Tom laughed,

"*Sabotaged your destiny*? This all sounds a bit melodramatic to me. It just sounds like a holiday fling that you chickened out on."

"Maybe so. And yet I think about her every single day."

Jann returned to the table.

"How was your steak, gentlemen?"

Tom ignored Jann and continued talking to his father.

"What's your point? You don't think me and Ophir have that connection?"

Jann's ears pricked up as he cleared the plates. He looked at Tom's face before taking the plates away and felt a trill of recognition. Spencer poured himself another drink.

"Only you can answer that, Tom. All I can say is that some people never do. But when you do you'll know that that person is who you were destined to be with. And if you do, you'll be truly happy. Miss Obasi is young, rich, beautiful and yours for the taking. The perfect bride. Whether you take her or leave her is entirely up to you."

"Would you like some dessert?"

Jann stood holding a menu and a plastic smile aimed at Tom. Spencer reached for his wallet.

"No, just the bill please. Here put it on that."

Spencer handed Jann a gold American Express card,

"With pleasure, sir. I'll be right back."

Spencer's phone began to buzz on the table top.

"Shit, it's one of my clients. Tom, I've got to get this. Can you sort out the tip and I'll meet you outside."

"Sure" said Tom, who continued to leaf through his text messages. Jann returned with the card and a receipt.

"For you, sir."

"Thanks. Could you get my jacket please?"

"Of course, sir."

As Jann walked over to the cloakroom, Tom began texting Ophir:

*Hey. I've been thinking. I'm sorry I was such a dick this morning. I miss you. T x*

Jann returned with Tom's jacket. He stood and held his arms out for Jann to put it on for him.

"Thanks." said Tom, heading for the door.

Jann scanned the table and called back to him.

"Sir. Just one thing."

Tom looked around surprised.

"Yes?"

"Service was not included in the cost of the meal."

"So?"

"Well, sir. You didn't leave a tip."

Tom frowned,

"I thought tips were at the diner's discretion?'

Jann cracked a passive-aggressive smile,

"Yes, sir. They are. But they are also how your waiters make ends meet. Tips are our livelihood, sir."

The warmth in Tom's face disappeared and switched to an ice-cold glare. He paced back towards Jann and leant in towards his right ear.

"Well here's a tip, Jann. Take some personal responsibility and stop blaming other people for the fact that you work in Borough Market as a fucking waiter."

Tom leant back and looked into Jann's eyes to see if he had made an impact. Jann's face began to redden. His work was done. Maybe just one more twist of the knife.

"By the way, the steak was overcooked. Have a nice life."

Tom turned and marched victoriously away from Jann, who stood statue-still in the now empty restaurant. Just as Tom reached the revolving doors Jann called out to him.

"I never congratulated you on your engagement."

Tom stopped still.

"What?"

"To Ophir Obasi. She is a lucky girl to have someone as special as you."

Tom turned around perplexed.

"How do you know her?"

"That's my business Mr Holden-Webster. All I'll say is this, I probably know her even better than you. In fact, I saw her this morning."

Tom took the bait. He stormed back through the restaurant, past the tables and back up to Jann.

"Tell me. Where was she?"

Jann gave a Cheshire Cat grin,

"I'm not sure what I know is worth much to someone like you. After all, I work in Borough Market as a *fucking waiter*."

Jann watched Tom's pupils dilate. Tom looked outside to see his father pacing back and forth on the black cobbled street, still engrossed in his phone conversation. Without hesitation he reached into his jacket pocket.

"About that tip."

He leafed through dozens of bank notes and pulled out ten. He held the notes in front of Jann.

"Here is £500. That's your tip for lunch."

Jann snatched the money from Tom's hand. Tom took out another bundle.

"Now. I'm going to give you £500 for every piece of information you can tell me about Ophir."

Jann didn't even blink. He simply leant into Tom's ear

"What if I could show you things about Ophir?"

Tom looked back at Jann,

"I'll pay you £5000."

For a moment the stand-off continued until Spencer called into the restaurant.

"Come on, Tom."

Tom handed Jann his card,

"I'll be back for dinner."

Jann grinned,

"I look forward to it, sir."

Jann returned to clearing the lunch services tables, safe in the knowledge that the footage on his phone was worth at least four months of rent. But he also knew not to waste such valuable evidence at the first sitting. It could be worth so much more.

Jann felt his phone beep. It was a text from Nancy:

*Jann. I am visiting my solicitor on Monday to discuss your eviction. You have 48 hours to settle your accounts with me if you wish to stay. I am sorry to have to do this but enough is enough.*

Nancy did not realise how sorry she would be. Jann uploaded the footage and hit reply.

Perhaps a bidding war should take place? Who was more willing to obtain the rights to his special little film? Perhaps a meeting was in order? A lovely reunion.

Jann picked up a wine glass and rubbed a napkin around the rim before placing it back in perfect placement on the table. His phone began to ring incessantly. It was Nancy. Jann ignored the buzz in his pocket and called over to his colleague.

"Martina, let's get these tables set for dinner. I think it's going to be a busy night."

Outside the restaurant, tourists bustled through the market stalls. Above their heads pigeons cooed and fluttered. One took flight and swept up around Southwark Cathedral, over London Bridge and up towards the glistening shard in the sky.

## Part III: Broken Futures

Tom arrived at the restaurant at 7pm and took a seat at the bar. Jann poured him a beer and handed it over to him.

"Do you know where Ophir is?" asked Tom quietly.

"You're her husband, have you not asked her?"

"Yes, I texted her. She said she was out with her friend. Why? Is she with a guy?"

"No. She is with a friend. And she's coming here."

"Tonight?"

"Indeed."

Jann began making a cocktail for someone. Tom began to look anxious.

"Does she know I'm here?"

"No, not yet. Would you like her to?"

Tom drank down the beer and ordered another straight away. He stared at Jann angrily as he juggled the cocktail shaker,

"Why do I get the feeling that you are wasting my time?"

Jann poured a thick, green liquid into two cocktail glasses before splitting a passion fruit and resting a shell in each glass.

"Tom, good things come to those who wait. You promised that if I showed you something that you didn't know about your wife you would pay me £5000."

"And I will. I have the money on me. Do you want it now?"

"No. I will let you know when. I have a big reveal planned. For now, she's just coming out to dinner with her friend."

"Which one?"

"Nancy."

Tom felt slightly relieved by this revelation. Not only was Nancy one of the nicer girls at work, but she also wasn't attached to any of the male pack at work. He threw back his second beer, trying to read Jann and get a glimpse of what he might be hiding. Jann brought him over a third beer.

"You should slow down you know. You don't want to miss the main event. I'll let you know when they arrive."

At 9pm, Ophir and Nancy entered the restaurant. They both looked nervous and shaken. Jann walked up to them smiling his fake grin,

"Ladies! So lovely to see you. Here, I have given you a beautiful view of the market here. By the window."

They were shown to a table made out for three. Ophir looked puzzled,

"Who's the other seat for?"

Jann whispered as he handed them their menus,

"Well, darling. That depends on how well you play the game. And how willing your lover is to protect all you hold dear. Can I interest you in a starter?"

"No," whispered Nancy, looking paler than usual.

"Very well," grinned Jann "Martina will be over shortly to find out what you would like to drink and I'll be back to take your orders. By the way, the meal is on the house. It's the least I can do."

"Why are you doing this?" snapped Ophir.

Jann leant in,

"Listen, I don't give a fuck about what you two get up to in her bedroom. I don't even give a fuck if your fiancé finds out all about it. I just want to protect what's mine."

He leant back with another smile,

"Now. I'll be back in 5 minutes and you can tell me what you want."

As Jann walked off Ophir looked up at Nancy,

"What are we going to do?"

"We're going to have this meal, Tom is going to arrive and then I'm going to leave."

"Why?"

"Because if I don't he is going to play Tom the video."

"I don't get it. What's in it for him?"

Nancy sighed,

"Because Jann hasn't paid rent in months I threatened him with eviction. In return he threatened to post the video of us being intimate on the internet and show Tom unless I let him live rent-free in my house."

Ophir looked shocked,

"That's all he wants? To live in your house for free?"

"That's what he says."

"How do you know he'll stick to that. You could have this hanging over you for the rest of your life."

Back at the bar, Jann poured Tom another drink. Tom was clearly starting to show the effects of Jann's hospitality. Jann placed the beer in front of him,

"Some Dutch courage? They're here by the way. I've sat them next to the window."

Tom looked over towards the far end of the restaurant. He swung his head back to Jann,

"Their table has three chairs. Who is joining them?"

"You'll have to wait and see. In a moment, I will pass you a bill for the drinks. You will then pay me the money, I'll put it into the till and then take it back when I cash it up later. I will then reveal everything you wanted to see."

"Fine." said Tom fidgeting. Jann stayed close,

"There is just *one* problem though."

"What?"

"Ophir knows that I am about to reveal her secret and has said she will pay £6000 to keep it quiet. Unless you can beat that I will tell them that you are here, they will leave and the secret will remain forever. So, what's it going to be? Do you want proof of her infidelity or do you want to remain forever suspicious of who was going to sit down in that third chair?"

Tom's drunken eyes began to thin,

"I don't give a fuck how much she is offering. I'll go higher."

Jann pinged the till and looked back to Tom,

"Excellent choice, sir."

At the table by the window Ophir continued to argue with Nancy,

"This is crazy, Nancy!"

"Ophie, if I don't do what he says he is going to ruin your marriage and your career. I am not going to let that happen. He says if I play by the rules he will delete the video and when Tom arrives he'll be none the wiser. I'll then make my excuses and leave. You won't see me again. It'll be easier that way for both of us."

"Why would you do this for me?"

Nancy looked up for the first time that night.

Jann arrived at the table,

"Ok ladies, what's it to be?"

Nancy, refusing to make eye contact with him, spoke quietly,

"It's fine, Jann. You can live rent-free. Just delete the video and leave Ophir alone."

Jann gave a high-pitched laugh,

"Thank you, Nancy. That's so kind of you. The only problem is that I have been given a much more attractive offer from Tom."

Ophir looked up scornfully. Jann continued,

"You see, I told Tom that I had a surprise about you and he has offered me a very sizeable figure for me to reveal it. Now I am very happy to do this for him. However, I am equally happy to tell him I was making it all up. On one condition."

"What is it?" whispered Nancy.

"Well, the rent-free offer will have to remain. But now I will also require £6000. From each of you."

Ophir laughed,

"You're insane."

"Is it really that much to ask?" remarked Jann "Think about your life, little lady. Do you really want to see it all go up in flames? Over this? If you agree to this I promise you your life can continue just as it was before."

"He's right, Ophie." whispered Nancy "There's no other way this can pan out."

Ophir reached over and took her hand, bringing Nancy up to her feet.

"Yes there is. Fuck you, Jann."

Ophir pulled Nancy towards her and passionately kissed her. There was an awkward silence followed by the restaurant unanimously erupting into applause. For a moment Jann stood, not knowing what to do. Behind him there was the sound of someone shouting;

"OPHIR!"

Jann turned to see a drunken Tom pacing towards him. He hurried up to him,

"There you are, Tom!" Jann said desperately "I promised you the big reveal. Now give me the m…"

"Get the fuck out of my way" said Tom, shoving Jann into a table. There was a hush in the restaurant.

"24 hours after our engagement party and this is how you repay me?"

Nancy intervened, "Tom, it's…"

Tom shot a finger towards Nancy angrily,

"Don't you fucking talk to me, you slut."

The restaurant was silent. Tom looked furiously towards Ophir,

"And as for you. You can take that engagement ring off right now. You don't deserve it. You don't deserve anything from me."

Ophir calmly took the ring off.

"Good. You can have it. I don't want anything from you."

She held the ring in front of him. Tom stared at Ophir,

"Why are you doing this? I don't understand. You're mine." he stuttered "You belong to me!"

"No, Tom. That is your biggest mistake. I am not your property."

Tom laughed sarcastically,

"No; clearly you're hers."

"No. I am free."

Tom began to cry,

"Who are you? I don't even know you."

"And that's the point. For years we have been together. You've given me everything anyone could ever dream of; a house, a car, a career. I'm sure in time you would give me a family too but deep down I could never hide from the truth."

"The truth?"

Ophir took a deep breath,

"When I'm with you I feel so lonely."

As soon as these words left her mouth she could see Tom shatter into a million pieces. His face began to show the strain of the revelation. He struggled to speak.

"I'm…leaving. I'm leaving now. You can come with me and we can talk about this or you can stay here. If you do you'll never see me again."

Ophir stood next to Nancy in silence. Seconds began to feel like hours. Tom nodded gravely, "Fine."

And with that he left. Ophir watched him stand outside the window and wait for a cab. She turned to Nancy,

"I'm going outside."

Nancy frowned,

"Ophir. Don't. Please."

"It's OK. I just want to give him this ring back. I don't want it to finish like this. I didn't want to hurt him."

"I know you didn't but you have to let him go right now. He's drunk. He won't listen."

"Just let me do this, Nancy. I have to try."

"OK. Just promise you'll come back."

Ophir kissed her gently on the cheek.

"I promise."

Nancy watched Ophir head out onto the cobbled market streets. Through the window she could see her stand next to a desolate Tom. For a moment she could see them talking. Nancy then turned her attention over to Jann, who was trying to head back to the bar.

"Where do you think you're going?" she shouted.

Jann froze on the spot. Nancy raised her finger and her voice,

"This pervert filmed me having sex and then tried to blackmail me for the footage."

Jann, feeling humiliated, tried to head towards the kitchen. Nancy called after him,

"He tried to ransom me for money and rent! Well guess what Jann, I'm changing the locks. Your eviction is effective immediately! And I'm reporting you to the police!"

Throughout the restaurant Nancy could hear vocal support. She felt good. She looked outside. Ophir handed the engagement ring over to Tom as a cab pulled up outside the restaurant. Tom opened the back passenger-door and jumped in. For a moment he held it open, offering Ophir one final chance to lead the life that had been laid out for her. Nancy watched as Ophir shook her head. The car door slammed shut and the cab drove away.

What Nancy remembered next is somewhat fragmented. She remembers Ophir turning back to face Nancy through the restaurant window, smiling. They made eye contact through the glass divide and revelled in their personal victory. The future was theirs. And then, like that, it was taken away.

A few diners had started to nervously check their phones around Nancy, distracting her. When she looked back up Ophir's face was frozen with fear. Nancy watched as Ophir was pushed to the ground with deadly ferocity. The diners screamed and ran for the back of the restaurant. Nancy tried to run against the tide of people to help Ophir but was dragged backwards by the momentum of people fleeing whatever was happening outside. People began to shout,

"Lock the doors. Head for the kitchen!"

Nancy crouched down amidst the stampede. Outside she could hear hysterical noise. And then, amidst the maelstrom she heard a popping sound; like firecrackers.

As the banging stopped Nancy pulled herself back onto her feet. She ran over to the window to see Ophir lying motionless. Her face was like a doll; empty and still. Around her was an expanding pool of blood.

Nancy screamed and ran to the door. It was locked. She shook and shook it hysterically until Jann let her out. She ran towards Ophir and cradled her lifeless body in her arms.

"Ophie. Ophie!"

She brushed Ophir's cheeks and felt no warmth. She gazed into her empty eyes searching for her lost love. She became so frantic that she couldn't feel the hands of someone trying to prise her away.

"Let go of her. The paramedics are here."

As the ambulance arrived Nancy fell onto the floor next to Ophir and wept. Next to her they worked tirelessly to bring her back but it was too late.

She was gone.

Nancy's tears fell onto the cold stones of the market streets. Around her blue lights flashed and her wails were lost in sirens.

# Thoughts and Memories from the Beyond the Shadows of the Flashbulbs

## Final Reel

It was Christmas Eve and down in the locker room, Anwar and a group of the others were setting up Abdul's annual seasonal surprise. It would be different every year of course and this year they'd prepare him a confetti explosion of sorts by shoving porn cut outs behind his locker door, knowing he'd be down there in a few moments for prayer.

In former years I would've joined such hilarious festivities with them but being Christmas and everything, the tensions between our faiths had become more prominent now and it would've been better to just stay out the way. Ever since that failed attempt at revolution back in 2009 had failed, they'd been looking for something to accuse me of in case of any future barneys and so I sank the last of the Smirnoff via hiding behind my open locker door. It had taken the edge off and I went back upstairs to face the endless hours of loneliness I had in my goldfish bowl of a box office.

Hardly anyone would ever come to the cinema on Christmas Eve of course and so I waited and waited in that place, staring out at the square's Christmas market with vodka-glazed eyes. After a while two characters emerged from the market and I recognised them; they came towards me.

"Oh no" I thought to myself "just fuck off".

It was my old mate Stanley and that girlfriend of his in one hand. I'd met her when they first got together a few years ago but hadn't bothered to contact him or any of them from the estate since and as a result, an invisible awkwardness must've haunted all our thoughts as to whether or not we'd still officially been friends or not. He smiled awkwardly as he approached.

"Alright Aaron? Still here I see. How are you doing mate?"

It hadn't even been an attempt at sarcasm but I wished it had been so that I could've justified my own bitterness a bit better.

"Yeah, I'm alright, what film do you want?"

His smile dropped at my bluntness.

"Two for *The King's Speech,* please".

The type of film everyone took their girlfriends to see. I then bluntly pointed at the transparent acetate floor plan that had been stuck on the glass. This made even her welcoming smile drop too. Even Ricardo, who'd come in temporarily to get some change from the safe, watched me somewhat suspiciously for the sheer disdain I now had for my customers. I swear, we didn't say another word to each other, not even a 'thank you'. Ricardo took his change, Stanley took his change and it was over, me back to my silence.

How long had I been in that place? How many films had I seen?

I'd been there almost five years by that point, half a decade, one year shy of the global changes caused by the war, I'd seen movie careers rise and fall here, I'd seen *Hers* rise and keep rising, time had moved on, everything and everyone had moved on except me and still she had a hold on me.

After a few moments, I could sense someone else approach, and I attempted not to make eye contact by faking that something was wrong with the ticket dispenser, so I reeled off the routine, by-now-robotic sentence,

"What film can I help you with?"

"How are you doing, Aaron?"

Jesus Christ, it was *Her*. She had concealed her celebrity behind thick wintery clothes and the Rastafarian hat that covered her famous, beautiful hair.

At first, I didn't know what to say.

"What are you doing here?" I said.

"Just spending Christmas this side of the pond, you know?"

The silence that followed seemed to stretch on forever.

"I just wanted to come here to say sorry to you".

"Sorry?"

I remember what she next said practically word-for-word.

"I'm sorry that I might've made you feel that there might've been something more out of what we were doing, I wasn't quite ready to accept the responsibilities that my job entails and I should've known how it might've affected other people. I'm just, I'm so sorry Aaron."

"How do you think you affected me then?"

She froze slightly.

"I don't quite understand what you mean"

"Oh *you* understand. You understand *now* because you're up there, sitting upon your mountain of success with your loaded boyfriend, looking down upon the world of the ordinary,"

"Don't do this, Aaron"

"You're trying to understand what a strange world all that had been and how awful it all now looks to you. You're so arrogant about it all you think *you* could affect *me* somehow? Can't you get it through your celebrity skull that I only fucked you for kicks?"

She just fell quiet and stared into my eyes angrily, intimidating me with that strange mystical aura of power that famous people have – I was helpless, a pathetic piece of cowardly trash to her but her gaze had a twinge of sadness about it too.

"Those nude scenes you saw of me in that film this place showed, they hadn't been scripted you know. The producers, and we're talking men obviously, *they* wrote those scenes into it as a selling gimmick and it sold Aaron, it *really* sold, and now that they know that, the same shit will probably sell again, and again, and again and I'll be forced to do it over and over again, probably in increasingly extreme ways until my 'Cut Out' date, do you know what that is Aaron? It's the age the studios see as standard to stop giving actresses sex scenes, do you think I have the power to back out of those things? I'm under contract Aaron. And so from that point on we're left to scrape the barrel for roles, roles that by then, are not of exactly high brow material, do you know what I mean? And yes, my boyfriend is 'loaded' as you put it, but do you think that if I choose to leave him my career will somehow suddenly rocket into the heavens? Quite the opposite. I'm stuck there Aaron, stuck in it until the press see a bigger, more attractive and sellable ideal to put me onto. So much for true acting, so much for true art, eh Aaron? You see, I'm just as expendable as you are and everyone needs a vent from these things, everyone has the rights to the privacy of their desires – but the cameras just see too far these days."

She then made a somewhat faked look of intrigue at that cramped box office of mine, and as a result its space seemed to shrink a little further.

"You can still get out of this place, Aaron".

I couldn't speak and she knew it, she knew that I could only think about what I'd always been concealing behind the multiple masks, walls and personas I'd built around my emptiness; "Don't go, don't go, don't leave me here" I thought to myself.

"Merry Christmas" she said with a smile before turning and leaving, revealing that from just below the eye level of the window, she'd been holding hands with some toddler. The two of them merged back into the crowds of other families as if no different or special to any of the others, open to the same problems, feelings and desires as we all were.

"I don't want a girlfriend, I just want you" was all my mind could conjure up from the more watery parts of my brain. Then, before they had disappeared nearly completely upon the periphery of Piccadilly Circus, I thought to myself, could there have been any chance, any chance at all, that that kid could've been mine?

I remember one grey winter's day from my childhood, when my growing curiosities about women had led me to sneak into my mother's bedroom – I didn't even turn the lights on and can't remember much of what I found in there – except for a shoe box full of letters. I quickly read the top of the pile to find a letter from a friend, talking about how without options, she'd been forced to turn to prostitution to feed her kids and was pleading with my mother not too think less of her. I remember feeling sorry for her kids, who had been a few years down from me in school, when those cruel schoolyard rumours would then turn to bullying of which, without much to do, I'd participated in also.

Then my Mum returned home and I quickly returned everything to their untouched position. The late-night glow of films would be the escape from these things, only those films would be my escape from then on.

Outside that annual festive market then shut down for Christmas, and as the sun went down in its silence, without its normal illuminations, it vanished into the darkness like a ghost from an older time.

Whilst *She* would forever to this day, be the subject of a beaming, digital projector light, projected twenty feet tall for the world to see, a star of sorts, all those other characters worth talking about; Paddy, Anwar, Big Momo, Abdul, Eliza, Clements and even the Yellow Hat Man had all disappeared into the shadows.

# MJ

That year, Gay Pride was being kicked off via a screening of *Can't Stop the Music* – an epically camp biopic of the Village People – at Soho's Prince Charles Cinema. This was to be a big deal for members of the gay community since it would simultaneously act as a precursor for the later World Pride Day in 2012 and so a turn out by as many people of our community as possible was simply imperative that day.

We had all got done up in the most ridiculous outfits we could find over at Mercedes' place in Bounds Green and now Julian, Sheila, Mercedes and I (as well as a few other of our gay friends) were hurtling our way under the city via the Piccadilly Line to Leicester Square station where the festivities were bound to be in full swing.

Our carriage consisted of nobody but a middle-aged father and his young son headed out on some day trip and two Australian girls wearing quite thick jackets and sharing a Corona, who were merrily singing *Summer Holiday* to rub in just how cold the summer here was when compared to their own.

At Wood Green, your typical posse of seven or so wannabe gangsters boarded and were larey from practically the moment the train pulled up; all hoodies, NY/LA hats, cheap bling jewellery and hip hop-blaring phones. Whether they were channeling their undercurrent of menace in our direction specifically was still hard to say but their presence slammed us and the ordinary folk into an uncomfortable silence ruined by bursts of their terrible music or incomprehensible, aggressively-toned jargon. Whatever they might had been saying, it was clear they wanted some sort of trouble with *somebody.*

Our train then screeched to a halt at Turnpike Lane and matters got worse when a large group of rowdy football men got on; you could practically hear them from the platform before the train had even emerged from the tunnel. They'd clearly already been drinking and had no regards for the tube's 'no alcohol' policy, instead continuing with crates of Stella in full use. Judging by their football scarfs, they were on their way to Arsenal some two or three stops further.

They were red-faced and slurring and taking the piss out of one of their obese acquaintances for his inability to get laid. The problem of course was that they were exactly what these rude boys had been looking for; a team of men equally as loud and obnoxious as they were who would make for the perfect alibi should they choose to break out into violence.

The doors beeped and hissed, sealing us inside our inescapable serpent and it began its journey onwards through that seemingly long, *long* stretch that runs the distance under Green Lanes between Turnpike and Manor House stations.

The rude boys were getting more and more pissed off at these football twats' ability to be worse than them and so their need to usurp them was polluting whatever confined oxygen this carriage still had.

"Jesus" we were all telepathically thinking; what if some kind of violence *did* break out in such a confined space? Those boys might have knives or something and what *exactly* could anyone do about it?

One of the football lot then caught sight of Mercedes' gorgeous, exposed Latino legs and started trying to make his move, clearly not realising her orientation.

"Listen darlin', may I just say that I think you're looking stunning tonight"

"Thanks" she said politely.

"Where you off to in that fantastic attire then?"

"Just to the cinema" she said in that wonderful Brazilian Portuguese accent of hers.

"Do you always dress like that to go to the cinema?"

"No, it's just the...occasion".

"What's your name then, love?"

"Mercedes"

"Like the car?" he joked.

"Is that the best you could think of?" she laughed.

He then planted himself in the free seat next to her and it was obvious that Sheila was getting pissed off about him now, and you *never* want to piss off Sheila.

"Listen Mercedes" he went on "my name's Dave, I'm off to the footy for the next two hours but I got time to kill before my next train back to Reading and was wonderin' if you'd like to meet up for a drink and talk and stuff, you know what I mean?"

Mercedes began pointing her finger between her and Sheila;

"Uh, I don't think that's going to work out actually"

Meathead Dave's eyes then cottoned to Sheila, then onto Julian and I and then our fellow costumed friends and understood what our outfits implied.

The rest of his mates then started sniggering under their breaths at his idiocy as if this might had been some kind of trick they'd pulled on him and he wasn't taking too kindly to it.

"Fuckin' hell, typical of London innit? You spend ages lookin' for a fit bird and the when you do they always turn out to be fucking dykes".

The word 'dyke' suddenly silenced the carriage completely, elevating the tension.

Then came the worst-case scenario; there was a loud screech from outside, the train stopped bang in the middle of the tunnel and the driver announced something about some sort of signal failure up ahead; now we were temporarily *stuck* here.

At that moment, the rude boys locked their scary, feral eyes with Meathead Dave's; now London was a tolerant place for gay people but those slight, sinister looks they gave him and his comrades might had appeared to be them somehow coming to our defence. The reality of course was that it had nothing to do with that; again, this had been the perfect excuse they'd been looking for, the police might have even supported them somewhat if their eruption into violence had been at the expense of defending a hate crime and it was even worse that everyone understood that.

The father and his young son moved further down the carriage out of the way and the son's incessant questioning as to 'Why?' just made the situation concrete and official.

What followed then was the ultimate Mexican stand-off. We looked at Dave and his football friends, they looked at the rude boys, they then looked back at us again and the other, neutral passengers just gripped at their clothing with white knuckles.

"Please, please let this train move" I could sense that we were all thinking.... but it didn't, our delay just went on, and on *and on.*

The door handle to the adjoining carriage then broke our terrible, silent eternity and we all turned in unison to see who had entered. Before us all was a character dressed head-to-toe as a Billie Jean-era Michael Jackson. He had the full tight black suit, the trilby hat, the shades, the polished dancing shoes with white socks, the white gloves, the lot. For some reason he'd painted his face entirely white and was wearing shades.

He was carrying something on his shoulders and we just kept watching.

He startled us all suddenly as he let cables of some description slip through his gloved fingers and allow two old-fashioned mini amps to slam onto the dirty floor either side of those shoes. We all just remained fixated on this ocean of possibilities; he reached inside his jacket and flicked on some kind of electrical device, within what felt like a fraction of a second he then kicked one dancing foot in front of the other as an almighty noise boomed out through those amp speakers.

The father grabbed both his and his young son's ears, everyone's eyes widened in surprise and a thick layer of dust was beaten off the 80's seat patterning as if suddenly freed from the same age as Jacko's heyday when it had probably been doomed to stay there.... the noise was the first funky movements to *Thriller.*

The guy then began attempting the Jacko moves... except not very well; his swinging limbs collided with the surrounding poles and he kept tripping over his trousers. This wasn't stopping him however, on he went to those funky, repetitive beats, without pain, without embarrassment and by the reactions of his flabbergasted audience, so far without harassment.

Then Jacko's lyrics kicked in louder than the beats. Slam, bong, screech, his dancing just went on and on, on the spot as if the 80s themselves were being driven at one-hundred-miles-per-hour by some reckless driver too excited to escape that gaudy time and reach the 90s. We could only watch, and watch, and watch, the collective eyes of all of us desperately trying to keep up with his speed.

Then, unbelievably, this unedited version even played the whole Vincent Price horror monologue stuff at its centre through which, his moves just *kept going.* There was a chance that that young kid, the one who'd been with his father, might not had known much about who Jacko was and would've subsequently questioned greater than any of us what the fuck might had been going on? He too was fixated.

As soon as the Vincent Price stuff had finished and the song went into that long horror-movie synth, - that part in the video when Jacko and his lady friend are being surrounded by the undead - this guy just collapsed onto the dirty floor and for a few seconds I could sense then, that we were all thinking there was a possibility that he might had been hurt and that one of us might have to stop this eccentric show and help him somehow. Then, with *really good* timing, he slowly started to rise, like a zombie, up from the floor and back to his original posture.

During this process I looked around at my fellow passengers, they were all frozen in their positions, *all of them*; the cocktail stick that had been protruding from one of the rude boys' mouths began to uncontrollably point downwards to the ground like some failed erection whilst his eyes appeared genuinely *scared*; Mercedes, who had gripped Sheila's shoulders in tension, had failed to notice that a small trickle of beer was falling from Meathead Dave's Stella can onto her knee, and neither had he since his jaw had practically fallen upon his beer gut.

Now at his feet, the beats kicked in again and he was back to his usual shapes, trying to do the Jacko spin but knocking off and quickly repositioning his shades, he painfully hit his knee on the door but just carried on and carried on until those final moments; *dah, dah dah, duuuh.* Then he went still, frozen in that famous Jacko pose, looking to the ground, his head tilted downwards to conceal his mystery behind that trilby and after the amps had stopped, the silence of the carriage felt like forever.

There was a slight screech from outside, and in that void, the train began moving forwards again as if powered by the power of dance. There was about another 30 seconds to Manor House and nobody knew what the fuck to do.

The array of wide-open eyes and mouths just continued for those continuing 30 seconds and neither did he, the man, the myth, move from his pose; just that sound of the rattling underground continuing all the way to Manor House. We stopped at Manor House and the doors opened.

Meathead Dave dropped to his knees, closed his eyes and clenched two fists as if his team had won ten nil; *"YEEEEEEEESSSSS!!!"*

With that everyone, and I mean *everyone,* the rude boys, the Arsenal fans, my costumed gay friends and the other members of the public, *everyone* jumped to their feet in an uproar of applause!!

"That was fuckin' *sick!!"* shouted the ring leader of the gang members across the carriage. This character coolly picked up his amps and left the carriage and a legion of followers did so too, momentarily blocking the doors as they went in pursuit of him – unaware perhaps, that they were probably at the wrong station.

One of the football men kissed him on the forehead; "We *LOVE* you!!"

Another of the rude boys gave have him a gangland handshake and everyone walked across the platform together as happy as pie.

Then the doors closed on my friends and I and the Piccadilly Line continued its journey.

Many tribes reside within London, and whilst the three tribes of that particular train ride might had been capable of forming armies in their greater numbers, Jackson, whose eccentricity and controversies positioned him in a grey area somewhere between race, gender, culture and the accessible with the inaccessible, had been something of a king of his own time, and not just of pop.

Five days later, on the 25th June, 2009, the real Michael Jackson would die.

# Transitional Noise

Nine hours ago, on the runway of JFK Airport, I fell asleep for the night flight; the only way I could truly get the divorce from Janine out of my head. Dreams never really have the effect you'd like them to have though, instead, those few seconds that she drove the truck away simply replayed and replayed. I know now then, that they shall always be replayed and then reanalysed by my memory banks for the rest of my life. I slept and I slept and then, with a bump, I awoke at Heathrow.

## *Part I: Arrival*

I'd forgotten just how foggy this place could get, it must've been around an hour since the cab departed and still the stuff hasn't cleared. You know that way how certain things just trigger memories? And then those memories are so potent it's like they have a flavour? Well that's what this fog is doing, I'd only been back to my place of birth for the odd brief spell since I'd left for Brooklyn something around twenty years ago, and every time it's the weather that takes me back, like I'm suddenly not the American I see myself as but another component of that strange melancholic ambience that seems to seep into everything to unify all urban Brits.

The cab is on the inward flyover and just briefly over the wall, I can make out the triangular rooftops to those claustrophobic red-bricked, terraced houses they all reside in; crammed in back-to-back, and trailing off to an invisible horizon. Their roofs resemble gentle waves moving undisturbed across an ocean of flat grey as if searching for land. There's no way of making out that iconic skyline yet though, it would've no doubt acquired several new additions since I last came here but it's just impossible to see, the fog is just everywhere.

On terms of longitude, New York isn't too different from London and in a physical sense, the weather's not too different either, it's only what it *does* to the city that makes it different.

I prefer New York of course, the place is home now, but take any aspect of any big city; finance, architecture, culture, politics or even crime and New York is sort of very 'matter of fact' to quite a boring degree; its streets and buildings are aligned in parallel to serve no other purpose but business, most of it looks the same and crime is the just the obvious shit of drugs, guns and 'don't go there', on this level, it's an easy place to get. London however, is the old world, the *really* old world, the *weird* old world, and no matter how much people try to stamp modern slabs of steel and glass upon it, the remnants of those older times, growing and festering through generations and generations, simply break through its concrete veneer like weeds; its streets are labyrinthine, laws and businesses are dictated by the words of rotting old scrolls, and from my childhood memories of Hackney, crime was the twisted stuff of a more feral and brutal age; whatever the government do to make progress here, they're always pissing on the graves of the past and the disturbed souls of its dead live on in this fog like ghosts.

"So mate, you sound like a yank, where ya from, New York?"

"Good guess man, but I'm from here originally."

"Lost ya accent then, haven't ya? Where was that then?"

"Hackney"

"Hackney? It's all changed 'round there now mate, gentrified to fuck. What brings ya back? Family?"

"Well, sort of, but it's work actually. I'm a culture journalist, I'm in town for a couple of days but I still got cousins and shit over here so my company, you know, thought it would be cheaper to send me here than put someone else up in a hotel."

"A culture journalist eh? What you covering?"

"Do ya know this chick, uh, Salome Jones? An actress on British TV?"

"Nah, I don't".

"Well I gotta interview her tonight".

"Who is she?"

"How much British TV do *I* get to see, man? I was hoping you could tell me; she's a fellow New Yorker originally which is why my magazine's interested of course but the weird part is, there's all this buzz about her 'cause she's kinda making this transition into politics..."

We nearly hit a truck, both horns just start blaring out and he's done the window down.

"Learn to fackin' drive, you fackin' cunt!!" He shouts out the window. I had forgotten just how casually the Brits use bad language.

He turns to me; "Sorry bruvver, I missed you there, you say she's moving from actin' into politics?"

"Yeah"

"That's a bit odd innit? What you gonna ask her about?"

"I don't know yet. I know she's left-wing but there's this set of pre-written questions I gotta pick up at the Shoreditch Office. You know the way there?"

"Can take you there directly if you want but I'll warn ya in advance, once we get off these main roads into the centre mate, the traffic's bloody horrendous".

"Ok so what about the subway?"

"Best bet is if I drop you off in Victoria; you get on the Circle Line and take it up to Liverpool Street and then work it out from there. Couldn't tell ya exactly mate except for the fact that they call it the Tube over 'ere."

Out of the fog come the same old suspects that I remember, the RAC building, GlaxoSmithKline, Sega and those ugly English High-Rises that loom over the flyover like exaggerated tomb stones; it's as if those gentle waves of triangular suburban rooftops suddenly lap off the bases to these anchored hulks of big businesses and rough London living.

"Listen mate, what do you make of London these days then?"

"I only really have distant memories of it to be honest. My Mom's American so I left around 1996, only been back in occasional, brief bursts."

"Ever considered coming back here?"

This is actually my secondary reason for coming here, could London be an option post the divorce? But I'm not bringing that one up with *him*;

"Never thought about it"

"Well don't. This whole country's gone to the dogs now mate, especially London"

Like the weight of the approaching city, something's about to surface in this guy.

"They've handed it over to all the fucking foreigners now. I mean, you're from New York right? You *must* know what I'm on about, with regards to the Muslims and all that?"

Ah shit. Here we go.

"I mean if you're British, and I'm true British working-class right, you ain't entitled to nothin' no more mate. *Nothin'*. Yet, if you come over here from Bangladesh or what have ya, the government give you everythin'. You'll notice that when you're here, that not many people are British here no more."

I look at his plastic-laminated I.D badge since I can't make out this guy's face properly but it looks like he has some kind of Asian heritage himself. Where the fuck's this conversation gonna go? Might as well see what I can get from it.

"So what are all you Brits sayin' about it? You guys have an election to leave the European Union comin' up right?"

"That's right, yeah. And I shall be firmly voting Leave, my friend."

As we stop briefly, it's as if he's trying to work out which side of the conversation I might swing (culture journalists are usually always on the left), yet I wonder, if he doesn't like Arabs much, what does he think of people of *my* extraction? London had always been a hotpot, I left around 1996 and it still was even *then*. What does he make of Americans for that matter? We're usually at the brunt of the blame for most global troubles even though most true Americans aren't really aware of it.

One hand comes off the wheel and he begins aggressively slamming a finger into one of those stickers that he has stuck all over the place. It reads EDL.

"You see this group here mate? E.D.L, it means English Defence League, you have to vote these now if you want any kind of change at all. *E.D.L".*

I thought it was a football team.

"These blokes, they're only small but they're growing mate. Everyone's getting sick of the Muslims takin' over and we want our country back. If you want my political standpoint, these are the way to go, you should say that to your political actress bird when you interview her, you should tell her that I say they're all too fackin' soft. EDL's the way, bruv. Tellin' ya".

I know I'm a professional interviewer and stuff, used to winging it, but I don't know what to say to this guy, I can't even improvise. I don't remember anywhere here ever really being particularly extreme; what the hell happened here whilst I was gone? Like I said, back in the States, at least even racism is clear in its definitions.

I'm just as frozen as the mist as the city grows higher and denser around us, a strange sense of menace emanates from all sides as the road descends into it.

It's like, if before, the vehicle had simply felt like it was gliding *over* the surface of a choppy, grey ocean then now we were like torpedoes being fired *into* it. Now we're amongst its weird fish and sharks.

My driver and I lock eyes occasionally in the mirror, expecting an extension of this conversation but nothing happens. I give up on the guy and ask to be dropped off at Victoria, our conversation went no further than his last comments.

Inside Victoria train station I sit outside a Costa Coffee, caffeine and a melted-brie sandwich wake me up and I'm getting my shit together. Stress comes in waves and the divorce washes onto the shores of the psyche like a riptide. Fuck me, how did life come to this? Our arguments were about the same old shit as every other marriage; when were we going to move up in our lives? When would our jobs be less busy so we could see more of each other? But a *divorce*? I never saw her pulling that one on me. I've questioned her and questioned her about it but now she's adamant. We'll have to separate the house, we'll separate our finances, thank god we never had kids. How much is this all going to set me back?

And now I've got to deal with this amidst this Salome Jones stuff; Salome Jones, American-British actress transitioning into left-wing politics. How the hell am I going to conduct this one? I don't know much about where she's come from and despite my knowledge of films currently being made, can't even say I've ever heard of her. Has such a transition ever truly worked for that type of person? Has it even been *done* for that matter?

One method of winging an on-the-spot interview, which is no doubt what I'm gonna have to do, is to make an assessment on your subject according to how much visual information you have and so I look out at the vast spaces and inhabitants of this station to see how much can be inferred regarding London as a potential future lifestyle.

I'm only here for three days so I guess I have further time to assess this beyond the jet lag but so far this place doesn't seem any different to Grand Central, except the famous modernist architecture of that place has here been replaced with a sickly flat white from which colours are only added by the protruding heavy-lit shop fronts. The main thing so far, however, is that everyone seems to be more angry. I guess it's still rush hour because the place is packed, guys with suits and Europeans with backpacks seem to be staring upwards at the display panels. Like a successful game of Tetris, the word 'Delayed' forms an accurate row from one end of the panel to the other.

My laptop springs open and in my inbox there's an email from Genevieve. I open it and, again, there's no information just simply an address; 51 Chance Street, E2, the name Genevieve and a reconfirmation that they'll have all the details ready upon my arrival. Why? What's with all the physical meetings bullshit? When else am I going to get the time to prepare this stuff? Couldn't they have just emailed me everything whilst I was on my way here? I must admit, this is not the type of politeness I'd come to expect here. Maybe it'll improve when I get to Shoreditch.

I close down the laptop to see a man slam his briefcase to the floor in anger, I lip read another saying the word 'fuck' and of course, an announcement in a posh robot voice booms through the station's echoing chambers:

"We are sorry to announce that all services heading in both directions to and from Southampton, Portsmouth and Penzance are all cancelled due to an engineering fault and a shortage of staff".

Are you for real? It goes on...

"We would like to apologise for any inconvenience this may have caused."

...and then it just stops. No alternative solution, no promise of refunds, *nothing*.

The hordes of people then storm the ticket booths in anger and there only seems to be one person there to deal with them.

Really? This tiny country of non-extreme weather can't even get a single train from one town to another? Because of a *shortage of staff*??!! At *rush hour?!!*

Everywhere I look these days, New York included, I only seem to see our tragic inability to pull things together; whilst globalisation seemingly intends to unite all the world's communities, it just seems that everything's instead in a rush to either arrive or depart. Staying put and waiting, as these suited gentlemen have now found themselves, seems to be seen as a problem.... no wonder everybody's getting divorced.

Fuck, I'm tired.

I descend into Victoria Subway Station to search for one of those Oyster Card things my cousin Gerard had told me about, they never existed in my day. Jesus, this place is *rammed!* Beneath me, people are crammed up shoulder-to-shoulder, they seem to push one way, then another, before some immense pile of luggage seems to block any sense of direction whatsoever. Why is this happening when there seems to be numerous clear ways of leaving? Across them there is a consistent, deafening ping as barriers fling open aggressively to allow access to further escalators below whilst next to them a transport worker, identified by a fluorescent orange jacket, shouts them through one by one like a military commander. This is truly, *truly*, the bowels of a rush-hour beast.

My bag and I make our way through the crowd, upon the floor I slip upon an assortment of small paper maps, resembling the papers that might scatter the pits of a stock exchange, and I finally reach an immense queue of sorts.

After something like fifteen minutes, one of the two working clerks out of a row of six closed ticket booths signals me over;

"Hey man, why you only got three booths open at rush hour?"

"Yeah, I'm sorry, sir, just seem to have had some issues this morning. How can I help you?"

"I'm just in town for three days, what's the best Oyster deal for me?"

"How many zones you travelling to?"

"Well I gotta get to get to Hackney at some stage".

He turns to his computer.

"Right, well that'd be zone three so I guess your best bet is to get the weekly one".

"Which'll be?"

"Uh, that comes to about..." he gulps down some coffee "...pounds"

"How much?"

"Forty seven pounds"

"Jesus man, that's about sixty dollars"

He laughs through a strange mix of awkward politeness and sarcasm.

"Well yeah, but that's London prices for you, isn't it?"

As I finish paying and walk away, I hear more sighs of despair as this guy too, pulls a curtain down over his window, leaving the rest of *that* queue now solely to a single window.

If there's one thing that a man should never forget about London, is that its prices are and have always been absolutely ruthless and the other thing that has always pissed me off, even when I was a kid, was how everyone just used the term "London Prices" as if it were a way of justifying such things before quickly moving on to something else. I pass through the bleeping barriers into the Underground.

I emerge at Liverpool Street Station. I'd forgotten how hot it is on the British Subways; have they still not found a way of installing an a/c system? The escalator takes me upwards into the midst of the heart of the capital, the money-making beast itself and man has it changed. Back in the 90s none of this used to be so high, maybe one or two buildings that could be considered to be skyscrapers but it was always just something like eight or nine-storey buildings; a stale comparison to Manhattan. Now however, the competition's on. For once I can sort of see how London might have something better, if Manhattan is something of an art-deco metropolis, somewhat stuck in the 70s, London, or at least here at Bishopsgate, might actually surpass it as something futurist, everything is silver metal and reflective glass; its shapes unusual, The Gherkin and the Walkie-Talkie making the place look like some kind of off-the-wall theme park rising into the fog.

Anyway, I can remember the direction. All you have to do is work out which way the river is and follow the main streets north and you get to Shoreditch. As I walk on, the aesthetic opposite to these previous designs come into play; the fountains and corporate-funded sculptures that constitute the entryways to the big corporate buildings fade away, the buildings get lower, the old red-brick railways return along with the dilapidated buildings whose ground floors support flimsy, independent outlets. The fashions change from expensive suits to either worn out tracksuits or goth-rock T-Shirts; a spit-and-sawdust reality sitting merely a mile behind the silver millennium. Still Shoreditch has changed too, most of this used to virtually be a 'no go' area, but now it's any Start-Up's 'must go' area.

I GPS the address with my phone and am led further into the assortment of old pubs, exotic restaurants, Italian coffee shops and strip joints. Once these things start to fade, you know you've entered the realm of artistic London, a place where successful artists occupy the studios that situate the dusty upper floors whilst the less successful get more exhibition space by decorating the walls and closed-down shutters of the shop fronts with some pretty impressive graffiti. Now this is definitely the kind of place where you'll find the penniless British branch to an American Culture magazine.

These streets are weirdly empty, there are no vehicles, trash overflows from paint-splashed trash cans and this fog still hangs low, blocking any sense of where I'm supposed to be heading; is this fog or smog?

According to this, the office is on Chance Street. It's got to be somewhere near here but suddenly my GPS goes nuts, telling me to return the way I came.

Since I have no idea how long the prep for this interview might take I guess now is a good time to get some food and I notice a small Turkish stall making kebabs and falafel. Two guys are scraping meat cleavers together as they prepare for opening, the sounds and smells start to make me salivate.

"Hey buddy, you open?"

"For you sir, certainly, what you want?"

"Could I just get a lamb and falafel wrap, please?"

"Certainly boss. We've just opened so will take just five minutes if that's ok with you?"

"Yeah it's fine man, hey, do ya know if 51 Chance Street is around here?"

"Just around the corner boss."

"Thanks" I leave him ten pounds and decide it's time to call my cousin, Gerard, to sort out tonight's accommodation.

Gerard picks up. "Yo Gerard, it's Maurice man, I'm here in the UK."

"Ah yeah bruv, was wonderin' what time you was gonna call? Where you at?"

"I'm in Shoreditch tryin' to find my office, gettin' a wrap from some Turkish street vendor."

"Ah shit bro, don't eat that crap."

"Yeah, whatever, listen man, it's good to hear from you but I got to make this quick since I need all my phone battery for the next few hours. You're still livin' at the same address, right?"

"Yeah bro, everyfin's the same as before."

"Ok, so I'll do what I need to do with work and I'll call you guys later okay, you're going to be in right?

"Yeah, all day Maurice. Sick.".

"What d'ya mean *sick?*

A van suddenly screeches out of the fog at high speed and halts right before me.

"It means cool, Maurice, *cool.*"

A side door jerks open and from inside an almighty football horn deafens the street, everyone takes notice but this 'everyone' seems to just be me and the Turks who're happily working away at my wrap regardless. The wrap is interrupted by a booming mega phone and we hear...

"Everyday, animals are kept in harsh conditions and killed in a systematic, holocaust-like way and yet you continue with your rancid businesses!!!"

A woman with a shaven head has appeared from out of nowhere holding a banner with a picture of a mutilated cow on it.

"*Is. This. Right!!?*" she chants in a rhythmic motion. The megaphone goes on...

"How long must blood be spilt before you take notice?!!

*"Is. This. Right!!?"*

"What's happenin' Maurice?" says Gerard, but I'm just like, totally frozen and so are the Turks.

From out of the van come two others, one male, one female; they dash at the vendor with what looks like a large tin of paint in each hand.

"Fucking nazi scum!!" They shout at the Turks before what feels like seconds, they, their establishment, their meat supply and what had been made of *my fucking wrap,* have been covered in red paint.

"This is what it's really like to have blood on your hands!!" booms the megaphone, before it seems all of them have, in an instant, bailed back into the van.

With a deranged scream of anger, the paint-splattered Turk is out in the street wielding a meat cleaver over his head. The tyres screech and the van disappears back into the fog, the Turk merely raises a middle finger to their direction and screams;

*"Every Fucking Week!! Every Fucking Week*!! You bastards!!"

He turns and looks at me with the eyes of a man whose only shot at business in this financially hard city is due to fail. Deep down I only really care about gettin' my wrap but I hang up my phone to declare;

"I'm sorry man, you can keep my change".


I find the place, sign in with security and make my way in the lift to the second floor. I step into a smallish office of dusty air, missing ceiling panels and endless IT equipment. An ugly middle-aged guy steps towards me endlessly rolling a cigarette...

"Can I help you?"

"Yeah, hi, it's Maurice from the New York Office."

"Martin."

I shake hands with Martin, his palms are clammy.

"I'm looking for Genevieve."

"Oh right, well, I'm afraid this is a bit embarrassing but Genevieve was *let go* last week".

For real? He just stares at me with an awkward form of silent politeness as he continues to roll that cigarette. This is pissing me off and he can tell.

"What do you mean *let go?* I've just flown all the way here and she was the contact I was given".

"Yes, I know. My apologies, Maurice."

"Well when was someone gonna tell me?"

"Yes, we've been having some issues I'm afraid, our server's have been down and none of our phones seem to be connecting".

*More issues?* What the fuck is wrong with this city? An overground train rattles past somewhere near us and the office shakes briefly like it's in an earthquake; dust trickles down from the open ceiling panels, telling us both how old and what temporary rush jobs these down-market offices are. Martin finally finishes rolling that cigarette as he concludes.

"Yes, Lewis thinks it might be something to with us being too close to the train lines. Can I get you a cup of tea or something?"

Martin automatically leads me into a kitchen of missing cupboard doors and a sink with a *"Do Not Drink"* sign.

"No thanks" I say as he begins boiling it anyway. The kettle is lime-scaled to fuck and flying ants crawl along sticky surfaces.

"So if Genevieve's out of office, who am I supposed to make contact with?"

"You'd need to talk to Lewis".

"Who's Lewis?"

I notice that this weirdly disturbs Martin as if somehow afraid of the question, an unspoken side to people that you pick up on after you've asked too many celebrities about their personal scandals.

"Lewis has, uh, taken over from Genevieve".

"Well, I'd assumed that was the case, but where can I find the man?"

"He's also out the office at the moment I'm afraid, won't be back until tonight."

"You gotta be shittin' me?"

"But don't worry, everything's been prepped for you!"

I can tell my question about Lewis has made him want rid of me. He turns to the edge of the kitchen and calls out across the floor of twenty or so outdated PCs.

"Frank!? Frank!?"

An eccentrically dressed man stands up from behind one of the final ones.

"Frank, Maurice from the New York office is here, do you have the notes that Lewis prepared for him?"

Frank makes his way over to me with a friendly smile and shakes hands... his palms are also clammy...but still he's someone with an ounce of warmth about him. And then he opens his mouth...

"Hello Maurice, a big welcomes to yous, how was your flight, everything ok? I have your stuff with me, please follow me."

Now, it's not that I don't understand *what* he's saying, it's *why* he's saying it in the way that he is? He's perfectly polite, but it's just that, it's too fast, like there's no spaces between the words. Maybe he's just got asthma or something.

"Sorry pal, could ya say that again?"

"HelloMaurice, howwasyourflight, everythingok? Ihaveyourstuffwithme, pleasefollowme."

Uh, *what?* I can't ask him to repeat it *again* so I just nod and he leads me to his desk. I'm introduced to a few people who I'm never gonna meet again before he's opened up his drawer and handed me an ipad, an ipad holder and a page of notes.

"I printed the notes for you since the bloody internet's been on the blink. As for the mic, I believe you should be getting that once you arrive there".

Why *does* he talk in that weird way?

"...Lewis may have altered some of them since Gene was in charge but it all looks easy enough, you know the drill, don't you?"

"Yeah. Hey, urm Salome Jones, I heard you met her, right? What's she like?"

"Oh Salome's lovely, verylaidback. Just so long as you don't make the fatal mistake about knowing which way she's turning, I think you'll be fine".

This time, a kinda camp laugh is mixed with his speech, and I can't hope to understand a *single fucking thing*. Did he just say to not make some sorta fatal mistake? Whatever.

"There's going to be a fair few celebrities at this bash tonight, one of our other journalists is interviewing another and so Lewis thought it best that you meet with him first so he can show you the way. You'll be meeting nearby at a pub called The Crown on Brewer Street, Soho. Do you know Soho?"

Thank god I understood that part.

"More or less, yeah."

"Good, if you could get there for 17.00, that'd be great."

He stands and begins putting on his jacket.

"Now, I have to shoot out for a few hours..."

"Who's this other guy? The journalist?"

"His name's Gyuri, you'll like him, a nice guy."

"Do I *need to* meet him? Couldn't I just like meet him at the venue?"

For some reason, his fast-paced nature then stops, the hang of his jacket seems to freeze in mid-air and that same air of disturbance comes over him in the same way it did the other guy. Even his speech is suddenly crystal clear.

"No. Lewis has left *strict* instructions, you *must* meet Gyuri and you must absolutely, under *no* circumstances, attempt to enter this venue without him. If you're alone, you'll be denied entry, is that understood?"

Not really but it seems simple I guess.

"Yeah, I guess man but do I get to speak to this Lewis first? I mean I have several hours, don't I?"

A train rattles the place again, the electrics flicker and I miss what he says, whatever it was, he's making the physical excuse of looking like he's lost something before using it to back away from me and leave the office.

I turn to one of the girls he introduced me to.

"Hey, uh, I'm a little jet-lagged from the flight, I was told there'd be somewhere I could crash for a few hours?"

"Sure" she says, pointing me somewhere, "if you go through those doors, there's an old staff room out there with a sofa, if you want, I can call a cab and have what you don't need taken to wherever you're staying, or you can leave them in there, it's up to you."

"Oh yeah, that'd be great, thanks."

I dump my luggage next to her and write Gerard's address down.

"You're welcome, I'll make sure everybody knows you're in there".

Maybe this place isn't so bad after all.

"Great, thanks".

It's another, dusty, shabby room again of course but the sofa's more or less comfortable and there's an old blanket already there as if this might be the sofa's frequent usage. A paper-thin window looks down at the rubbish-strewn streets below, and still the fog is so thick I can only just make out the base of the Bishopsgate skyscrapers about a mile away.

I put my feet up and begin studying the twenty questions, everything looks easy enough, I assess my chosen tone for later and I settle in for my early afternoon nap.

I am comfortable yet my peculiar sense of my unease for the night ahead grows and grows.

### *Part II: The Surface*

The alarm goes off, it's 15.00. I have a text from Gerard to say my luggage has arrived ok, although I can't understand a word of that damn slang he uses.

Janine driving away in my truck is the last thing I can remember of New York.

Man, I'm hungry; I wonder if that Turkish guy caught those activist punks? He'd be avenging me as well as them. I guess I'll just have to get something on the way.

Anyway, the first major stresses are out the way, it's time for work and I feel ready.

I put my shoes on and check myself out in the broken mirror. A quick go on the dental floss, a quick wash and me, my dreads and the new suit, all look cool.

I grab my ipad holder, stuff the new equipment in, and I go.

Everything about Piccadilly Circus just reminds me of how much London and New York copy each other; Piccadilly Circus would've been around first of course but Times Square must've been the first to show off its stuff, the first realm of any global city that would utilise so much electricity, so much neon, it would effectively be in light for twenty-four-hours.

Piccadilly Circus now replicates it of course, day and night, those enormous neon advertising panels act as an artificial sun for the intense traffic, the tourists, the police, the theatre goers, the bums and the wrong-doers. The reality is that the immediate world this has helped to illuminate is mostly just one of sensationalist crud; gift shops bearing union jack T-Shirts and key rings of the Queen, overpriced restaurants, overpriced cinemas and cheapo gimmicky museums; a five-block tourist trap if ever there was one.

Like most mainstream rivers though, it is upon its embankments where its true samples of life are washed up and found and so something of the real London exists in those narrow back streets behind the neon; the shadiness of Chinatown, the sheer obviousness of the porn world, the pimps and whores and probably the only place in the world where gays can outnumber the straight. Admittedly, I had been too young and too broke to truly experience it in my youth and whilst right now it's late afternoon and still relatively normal, by night, I hear the place can be a jungle. Into Soho I go.

I navigate this maze of virtually identical passageways, consisting of either pubs or the backs of pubs, after sifting through the blockades of black cab and tuk-tuk services competing for customers via increasingly absurd designs, I finally locate The Crown behind the sea of people who've carried out their drinks onto the outside streets.

Inside, I find Gyuri sitting upon an old leather sofa in a dimly-lit corner. He acknowledges me immediately – I guess they told him to wait for a black American guy.

Before him, upon his puddle-soaked wooden table are two or three empty beer glasses with the remains of their heads sinking down the insides, telling me that they're freshly drunk and that he's just about to finish his *third.*

"You must be my partner" he says in a fashion that mixes a drunken slur with broken English.

"Gyuri huh? How ya doin' pal?"

"I'm good, you know this place? I forgot how spoilt for choice we are in this city."

"I'm not sure man, I haven't been back to London in years, let alone Soho. I hear you're from Hungary, right?"

"Originally yes, but you know, the freelance existence sends me all over Europe. Done it for years now."

"I know, nobody's settled anymore, right?"

"Not in the 21st Century no. And London, you know...phew". With that he sinks the remainder of his third drink in one go and I note that his eyes are already beginning to roll.

"What d'ya mean by that?"

"It's hard my friend, like those parts of the ocean where the two hemispheres collide and create hurricanes; it moves some people this way, some people that way, carries the entire world through its chaos but leaves it incapable of settling. Don't like coming here anymore."

An A-typical alcohol-induced attempt at philosophy happening here. He stands...

"You want drink?"

"No man, I don't want to drink on the job."

He laughs, it carries a somewhat aggressive tone.

"You call that respectful? *In Europe!!*?"

"I believe my subject's American actually."

"That's even *worse!* Come on, this is high-profile party, everyone will be on something by the time we get there."

"That's a fair point. Just one then".

This'll not serve my hunger situation too well.

A slight smile of brotherly camaraderie shows on the corner of his mouth and he disappears to the bar. I scan the crowds in this place, a dirty piece of white trash, some teenager, is flitting between the clients asking for money with a broken McDonald's cup. The Brits are all making their typically polite refusals and he flits over to another group, a group of rowdy-looking men, football fans of whom I'm not sure are celebrating before or after a game. This bunch's strain of politeness comes out as "fack off!!"

The feisty barmaid approaches this little scavenger from the outside world; "Right, you, I've told your lot before you're not allowed back in 'ere so get out, *now!*"

The little bastard then disappears outside where through the window I see him go on to pester the drinkers on the street.

British pubs are such an unusual thing, in the States, each bar seems to be used by a certain type of synonymous character, here, just about every walk of life descends upon it like a like a social experiment petri dish, and then they just *stay* there, like it's an eternal living space.

Gyuri reappears and clunks two beers, heavy ones, before me, plus two tumblers of spirits.

"Oh maan, what the...?"

"Welcome to England" He laughs cheekily.

"These are gonna fuck us up Gyuri."

"That's not all, check this out" - He refers to the glowing screen of his smart phone – "Lewis has given you second assignment."

"Oh what the F?"

"No, look". He hands me the phone. An email reads.

*To: Maurice....*

*Hi Maurice. I have an extension to your evening. Following your interview with Ms Jones, I'd like you to cover an exhibition opening at Top Floor Terrace, The Skyline Gallery, 26 Tyers Terrace, Lambeth, SE11? All you would need to do is a series of brief interviews with the artists covering their lives and inspirations behind their works. There are six of them in total and their names shall be presented to you upon entry. Please be there before 20.00 and under no circumstances arrive late.*

  *Regards,*
  *Lewis.*

I'm pissed now, *really* fucking pissed. Who is this *Lewis?*

"Who is this guy man? What happened to Genevieve?"

"No idea. I never met Genevieve, heard she was lesbian" he smirks an immature smirk.

"And *Lewis?*" He's drinking his beer like water.

"I've never met him either."

"Where did he come from?"

"You mean the office didn't tell you?"

"Tell me what?"

"I don't know. I meant, they didn't tell *you* anything? Because I was hoping you knew."

Gyuri's plump face just freezes, I do the same and probably look equally as stupid. The sounds of the rowdy football guys dominate the place.

"Well, he's not keen on his pleases and thank yous, is he?" I say.

It's just one night, Maurice, you've got through worse.

Gyuri speaks; "I know that he works throughout all of Europe, for several magazines at once, all types apparently."

"But shouldn't a boss, I mean editor, be more sorta, you know, *fixed?* I mean with at least, *one journalistic angle* to stick to? I mean, that's weird, isn't it?"

"Don't know, I've never met anyone else who's met him either. Oh what the hell" He sinks another unusually large swig "I just do what I'm paid to do".

We go quiet again, the football guys get dominance over the sound of the place again. Okay, let's just change the conversation and get on with this shit.

"So, you know where we're supposed to be going tonight, right?"

"Sure" He checks his phone "Number 20, Meard Street, Top Floor, we have one hour"

"And who are you interviewing?"

"I'm not, just reporting on events of party itself, what happens, who's there, that sort of thing. I'm the environment, you're the content I guess. I think Lewis wants to merge two together as one article. Like two eyes in one".

"Does he now?"; I say to myself. I need some time out; "I'm going to the bathroom".

"Hello sir" a Nigerian man says to me as I enter the bathroom, and I see him dressed head to toe in an expensive suit whilst sitting next to the sinks with an assortment of soaps, aftershaves and lollipops; is he a doorman?

"You havin' a good night boss?" he says.

To the left of him the urinals are taken up by some of the football fans from upstairs, they belch and talk aggressively about some shit I don't get. My shoes slop through a pool of piss, past the fans, towards the urinal at the end, I work out the guys are involved in a sports conversation with the Nigerian, and so I can assume they're regulars and so to pray that they don't ask me anything about soccer, I just stare at the wall before me.

I have to sober up a bit, how the fuck am I gonna get that Gyuri guy to do this in one piece? I wish I hadn't taken this fucking job. I read the graffiti before me;

*Tories are cunts.*

Someone responds beneath.

*...and I just fucked your Mum.*

Very pleasant.

Suddenly there's some commotion from the door and the meatheads start going mental. I look round and see one of the fans holding a younger one by the collar.

"'Ere lads, Jimmy just stood in the Wanker square" the older one says.

The line of meatheads go quiet and they turn in unison to this young guy.

"Oh, Jimmy, Jimmy, *Jimmy*."

The Nigerian also stands from his chair and pulls a big toothy grin at this 'Jimmy'.

Judging by the way his half-drunk beer tilts from one of his hands, in this Jimmy, I see the face of a young fan who's drunk enough to stupidly break one of their stupid rules. I think he knows what's up but Jimmy looks at me with the wide eyes of a young innocent in search of help. He looks like that cat from the *Shrek* movies.

"Jimmy, Jimmy, Jimmy," says the ringleader, stepping towards him, "we all know fair and well, what has to happen to those who stand in the *wanker square*." The ringleader pulls his cock out again and flips it over the rim of Jimmy's glass.

Jimmy lets out a whimper and tries to break free, but the man holding him instead hands him to the seemingly more powerful grip of the Nigerian. A small trickle of piss then begins filling up Jimmy's beer level before, I guess, just trickling out. They then lift the glass,... *to his mouth*!!

I feel a bit of hunger-induced vomit beginning to rise in me.

"Hey, don't do that man, please"; I plead with them.

They all freeze, the glass halfway to its destination, and instead turn to look at *me*. Am I to be their new victim? What have I done? Oh Jesus.

The Nigerian speaks;

"Sorry sir, you cannot help him, he stood in *the wanker square.*"

The Nigerian points through the toilet door to a part of the floor identified by a small mosaic square. Next to it stands another of the fans just looking at it, shaking his head in shame.

"Rules are the rules" The Nigerian laughs, his grip on the boy getting tighter.

Did I stand on that square myself on the way here? I can't remember.

Another of the meatheads then interrupts the laughter.

"Wait, Jimmy did step on.... *the Wanker Square!!* Piss, ain't enough lads".

Oh God, what was going to happen now? And I take it this guy has some *real* grudge against Jimmy.

The man in question then barges into one of the cubicles and reaches down for the toilet brush.

Oh Jesus. With a trickle of dirty water, he pulls it out and begins carrying it to the glass. Coiled in the brush I can see old wraps of toilet paper and yes, the brown stains of shit.

Oh man, *oh man*.

The guy carries the brush to Jimmy's piss-filled glass, the others are all smiling horribly, the Nigerian, like some twisted elected king, is handed the brush and begins plunging it in and out of the splashing beer.

The wanker square comes with its own soccer-style song, and now they're singing it.

This cannot be, this just *cannot* be.

They finish, Jimmy looks to me, I shake my head but I know he's done for, there's no escaping this lot, I can't watch.

"Wanker. Wanker, wanker" they start chanting as the beer's given back to him like some cold-hearted, experimental soup.

Time freezes, and yes, the terrible happens, Jimmy sinks... *the lot.*

The guys all cheer and the Nigerian hands the yacking Jimmy a free lollipop.

I try to avoid it but I can't. That hunger-induced sickness returns and I blow chunks all over the urinal wall; empty, liquid-based spew now drips down the graffitied tiles and back into the urinals. After a short pause, the guys suddenly start the most ferocious laugh I've ever heard and as I gain my strength, they're all patting me on the back as if I'd given them the funniest moment of their night.


The hunger and sickness are taking their toll now, I wobble as I make my way back opposite Gyuri – he's drinking again.

"You okay?" He says, laughing again "you look sick, my friend, you only had one."

"I'm fine... I haven't eaten much today".

"No problem, we can get food in here" He turns to the Spanish girl who's leaned in to collect glasses "Hey, Spanish princess, we can still get food?"

He's staring right down her top as she leans in.

Her face is frozen with a look of resentment, Gyuri will not change his gaze so she returns to her standing posture.

"Anything you order now's going to take maybe up to an hour, the chef is overloaded."

It's not enough time – hopefully they'll have something at the venue.

"Can't you do special favours for us?" He winks at her inappropriately, "we're journalists you know".

"That's the way it is" she says.

Then, as she turns around, he slaps her on the *ass*.

She turns back, *ferocious.*

"Hey, you don't do that ever again!! You fucking bastard, I'll *fuck you up!!*"

She storms off and Gyuri's looking at me as if expecting me to be *in praise* of him. I'm just shocked, it's been a long time since I've seen his behaviour within any type of civil world. Then, I guess he sees how unfunny I'm finding things and his smile drops, as if angered by my embarrassment or something. He silently takes another gulp through a shitty expression. Get him back on the job, Maurice.

"What do you know about these people we're interviewing? Know anything I don't? "

"No" – he's turning weird now.

"I mean, I like to think I know my shit culturally speaking man, but, I find it a little odd that I've never heard of any of them. Are they more famous in Europe or something?"

"They're just performers" his response equally as blunt and bitter, he lifts what must be now his *sixth* drink, "performers are all the same, done millions of interviews like this before".

I take the glass from his hand and return it to the table. It's time to intervene.

"Don't you think, uh, you oughta, slow it down?"

"What do you mean?"

"I mean, without being too frank, be a bit more *professional*";

"Who do you think you are? Telling me how to conduct myself? You Americans are always trying to dictate to us..."

Here we go.

"Come on, don't take it like that man, we got a job to do. What if they don't let us in?"

"You can't dictate to *us*, this is Europe, we're older, wiser and more experienced than you. Your people voted for Bush you fucking idiots."

He drinks from his drink again.

"That's it, you drink what you want, I'm goin' outside and I'm calling Lewis, sortin' this shit out right now" I slide the remains of my drink across to him "finish mine too".

"Ok, you go, see if I care."

I don't, I don't have to work with this shit. I get up and head outside. Maybe the fresh air will sort me out.

Outside is difficult, the football guys have spilt onto the street, they're loud as hell and happy to see me, slapping me on the back again.

"Hey look it's the yank who spewed" one says to the other, a cigarette wedged in his lips.

"Legend! Legend! Legend!" What a strange thing to celebrate.

I make a gesture that I need some silence and to my surprise they respect it, allowing me free to my own corner. This'll still be difficult though, I find the number I was given and call it. You'd better answer, I bet you're a right, short-ass little prick. It's ringing, I wait.

Suddenly, my surrounding festivities stop, everyone falls silent as the booming sound of Pavarotti begins rebounding off the brickwork walls of Soho's narrow streets. All I can understand is that this booming opera is coming closer and closer and is accompanied by a nuclear fluorescent green light.

There is a bearded man driving an empty Tuk-Tuk; only this is no ordinary Tuk-Tuk, this is no ordinary man and he bears no ordinary beard. He appears to be wearing gladiatorial-style armour and a Viking hat and every time he peddles, he activates some kind of dynamo that fires a type of luminous green Christmas light up from the peddles, through his feet, up his armoured legs and body, up to the tips of his Viking horns and (I'm sure I'm seeing this right) through a beard that must be constructed entirely from some sort of fiberoptic conductor. The dynamo similarly then powers that kick-ass speaker attached to the Tuk-Tuk; is he from an ancient gladiatorial past, future, or both? This man, whoever he is, has in a matter of seconds, commanded himself the king of the Soho Tuk-Tuk services. Then, like a beautiful peacock spotted between the trees, those lights and that music have vanished back into the woods.

Everybody looks at each other with looks of clarification as to what the fuck may have just happened... then it's business as usual, the crowds spill back out onto the road, their drinks are drunk and their banter continues. Fuck me, outside's as weird as inside.

The elusive Lewis still hasn't answered of course so I hang up. Why the fuck is everyone so intimidated by this guy? I want answers.

I turn back to the entrance and see that everyone has crowded around some kinda drama at the bar.

Gyuri is slamming his palms on the bar exercising his apparent rights to be served against the landlord's refusal. His plump face is red and withered up in anger. Then the Spanish barmaid starts to lay into him and then there's a crash; the totem pole of glasses she'd collected shatter upon the floor as Gyuri's now grabbed her by the fucking *hair*.

She screams as she tries to knee him in the groin and in what feels like time travel, the Nigerian guy from the bathroom has appeared and grabbed Gyruri. Gyuri's still got hold of this chick's hair and everything's slowly making its way back towards the entrance again.

Then, I notice a sorta change in my physical state, like a sudden weight has just been lifted and I notice my ipad is missing from my holder.

In the corner of my eye I notice someone trying to push back through the crowd and I see that hawking white-trash fucker from earlier cutting through the drinkers with the speed of a pro. He has my ipad, he's taking *my fucking ipad* – no doubt being temporarily freed from the eyes of the bouncers he's spotted his chance. He winks at me, that cheeky little asshole, just to rub it in. This, I can't take, I make chase, nobody notices of course 'cause they're so distracted by Gyuri's exploits but I can do it on my own, those hours of the treadmill and boxing classes are gonna come in handy on this fucker's face if necessary.

The kid's fucking quick, restaurants and bars dart past us as he cuts through their outside crowds with the competency of a well-practiced day job. Then, like a rat, he darts to his left into one of Soho's more obscure, darkened streets. He thinks I haven't noticed. He thinks I won't follow. Think again you little shit.

I still see him, the dirty whites of that baseball hat vanishing behind walls but I'm still on him. Ventilation steams and the smells of the bins come and go. I'm getting closer and he isn't expecting it.

He leads me into this sort of closed-down square, Soho Square it might be, and I think he thinks I've given up 'cause he's handed my pad to this other kid who's trying to put his leg over the closed off square's iron fence. You had your chance, prick, here's mine. I charge forwards while Kid 2 has one leg over the railing, my reflexes are like a ninja. I've snatched the pad out of his hands and am on my way. I see, very briefly, a look of shock and disappointment come over the kid's face, like this kind of unexpected retribution isn't supposed to happen and then behind him, amidst the darkness in the centre of their square, where there would, no doubt by day, be workers having their lunchbreaks, I see a number of figures rising to their feet. I run on, only to feel the smack of a heavy fist crack across my jaw. It's Kid 1 again, a similar face of disapproval upon him but my legs are quicker than my thought processes and I just get away into another adjoining street, my pad still with me, my assignment, so far, still do-able and that's all without eating and feeling sick. Respect to this yankee black avenger!

I run on down another street since I figure if there were more of them, I should really be getting lost and quickly. Time to return to civilisation. Where the fuck am I? And what happened to Gyuri? Jeez that kid had a punch, what was he? Fifteen? Sixteen? I hadn't felt anything like that outside the bigger guys at boxing class. I stop to get my breath, my lip and nose are bleeding a little and I guess the hit must've dazed me since this street seems darker and quieter than what it should be in reality, and what the hell is that rancid smell of piss?

Then I see him, a huge, lumbering man, striding out of a nearby alleyway towards me, his face is unidentifiable behind thick messy hair and his clothes are seemingly from some medieval time, tied together with string. The bums here were always pretty reasonable, never much trouble, you just gotta say what you gotta say and walk away. He leans in;

"Brother, I've got some shit going down. Can you spare us a couple of quid?"

As he leans in, some sort of light catches his face; I see that it's ridden with boils and coated with dirt and that his hair, both facial and upon his head, have locked together into a giant, stinking matt.

"Sorry man, I really gotta be somewhere".

"Ok brother" With every laugh he then makes, I breathe in an intoxicating mix of booze and piss. In this dim light I also notice that something on the side of his head, something beneath his congealed matt, appears to be moving. With a hand he brushes his hair to one side, an even fouler smell emerges from behind and I see what's moving, a swarm of bluebottles have been released and take flight into the Soho night, and behind it, so congealed as to resemble black ink, is an infected orifice where an ear used to be. I want to spew again and begin upping my pace back down the street to fuck knows where.

I still hear him laughing manically in the background until gone.

I rest upon a railing outside some building and I can feel my weakness again, will I vomit? My God, if only I could just get *something* to eat. I hope they've got something at this party.

"You alright there, babes?" This chick's just appeared from outta nowhere and is stood in the doorway, she wears a skin-tight red leather skirt and a top that reveals a little too much beneath. I know the score. Still, thank God she's local.

"Yeah, I'm cool, just need to... listen, I'm looking for Number 20, Meard Street, can you help me out?"

"Sure, I can help you out, why don't you come inside? Sly like."

"No look, I'm not looking for that."

"Why, what's wrong wiv ya? You into men or do ya just not like English girls?"

"I said no, do you know where it is or not?"

"I said I could help you, didn't I?"

We both go quiet and I question once again, what the fuck is wrong with tonight?

She points upwards and up and beyond the Victorian lampposts, the towering, grey-bricked walls and the red lamps that glimmer unsubtly from the windows, I can make out what appear to be Batman-like spotlights in motion on a roof that's something like eight stories up. If I concentrate further, I can also make out distant music too. Surely she can't be telling the truth? Is this *really* where I have to be?

"No, I'm looking to get to a high-profile event, it's at Number 20..."

"And I said that's *here*" Then she refers me to the door number, number 20.

"You wanna come in or not?" She continues.

I check my GPS and what the fuck? This *is* it! Is this the same entrance where everyone else had gone? Gyuri? The others?

"Is there, you know, some other way in?"

"There's many ways into everywhere if you know what I'm sayin'? Now, I've got more business to be gettin' on with tonight so if you want me to help, I can take you up there now or otherwise find your own way, choice is yours."

Too many thoughts and Gyuri is not the main one; what scares me now is that if my ipad has already caught the eye of one thieving little fucker tonight, then if I step in here, I'm prey to *many*. Perhaps the two parties are even working together?

For some reason I step inside regardless; the foyer is nothing but a narrow corridor lit by dim, overhead electric lights, it leads towards an even narrower, upwards staircase.

As she shuts the door, the two of us become awash in a seedy electric glow.

"So, you from America?"

"Sorta yeah."

She walks up the staircase before me. Up we climb; this building's seen better days. Soho was once known for its porn world back in the sixties and by the look of things, going by my first look at its 'insides', nothing had changed much since; crap wallpaper still peels from the walls revealing dark green surfaces beneath, the designer foliage of the stair banisters was once meant to weave together into a series of intricately-designed, patriotic lion heads but without the repainting, these British lions now appear battered or unnoticeable in the darkness.

Upon each turn of the stairwell, the sights, sounds and smells before me are telling me to simply get out; further girls (African, Asian or Eastern European-looking) line up along the walls as if queuing or, God help me, preparing for ambush, and every time we pass a door, the sounds of bed springs, screams of penetration or electric buzzes feel too close for comfort and, indeed, are they of sex, violence or both?

A Japanese businessman, the only other remnant of normal life outside of this world descends and pushes past us in a state of excitement. We tower up further, must be on the fifth floor now, and my sense of the building's carnal exploits start to dissipate and are replaced by worry. I'm too far into this abode now, too far from the entrance to make my escape and the corridors are too narrow for me to dodge anybody. Fear hits me, anybody could now appear from anywhere, they could knock me out and I'll wake in a fucking trash dumpster with all my equipment gone, or my goddamn *kidneys*.

"You don't talk much for a journalist;"

Alarm bells ring.

"How did you know I was a journalist?"

"All the events up 'ere are high-profile, you're either aristocracy of some sort or a journalist" she stops suddenly so that I walk into her, her ass now pressing up against me; "and you don't seem like aristocracy".

"So these guys, they're all politicians right?" I say to keep things normal.

"Something like that, just high society mainly"

So I *am* in the right place; that's journalism I guess, always taking risks to get the best stories. "Where do you think I get most of my business from?" She concludes.

We ascend a bit further and reach another closed door, from behind I hear that same music I heard from below. If anything happens, this'll be it. She opens it.

"Welcome to high society".

It merely leads to another corridor, a more upmarket one this time, which then leads to yet another door. No sense of threat yet evident.

"A fanks might be nice".

"Fanks"

"No problem, just knock on that door. Maybe you can write a story about me sometime?"

I have nothing else to say so I just nod with possible enthusiasm before stepping inside. She closes the door behind me and I step forwards through a corridor of red to that second door. I knock and hear the music from behind.

## *Part III: High Society*

The door opens and the music is as loud as the two Russian doormen before me are intimidating; filling out their designer suits and with wraparound shades fronting crew-cutted blocks for heads, the two of them are practically spitting images of each other. It's also here that I realise I've emerged at some obscure corner of the venue.

"Evening sir". Says the first Russian.

"You on guest list?" says the second, as he browses the list before him.

"Yeah I should be, I'm a journalist working for, I'm here to interview Salome Jones..."

"Sir, all journalists must be in twos to enter."

"Yes, all journalists must arrive in twos, where's other journalist?" repeats the second.

"Yeah, I'm sorry about that, I had a few problems downstairs..."

"No" interrupts the first "if you're not in a two then there's no entry tonight"

I just fall quiet, have I come all the way from New York for *this?* It's not happening on my watch man, I've got past worse than this, my mind's thinking up all the on-the-spot journalistic tricks I can think of.

"Do you understand?" He confirms.

"Yes but..."

These guys are gonna be tough.

"Then please go away, this is strictly private function".

Then I think of a trick. Surely it *can't work?* Fuck it, I'm all outta other options.

"Do you know who I am buddy?" Confidence can win in any situation.

The first Russian now squares up to me. He's definitely ex-special forces or something.

"We don't care who you are, if you're not in pair, you *don't* come in."

"I don't think you know who I am." my confidence is beginning to fail.

"Do you want us to make you leave in professional manner, or personal manner?" says the second.

"Listen guys,.."

Just do it, you can always run,

"I'm *Lewis.*"

The two of them are suddenly taken aback. They look at each other like a couple of terminators.

"*You're* Lewis?" asks Terminator 1.

"Of course, you were told I was coming through this private entrance, weren't you?"

They go quiet again.

"Do you mean you *weren't told?*" I say sternly. Jeez, Lewis puts the shits up everyone.

"We were told..."

I interrupt Terminator 2 with...

"Told what? Honestly man, who's your superior here?"

"Sorry Lewis, there must've been mistake" they part the way to let me through and Terminator 2 turns to Terminator 1 and says;

"Why didn't you tell me Lewis was arriving *here*?"

"I didn't know" claims Terminator 1.

"and yeah I should be on your goddamn guest list" I say.

"Come in, come in, Lewis, sorry for misunderstanding."

He ushers me inside. I don't know how the fuck I got away with that one but I better not get found out. I step past them into the music.

How by the love of Christ can what I see before me exist in the same place as a whore house? A large square palace-dancehall decor, mirrored walls, statues, concrete pillars all spreads out before me. Surrounding its central dance floor (which is empty for now) are an array of bars where smartly-dressed people are gathered and socialising. Whether they're Lords, CEOs, Royal associates, it's hard to say but their unfamiliar faces and auras of meanness would suggest that these are mostly the types who exist *behind* the scenes we know of.

Whilst there appears to be a roof of sorts, we also appear to be on some kind of extended rooftop area and knowing where one ends and the other begins is hard to say for two or three further levels of industrial mezzanine floors confuse my view of its upwards geography. Through the railings of these levels, further opulent types, from the young and the old, stare down at this dance floor like gargoyles; even further up, although I can't work out if it's being created by some kind of smoke effect or by the open air, the higher levels to this structure disappear into the fog.

The waitresses, appearing exclusively as a number of stunning young Eastern Europeans by their appearances, move about the place serving hor d'oevres or champagne glasses from luxury silver trays. I take one each and head up a staircase to the first-floor mezzanine; here, the presence of electricity is so dominating you can practically smell its static, thick cables and Christmas lights are wired up both the infrastructure and the decorative fake plants, and projected onto small cinema screens are strange geometric laser patterns that flash up, change colour and appear to rotate in a hypnotising fashion, in this semi-darkness, they hurt my retinas to look at; needless to say, if this fog turns to rain, we're all fucked. What else is going on in this place? Nothing about this seems to make much sense. Gyuri, how the hell would a dumb-ass drunk like you be able to muster the correct prose to describe this place?

I'm still fucking hungry and that hor d'oevre just wasn't enough; my hungry eyes then spot that everyone here seems to be chowing down like kings on plates of assorted salads. Where are they getting it all from?

From the dance floor below, a host taps a microphone and both music and chatter immediately stop. I watch from the railing and the fat political guy to my left has no table manners, salad falling from his gluttonous lips to the floor below.

"Ladies and Gentlemen" our host announces, "I hope you're all enjoying the evening" shouts and whistles of support follow; "for our next act, I present to you, a Circus like no other, Mr Ryan de Seville".

Everyone claps and this little topless gay guy, his nipples painted blue to draw attention to his lean torso, emerges from nowhere and begins a fire-breathing spectacular – fire balls bellowing upwards to almost hit the railings of this upper floor.

"Who are you?" a well-spoken voice asks from behind.

I turn and see this ageing, overweight guy eyeballing me from behind authorative, slipping spectacles, sweating from the physical exertion this vertical environment has brought to him. Clearly, he's got some form of authority over this place and I guess he's the boss of the two Russian Terminators, should I run now, or wait to run later? I don't think I should try the same Lewis trick on him.

"I'm Maurice, the journalist from *Forwards*, I'm on the guest list."

He refers to the clipboard he grips under one clammy arm and runs his finger down the list until finding my name.

"All journalists were strictly supposed to arrive in twos; where's your partner?"

"Yeah, there was a bit of a mix up man, he wasn't allowed in" I mix my bullshit with a likely truth.

"Then why are you here?"

"I spoke to my editor and he said to just go ahead anyway".

"And who is this *editor?*"

Here it comes again...

"Uh, *Lewis*".

The guy just goes quiet and as predicted, his authorative stare turns into something unreadable but beads of sweat crawl down his face implying better-resisted nervousness.

"Lewis said that?" He goes on.

"Yeah, that's cool, right?"

"The name's Tony" he says, grabbing my hand and shaking it "welcome to the party, I'm in charge of this place tonight, what do you make of our little show here?"

He watches Ryan de Seville with me.

"It's certainly not what I expected for a political celebration; it's better I mean" just to be polite.

"Well, one must make an effort for the rooftops of Soho, mustn't they? If you go to the top floor, you'll see the competition, some more of my flattering talents shall be on display later too."

Then he snaps out of it.

"Have you met Salome before? In the States perhaps?"

"No, never."

"Then I must apologise my dear boy, I was under the assumption you knew what all this was about. Let me show you around".

He then begins leading me up further staircases onto the second, then the third mezzanines; the artificial metallic flooring seems to become more unstable here and the lights become more blurred as we ascend further into the fog. Now we're on the roof, looking over the edge, and the lights of the city have a similar effect.

"A tremendous view don't you think?"

He's right, what's visible of Shaftesbury Avenue's neon glitz is impressive; then something strange occurs to me; although we're here, staring immediately down upon the typical traffic of Shaftesbury Avenue, I don't remember the entrance to this building being anywhere particularly close to Shaftesbury Avenue. How big are these upper floors?

Nearby I hear sounds of excitement and through further dimly lit lights I'm led over a rickety walkway to yet another floor space. A TV crew are there amongst a group of further onlookers, holding what appear to be kite-like structures to the ground and yes, they're all eating salad. This middle-aged hippy chick with blue dreadlocks appears to be their director.

"This is Agnes" says Tony, "she's in charge of everything media-related tonight".

Agnes gets up from what she's doing and rushes towards me enthusiastically.

"Hi there, I'll set you up as soon as I can but would you just mind helping us with something for a moment?"

"Well, you know. I wouldn't mind getting something to eat first, where's everyone getting all this salad from?"

"All in good time," she says "we have to get these things launched now if we want to stay on schedule, would you mind?"

"What are they?"

"Chinese lanterns, we're going to send our promotion out into the city."

"What in *this fog?* The best you'll get is a UFO report in tomorrow's paper".

This only gets me mildly shitty looks so I squat down and grip the edge of the candle frames.
"Well, I'm sure you noticed all the installation screens on your way up here?"
I nod as the camera guy attaches a load of GoPro cameras to the bases of these things.
"Well, there are others throughout several venues in the city tonight; whatever these Go Pro things end up showing shall be projected onto all of them".
Another member of the crew then flicks a switch and upon a tiny monitor I see our shoes.
"Why?" I ask.
"Wherever they might end up, up there" pointing upwards "it shall always be from 'our view'" she explains doing that irritating inverted comas gesture people always do, "get it? Pretty clever don't you think?"
I nod again.
"Well I shall leave you lot to it" Tony says before vanishing. Another then comes forwards and lights the candles. Their parachutes flare up and each of them slowly take lift off into the foggy air. Everyone cheers.
"Come and have a look" Agnes says as she brushes the branch to one of the artificial plants to one side and reveals the footage showing upon another of the installation screens, upon it all we see is fog as thick and colourless as a stone wall.
"I knew it" says the Gaffer "such a shit idea, all we were ever gonna get tonight was the fog".
"Wait" insists Agnes. The fog just seems to go on and on, only broken occasionally by the distant lights of a faraway aircraft.
Finally, there is a breakthrough; we are above the fog and the entirety of the city can be seen, neon lights revealing and revealing a 21st Century eternity.
Right now, within the fleeting space of every human lifetime, the universe is shrinking, star constellations are pulling ever closer together. The stars of Soho and the West End, Bank and then Canary Wharf all pulling together as one sun behind a blanket of fog. Everything is either coming together or coming apart, there is no alternative.
Then, like the opening credits to some type of exploitation film, red, intimidating fonts appear before us;

*"The Whole City seen from one view. The Best View. Salome Jones."*

Upon the appearance of her name, uproarious applause floods all the levels of this strange place. Everything in our world, no matter how beautiful it might seem, will eventually have its purpose rooted in either political or financial gain.

"Salome will see you now" Agnes says as she begins attaching a mini mic to my jacket.
Across another flimsy structure that could be leading to an entirely separate Soho rooftop myself and Agnes' media crew step towards a temporary shed-like structure coated in plastic sheets and Christmas lights. Another PR person welcomes me inside.
Inside it is cozy and welcoming. Salome sits around a small round table and two glasses of spring water have already been placed before us. Despite the sense I get that she's tiring of all the interviews she may have already had today, from both the cultural and political sides, she seems pleasant enough. She's tall, blonde, cute and dressed ready for politics, standing with a welcoming hand in an appropriate way.
"Salome Jones. Nice to meet you" she says welcomingly.
None of these things detract from the fact that I still don't recognise a single fucking thing about her of course.

Agnes does her stuff with both our microphones and I set up the voice recorder which then feeds back to the iPad hidden at the base of my feet. Standard stuff.

The cameras whirr and Agnes does one of those three-second countdown things. We're on. "So Salome it's good to meet you at long last, what an incredible thing they're all holding for you here. Now we're both British-born Americans, how do you feel about coming back to the motherland?"

She laughs, which is a good sign.

"Well, I've been here for a *long time* actually. You're from New York too, right?"

"Yeah"

"I mean I don't know if it's just me but I sometimes struggle to differentiate between the two places."

"Well Salome, I'd love to tell you what London has brought upon *me* today, but that'd just be too much of an interesting interview so I won't."

"I mean" she goes on "if you're walking down West Street you feel like you're just gonna step into Canary Wharf, the two cities are like mirror images of each other".

"Yeah, one has a river going *through* it, whilst the other has it *surrounding* it, whether that unconsciously creates some kind of different sense of identity I don't really know" I impressively improvise for myself.

"My memories of the place are a bit too distant now to say with any accuracy I'm afraid, my career's been fixed here for a while now so I feel more European in my sensibilities" she says.

"And were British politics something you'd always planned to move into?" I ask.

"You mean in relation to *American politics?*"

"Well, I mean it seems to get a lot more glitz over there."

"Well, they're doin' a good job here too" she laughs "but, y'know, I think in any job, once you're focused on doing it, you sometimes fail to see that there are ways to move sideways instead, and sometimes those doorways whether they be left, right, up, down, diagonal freefall, you see that they might have as equally illuminating possibilities for you that, who knows, may offer more than the place you're in. It seems like the world is moving in so many directions at such a great speed, that we might as well start thinking that way too."

I'm thinking about Janine leaving with my truck.

"I think of it as a little stuffy and old to be thinking in those ways and I guess that's the way that I'm, hopefully, modernising my field". She concludes as my brain drifts a little.

"That's a nice way of putting it and I'm sure that'll pick up fans; now, as you know, since I'm writing for a culture magazine I have to ask you an inevitable question I'm afraid."

"That's ok, go ahead."

"Okay, so, now traditionally, the worlds of art and politics have been sorta coined as enemies of one another and so I guess making that marriage is something that's somewhat historically radical"

"Why thank you."

"What do you see to be the connection between those two worlds?"

She leans in slightly closer as if this is some gesture of romance but I know that what she's about to say is serious and rehearsed. I don't know why but the way she says it has some kind of hypnotic power over me.

"Look at the modern world around you Maurice, look at London, there's a million things going on at once here now, the more you probe into politics the more you slowly hold up a mirror to something else or indeed, its exact opposite. Art and politics might be opposites yes, but without that notion existing, without that fight, neither can progress."

She relaxes again slightly before continuing. I'm *still* hungry.

"No singular magazine article can ever truly encapsulate this city anymore" she goes on, "the space between one faculty and another has narrowed, you can no longer talk of politics without talking about art, you can no longer talk about America without it somehow connecting to, let's say, France. Where the world once resembled perhaps the atomic structure of a liquid, with its particles moving freely and separated, it's now come to resemble a solid, everything has become connected."

Wow, this chick is deep and I've sort of lost my sense of direction over how I was structuring the interview. I feel like we're developing something of a bond however so I just jump in and throw a personal question on the subject I'd kind of been thinking about this whole time.

"So going by that, do you believe that your ideas or policies might be better propagated through politics rather than through art or acting?"

Her friendly expression drops and I notice that from behind the camera that's now moving behind her, Agnes is making silent gestures for me to move on. What did I say?

"What's that supposed to mean?" Salome says with a fixed glare.

Just give her what she wants to hear.

"I mean, I kinda agree with you, I think people are more likely to take a politician seriously than an actress these days, don't you think? I mean they're actually more likely to be accused of fame-grabbing now in some ways".

Her angry silence continues and I don't understand.

"What the fuck is *this*?" she says looking up to Agnes who's trying to stay purely technical.

"What do you mean *fame-grabbing!?* What do you mean about ideas being better promoted *through politics rather than acting?*"

Is it the hunger or the jet lag making me do this? I double check myself.

"No, but that *is* what you're doing, right? You're going from acting into politics?"

Agnes is now behind me and I can hear her suck her breath in through her teeth and Salome's looking at me like I've just punched her.

"You know what I'm sick of in both worlds?" she asks "the fact that it's a six-hour flight from JFK to here and hack reporters like you still can't be bothered to do your research".

She stands, disconnects her mic and shit is just going wrong with a capital 'ong'.

"I don't come here for hours at a time, to have people like you use these interviews as a means to criticise my choices".

With that she throws her glass of water over me and through the fritz of my failing microphone I hear her say "Excuse me" before leaving through the plastic sheeting.

I wipe the water from my face and for some reason, turn to Agnes for comfort. Her and all her crew are gently shaking their heads in disappointment.

It was politics *into acting*, not acting *into politics*, and I've just called this step of hers *backwards.*

"Always make sure you know which way she's going" was the only useful piece of information I'd got out of my otherwise useless, weird-voiced Shoreditch colleague of mine, and it was the only one I'd forgotten while in here.

I grab a free beer and head down to the second mezzanine floor in the hope that mingling perhaps with some other journalist might bring some normality to my dilemma and grant me a protective crowd should the 'birthday girl' herself come my way again. I find nobody of familiarity but in my search I suddenly notice that what was once a cold-feeling party occupied by the aristocratic types has now turned somewhat playful; Agnes and her crew are now mingling and drinking with the others very merrily indeed but there's a new feeling of strangeness in the air, different and perhaps thicker than before, like it might have a consistency of many levels.

Then I notice what it is, in the foggy shadows of this domain, behind its extravagant decor, there's something that had previously been invisible to me; there's a *further* camera crew covering this place; not Agnes' crew, because they're now all mingling, but some sort of second unit with all this high-tech equipment, proper big-budget, Hollywood shit, I can make out how the lights of this place reflect off their gadgetry to expose their faces flitting about behind the scenes.

Agnes immediately gets everyone's attention by climbing up onto the perimeter rigging of this level, facing us all with her back to London.

"All of you lovely people who've been working with me all these months on this project..."

She's gripping the unstable scaffolds at the base of the upper level and her shoes seem to wobble as she tries to support herself. Despite the fact that she seemed totally normal before my interview she now seems like she's had a few too many and about to perform one of those party tricks gone-too-far.

"I'd just like to say a huge thank you!"

I tap her Gaffer on the back.

"I think we ought to get her down buddy, that doesn't look safe."

"It's ok" he says back to me; the first time a man's calmness has managed to unnerve me.

"I mean it man, we gotta get her down, look at her."

He just gives me a hand gesture to imply the exact same thing as before.

There's a sheer drop to Shaftesbury Avenue over there, I stood there myself, a *sheer drop!* The wind is in her blue dreadlocks, she now only has one supporting hand since the other has come free to drink from her glass and her stability gets worse and worse.

"It's been a tough project for all of us but I love you all!! So until next time gang. To Salome Jones!!"

She raises her glass and everyone but myself just casually toasts like nothing strange's going on.

"Goodnight and good luck" She shouts.

Then, as if like some bizarre company ritual, everyone raises their hands and begins waving monotonously.

"Goodbye Agnes" They all say, before *she spreads her arms and fucking jumps!*

It seems like slow motion as I focus in on her disembarked glass going with her.

Another immense applause echoes through the venue and I've cracked my beer bottle through tension...

I'm just staring out at three rows of her crew, just *clapping and laughing* and beyond that, London, the fog and my first sight of the long-awaited Shard in the distance. I'm too head-fucked to care now.

What the hell was that? Gone into the air with a wink like Tinkerbell? I shall relive this moment forever.

I sense movement from behind me and as I turn I see that all those subtly hidden camera operators have appeared out of the shadows to capture everything that I've just been witness to.

Is all of this, no it *couldn't be*, is all of this some sort of *movie set?* A movie set of which I'm an unwilling component? Only, and I swear I'm telling the truth, I can hear the beeps and honks of a disrupted Shaftesbury Avenue down below.

Salome Jones, left-wing political player turned actress, top floor of 20 Meard Street, a building of more faculties than I can even understand.

I need to find that salad bar and calm the fuck down.

I head back down the stairs to mezzanine one and looking down on the two levels beneath I can see that the party's now in full swing, people are drinking and lines of coke are being snorted without interruptions off a good many of the tables; I'd visited many a hedonistic movie party in my career and this is kind of what they generally look like; only, had this been going on the whole time?

I bump into Tony again.

"Maurice, how did it go?" he asks.

"Not too well if be honest";

"I heard"; his stern face of disapproval returning.

"Anyway, what can I do? I guess I got, well, *something* to work with".

Let's get off this subject before Salome herself walks into it.

"What sort of act you got on the dance floor next, Tony?"

"Act?"

Where there was once a guest list on that clip board of his, there is now what appears to be, uh, a movie script. He fingers through it, frantically.

"But the script's saying the dancefloor should be empty here" he goes on, "do you think it'd be better if something were to happen?"

What?

"I was thinking the same thing my boy, let's make something happen, shall we?"

Suddenly the guys also got a walkie talkie. He speaks into it.

"Could we get another act upon the stage please?"

I just want my salad.

Through a static cackle I can make out some sort of complaint or rather.

"What do you mean we have *nothing else* scheduled?" Tony says enraged "well that's just absolutely fucking out of order! Pack up your things Jerome and get out of my establishment!"

One of those beautiful waitresses has approached us again and Tony's caught her in his eyeballing stare.

"You?" he says to her "We've had some unexpected problems, want to earn some higher wages?"

She stands somewhat taken aback by his sudden abrasiveness.

"What you want me to do?" she says coyly.

"Get down on that dance floor and start dancing, would you?"

"*What?*" She asks.

"You heard me, I said get down to the dance floor and start taking your clothes off"

"I'm not a stripper."

He takes the tray off her with immense force and begins leading her by the arm down to the dance floor area.

"No. but you're on my payroll are you not?"

"...but..."

"Then that means you do anything I tell you to do. You came to London to make money, didn't you?" he pushes her onto the dance floor and everyone takes notice "then make some money".

She begins an awkward attempt at erotic dancing and the jeers of both male and female rear up like never before. I want to help her but what can I do? The jeers and the first electric beats to *Suicide's 'Wild in Blue'* have her writhing like a cobra under an Indian chant – she starts shaking and I can feel her pain like it's my own. She looks up to me for possible help but I just can't be bothered to have anything more to do with this place.

I feel a repressed tear of shame trying to push its way through as I ignore her and she peels her top down to her bra and just continues. Cheers flare up for more.

I take the wrong turning and, hallelujah, I'm there. In the corner of some tight, dark room, beneath a neon UV strip, is the ever-elusive salad bar. A few people have followed in behind me but there's still plenty left; my hunger turning this standard arrangement of lettuce, olives, tomato, garlic potato, pasta swirls and feta cheese into something like an expensive still-life painting hung here to symbolise a passing age of woe and famine.

"Hello monsieur" says the friendly French caterer, almost erotically beneath that neon UV light of his.

"Oh thank god I found the place, I'm practically passing out man."

"You 'ungry Monsieur?"

"Yeah. Could I just get a mix of everything?"

"Sure" there's no more of the silver containers everybody had been eating from "Just need to find a new container. One second".

He's disappeared behind the counter and I wait.

*Wild in Blue* is shaking on through the place; cool tune although I know that now I shall forever associate it with my own cowardly complacency.

A foghorn sound then blares out of nowhere as if telling *Wild in Blue* to get fucked. It's weirdly familiar.

Then, I notice that it's coming from a few of the people behind me; dreadlocks are protruding from Salome Jones paper face masks, the fog horn is being replaced by a loud speaker... *oh no*. I recognise them instantly;

"Every day, fruit and vegetables are systematically cut down and butchered for your consumption!!".

*"Is. This. Right?!!"* Another is shouting at the confused other members of the queue.

"They belong with *the Earth!!*" Shouts another.

The Frenchman has reappeared with a similar 'what the fuck?' expression and I know what's about to happen. The quieter of this bunch are now pulling out what look like industrially-sized spray cans...

"Get outta here!!" I call to the Frenchman but everything's just happening too quickly for him.

I try to dive in and shield his stock like some kind of absurd salad martyr but the spray cans are too many.

"This is what it feels like to have the sap of mother Earth spilt like blood across your hands!" I swerve out the way as the cans let loose like unleashing a multi-coloured luminous gas...

"And to eat the cheese of the She-Goat's teet!!" shouts another as the white cubes of feta and everything else on display, including the Frenchman, are suddenly covered in a gas of fluorescent colour.

The silence of the Frenchman, the other bewildered members of the queue and myself are all the result of their shock tactics before...

"You communist motherfuckers!!" shouts the Frenchman before wielding a knife and trying to get around the counter to get to them.

The two Russians terminators are here in a heartbeat, they practically push me palm-first into the paint as they barge past. These activists (what the fuck do they *actually eat*?) have, like myself, and everyone else here, got themselves lost in the dark and the one at the end has already been caught.

"Fascists!!" he manages to shout before a fire exit door explodes open and out they go, the other Russian and the angry French caterer going after them.

I look at the modern art remnants of that sad, sad salad bar, the UV light strip illuminating the fluorescent paint upon them, *nothing* has escaped it, not even a single olive, and I feel my hunger even more. A child-like frustration overwhelms me.

I *really* wanted that salad.

I turn and leave the way I came.

## *Part IV: The Mirror*

Of course, the food outlets in Soho and Leicester Square were rammed and so I decided to simply continue my journey to this Skyline Gallery in Lambeth, the quicker I get this part done, the less I hold up Gerard's generous hospitality.

Hunger, sickness, something has now truly kicked in and now outside again, the woozy, neon glitz of the West End appears to sway as if their gleaming panels had been attached to the fronts of palm trees and been left to sway in wait for a hurricane.

I take the tube, its bleaker confines seemingly less intense. Now however, whilst navigating these draughty tunnels of the underground on my way to the Northern Line, I am reminded of how empty my guts are. I begin to feel shaky, nauseous, and those geometric neon grids that had been projected upon those installation screens on that strange rooftop seem to match with the columns and rows of the dirtier alignments of the subway's wall tiles.

Now I'm on the platform and on the curved wall opposite, the wear and tear of the passing trains have turned its assortment of billboard-sized posters into something indefinable; the images of their most current layers ripped away to reveal what came before and it reminds me of that millisecond of a moment when you used to switch channels on old-fashioned TV sets and you'd briefly catch the ghost of your previous channel carried over to the next; both images overlaid make no sense at all when put together but they take on a peculiar, abstract beauty of their own, as if everything that's chaotic about the modern world could just be caught, frozen and meditated over in a timeless silence. How I wish such a thing were possible within the strobe-lit, nauseating stimuli of the 21st Century.

There's a rush of wind and the train appears, I board and think about a) how much did I really get of Salome's interview to which anything effective can really be made from? And how, to my great frustration, I would now be pressured to do a good job of b) *this second fucking assignment* of which I've been given about three hours' notice for. An exhibition launch atop *another* rooftop party? I'd done a million of these things in Brooklyn alone, the only thing to make it any more difficult than my routine day job being that now I'm in an absolutely *foul* mood.

Towards the other end of this carriage, this black kid gets up and steps into the centre and places this shoe box before him...

"Excuse me Ladies and Gentlemen, ma name's Benjamin, I bin workin' on my music against all tricks and fings and I'm tryin' ma bestest to raise the cash to release ma first record; I'm gonna give you a sample of ma lyrics and if you can spare me just a little bit 'o cash, it'd be much appreciated."

The kid then starts rapping his stuff in front of everyone. The few people of whom occupy the seats down this carriage just ignore him, hiding behind their papers or probably not even understanding a word of English let alone what he's on about.

In the anti-social silence that's synonymous with these journeys I listen a bit of course, not much of it is that good, just Brit-slang-heavy stuff about being kept down by the system again, the same old clichés.

We hit Embankment Station and a large number of people get off; in fact, *everyone gets off!* The doors close again and it's just me and him, he's rapping onwards and the train proceeds into the darkness of the tunnel.

How can I ignore him now? Come on Waterloo. Implying that just because we're the same race and that this stuff *must* be resonating with me, the kid just keeps staring at me as if I might be somehow betraying my people by not supporting him. Instead, without a paper to read, I just stare at my own reflection in the darkness of the opposite window.

Oh who the hell am I to speak about the authenticity of hip-hop? Like I ever helped alter the direction of things. I'm a journalist with the potential to make a change on our readers' perception of culture and even I'm just a pathetic cog in the wheel, forced into doing what I'm told by some asshole who might as well be Mickey Mouse. What the fuck does it all matter anyway? Salome had been right about one thing, the walls that once separated one section of society from another have fallen, everything's bled into its neighbouring body, the influence of each no longer isolated to its own path. How the fuck are we supposed to package and market *that?* Is that the future? And do we even have the mental capacity to consume it?

*Crunch!*

Before I come to any sort of conclusion I'm thrown sideways and my face hits the dirty seat cover.

The kid has been thrown off his feet entirely and has landed face-first down on the seats opposite.

The train has stopped.

It's done an *emergency stop.*

"You ok kid?" I say to him.

He peels himself off the seat, he looks pissed.

"What the fuck was that bro?" He's physically fine at least.

"I don't know."

There's nobody else in this carriage to consult with. We wait for an announcement. There's nothing.

"Did we hit somebody, or something?"

"Maybe, but we ain't nowhere near the station bruv, you know what I'm sayin'?"

"Somebody was inside the tunnel maybe?"

Ben's just gone quiet. We wait further for an announcement but still, there's nothing.

All kinds of thoughts race through my head as to what might have happened, but if I'm to go over that brief sudden moment again, it definitely felt like we had impact with *something?* And if we have, where's the immediate announcement? Has the driver been harmed? And if he has, who the fuck gets us *out?*

Ben looks into the last carriage directly behind this one and there's nobody.

"Shall we move further down the train?" I suggest.

Without answering, we're moving from carriage to carriage closer to the front. This isn't good, this isn't good *at all,* there is *nobody else* on this train. Further we go, the lights to some of the carriages are flickering as if damaged until we reach the locked door of the driver's compartment and again, there is *no one.*

"What we gonna do?" says Benjamin.

I pull the emergency lever, it has to contact someone, but not necessarily immediately.

"Shall we knock on the door?" I say.

Benjamin nods and starts hammering on the driver's door.

"Yo boss, you in there? What's goin' on?"

We wait for a few seconds but nothing happens.

We do it again, they had to have heard us but still, nothing happens.

"They have to know somethin's up, the trains are all monitored by TFL somewhere". Ben informs me, although I'm not sure how a hundred percent he is of this.

"So we just *wait* here?" I say.

"Yeah, I guess" and so we take seats opposite each other.

Now, it's only when you stop moving and contemplating things that claustrophobia begins to sink in. All I really see is a long, white empty corridor, an elongated coffin basically, with sealed doors leading to dark walls, and how fucking *deep* are we? Twenty, thirty feet beneath the city? There's no signal, we're absolutely at the mercy of a society that judging by tonight's experiences, doesn't operate on any kinda logic I can rely upon.

He's difficult to read this kid but I wonder whether he's cool with all this? Does this happen a lot here? Is this normal? And if so, how long until things sort themselves out? Am I simply being paranoid?

I analyse where my paranoia might be coming from and it's not just from my unfamiliarity with the place, it's because for the first time during my flight through this city, I am actually motionless, and to not have any immediate answers to anything, now *that's* a journalist's worst nightmare.

Don't think about it. Make conversation.

"So, maybe you can write lyrics about this when we get outta here, huh?"

"Perhaps, yeah. You from America?"

"New York, yeah." I'll save my Hackney origins for later.

"Sick. What part?"

"Brooklyn."

"Yeah? I had some family over in Queens."

"So you've been over there, right?"

"Nah, they're all dead now."

Why the fuck did he have to tell me that? – The walls come in a bit closer and it's hot down here.

"I'm sorry to hear that."

"Yeah, drugs innit? So, what you doin' here?"

"I'm a reporter, had to interview a politician up in Soho."

"Oh yeah, which one?"

"You know Salome Jones? She's new"

"Nah man. I don't know much 'bout politics."

"No?"

"Nah, fuck those pricks. I'm from Clapton, y'know in Hackney?..."

Certainly do.

"...an' dey never gave a fuck 'bout me and ma estate man. You know dis situation we're in now man, this ain't no different to anyfink up dere."

"Oh yeah, what d'ya mean?"

"You must know 'bout the same fing in New York. If you're born in the ghetto you're dere for a reason, government want you to *stay there*. Standard."

Why does he have to assume I'm from the ghetto? Don't talk about this, don't talk about this. Fuck.

"It's true blood, the government don't want you movin' legitimately."

"I think you've been listenin' to too many rap tunes man;" I say as I stand and begin pacing up and down this part of the carriage – fuck, fuck fuck, I start believing the little fuck, a paranoid fantasy about the government deliberately leaving people down here, shit man, the walls are closing in.

"Well, what else is it den? An incident's 'appened down here, there's two people left on the train an' nobody's doin' anyfin'"

"You don't know that, they must be. How long have we...?" I interrupt.

"Twenty minutes at least bruv, maybe half an hour." He interrupts.

Shit starts to slowly spin, and this whole train, this whole tunnel even, now feels like it stretches no further than just one carriage.

Suddenly he stands up with me.

"I know what this is bro, if this ain't a system problem, then it's gotta be a fuckin' *terrorist attack*"

Ah fuck, why did he have to say it?

"I don't necessarily mean down here bruv, I mean up there, on the streets, innit? It's Waterloo innit? The next station's too dangerous to pull into."

"The fucking driver woulda told us then!!"

"He's done a runner bro. He ain't gonna stick around to evacuate two people who were sat at the back of the train."

"You're not helping kid, they have to break us out, they *have to.*"

"Bruv, I ain't bein' funny, but two black guys buried twenty feet down, we'd be lucky if they sent a dog down here to break us out."

"Then what the fuck are we gonna do then?!!" I shout. Benjamin just goes quiet.

I had known even since this morning, that as I was descending from that flyover into the concrete of London, back into my homeworld, further and further back into the trash-strewn womb, my racist cab driver with me, that I was possibly about to meet my doom. Perhaps my driver too had met his in some alternative sort of a way, locked up and trapped like me at the bottom of the concrete whirlpool.

The walls come in further, tighter.

I bang on the windows, walls and that driver's door again.

"Help! Help!" ...it amounts to nothing, just *nothing.*

"I fink you need to calm down, bruv".

The carriage is now the size of a mere elevator and there's nothing beyond it. Is this all karma because I didn't help that waitress back in Soho? Or the stripper? Or Jimmy? Black spots fill my vision. Hunger. Fear. Reality and paranoia converge on each other and I pass out.

I am back in Brooklyn, only at an earlier time in my life, a happier time and by the sheer ambience of the scene, I can sense that none of it's real.

The breeze of a beautiful outside world disrupts the drapes, that vast, wonderful and new outside world of old America, it cools the sweat of our post-sex naked bodies that wrap around each other. Outside the neighbourhood has fallen calm but we're both unaware if this is the way it normally is or whether it's just our own unified euphoric take on it. We're somewhere in our mid thirties and have only been married a short while.

She leans towards me and her beautiful purple lips break the silence.

"Do you think we'll be together forever, Maurice?"

"Sure" I laugh.
"Do you think we'll always be in this building?" she asks referring to the spiders that occupy the cobwebs in the corners of this old block.
"We'll have to make friends with the spiders if we do".
I slowly run fingers down her spine; her sweat builds between my fingers the lower it gets...

I see the two or three mezzanine levels of that Soho rooftop establishment before me, its lights gleaming dimly through the mist like before, and the lights of further London beyond. In slow motion, the rigging of the structure sways uneasily before collapsing, taking its electric wiring down with it, down, down, into ever-rising water that appears from below. The artificial plants topple and are crushed by the falling scaffolds, the electrics spark and explode as they fall into the sway of the water. The electrified water rises and rises before spilling over the edge of the perimeter wall, carrying its chaos over the edge into the streets below... into London.

I'm back in Brooklyn, I'm standing naked, looking through the drapes at the neighbourhood around me awash in an orange twilight. My curiosity dares me to look beyond Brooklyn to the slowly ascending structures of Manhattan further away.
From the twilight orange, an aircraft flies dangerously close to the height of The Freedom Tower, threatening to restart the 21st Century all over again and without control I say to Janine:
"I still love you".
I turn around to see her holding *me*, a past version of me that is, we're naked and her beautiful purple lips break the silence, talking to *him* but not me.
"Do you think we'll always be in this building?"

"Bruv. Bruv."
Benjamin comes into focus.
"You alright bruv?" He gives me some water that he's seemingly found.
"Are we outta there now?"
"Nah, but I think I've found a solution."
Okay, get your shit together Maurice, maybe this guy's onto something.
"What is it?"
"Look at dis".
I pull myself to my feet, too weak to really move, I need to eat. Ben leads me one carriage back and I notice that the electric lights are beginning to dim further. He points out the window towards one of the outside walls.
"Down there, I can see like an alcove fing, it's got some sort of service door".
He's right, a little further down, along the edge of the train, the wall of the tunnel has a little inlet with what, indeed, looks like a staff door.
"How do you suppose we reach it?"
"I need your help gettin' dis door open, and den we need to scramble along the wall towards it".
"No way kid, if this train starts up again while we're doing that we'll get ripped in two."
"It'll take us three minutes each to get there."
"No way man!!" I scream "Somebody *has to* come eventually."

"Bruv *look*" he points upwards aggressively. "Those lights, are beginnin' to fade, d'ya know how long we been down 'ere? *Nobody* is comin' for us bruv, you get me? We gotta do dis now before those lights go out."

He has a point, most of the time in life, people tell you that everything will be alright no matter what you do, that we can always rely on our system to fix things for us, to help; other times, however, the Benjamins of this world are actually right, they're used to unstable worlds, and sometimes, like tonight, you've been left to burn and *you* are all you have.

"Also, I need your light, my battery's nearly dead", he goes on.

I slide my iPad onto my stomach and fix it there, an effective square of white light shines out before us. Ben grins at me.

"Let's do this shit."

You find your strength when you're convinced you have to survive, with our backs we've prized the train doors open, they freeze and go into some kind of emergency state.

"Now" cries Ben and we squeeze outside against the tunnel wall and after a bleeping sound the doors close shut again. There's no turning back now.

By the backs of my feet I can feel the iron rails and smell their static, the palms of my hands squeeze through ooze as I grip the piping or cable work that lines the wall and with minimal light we squeeze our way through this thin, three-minute slip of a passageway. Gripping those pipes, Ben shuffles forwards, he's slow and fear hits me again; imagine if the train started up again *now?*

"Hurry up man" I command.

"I can't get my footin', I can't see a fuckin' thing."

"Just get a move on".

We squeeze forwards, the cold curves of the train's surface against my spine, the grease of the wall congealing upon my front. Ben's made it, hopping off the wall into the alcove space.

"Come on, come on!"

A few more squeezes further and I make it. The worst part now being that if we can't get through this doorway, we're in the exact same situation as before...only with less.

In our light we see a faded Emergency Exit sign so covered in grease it implies that it hasn't been used in ages. Ben pushes it and it opens slightly.

"It's quite loose, I reckon we should kick it in".

"Ok" I say and with whatever force I have, I kick the heaviest foot I have and smash the thing open. Mice jump in every direction and the base of the door screeches through the grease and dust to form quarter circle of cleanliness in the dirty floor.

Before us now is some kind of old, industrial chamber containing nothing but an iron spiral staircase descending from the ceiling. The walls are so dank in decay, their rust forms an entire colour spectrum of its own, bearing yellows, oranges and reds like it were some prehistoric cave at the centre of the earth.

"What's this place, bro?"

If I had an answer, it would be the obvious one of one of London's old disused chambers but somewhere up above, more questions need to be answered, for above us, we hear the sounds of human commotion, of shouting, banging, I look at Ben and he looks at me, fear is in both our eyes, had he been right? Had the surface really gone into some kind of societal meltdown while we were down here?

Our shared looks just said we didn't have much of a choice but actually, during our time together, I feel that this Benjamin and I could make a pretty much effective team in self-defence.

Fearing tetanus, I carefully handle the rusted ironwork of the spiral railing and lead the way up to whatever is above. Whatever it might be, it stinks to high heaven.

The staircase only goes one level and I appear in another chamber, this time pitch-black and with my hands and breath I only sense damp. As I stand to my feet, the height is ok, but the space is narrow as if difficultly crammed into something smaller, and as the ipad light catches up with me, it illuminates walls made up of damp cardboard. Rats and insects scatter about on a floor strewn with newspaper and rubbish but at least it unfolds a few feet further. We're not *trapped* here, at least for now. Ben appears behind me and I feel him shake in horror for the sounds we hear up ahead.

"It's ok, stay close" I tell him.

Kicking rats out the way, we step forwards until we find ourselves at an intersection of another corridor, made out of cardboard again, going both left and right. More civilization has been here, the floor is coated with sleeping bags, shopping bags, magazines and piles of moulding books. There is more light too, small gimmicky, gift-shop candles create a morbidly comforting flicker of direction. Then I hear a thumping sound, not from the punches of fists but of flat feet, they thump closer and closer. Benjamin, once my saviour under claustrophobia now shields himself behind me as if assuming I might be better at handling such alternative threats as the unknown and to be fair, I owe him one.

My boxing memories come back, ready to knock out whatever fucking monstrosity might reveal itself from this abyss. A silhouette comes closer at great speed, and we back around the corner of the corridor we just came. I make it out, a male form of almost anorexic frame, then I make out a torso of tattoos, it comes closer, it's naked, except the flat-footed thumps clearly come from heavy boots. I can make out in his strides and upon his head is something more, something blocky, it then runs not towards us but as if going past us and I see he's wearing a police riot helmet. He turns to us as he passes and with a cockney accent...

"I fuckin' got his 'elmet, the cunt".

...and then he disappears past us. The place he came from was the place of the commotion. Is that the way out?

"Fuck this!" shouts Ben "Fuck this, whatever the fuck is up *there,* ain't right, bro."

Ben begins to panic and runs in the same direction as the naked guy, a direction from which I notice in this cheaply assembled corridor, is slanted slightly downwards and I feel scared *for* him.

"Where are you going?" I shout but he's disappearing, quickly; "the only way out is up" I call.

"We've got to get out of here bro, we've *got to* get out of here". He's shaking and he's gone after the naked guy.

"Ben, come back! Come back!"

The corridors of lowering ceilings I see that direction leading to can't be a good sign and above all we'd just been through, it struck me as strange that the one thing to make Ben panic was the bulky image of a police riot helmet. Or was it the naked man? Probably both. I see Ben running, and then, as if he'd just become a part of this place itself, he's gone, no way of getting him back. I look back towards the correct way, the way of the commotion and I realise that up or down, higher or lower ceiling might not mean anything in navigating *this* place. What the fuck *is* this place?

I then realise why the naked guy looked at me, with this rectangular ipad light shining before me, and now with a smart phone light fixed to my chest, I must look like some kind of absurd dreadlocked robot. Still, it lights the way and I creep forwards to an oddly familiar smell.

I reach another turning and I see a group of homeless people sat along opposite walls of this cardboard; as they notice me, an exhale of smoke flows from one of their mouths like a seductive serpent before they hand a makeshift pipe to the person next to them.

Shit, having expensive equipment is not the right situation to be in down here and so I barge through them before they can comprehend the end of one hit and getting the means for the next one.

This place is thick with crack smoke but I storm my way further until it fades. This was not where the earlier noises were coming from however and from further up I make out the words;

"We still have each other!!" someone cries.

"We shall rise again!" I hear from another.

The walls thin further and I begin to fear that Ben's chosen direction was correct.

Now before me, my light shines upon an elderly man sat upon the floor, his eyes are glazed over as if blind but his face is terrified. Before him I notice a pigeon with one foot attached to a rope.

"Brother, Cardboard City Three is coming to an end. You must leave! You must leave!"

I scramble on and the corridor widens again. More graffiti provides a perverse decoration to the place, then I see that they are the words of Shakespeare, Keats and the bible itself. This is a place where literature has been used as guidance, both figuratively and literally in this labyrinth of a place.

I come to another junction, I decide to go left and I see, before candle light, a group of homeless people are kneeling before another. He stands before them as if like a priest, they grasp his palms while looking up to him with expressions of desperation. Dogs whimper at their feet.

"My friends, once again, we have fought" this 'priest' says "we have fought for our ways but Cardboard City Three is to collapse, the end is here and we must return deeper into the underground."

I just decide to keep going and then I hear.

"Let us not forget the man who established us, we shall return to him"

"Lewis the Earless!!" They begin to chant in unison.

"Lewis the Earless. Lewis the Earless will find us again!! "

*Lewis the Earless?! Lewis? Again?!*

"Lewis the Earless, who united us in our loss and built us a place where we could stay!" the priest goes on "we are the vulnerable, the neglected, and with god's help, we shall rise again".

I can't take hearing the name Lewis again and so I trudge on. I step in something shitty but keep going, something tells me this ongoing corridor has to be the way out.

From out of nowhere, this policeman just appears, he's dressed in riot gear but his helmet's missing, he sees me, and puts a truncheon to my throat, pinning me to the cardboard wall, a maddening stubbled face stares deep into my eyes.

"Listen, I've lost my unit, where's the way out of here?"

"I dunno what you're talkin' about man!!" I say.

*"Tell me!!"* he screams as he pushes the truncheon in further, choking me, and then I realise, I'm covered in dirt, I'm slightly drunk and I must stink. He thinks I'm one of them!

"I've been down here for hours now stop fuckin' about and show me!!" he screams.

Suddenly a dog just bites into his arm and he attempts to hit it with the truncheon using his other arm. The Pitbull won't let go and he just kind of dances off into the depths of the labyrinth screaming.

I worry again as the labyrinth begins to descend downwards and lights darken. I have no other options and just sense that something really bad is going to happen so I just keep going.

I then find myself in another square-shaped, low-ceilinged compartment; it is concrete upon three sides with the cardboard only making up for one side. All of it seems to have been constructed around some other abandoned system, I don't know if it's the sewers or something else but the stink is getting to me.

Wherever they've just come from I can't make out but two older bums then enter this chamber and start fighting; one uppercuts the first to the guts and so the second lays him one back to the face; there is a push, a shove and one of them falls back against the single cardboard wall, causing it to collapse and fill the chamber with dust. Coughing through it as it fades, I see through my ipad light, yet *another* compartment taking focus in the shadows.

I then make out several or so people in a squatting position pulling back up their trousers.

"'Ere, I thought this was the designated toilet area, some privacy would be nice".

"What happened?" One of the old bums leans in to say to me, also coughing from the dust. His opponent scarpers away back into the labyrinth.

From a tiny entrance not far behind this, torchlight appears and a woman enters holding a pile sleeping bags and a bag filled with food, the torch gripped between her teeth. She passes it to the others and appears in a state of panic.

"They're coming! Grab what you can, we must move all the supplies back into the underground, now!"

"What's the point, it's over! It's over!" cries the old, remaining fighter. She turns to him aggressively.

"The location of Cardboard City Four has been decided you wanker now get moving!"

With that, as if under some kind military formation, everything they might need is collected up and they've scattered like mice towards the direction I just came. I notice that the small entranceway this woman entered through appears to head upwards and so I go through it and seem to go up a level.

I find another junction and upon each one, the tunnels widen a little more and more, now more like something akin to the width of a regular subway tunnel. I turn another non-specific direction and then I find...*a family*.

A middle-aged man and woman and two children are aimlessly following a map. From their fanny packs and baseball hats I can already tell that they're American tourists. How the hell did they get down here?

"Excuse me sir" the father asks "we're looking for Leicester Square. Is that around here?"

"No, absolutely not, you need to get out of here".

"Oh, are you American?" He asks enthusiastically.

"Yeah, I'm from New York, but listen to me..."

"Oh we're from Florida but boy is it good to see another American citizen" he says without listening.

"London's so beautiful, but my God is it confusing" says the woman.

"That's because you're lost, you're *really, really* lost. Look, you *have to go back the way you came*".

"But the map says Leicester Square is this way, is that *true*?" he says referring to *the same direction* he was heading.

"No, it *isn't*. Look; you and I, we *all* shouldn't be here, now please, just turn around and head back."

"Oh well, I'm sure we'll find it anyhow" says the man before, they just *continue,* completely not listening to a word I've said.

"Look around you man, is this a *normal* place to you?"

"Well, it's Europe you know. We've never been outta the US but, I'm sure we'll find it, won't we kids? Thanks for your help, sir."

And then...they just continue down the same fucking cardboard corridor, the family's enthusiastic banter just drifting further and further into the darkening bowels of the city in the same way that Ben did.

Suddenly I hear an immense sound coming towards me, like a grind of sheer metal. What now?

As if coming down a slope from a higher level, a militarized row of torch lights then appear, and then I see, like a clump of metallic vehicles pushed together as one indefinable unit, that they're riot police, lots of them, their plastic shields pushed before them.

Forgetting that these are unarmed British police, I automatically put my hands up and squint before their torchlight. They stop.

"Who are you?" They ask, a single truncheon pointing at me face-first.

"I'm just a journalist, I got lost down here."

They shift to one side and point their truncheons towards the direction from which they'd come.

"This way" they declare, and so I go.

Individual faces of amazement looking at me from behind the shield visors of their helmets as I make my way past just as casual as pie. Finally, behind the police, as more light seems to illuminate the area, I see a singular suited man in a suit smoking a cigar.

"Are you a journalist?" he asks in a well-spoken tone.

"Yes" I say.

"What the bloody hell are you doing down here?"

"Well man, you know you've still got trains down there with people in them? I nearly got myself killed trying to get outta one because you guys weren't there to do it for me".

"Right yes, we're still working on that. We've had all kinds of issues today I'm afraid".

"There's a family of tourists, just down *there"* I say pointing out the direction.

"Yes, not to worry, we'll find them too I can assure you".

"What the hell's going on here?" I ask.

"Cardboard City has reappeared again, there was one a few years ago not far away from here and they had to destroy it to build the IMAX cinema. Every two years or so, it reappears at a different location, this is the biggest one yet, the boss says there's never been anything like it, but they're building a bunch of flats and one hotel on this site and so it's time to level it again".

The roots of the old city, I think to myself, shall always grow back.

My conversation with this man then grows awkward.

"So, where's the way out?"

"Keep going, take a left, then a right and then you're there".

I feel like I'm owed both some sort of explanation followed by an apology at this stage but as I begin to open my mouth and say something in anger, the same very weirdness of tonight seems to affect my ability to do so, leaving my answer just as weirdly unsatisfactory as all the others that might had been floating about tonight.

"Thanks" I say in the fashion of a truly failed journalist before just leaving this man to carry on commanding whatever the hell he might be commanding here.

I follow his left, then his right, the corridors widen properly now, those rancid smells dissipate and the cardboard slowly rots away from the walls, revealing the extinguished glass strip lights and regular concrete greys of civilian underpasses and then, like I was on some totally regular pathway, I'm led out into a perfectly normal construction site where all around me stand the first columns of steel that shall be the framework to these future high-rise buildings.

How nice it feels to breathe that unpolluted air once again, how nice it feels to taste the fog but...still...where the hell am I?

Curiously enough, despite there being no sign of anyone around in this concrete basin of a site, there is still noise, similar, though not the same as the one's I'd heard with Benjamin when we were far down in whatever-that-place was. The noises of people, huge hordes them, in motion, and it's bigger.

Directly above me, beyond the warning lights of these great scaffolds, through the fog, the spotlight to a police helicopter illuminates the way towards whatever else might be going on. This entire site seems to have no security gates, no barbed-wire fences, no nothing, and so I just step into... lo and behold, Waterloo!

I'm in that quieter bit where the Premier Inns, the coffee bars and the back sides of the pubs all converge but from which, just around the corner, is perhaps the most touristy place of the entire city.

I step around the corner to see that this helicopter has hovered its way over Westminster Bridge and towards the wondrous illuminations of the London Eye.

At its base however, I notice an array of armed policemen beckoning hordes and hordes of tourists away from the mainstream areas, towards Jubilee Gardens and into the wider realms of the South Bank beyond. Not only are they being led away, they're being cautiously inspected as they do and some, it seems, are even being bundled into the back of police vans, why nobody is leaving via the direction I just so easily arrived from I have no idea but everything resembles some kind of militarized refugee zone. Then I hear what one of the police are saying into their megaphone...

"Anyone who'd been residing in the Cardboard City please make yourselves known!"

I then realise that in my current state, I should probably stay away from them; me and my precious dreads are covered in grease and shit, I stink, I'm mad as hell and I'm simply drawing too much attention to myself via having two neon screens, one small and the other large, beaming out of the front half of my body like a homeless robot. I could easily be mistaken for one of them.

I turn off my light sources, there's still just about enough battery to record some smaller interviews if they ever fucking let me in to this art gallery place.

The fleeing crowds are becoming less and less and so I turn my attention to what I can see of the water behind them and another spotlight, this time from a river police boat, cruises up the embankment and another announcement practically echoes through the entirety of Central London.

"Everybody!! We need you all to leave this area as quickly and as silently as possible!!"

People still flee and flee until the area is practically empty.

Then, *Riiip! Kaboom! splash!!*

Whatever the fuck created that indescribably unnerving noise from beneath my concrete footing, I know what it means;

"All done lads" Calls someone from another department.

This would all signify, of course, the end of that labyrinthine hell hole I'd only just got myself out of, somehow destroyed from below as quickly and simply as crumbling some giant leaf.

What if I'd still been down there?

Presumably their job was to get everyone out so I would've been ok but what about the others? What about Benjamin? What about the Floridian tourist family?

Now, in the darkness, all that is left is one form of shape, metallic and fast, (the police) chasing down and wrestling to the floor some more of the ragged, frightened homeless and I decide to make my exit, after all, having come this far, I'm going to complete this assignment.

My GPS leads me further and further on through the fog-strewn streets of Lambeth, across quiet roads, under railway bridges and through narrow streets of shut-down offices and I know I'm late, I know I'll be in serious shit for turning up like this, and I know that I'll be in further shit for having such an unbelievable alibi; they'll all just have to wait for tomorrow's news to prove that one I guess but right now, I don't give a shit, I'm finishing this job and then this ever-mysterious *Lewis* can go fuck himself.

I don't know whether it's because I might look scary or whether it's because the police are clearly out and about tonight that nobody seems to be around, even the fast-food chicken joints are shut and I'm fucking *dying* of hunger man.

Then, down another narrow brick-work street, I see it, finally, a corner building of brick and glass display windows, a sign reads *The Skyline Gallery*! The only thing is, it looks empty, all the lights appear to be off and there's only the mild sense of movement from that fifth-floor rooftop where this thing's supposed to be happening.

There's a few other lights flickering about through the windows of the lower floors but these look more like luxury apartments than anything to do with my being here.

I check my GPS, I check my instructions, 26 Tyers Terrace, Lambeth, this *is* it. Nothing can surprise me now regarding these establishments, especially after the Soho whorehouse thing but what's this? Did I miss it?

The front door is locked, no doorman, no anything.

I ring the buzzer for the top floor.

There's nothing.

I ring it again.

Nothing.

I notice a small arrow chalked into the wall next to the buzzer box, it points to my right, to the display window, it's dark inside...

An array of pretentiously arranged light strips then flicker on as I approach and light up a canvas that's on display just behind the glass. As I lean in to see it closer, it merges with my reflection, it's not much, just a bunch of crappy, abstract shapes and colors merging into one another, it's not much to look at.

Then, for what I first assumed to be a single square of yellow colour, I then notice is a small postage note with some writing on it.

I lean in closer. It reads;

*To Maurice,*

*We're very sorry you couldn't make it but there's no excuses for lateness.*

*Lewis is <u>very</u> angry.*

The word *very* had been aggressively underlined as if the pen might had ripped straight through the paper and damaged the canvas.

*Who the fuck are these freaks?! Who would do such a deranged thing?! And who the fuck is Lewis?!*

I slam the window and an alarm starts blaring out into the empty streets. A man calls out from a window nearby.

"Oi, bugger off, will ya, the party's ova! Have some respect for your neighbours".

"Yeah, bite me!" I shout as I turn and walk away.

Fuck these assholes man, fuck this weird, *weird* old town, you're getting nothing outta *my* talents.

I just want to find a taxi and fuck off back to Gerard's place.

I make my way to what I assume to be the nearest main street to contain cab services, the sounds of the alarms slowly dying out behind me the further I walk.

Then, out of the fog, like a firefly, a tiny light seems to be spiraling down towards me, a flame of some sort. Something falls behind it like a mini parachute and it gently settles on the silent sidewalk before me. Its little flame burns out, darkening my view of it and then I notice what it is, a Chinese candle with a tiny GoPro camera attached to it, a tiny GoPro camera looking right up at me.

Is this thing still transmitting to all the selected venues currently still partying throughout the city? Because now it can see me bearing down on it, and only me.

"One vision of London. Kiss my ass." I say, as I stick out my shoe and crush it.


I've made it onto a more mainstream street and the fog has thickened, it's hard to say of course but I'd say it's still just as empty as all the others. Through the fog I notice a line of black cabs, behind the wheel of the first one, a grey-haired driver sits behind a newspaper. I knock on the window and he winds it down.

"Hello fella, how can I help ya?"

I recognise the accent, it's from Liverpool.

"Can you get me to Sandringham Road, Hackney, E8, I think?"

"I certainly can, 'op in!"

I jump in the back and can make out the guy's eyes in the mirror. He looks friendly enough.

"Listen mate, are you 'ungry?"

"Am I *hungry*?" I can hardly even speak because of it "buddy, I'm starving"

"Do you want these chips? I can't finish 'em"...and next to him, is practically a *whole bag of British chips!!*

*"Do I?"* I say before the hands of Jesus pass them through the hatch to me.

"Ye very welcome to 'em, I don't know what you make of our crappy food but these ent a good example of 'em, gotta get 'em up on the North West Coast where I'm from to get 'em good, tellin' ya."

I'm eating like an animal as he turns the ignition and pulls out into the street.

"Man, if you knew what I'd been through tonight, you wouldn't even care."

"Well, I was meaning to say mate, and I don't mean to be funny, but have you taken a bit of a ham sarnie to the face tonight?"

"A what?" I ask as he pushes a packet of Kleenex through the hatch too.

"An ham sarnie? You know, a punch? Check out your nose mate."

I look in the mirror and the dude's right, my lip is swollen and my nostrils are filled with red.

"Ah shit" I grab the Kleenex and start cleaning myself up. I remember now, back in Soho, that little white piece of trash who tried to take my ipad. How hard did he hit me?!

I can't even say what the most peculiar event of the night had been, but I suddenly see something further in the mirror, beyond my blood, that sorta tops it all off. I notice that, I'm suddenly *completely normal!!!* There's no dirt, no smells, absolutely nothing to prove where I'd been.

"Meet some of my unfriendly Southern cousins, did ya?"

What the hell? What happened?

"Is this the right way to Hackney?" I ask.

The driver double checks something.

"Aye shit, you're right mate, sorry. Just a sec, gotta find a way of turnin' round" He continues onwards "So come on then, it's not often you yanks 'ave something this interestin' to say, what 'appened to ya?"

Outside, beyond the passing shops, beyond the glowing cabins of the London Eye, I can make out the major lights of Bank, The Shard and even Canary Wharf trailing off into the distance like pinholes of light through a dark sheet of blindness, and as I think about an answer to this man's question, I can honestly say I don't have one except for...

"Ya have some strange shit goin' on this country right now."

"Ya can say that again mate? You a citizen here, are ya?"

"Yeah."

"Then if you're gonna live 'ere"

The bloke then begins pointing at some stickers he has stuck all over the insides of his windows; they read *Vote Labour, Vote Corbyn.*

"If you're gonna live 'ere, you got to vote for this bloke. Jeremy Corbyn his name is and I'll tell ya somethin', he's gonna save this country mate. We need the workers' rights back, we need the Unions back and we have to get these fuckin' careerist Oxford boy toffs out of office. Save the country, that's what I say. Vote for 'im"

"I still think you're going the wrong way" I say, gripping my chips.

"Aye shit, sorry, you distracted me".

He halts the car and looks in the mirror.

As I continue to look between him and the passing shops, I question whether I should return here for good. Leave my issues in the US and start over. I just don't know.

The driver does a three-point turn and begins heading north.

Not yet, I decide for myself. First this country has issues of its own.

# South Mimms Services

Some dream of Venice, some wish to see the Taj Mahal or the Great Wall of China but for this humble traveler it really does not get better than South Mimms service station. Like a proud diamond at the northernmost tip of the M25, this outstanding station is a testament to tireless innovation and exceptional design. It is a shining beacon of accomplishment.

Its architecture is similar to a mighty aircraft hangar and beneath the crest of its arching roof is a romantically designed pebbled pathway leading to the entrance. Housed within is, in my opinion, everything one could possibly ask for and more.

The main hall is palatial in stature, allowing the entrant an unrestricted view of all it has to offer. In the centre of the room are dotted little islands of leather seats creating a relaxed and informal environment. Just to the right of this is a giant screen that serves not only to keep guests updated with traffic news and world events but also plays short movies showing how guests could enjoy themselves eating burgers and topping up fuel. These short idents create a sense that one has found a modern utopia.

Whereas other service stations may offer one or two superior brands, South Mimms houses dozens of consumer favourites. We have some serious titans standing shoulder-to-shoulder here; *Waitrose, Pret A Manger, Subway, KFC* and *Harry Ramsden*. The selection is dizzying and deeply satisfying.

The station has not one, not two but three branches of *Starbucks*. I chose the one just to the left of the entrance and ordered my Chai Latte (*expertly* made). The seating is comfortable and the surfaces are oh-so-clean. The entire station is spotless.

The cafe segment itself is open plan and minimalist, allowing space for guests to roam. On the wall is a mural documenting The Coffee Belt, which details the locations that *Starbucks* Coffee is sourced. I found this touch considerate, enlightening and informative.

Venturing further I headed towards the toilets, passing the *Gaming Zone* which was filled with exciting distractions and impeccably designed; discreet yet inviting.

The toilets were extensive enough to accommodate a couple of dozen guests per row and the seal of quality had to be the *Dyson* dryers that have been installed. My hands were dry within seconds.

Back in the main enclosure I wandered around some more, taking in the sights and sounds. The more I discovered the more I realised that I had found what my soul had been craving; perfection. Clean, marbled, brightly lit, aromatic and smooth perfection. I began to feel quite overwhelmed. I wasn't aware at first but I must have been crying with joy as a few people turned around in the central dining section. One woman pulled her young son close to her and cradled him.

A couple of security guards approached and asked if I was alright. I have to say they conducted themselves in a very professional manner and their uniforms were in a spotless condition. I explained I had a reservation at the *Ramada* next door and they selflessly escorted me outside. I thanked them for their assistance and took a moment to enjoy the late evening sunset on the pavilion decking outside.

I felt hungry so headed to the wonderfully quirky *Ed's Diner* next to my hotel. The concept of the restaurant was a throwback to 1950's Americana, with pictures of Cadillacs and Jukeboxes. In the background an Eddie Cochrane number played as I was shown to a booth by a young waitress called Debbie. Debbie did her best to play along with the style of the restaurant and had a lovely smile but I couldn't help but notice how tired she looked. On her wrist was a small tattoo of a crucifix and the name *Simon*. She asked me what I wanted to eat but there was so much choice that I became agitated and spoke out of turn.

I glanced around the diner and read the witty quotes on the walls. One said *If you're smoking in here you'd better be on fire!* which, despite being a witty play on words, conjured up a rather distressing image in my mind. I could see that Debbie was pointing over at me and talking to her manager, who was nodding sternly. She was no longer smiling so I decided it was time to leave.

I went outside for a cigarette and walked around the back of the restaurant. Outside the open door of the noisy kitchen was a large ventilator and a plastic chair, similar to the type you would find in a school. I rested on it and lit my cigarette.

It was then that I spotted it.

In between the service station and the hotel was a small concrete path leading to a gate. The evening sun lit up the words displayed on the fencing.

### Wash Lane Common

Surprised to see something so alien to the industrial surroundings I ventured towards the gate. On the opposite side was a quiet country lane. Across from the path was a sign detailing the history of the Common.

*Hidden behind South Mimms M25 Services, Wash Lane Common is a linear area covering approximately three hectares. The common is made up of grassland, marshland and swamp and includes some uncommon species to Hertfordshire.*

Beyond the sign was a luscious, verdant swathe of trees and a narrow mown-grass pathway leading into a wooded area. Something deep within my being began to stir like a sleeping giant. I headed towards the reeds.

As I ventured further away from the station the green path twisted and turned, occasionally opening out into perfectly secluded ardent spaces where only a distant hum from the motorway could be heard. Upon hearing the gentle sound of running water I ventured further. I chanced upon a quiet brook and followed its stream towards a bridge hidden by overgrown weeds. I cut through the branches by holding my briefcase with two hands. Eventually I got a glimpse of the light beyond. The overgrowth opened out into a beautiful meadow of long grass. I felt a pang of anxiety and concern that I had ventured too far from my comfort zone and considered turning back and checking into the *Ramada*. It was then that I spotted four figures on the opposite side of the meadow.

At first, they were too far away for my eyes to focus upon but as they drew closer I could make out that it was a man, a woman and two children. As they slowly walked towards me I could see that the man and woman were dressed much like me; in expensive suits, only theirs showed the wear and tear of the outdoors; grass and mud from top to toe. The man had a handsome face and a dappled beard. On his head, he wore a majestic crown made from the antlers of a deer. The woman wore a fox's tail around her head like a bandana. The two children were clothed entirely with animal skin; the youngest, a girl, wearing rabbit's fur and the older one, a boy no more than 6 years old, wore a badger's pelt over his torso like a poncho.

I froze still as they approached me, holding my briefcase tightly in my right hand, ready to swing it if necessary. The adult male approached me first. He smelt either side of my neck before resting his hand on my shoulder and smiling like a long-lost friend.

"Hello, brother" he said.

"Hello." I replied

"What brought you to the meadow?"

I hesitated and stumbled over words,

"I... lost my way."

The man laughed and his family smiled. The woman joined the man next to me and placed her hand on my other shoulder. She stared into my eyes intently before speaking,

"You've seen us before, haven't you? In the fields and trees?"

"Yes," I whispered.

"What is your name, brother?"

I told them my name and found out theirs. The man used to be a software engineer. The woman was his wife, who had been a successful project manager. They had visited the service station in 2014, en-route to a business conference before deciding to become what they described as *Border People*.

"Initially we were searching for a secluded spot to be intimate but we discovered so much more. We decided to stay here in the fields and meadows."

I was distracted by the young girl stamping the ground. She lifted a fat dormouse up by its tail and without hesitating bit into its side like an apple. Blood covered her mouth as she chewed and gave a big red grin. Her parents looked at her and smiled.

"Don't be alarmed. Our children were born out here in the borders. They have no connection to your world."

Despite feeling shocked I remained entranced by these strangers. I tried to make some excuses.

"I should go back. I have to complete my review of the service station."

The man looked at his wife.

"You know, there is another way. Another life for you should you wish to stay."

"I can't. I mustn't."

The woman gave a patient smile.

"We've watched you from the outskirts. I can see how lonely you are. There is nothing back there. The world you know is not what you think it is. There is a life for you beyond the orbital. And you will never be alone."

I could feel hot tears streaming down my face. The man and woman squeezed my shoulder tightly. Beyond them in the fields and trees I could see others just like them. Some in clean suits, some in faded police uniforms or hospital scrubs whilst others were in a more primal state. A few were sat on top of horses. They all stood and watched me in silence.

I listened to the buzz of the motorway in the distance. A beautiful sunset was giving way to dusk and I could see the lights of the *Ramada* hotel switch on. I took one last look at South Mimms services before looking back at her.

"Take me with you. I'm ready to go."

She smiled.

"You may follow us. All we ask is that you leave your worldly possessions here at the border. This will be your ultimate sacrifice."

And with that they turned and started to head back into the long grass. One by one I watched them disappear into the bushes and trees.

She is looking back at me as I type these final words, holding out her hand.

Night is falling.

I must go now. I am leaving this phone by the bridge.

This will be my last report.

I am going to live beneath the stars.

Twitter: @BatteryLifeBook

32967586R00188

Printed in Poland
by Amazon Fulfillment
Poland Sp. z o.o., Wrocław